CANAAN

A NOVEL BY
CHARLIE SMITH

SIMON AND SCHUSTER
New York

Copyright © 1984 by Charlie Smith
All rights reserved
including the right of reproduction
in whole or in part in any form
Published by Simon and Schuster
A Division of Simon & Schuster, Inc.
Simon & Schuster Building
Rockefeller Center
1230 Avenue of the Americas
New York, New York 10020
SIMON AND SCHUSTER and colophon are registered trade-
marks of Simon & Schuster, Inc.
Designed by Barbara M. Marks
Manufactured in the United States of America

10   9   8   7   6   5   4   3   2   1

Library of Congress Cataloging in Publication Data
Smith, Charlie, 1947-
   Canaan.

   I. Title.
PS3569.M5163C3   1984   813'.54   84-13993
ISBN: 0-671-53295-2

To H. P.
AND TO THOSE WHO TRUDGE THE ROAD . . .

ACKNOWLEDGMENTS

To these four I owe a debt of love and gratitude which I will never be able to repay: Ken Chacey, Dick Ballard, Reynolds Price and Larry Smith.

For their support and encouragement I would like to thank Jim Cleveland, Lynne Sharon Schwartz, Doris Grumbach, Leon Lyvers, Margaret Erhart, Gary Whittington, Nancy Hamilton, Jim Delaney, Doug Lowery and Amy Godine.

I am grateful for the James Michener grant from the Copernicus Foundation and for a fellowship from the University of Iowa Writers Workshop which aided in the completion of the novel.

PART
ONE

1 Jacey Burdette was born in Hawaii, but he was a southerner nonetheless. As a child, newly moved to his father's home in Yellow Springs, Georgia—and for years afterward—he was bothered by the fact that he had been born on an island in the Pacific, unlike his playmates, who, except for Roy Moscova, who was from Philadelphia, had all been born right there in Yellow Springs, on the third floor of the Burdette Memorial Hospital.

Jacey saw the light in the white one-story naval hospital in the green-and-red hills above Pearl Harbor, and his mother liked to recount the story of how with him in her arms she had stood at her window looking out at the blue Pacific where his father's ship, the cruiser S.S. *Boston*, rode at anchor in the roads beyond Battleship Alley. That was in 1945, in late November, a month in Hawaii when the skies are especially blue and there is a subtle and delicious feeling of change in the air. That change is the coming of the *kona* winds, southwest breezes that bring rain, and sometimes storms, but in Hawaii, the rains are freshening and the storms are short-lived. In Georgia in November, the rains that come are the drizzling, cold rains of winter. Jacey's mother hated the rains—she hated everything about Georgia, in fact—and that is why she liked to tell the story of standing with Jacey in her arms at the wide window of the sunny naval hospital in the hills above Pearl watching the movement of the great ships in the wide blue harbor. "For the contrast," she would remark, her full lips pursing in disgust as she related the story against the obvious and relentless background of the gray late-fall Georgia drizzle where if anything moved at all it was probably a crow.

Jacey—Jackson Coleridge Burdette IV, called Jacey to differentiate him from his father J.C., his grandfather Jack and his great-grandfather Jackson—had to learn that he was not Hawaiian. The recipient and repository of nearly two hundred and fifty years of unsullied southern blood

9

and breeding (a hundred years in Charleston, one hundred and fifty years in the south Georgia cotton and tobacco country), he lacked only the ingredient of southern birth to complete the skein of pure southern heritage he was heir to. It was an ingredient whose lack, however, could be troublesome.

"Are you an American?" Danny Burskeen, smart little wiry son of a sharecropper, smelly and quick, had asked Jacey on his very first day of grade school. Jacey had looked at Danny, who, with stiff, outgrown crew cut and dog-chewed cuffs and the thin glint of light in his eyes, looked like a pale and refugee guerrilla, no American he knew, and answered, "I don't know. I was born in Hawaii." Danny beamed triumphant. "Hawaii's not in America," he said. Jacey was crushed. Like a wound under his clothes he carried the knowledge of his foreign birth throughout that first day of school, frightened, biting back tears, horrified of making trouble, lest his teacher, Miss Hurdle, a great blue-dressed, white-haired, humpbacked whale woman, accuse him and send him away—until the final first-day bell rang at one forty-five when he reeled from the building into the deep red leather of his mother's Cadillac (and a second later into her bemused arms) and spilled the beans of the guilty not-so-secret secret he bore.

His mother, aroused from daydreams, had, in her random, reckless way, tried to comfort him. Elizabeth Bonnet Burdette, the final tart plum of the Charleston Bonnets, was herself the heir to three hundred years of southern pomp and circumstance. A brilliant, ingenious, self-absorbed woman, known in her teens as the Beauty of Charleston, she had chosen, quite consciously, to live her life as if every day were a cotillion.

Jacey was madly in love with her. Everything about her fascinated him. She was (if mainly, and finally only, in his fancy) the end and the beginning for him: lover, sovereign protector, playmate, storyteller. She was his only available mother, and if he created for her a role that she never in her actual life played, it was a role that beguiled him, that took him years to dismantle. When, sobbing against her breast, he told her what Danny Burskeen had pointed out to him in the schoolroom, he did not mean for her to leave the car, seek out and find six-year-old Danny (eating an apple at the end of the catwalk) and barehandedly paddle his small bottom ("within an inch of his life," as she gleefully told him afterward), but he was not surprised. He had grown used to her sudden attacks of hot attention.

10

There was a curious, ambivalent, retardant closeness between them, mother and son. Fostered possibly by Elizabeth Burdette's rage and fear at finding herself at thirty trapped in the maze of feudal country society that her marriage to J. C. Burdette brought with it, and certainly by the fact that for four years after her marriage she had lived alone with Jacey in Hawaii, it was a closeness of more, and often less, than proximity. She had not come home with her husband when the war was over. "I'm not finished here," she told him, and she had stayed.

She was, when they met, the fiancée of his executive officer, Haven Holderness Laurens, another slim scion of an old Georgia family. Societal ties had not hindered J. C. Burdette's pursuit of the black-haired Beauty of Charleston, nor had the barriers of rank (J.C., a thirty-year-old lieutenant, was the cruiser's assistant gunnery officer, a notch below Haven). They were introduced at a ball at the Pearl officers' club, and though J.C. danced only once with her, he was standing on the veranda of her cottage the next morning in spanking whites carrying a bouquet of bougainvillea and plumeria blossoms. "For the first time in my life I knew exactly what I wanted," he told Jacey years later, years after Elizabeth Bonnet Burdette was gone, years after the fields and houses of their ancient patrimony were no longer marked with the name or presence of the Burdettes of south Georgia.

The courtship was brief: a month after they met they were married. When he was not at sea, J.C. lived with Elizabeth in her tiny white cottage in the hills above Pearl. From their veranda they could look across the bay to the line of muscular hills that rolled toward Honolulu and Waikiki. The sun rose over the hills firing their green backs into gold, and it was a view that J. C. Burdette loved, though he quickly discovered that it was a view he usually saw only on their way in to bed—or occasionally, if there was an early call, on his way in to duty. Elizabeth had no intention of changing her fanciful ways because she had married. Just as at sixteen she had been the Beauty of Charleston, she was now, at twenty-four, the Belle of Honolulu, and no marriage would hinder the celebration of herself and the adventure around her that her life had become. If she danced naked on the beach, if she swam after midnight with the island boys in the high flower-scented springs of the Halieva River, if she drove a motorcycle and rode the roundhouse waves off Makaha Beach, if she continued to see Haven Holderness Laurens and vent in his elegant arms the passion that even J. C. Burdette's bone-deep ardor could not subdue, she felt it was only her right and her way. She would change for no one.

Jacey's memories of Hawaii were vague and pleasant. He remembered light and the wind, and leaves like frogs' feet. He remembered the clear sparkle of the water inside the lagoon at Waikiki and the feel of it, warm and salty, on his skin. He remembered the deep rusty red of the pineapple fields on the Schofield Plateau and the green cliffs of Koolau that soared into the mists. He remembered leaning his face against the warm white clapboard of their tiny cottage and the smell of the white and yellow blossoms that grew on the plumeria bush by the front door. He remembered the color blue which was the color of the walls of his room and the smell of his mother's hands and her perfume, and the sound of her voice when she would wake him just after dawn as she returned from her nights of frolicking. He remembered—tentatively—the frolics themselves, the ones she would take him on. There was a haze of faces, smiling white and brown faces, that seemed to hover over him for years afterward, faces that came to him at night as he lay in his bed in the big house of Canaan.

For Elizabeth Bonnet Burdette, party girl and adventuress, her marriage, and the incidental, almost immediate pregnancy that followed, were new grand frolics, and she welcomed them as she would a picnic to a forbidden beach. She suffered little from morning sickness, and she carried her smoothly swelling belly to parties and dances with an unwavering boldness and delight. Until the final week of her pregnancy the progress and style of her life were undeflected by the sleeping child she carried beneath her heart. For all of his life Jacey kept with him a photograph, made in the last week of the pregnancy, which showed her standing on a beach in a two-piece bathing suit, her great belly ballooning from her like a ripe fruit. In the photograph she was looking along her shoulder at the cameraman, her long hair loose down her back, arms stretched and hands clasped behind her. Her fine, high-boned, risible face, the strong chin tilted upward, the eyes looking directly into the lens, was flushed with pleasure.

He had no friends in Hawaii—he was mostly too young for that, and too isolated—except for Rufino Atalig, the Guamanian yardboy, whose job it was, more often than not, to care for him. Rufino, a small curly-headed man who walked as if he expected the ground to begin suddenly rolling beneath him, hated Hawaii and all Hawaiians. Sent there to learn to operate heavy construction machinery, he had been stranded by the war, and though the island was filled with heavy machines he had not been allowed to operate any of them. Too old for military service, he had become a yardboy for Navy personnel, a job he kept until the arrival of Elizabeth Bonnet, who as a Red Cross nurse was not attached to the Navy, but who liked Rufino and who never planned to live her life anyway without a gardener and who as the youngest daughter of one of Charleston's tenured and richest fathers could *afford* a gardener and so was able to pay Rufino, for the first and only time in his life, what he thought he was worth.

In the mornings while his mother slept, Jacey and Rufino would go on excursions of their own around the fields and woods near the cottage. Rufino taught Jacey the names of native plants, showed him the difference between male and female papaya trees, explained the various ways to prepare breadfruit and told him the one hundred Guamanian names for the coconut. He showed him how to catch a lizard with a noose made of pandanus fiber and how to weave a sleeping mat, and he taught him how to drink *tuba,* the sweet piercing wine made from the coconut flower.

Though in the years afterward Jacey was to forget much of the lore Rufino had taught him, to remember only that he had once known the names of flowers and trees that were now foreign to him, processes that escaped him, he remembered, as if it were engraved on his insides, the taste of coconut wine. When he had his first Stateside sip of an alcoholic beverage (from a bottle of saki he and his cousin Burleigh Burdette stole from his uncle's pantry and drank under a pine tree in the Canaan woods) he was slammed suddenly backward into the old Hawaiian time, the taste of the wine burning like a current along a wire to the days when with his teacher and protector Rufino he had sat on the steps of a ruined temple in the hills above Pearl and tasted for the first time the tough, pungent flavor of the island wine.

His mother didn't mind Jacey's excursions around the viny woods and the fields that surrounded her cottage in the hills—free herself, she wanted and expected her son to enjoy the same life, and she let him run as he would. In the first days after his birth, when she lay again in the wide bed in her white bedroom, she listened with amused detachment while her husband told her of his plans for their son. J.C., who, on his return from Harvard in 1936, had begun the relentless hammering attack on the until then steady, though dilatory, direction of the family enterprises (farming, naval stores)—an attack that first amused, then baffled, then threatened, then frightened, then swept away his own father (until by 1942, when, excited by the war fever, and his own hot dreams, he had entered Naval OCS in Providence, Rhode Island)—had for his son, Jackson Coleridge Burdette IV, in his mind and on his lips as he lay beside his ravishing and amused wife in the big teak bed, a plan, solid in conception, elaborate in promise, strenuous in execution, that would, he believed in his bones—though he would not, could not say *this*—drive the name and influence of the Burdettes of south Georgia far beyond any heaven his father, or he himself, had, or might be able, to reach. "New York," he whispered as he stroked her arms, "the big leagues—where the Yankees are."

Elizabeth Bonnet Burdette listened to his voice rise and fall in the darkened room, and as he spoke, his words became for her the droning, pleasant background of her dreams. She had no plan for her son, just as she had no plan for herself. She had only an attitude, a response, an approach, and it was not anything she ever had to teach herself or explain to anyone else. She turned her face, and through the white slats of the crib beside her she gazed at the sleeping face of her son. A great man?—he would be that, she knew. Fierce guardian of the Burdette empire? Bold entrepreneur?—possibly, if it pleased him, if it was his play. She had other things to teach him, other worlds to show.

Her decision to stay in Hawaii had not been made beforehand. She heard J.C.'s quick, solid footsteps up the cottage steps as she stood over her son changing his diapers, and when her husband entered in his rumpled khakis and pulled from his leather case the orders that would take him away she heard him speak with her mind still focused on the vigorous, wide-eyed child squirming on the bed under her hands.

"It's in two weeks," her husband said. "They give me time to conclude business here."

She looked up, her slim hands smooth and whitened with baby powder, and, smiling, her eyes full of her perpetual gaiety, and with no foreknowledge of her words, said, "I'm not coming. I'm staying here."

In their year together J.C. had learned that she meant whatever she said. He was driven grieving and speechless from the room. The nights of the next two weeks were long and hopeless for him, and though he talked earnestly, desperately, angrily, at times hopefully of their future together—of his plan for it (it's *normal*, he would plead)—she would not, did not, change her mind. She saw him off, wearing a white dress and a multicolored belt woven for her from pandanus fiber by one of the island boys she swam with in the mountain streams, and her farewell was fervent and loving. She remembered always the perfume of the plumeria blossoms from the lei that they crushed out between their bodies as he held her to him in the moments before he boarded the launch out to his ship. She had lost no love for him, nor was she to lose any, and if something in him understood that—appalled, totally bamboozled—something else in him hardened and turned from her, something that would never turn back. She saw the turn, felt it like a grazing blow, but she was strong in the light airs of her way and whimsy.

She let her son run wild. For his first three years he wore no clothes at all beyond the cotton diapers she and then her yardboy Rufino changed regularly for him. She didn't think to give him playmates—beyond Rufino—and he never asked for any. She took him often with her to the parties she attended—parties which with the partial dismantling after the Japanese surrender of the Hawaiian congregation of military war enterprises became increasingly the *hoolaulea* of her island friends—and she let him run as he would on the newly opened beaches, into and out of the arms and presence of her friends.

Jacey's memories of the Hawaiian time were vague, but the tone of the times stayed with him all his life. He knew little restraint in those years, and like Elizabeth, when they had returned to the fields and orders of Canaan, to the stricter confinements of the world created and occupied by the south Georgia Burdettes, he fought hard against any diminishment of the freedom he had accepted as birthright in the sweet country he was born in. When, after a morning-long excursion to pick papayas, the yardboy Rufino brought him home drunk, having allowed him to swig his fill of the sweet wine he made from the coconut flower, his mother was not angry, either at Rufino or at Jacey. Though she scolded Rufino, she was laughing when she sent him back into the yard to continue hoeing out a camomile bed, and as she settled her burbling four-year-old son into the crib he still sometimes occupied between her bed and the wide jalousied windows that looked down the long sweep of hills to the harbor and the southward-stretching Pacific roads, she was smiling, well amused. She stood beside the crib in her red silk kimono and watched until he fell asleep. She didn't punish him—then or ever.

On the Hawaiian mornings, which he always remembered—apocryphally perhaps—as fine and fair, Jacey was the first to arise. He would wake shortly before Rufino pedaled up from the off-islander *kahi* shack he occupied with his Chinese wife. In shorts and T-shirt, barefoot, Jacey would race from the house to join Rufino in his morning round of chores. Toward midmorning, the chores would include the preparation of breakfast for Elizabeth Bonnet Burdette. Jacey would sit on a stool in the kitchen while Rufino padded around in his black double-toed Japanese tabbies preparing the native fruit juices and sweet rolls she liked. He would follow him as he carried the tray to her bedroom and, once she had responded with her sleepy gaiety to Rufino's knock, would race past him to join her in the big bed. Her black silk sleep mask pushed up on her high forehead like a pair of raffish aviator goggles, she would take him into her arms and across his in-curled body eat and drink.

On her night table she kept a photograph of his father, nearly a foot high, in a gilt, velvet-backed frame, and Jacey would watch the picture as his mother ate her breakfast. He knew the picture well—it was always there, had been there when he slept in the white crib beside her bed and there later still, when he moved to the cot in the corner under the window. In it, his father stood on the bridge of his ship holding a pair of binoculars. His fair hair was blown back from a high clear forehead, his eyes were light-colored, his nose broad and straight over a thin but soft-looking mouth and a short, square chin. In the eyes, looking out to sea, there was excitement and delight, and the hands that held the binoculars against his chest were rough-knuckled and strong. For Jacey, the picture, of a man he had never seen, was a fabulous artifact. Alone in the room, or alone as his mother slept, in the mornings, when before he joined Rufino he slipped in beside her and lay with his head on the pillow next to hers, he would reach across her sleeping body and trace the strong contours of his father's face. He could not find the face or any trace of it in the faces of the men who visited them, nor in the men they met on the beaches and by the highland streams in the afternoon and the evening parties she would take him to. There were no men in those places who were anything like the man on the ship's bridge. Whether in the starched whites of naval officers or the flowered shirts of the islanders, none wore the clothes or the look of the man in the photograph. Jacey wondered about his father always. He stood, tall as a house in the foreground of dreams, and he came to him—in the dreams—as a presence, so strongly that sometimes he was stung from his sleep by the power of the image. He asked his mother a thousand questions about his father, but she would not tell him much. What she said was always full of affection and some scorn.

"He was the most dashing man I ever saw," she would say, and the laughter that came into her voice frightened as often as it soothed him. Letters arrived from his father several times a week, and always, in each one, there was mention of him. He was "my fine boy," "my beautiful boy," "my sweet boy," in the bold black script he could not read. When his mother was away—at least in the last year they were in Hawaii—he would climb a chair and take from the top drawer of her dresser the packet of letters and carefully turn their pages, looking for something. They carried a scent he was not familiar with, if only because it was not the whimsical perfume his mother wore—and a feeling would grope through him that became larger and stronger as he held the pages in his hands. There was a mystery he could not understand, and if it was a mystery that drove him twice more in his life to study those same letters—kept during the years of his mother's life in the same drawer of the same dresser in her second-floor bedroom in the big house of Canaan and later in the flat wooden trunk that had belonged to his paternal grandmother—it was never clearer to him, or more needful of solution, than it was as he stood on the chair alone in his mother's bedroom, reckless and illiterate, turning the smooth white pages in his hands.

Elizabeth Bonnet Burdette made no attempt to explain her actions to her son. She made no attempt to explain them to herself. She saw the world not as a place to conquer, a beast to tame to her hand, but as a delight to experience, a confection not meant to run out. If her husband saw it differently and sought letter by letter to change her, to bring her around through the relentless strength of his love, she was not particularly moved. She had believed since she was a girl that a current flowed inside her that was unaffected—in any way she could see—by what went on around her. She made her connections, settled her choices with neither forethought nor worry, and she accepted the consequences that came. So she believed. When Jacey asked her years later why she had stayed so long in Hawaii, she first gave him the same answer that she had given his father: that she wasn't finished there. He thought she meant that she still wanted to run wild, and there was much of that in her reasons, but as he stood above her (as she lay, wine-drunk, in the bottom of a johnboat in Lazarus Swamp) she began to amplify the single sentence of explanation. "What I liked to do," she told him, "more than I liked the parties and all that fun"—she smiled then the old impish smile of those days—"was to sit out on the porch looking at the ocean." Her fey gaze shifted then to her cabin, risen like a native hut from the river ferns, and she smiled, as if through the late-winter drizzle she could see Hawaii. "I wasn't even looking at the ocean," she said, "I was just looking. That was what I liked to do: sit somewhere pretty and look around me. Your father couldn't stand that."

Jacey could understand her love of simple *being*, but he felt always and at the same time the tug of his father's energetic, explorative, quest-ing way of life. Letter after letter had come to the cottage in the hills—if nothing more, the energy of his father's unfaltering assault reached him. When later, as a teenager, he stole the letters from his mother's drawer and read them beside the watercourse behind the house at Canaan, he found what he would have expected: his father's ardor—on the page—was desperate and deep—like a June bug on a thread, it buzzed and flew around the source that held it in thrall, ever returning, exhausted, inevi-tably, to Elizabeth. "I love you completely" was the way the letters ended, letter after letter, and Jacey was sure that his father meant what he said. Six thousand miles was a distance he would somehow conquer. He would throw a line of love that was strong enough to reel her in. And he believed, Jackson Coleridge Burdette III, as he told Jacey in later years, that his love—fierce and unfailing—had broken her loose from her island fortress and pulled her home.

Elizabeth laughed at that. What she was never able to explain—and saw no need to, beyond the demands for explanation that her husband placed on her—was that her love for J.C. had never wavered during the Hawaiian time. "He was what I wanted, too," she told her son, long after he had stopped believing her. But her husband was only one of many things she wanted. And for that she was never forgiven.

J. C. Burdette returned, as he told his friend Haven on the long passage through the Canal, "burned all over," but he had returned to the life of enterprise that had thrilled him always. It took him most of the four years of Elizabeth's exile to consolidate his hold on the Burdette empire.

Elizabeth knew of his plans—she knew his capability; she knew what he was doing. In the letters he told her everything. She would walk out on the narrow porch and sit in a rocker and read the pages. From

18

time to time she would look up and gaze for long moments across the hills to the bay. The ships were fewer now; even from this distance she could see the effect of the dismantling of the war machinery. The Navy had swept on to its new, or newly refurbished, bases in the Far East, and Pearl was, she knew now, only one more stop on the line. She had come here because it had been as far as she could go; it had been the farthest-flung of the picket lines. Now it was something else. She had never been to Georgia, never seen Canaan. Her own family's plantation on the banks of the Ashley River thirty miles upstream from Charleston was nothing more than a summer house, the land rented out to tenants. Her family hadn't farmed for generations. That life—or what she knew of it—was nothing she missed. And she had no desire to live in a small southern town, no matter how much of it her husband owned. That world, no matter what the Burdettes' two hundred and fifty years of grasping and holding had made of it, was hardly different from the world she came from. Certainly not in the number and strength of its chains. Still, it was new. New land. And this was done. There was more, there were other reasons, but she did not look at them, then, her son was to learn, or ever.

She would let the pages fall loosely on her lap and she would push back in the rocker, setting herself in motion. It seemed a fierce blue day always, there in Hawaii, under the widest sky in the world. Coconut fronds jumped in the wind, popping as if something were being shaken out of them. What could anybody do to her? What could anybody do? Into her eyes would come the fine gay light. Let them try to change me, she would think. Just let them try.

And try they did.

2 So they left Hawaii. In late August of 1950, on a silver TWA transpacific airliner, they flew eastward, toward America and their new home, Canaan, the 25,000 acres that were left from the original grant awarded by King George to Jacey's greatest great-grandfather, Langston Rooley Burdette. Canaan, always so named, had once been much more than the nearly forty square miles of cotton fields and pines the Burdettes now owned. Anchored originally on the banks of the Withlacoochee River, which cut like a stake through the bottom quadrant of Georgia, the original grant had run in a twenty-mile-wide band almost to Alabama, 120 miles away. The heave of land, its dark gray forested soil, rolled up and ended only at the high granite cliffs of the Chattahoochee, beyond whose dark wide water lay the slumbering grasslands of Alabama.

The Burdettes would have crossed the river and taken that land, too, augmenting endlessly if they could the 2,400 square miles of territory they already owned (a million and a half acres, Jacey was to discover, in awe and delight, one afternoon during a third-grade arithmetic class), but before even they could subdue the forests and rivers of the original grant it was taken from them by the redheaded scoundrel from Tennessee, Andrew Jackson. The Burdettes had already owned the land for sixty-five years before Jackson made them give it back. Had owned it, but it had never been theirs. It was run through by Indians, the forest Creeks who lived in mud-thatched log houses along the rivers, in clearings surrounded by the rotting bones of animals and enemies. With the Creeks there, the Burdettes were never able to do more than *know*—and *say*, if they wanted to—that the land was theirs. With the Creeks in residence, fierce and intractable, they were never able to do anything with the land. When the Tennessean, as President, finally sent soldiers first to whip the Indians, then force them to pack up and march to Oklahoma, and the land became theirs for the using, there arose such a clamor from the vigorous landless folk who were champing at the bit to move westward and who saw Canaan as either a barrier to their movement or a treasure they lusted after that Jackson ("spineless as always," his great-grandfather had said, "before the will of rascals"), in a handwritten decree still in the possession of Jacey's father, rescinded the grant—except for 25,000 acres running westward from the courthouse square in Yellow Springs to the banks of the Okeekee River—and the Burdettes had had to make do.

Make do is what they had done. First there were the woods themselves, the soaring stands of yellow pine. They cut the great trees for houses, then they cut them to make way for fields when the mechanical gin made it possible for cotton to generate money. The houses of brothers and cousins soared up across the forty square miles of Canaan. The houses were of timber mostly, though some were of brick and one was of stone. The first Burdette to take the lands—Rooley, wild son of Langston—had ridden, on his first day there, the length of the territory (from the Sunskin Trail station house beside the clear, cedar-ringed spring which was to become the namesake of the town that grew up around it), the fifteen miles through the pines to the bank of the Okeekee River where the sundered grant ended in the briars and black mud and snakes of Lazarus Swamp. There, in spite and meanness, he had staked ground for his house. He had raised a family there, beating backward daily up the land to wrench the tangled woods from themselves, battering down forests to make the wide fields that grew the short-staple cotton the Burdettes were to make their first real money on.

Rooley's house had fallen, eaten by the swamp and by the distance from it to the warehouses and Negro shacks grown up alongside the high road (later railroad) in Yellow Springs, but the impulse that had sent him that first summer morning hurtling through the viny woods against the barrier of Lazarus Swamp raged in the blood of the Burdettes that followed. They were not high church, the Burdettes. Baptists—even in Charleston where they had held out against rebellion until war itself was a fact—they were of the same Cracker blood as Jackson himself, the same Cracker blood as the knife-boned, ravening woods runners whose own relentless ambitions had split the land from their hands in the first place.

They hated the other Crackers, the Scotch-English jump-bloods who had followed them into the southwest Georgia (soon-to-become) cotton country. The Negroes the Burdettes owned (120 in the 1860 census), hauled in wagons overland from the docks in Savannah, were their work force and the means of the isolation they created. The Negroes were protection from the flood of ambitions beyond their boundaries, ambitions which, the Burdettes feared, could only hinder their own. Their ambition was to get everything their nubbed-off territory could give them. Not to ruin it—though for years, in the subduing, that had seemed impossible anyway—but to transfuse their own lives with the power and abundance of it.

"I would eat it if I could," Wheeler Burdette, son of Rooley, had said. All the other Burdettes understood. Brothers and cousins, they had worked the land with an energy that the land itself could finally not contain.

Wheeler's son Jackson, J.C.'s grandfather, born in the brokenhearted days following the War, administered, along with his bachelor younger brother Eustace, the empire the fathers had created. Jackson and Eustace were the first Burdettes to fight over control of the lands, reaching a point finally, late in the century, when they carried revolvers to protect themselves from each other. They constructed a division of the lands, drawing a rulered line from the courthouse to the swamp that they marked at hundred-yard intervals with squat brick pedestals, a line they fretfully patrolled for ten years until Eustace, unable finally to bear up under the pressure of brother enmity and the rising energy of Jackson's son Jack, caved in, dissolved the fight, and followed. Jackson died of renal failure in 1930, but Eustace, soul and heart eased, lived on, long after the reins had passed from his hands. In late years he loved to remind the kin that he had been born in the final winter of Andrew Johnson's Presidency and he was still here, still, he crowed, walking the planet.

First there were the trees, cut for houses, then there were the fields, 15,000 acres finally, then there were the trees again, in the '80s when turpentine became an industry, then diversification in the '20s into to-bacco, peanuts and corn, until, in the late '30s, the land wrested finally and completely from its virginity, J. C. Burdette had begun the push into the wide world that would carry them all (he believed) over the created threshold of any land's end into a new sure mastery of their life and time.

Home from Harvard in 1936, he had set about having his way. His father, and the rest of the Burdettes, had been caught unawares. They had known that J.C., as the oldest son of the oldest son, would have his turn as emperor, but they expected the old rhythms to continue. If they had gotten used to an easier canter, J.C. wanted them to gallop again. He began with his own money, the money that came in the multi-way split at the end of each season. The lands, which according to Langston Rooley Burdette's will were to remain "ever undivided," provided, in 1936, a yearly gross income of nearly six million dollars. After expenses, the money was split by household along the bloodlines. Five-eighths (Lang-ston's decree again) was sent back into the lands for the coming year. In 1937, J.C., still living at home with Jack (his mother had died of drown-ing during his junior year in high school), had taken his clear share and invested in cotton warehouses. From the warehouses he began to buy and sell cotton that was grown off the lands. The next year, richer by half, he had refused to reinvest his portion of the Burdette gain. His father had spoken to him—to no avail. Arguments followed that grew bloodier as they grew more unreconcilable. Jack accused his son of ingratitude; J.C. accused his father of killing his mother. Jack ordered J.C. out of the house; J.C. refused to go. He discovered in the course of the fights that if he was willing to take the consequences he could say no to anything. The message of refusal, which he was to learn again at the hands of his wife, touched the deepest part of him. It became information quietly stored, always ready; no one was going to do anything to him if he said no. To his surprise, and relief, his father moved out. The patriarch, suddenly older, fled the house of his birth and his son's refractory will. He retreated into the lands, to the old overseer's house at the edge of the woods overlooking the pond.

He left on a Saturday afternoon in May, packing his farm pickup with clothes and artifacts. J.C. sat on the front steps watching. His father made a dozen trips from house to truck. He hadn't offered to help, and Jack hadn't asked. It was as if J.C. were invisible to his father. Magnolia blooms filled the air with their clear, sweet scent. Clouds the size of continents advanced, through blue sky, on Florida. Once as his father passed him on the way up the steps, J.C. felt an urge to touch him, but he restrained himself; he had won and he thought that a gesture of reconciliation would sully the victory.

Jack came back out carrying the large gilt-framed portrait of his wife, J.C.'s mother. He propped the painting in back against the cab, face out. J.C. had never seen the painting from such a distance. It had been done shortly after her graduation from Hollins. He had always remembered his mother's sternness, her self-absorption that had translated, ever more fluently in the years of his childhood, into the haughty silence that was his most enduring impression of her. He saw now, however, at a distance that made her nearly a stranger, that she had once been someone else. The painter had swept her fair hair lightly off her forehead; it seemed to float around her head. Below, her gray eyes gazed outward with hope, and with an openness he had never noticed before. He had never seen that look in them in life, not to remember it. The urge to speak to his father became a sudden craving. He knew something about him now that he had not known before. He saw what his father must have seen when he met his mother on the trip she made to Yellow Springs to visit a college friend. But J.C. didn't speak, didn't speak even when his father, struggling under the flat leather trunk that had belonged to his mother, brushed against his shoulder; he shifted a little to the side and let him pass on. Victory was more important than reunion.

The brothers and cousins were no stronger than his father. Meeting on the first Sunday of the spring quarter of 1938 on the second-floor porch of Jack's (now J.C.'s) house, as they had done since the beginning, again according to the will and practice of Langston, the kin listened and gave in to the new plans J.C. had concocted. There was mild resistance, from J.C.'s younger brothers Bryce and Franken, who were to become sub-empire managers under J.C., and a stronger, more grieved protest from Eustace, who could remember the old days, the great redemptive cotton days after the Civil War, when the feud with his brother Jackson nearly tore the family apart; but in the end he prevailed; the uncle and brothers and cousins went along. Pulled perhaps by their own greed, they also saw in J.C. the emblem and chance of their will. He was the same Burdette who in 1931, the year before he went off to Harvard, had made ten thousand dollars in a summer buying and selling tobacco as a speculator in the newly opened markethouse off the Square. There was a race in his blood that as family they all had seen, and if something in them kneeled to that spurt of ability and will it was because to them it seemed so clearly there, so clearly going somewhere they wanted to go.

His father returned to the main house only for meetings, and regularly to stone the house. Every few weeks, after midnight always, he walked the four miles from the overseer's house, where he raised zinnias and bees, through the cotton fields, pausing as he walked to fill a burlap sack with the red pebbles that covered the ground. Slipping through the back gate beside the spring, he would take a position in the middle of the yard and throw the pebbles at the back walls and windows of his former house.

The stones were no hindrance to J.C. Burdette. If in the beginning he had shouted down for the old man to quit and go home he now rarely bothered even to turn on a light. He was willing to acknowledge nothing from his father. He rarely spoke of him, and when in the family meetings the old man, in his increasingly ragged clothes, tried to take the floor and bend the discussion once more to his ends ("No off-the-land projects—this is where we were born to work"), J.C. ignored him. The women might have softened the blows of exclusion, but women were excluded from the meetings as a matter of course. The woman who succored Jack now—Mattie Bates, widow of a tenant—was not even allowed in the house. She, too, would have been willing to help in the stoning of his son's fortress, but Jack never brought her along. It was Mattie though who explained to Jacey, one afternoon as they pulled cobblers from the oven in his grandfather's kitchen, the *situation* of the Burdettes and their women.

"It's simple," she said. "The Burdettes always marry women too fine for them. All these women—like your grandmama and your mama—are so overbred they've got the sense of peahens. Not that there ain't a brilliance there—and that energy—it's just that what they are equipped for is life on some other planet than this one."

What Mattie was unable to tell him was that the women were only a singular element in the passion that drove the Burdettes. If the Burdettes were compelled to subdue everything that came to their hands, that everything included the women as well. And just as his father had not been deterred, at first, by the seeming self-sufficiency of his wife, Jacey was not to be stopped. When, years later, in the earliest of his wine dreams, he lay in the old teak bed with Martha in the apartment overlooking Tompkins Park in New York and spoke to her of what Mattie had told him of the Burdette women, he had watched the light in his wife's eyes coalesce—as the stars will when knowledge transforms them into constellations—seen the same fearless gaiety brighten them, and he had not, in the first years anyway, been frightened; it was delight he felt, wonder and joy at the prospect of struggle that lay before him. But this was before his mother's end.

With Jack corralled by his flowers and his impotence, J.C. brooked nothing in his thrust toward what held him in thrall. He wanted control of more than the Burdette crops. The warehouses and the buying and selling of cotton that he used them for were not enough. In an old truck yard behind them he built cotton gins, and on a patch of grassy ground beside the river he erected a sulfuric acid plant and a plant to convert the acid into fertilizer. Into white-stitched cotton sacks the hundred-pound lots of fertilizer were poured, and the sacks were loaded onto flatbed trucks and hauled to the farms in the county. J.C. was willing to sell the fertilizer himself. He walked farmers' fields to talk about Burdette's One Hundred Fertilizer. He coined a slogan, Richer Fertilizer for Richer Crops, and he repeated it to himself as he slogged through the musky unsown fields of late winter. Farmers would buy, impressed that a Burdette would cross their fields at any time of year to talk to them.

In the quarterly meetings the brothers and cousins still raised objections, but they accepted the harvest of money that the new projects brought in. They had agreed, after the first two years, to divert a measure of their own profits into J.C.'s enterprises. As the return grew they voted to transfer money from the lands' profits into the ventures. They were a part of the roll then, so that when J.C. in 1942 decided to go off to war, he was able to turn the leadership of the businesses over to his brother Bryce, freshly graduated from Tulane Law School, who in 1944, when he finally agreed to spend a minimum of time in service to his country, was able to turn the businesses over, for a year, to younger brother Franken, a Wharton M.B.A. Everything was intact when J.C. returned from the Pacific. Neither brother tried to deny him what they all accepted as his right.

He came home, riding the despair of Elizabeth's refusal, but carrying the steady intention to make his enterprises flower. He had newer plans, a wider reach. Late on the first meeting nights after his return, when the white porch rockers were empty and the call of owls drifted up from the woods beyond the spring, J.C. would stand alone on the porch and look out over the darkened lands. He felt in those moments—emptied, by the talk and the triumph, briefly, of his passion—that something was moving toward him, something fierce and ravening, but something, he believed, he had spun from his own hands, and if it was greater than any creation surging in the waves of the past, then so be it, let it come; angel or devil he had strength, he had will, he had nerve: he would win.

He couldn't shake Elizabeth. Not that he wanted to. What he wanted was to run on two tracks at once: enterprise and love; send himself hurtling breakneck down the parallel passageways of his desire. But Elizabeth crossed over. Even on meeting nights, when the kin were gone and he leaned against the screen listening to the faint calls of the owls and to the servants downstairs as they washed the crockery, even then, when once again brothers, uncles and cousins knelt to his will, she came to him.

She came, or desire. He wanted her always, but because she often appeared in the moments when he seemed to be looking farthest away, he was continuously surprised. If he reached to take a mug of coffee from his secretary and saw in the blank flesh between the woman's collar and jaw the skin of his wife, he was surprised. If he stood beside a drainage pond talking fertilizer with a farmer and caught the faint scent of sweet bay drifting over the water, sweet bay whose perfume was so like that of the plumeria bush by their old front steps, and he was tossed backward into that time with her, he was surprised. Once as he walked through a hall of cotton bales in the warehouse behind his office he had come on a work gang in the middle of a contest to see who could lift and carry a cotton bale the farthest. They asked him to try. Pressing his back against the bale, he reached behind him with hooks in both hands, snagged the top and managed to stagger half a dozen steps with 450 pounds of pressed cotton on his back. He was amazed that he could do it. He had seen black men who could hoist a bale and walk around with it as if it were no heavier than a sack of rice, but he had never known he could get one off the ground. Yet, as he carefully lowered the bale to the floor, the strain in his back—the strain itself—seemed to propel into his mind the image of Elizabeth, of Elizabeth standing over the crib, her hands wrapped in the blue hospital blanket that had swaddled the child, a look on her face of delight and wonder. He was so shaken that when the gang boss took the hooks from him ("You sure are something, Mr. Burdette"), J.C. had already forgotten where he was; he started at the man's words, stumbled against the three-bale-high tier of cotton and without answering fled the warehouse.

His reaction to it, to the weight-lifting scene, and to all the other scenes, was a fierce, mind-dissolving anger. On the days when Elizabeth reached up to him he left the office or the plant or the field and returned home, his fair face locked in a rictus of anger and dismay, saddled his horse and rode out over the fields of Canaan. He didn't ride so much as run. His horse, Michonnet, a stallion descended from the horse his grandfather Rooley had lashed across the pine barrens on his original ride, was willing. The long reins gathered in his left hand, he would beat the horse into a run with his hat. The hitting was release for him only; the horse ran on his own. Down the cotton roads, past the pond, through the pine woods, J.C. would send the horse in a run so smooth that riding him, he thought, was like sitting on a floor. When they reached the swamp, J.C. would dismount and swim in the river. On Canaan the river was barely a river, a canked, coffee-colored stream that wound between low hilly banks under overlapping live oaks. Cypress and alder roots stuck out of the water. A snaky, perpetually dark place it was, the opposite of the clear, blue-eyed spring that bubbled among cedars behind the main house, but to J.C. it was the place to throw his anger. He would shed his clothes and wade naked into the rooty water, swim out into the faint swirled current and float on his back looking up into the massed leaves of the live oaks. On the far side, downstream from where the path ran out, was a small sandy beach. The sand was white and hard, the deep scourings of undersoil—J.C. would float and paddle down to the narrow strand and lie just at the waterline, his head and shoulders resting on the

27

sand, his body flagged out in front of him in the stream. There he would let what thoughts came have their way. Excited nearly to terror by the ride, exhilarated by the swim in the gloomy stream, he would lie down under the romping images of his wife, defenseless. The theme was loss, always. The picture was Elizabeth standing on the dock at Pearl, her white dress blown against her body, the yellow plumeria blossoms swirled on her breast. In his mind her hand lifted to unfasten the single red hibiscus she wore in her hair. As the launch moved away from the dock she held the flower toward him, twirling it between her fingers. He couldn't reach it and didn't try. She smiled steadily at him, without tears. As the launch moved away it was as if for a moment the distance between them remained the same; her smile held its brilliance, the flower was large; he could see clearly the long pistil and its seedlike yellow stigma. He tried to hold the image, the flower and her smile, hold it as it hurt, but it would slip away and he would return, lying on his back, his hands scratching at the sand, the woods sounds twittering around him, to the reality of his life. He would rise then and climb the bank, and still wet, dress and ride the fifteen miles back across his lands to the house.

Lazarus Swamp was not his only bed of sorrows. At night, alone in the bed he had wrested from his father, he learned how fiercely the body could cling to what it no longer had. He had no reason to forget her—her letters, lighthearted and loving, came regularly—but as he lay in the bed he could feel his body releasing her (body that in the first days of withdrawal had burned as if skin had been blistered away), and he fought against it, fought knowing that to hold her so tightly would only secure and enliven his pain. It was not the body so much as the mind. He watched appalled as she slipped away from his skin. In the first days on the ship and later at the base in Miami (and even later when he was back at Canaan) her presence stayed beside him. He could feel her, like a phantom limb. Her skin is part of my skin, he thought, marveling that it was so. But she began to leave. So he fought. He lay in the bed and conjured her into life. He learned to shape her face in his mind, first the hair, so long and heavy that its natural curls were pulled nearly straight as it hung down her back; then the high uncreased forehead and the pure curve of her hairline; the arched, heavy, unplucked brows; the eyes that had in them the colors of plums and bruises; the nose, so straight that it seemed to carry a minute iron bar just under the skin; the wide mouth with the surprising fullness of the lips; the small, square, slightly cleft chin—and then her body: broad shoulders, the prominent wings of her collarbones; the rise of bone between her breasts; the breasts themselves, small and firm as a handful of meal; the nipples, no larger than his own, the color of strawberries crushed in milk—then all the rest of her depending downward: the protuberant ribs, the narrow hips enclosing the flat belly, the triangular feast of sooty hair; the legs, slim, so startlingly long. . . .

He had it all, in the long nights. He forced her into his mind. But he couldn't hold her. She slid away from him as she had done the first night they made love, when after it was over she slipped from the bed, climbed through the window and ran naked on the lawn in front of the cottage. She had a mole under her right bottom rib that was blue. There was a crescent-shaped scar high on the inside of her left thigh where she had fallen against a dock when she was twelve; one eyebrow was broader than the other; her palms were full of whorls and stars.

He sent her a letter in which he included his bedtime visualization of her—she hadn't commented. The description was only one moment in many letters. Stoked with a restlessness he couldn't contain, he would get up and at the desk under the high darkened windows write lengthy letters to her, letters that he became, as they centered more and more on his despair and his yearning, unwilling to send. She didn't write that way at all—her letters were gay. She wrote as if she were away for the weekend with congenial companions. She told him of picnics in the green meadows of the Koolau Range. She told him of learning to ride a surfboard in the waves off Makaha and Sunset beaches. She recounted the changes in Honolulu, the shutting down of the whorehouses and the tattoo parlors and the bars as the soldiers returned home. She was learning to paint, and she told him of her excursions to the North Shore, her first efforts to depict the old sugar mill at Poonoo, the crust of cliffs beyond Halieva, the notch in the windward mountains that the Japanese planes had poured through, the huge old banyan trees at Schofield Barracks, the fields of seaweedy coral beyond the North Shore cliffs. The letters struck him like blows. He wanted love and loss and yearning, not news. They drained spirit from him, something that he sought to win back behind the glass-topped desk of his new office and in the factories he had constructed and in the fields he slogged across beside irascible farmers.

For a year after he returned he wanted to go back and fetch her. But he knew that if he went to retrieve her she would laugh and kiss him and laughing send him away. He couldn't bear that, he thought, and live. He could, however, bombard her from here. So he wrote letters, almost daily, stringing a bridge across the fracture that separated them.

In Elizabeth's letters, along with the news, she included photographs. J.C. was grateful. He became increasingly unable to picture her. As the months, then years went by, and her letters continued to carry their gay, nonmoaning freight, he grew to be afraid to look at the photographs directly. He began to secrete them around the room, like a drunkard hiding bottles. He was afraid to see her face, but he wanted to—he chose surprise, the surprise of reaching into the pocket of a seersucker jacket and finding a picture of her, the surprise of finding her in a record album, or between the pages of a book. He carried hope always. The letters he sent were the insignia of the hope. If he could keep writing, keep putting the words of his love and need on paper, he could hold her until she gave in. It reminded him of the fights he had gotten into as a child. He had never been big but he had been relentless. His technique had been to grab his opponent around the neck and hold on, squeezing harder and harder, until he gave in. He could take whatever punishment he had to, to win.

Even the rocks his father threw didn't bother him. The bang of stones would wake him and he would rear out of sleep clutching at his wife's image. The awakened time gave him a few more minutes to work her up: her legs, where the silvery hairs began at the razor line; her toenails that were always painted bright red; the way she could whistle through her cupped palms. He would lie in bed as the stones pattered against the walls and would try, once again, to bring her into the room. Her body was gone, but her form was not, his longing was not.

On those nights and on many of the others, he would get up and write another letter. He tried to give news, but he wound up always relating loss. Whatever words went onto the page he waited only for the places where he could afford again to tell her he loved her. He thought he could write letters that were just that: *I love you* written down five hundred times. I love you, I love you. I love you. He had to ration himself; it was a discipline he came to admire. Something told him to hold back, and the ridge of his yearning was pressed against it. "I want to yell it in your ear," he wrote one night, "I want to lean over you and yell it into your ear: 'I love you.' " He wondered if it would have been that way if she had come back with him. She must be changed now, though in her letters she didn't seem to be. He wanted her attention, Elizabeth looking at him.

Often he would get up from the desk and walk out onto the porch. One night, leaning over the rail, he cried out: "Here I am, here I am." If anyone heard him—servants, his brothers in next-door houses—no one called back. The spring bubbled faintly at the bottom of the yard. The moon had turned the cotton plants silver, and clouds faint as dust cleansed the sky. A whippoorwill sang its three notes. It was his father's night to stone the house, but the old man had already come and gone. Medallions of yellow light lay across the boxwoods, tossed there from the servants' quarters in the basement, but no one roused to his call. He waited. Nothing answered. Slipping his hands inside his pajamas, he began to touch himself. His hands moved down his chest, down his stomach, loosened the drawstring and continued downward. If they could be other hands than his own. Elizabeth. Careening six thousand miles through the sky to me. Elizabeth. His hand tightened. Elizabeth. There was nothing else to do.

3 Jacey would always remember his father leaping out from behind a cotton bale calling his name. He would forget the long train ride across the country which his mother had chosen for them because she had not ridden a train for the eight years she had been in Hawaii. He would forget the ride and the country they came through, even the loquaciously green forests of the South that they entered beyond Texarkana, Arkansas, country that became greener as they crossed the rolling hills of Mississippi and Alabama into the north Georgia pine woods. They changed trains in Atlanta, boarding the nameless Atlantic Coast Line passenger train that headed south, through Forsyth, crossed the Fall Line at Macon, passed through Perry, Vienna and Cordele, to release them among the cotton bales and camphor trees of Yellow Springs.

As the miles wound toward Canaan, Elizabeth was surprised at the intensity of her excitement. She soothed herself, and, she hoped, her son with stories about her family in Charleston.

"You are from Charleston, too," she reminded Jacey as they passed a field of cabbages in Arkansas.

"Your great-grandfather built the first swimming pool in Charleston," she said, as they watched a flock of egrets swoop down over a pond in Alabama.

"The Bonnets have lived in Charleston for three hundred years, all the time in the same place," she told him as they passed through a peach orchard south of Atlanta.

Jacey wanted to know about the pool. "Tell me about the pool," he said. He pictured the lagoon at Waikiki, the level blue water that he could wade out in for a hundred yards.

"It had a screened roof and was filled from a big iron tap," Elizabeth said, "just like a bathtub."

Jacey laughed at that. "Did you wash in it?"

"Swim," his mother said. "People would come from as far away as Columbia to swim."

"Am I going there?" he wanted to know.

"Not this trip."

Not this trip or any trip soon. It would be fourteen years before he would cross the worn, ballast stone threshold of the old yellow house she had grown up in Charleston.

"The Lane of St. Louis," she said, her hand rising as if to touch the name.

"What?"

"Where we live. Half a block off the Battery up the Lane of St. Louis."

"Is it like Hawaii?"

"A lot of the flowers are the same." Hibiscus, called mallow in Charleston; oleander, whose red petals wouldn't fade when they dried; Chinese rain tree, yellow as gold; quince.

"It's cooler in Hawaii," she said.

"It's hot here. I'm hot."

She fanned him, with a fan given to her by her last lover, Kaui Hanaku, the twenty-year-old son of a pineapple cutter from Haleiva.

If Jacey was not to remember the trip across country, he would remember her fanning him. Maybe because she did it more than once. Maybe because in later years when his mother's mind had slipped its anchor and she became, both externally and internally, a kind of wandering ghost ship and his guts twisted as he tried to remember that she had once loved him at all, the fanning, in her broad bed in the breezy room above

Pearl, on the train to Yellow Springs and later in his bedroom overlooking the front yard in Canaan, became an emblem, proof that she had once been his.

The fan had a picture on it, of chrysanthemums painted the color of lilacs. His mother turned the fan constantly in her hands, showing first the flowers, then the blank bamboo, then flowers again. As below the Fall Line, the woods and orchards gave way to the row crops of south Georgia, Jacey watched the picture appear and disappear, flowers to blankness to flowers as the fields of corn and cotton and peanuts, the fields of tobacco and rye and sorghum, of barley and oats and millet, of soybeans and sugar cane passed by. There were nights in Hawaii when she would fan him, nights when the moonlight streaked the floor and the smell of plumeria and frangipani drifted from the yard, nights when they lay in the big teak bed listening to the chirps of the geckos and to the sound of the wind blowing off the Equator, nights when there were only two people in the world and his mother's cool fingers touched his eyelashes for sleep as she swung the fan, changing the air around him from hot to cool. If those nights were rare, he remembered them. If he forgot the train stations in Los Angeles and Atlanta, if he forgot the color of her dress and whether or not it was a rose or a gardenia she wore on her lapel, he did not forget her fanning him. Her end would drive him to that, would keep him there.

Cotton bales ringed the station court in Yellow Springs, and from the train window Elizabeth could see the green dome of the courthouse three blocks away. Above the dome, in an otherwise clear sky, a patch of small, round clouds floated, like smoke signals. The small, brown-suited man who had leaned across the aisle at regular intervals to point out sights whose magnificence only he could see sprang to his feet and took her bags. Absently she let him, her mind elsewhere, her body surging with an excitement that was almost terror.

They followed the little man out, stepping from the train into a day that was so bright Elizabeth had to close her eyes. When she opened them she saw the cotton bales and the blue sky, the little man bowing, pressing her hand and hurrying away, no husband yet. On the platform two men in identical Panama hats sheltered a stooped, gray-haired woman between them. A boy in short pants sat cross-legged on a cotton bale peeling an orange; bright shards of peel littered the bricks below him.

She wore a cream-colored linen dress, a hat shaped like a scallop shell and a cream-colored veil. She would always remember the dress and their arrival on a hot September afternoon under a clear sky. Cotton bales lined the sidewalks, awaiting storage in the warehouses; barricades, Elizabeth thought, protection for the good merchants from whatever might spring at them off the street. Above the bales, planted along the sidewalks and along the station court, were camphor trees and tulip poplars. The poplar leaves were already turning, going yellow high in the crown, some of them already turning brown, the way poplar leaves will before the whole tree has had a chance to yellow out.

She walked to the end of the drive, a black boy in faded jeans following with the suitcases. Uptown, a huge magnolia stretched over the street from the courthouse lawn. Across from it was the dense greenery of Canaan that she knew from her husband's letters: live oaks festooned with moss; a huge willow; Cherokee rose and honeysuckle sprawling over a wrought-iron fence. She plucked a leaf from a camphor tree beside the drive, broke it and pressed it against her nose. Simple balm. The fear became delight. There were gaps in the rows of cotton bales before each store. Men in shirt sleeves, women in light dresses, farmers in overalls and khaki crossed the street from one barricade to the other. She would like a procession down that street, the main street of Yellow Springs, spectators perched on cotton.

She turned to speak the thought to Jacey and saw her husband leap from behind a bale in the station yard. Clean as a whistle, she thought as ten feet from her he swept their trailing son into his arms. He swung the boy above his head like a trophy. As he lowered him, struggling, nearly frantic, their eyes met, husband and wife, and the distance-diminished days of their marriage seemed cast like peelings on the ground before them. For Elizabeth, there was no barrier; from her came all the feeling that had held steady and untarnished for nearly five years. Distance hadn't made her let her husband go. For J.C., as she saw, in his gray-eyed glare, there was anger and resistance, fear's consequence. Watching her, he stooped to the boy and took his head between veiny, farmer's hands.

"I've missed you every day," he said and his eyes rose from the tousled blond head to Elizabeth's face. "Every day," he repeated.

Before she could speak he looked at the boy again and his eyes softened. Jacey had gone shy. He twisted in his father's grasp like an animal.

"You'll have to let him go until he knows you," Elizabeth said, crossed the distance between them and handed him the broken camphor leaf.

He took the leaf without answering and tucked it in the breast pocket of his suit.

Years later, she would remind him that she had given him a camphor leaf as the first gift of reunion, but J.C. would be unable to remember it. "Maybe it was a poplar leaf," he would tell her, missing again the totem of the camphor's balm. "A medicine," she would say. "Balm. A symbol of healing."

"Nothing was healed," he would remind her, his jaw working.

And then, even then, as she felt the distance waver and grow between them, as the odorous, cold Charleston wind blew around her, she would laugh.

"You miss everything," she would say, and laugh again, at her life, at the path she had taken, at her husband whom she couldn't help loving.

He didn't understand. In a window seat in her childhood bedroom he sat looking out at the rain. It was late winter and the wind cut the rain with scythes. From the window he could see the ships in the Charleston harbor, white as doves, gray as whales. His thoughts drifted to the time when he had stood on the flying bridge of the cruiser *Boston* watching the Pacific swells sweep toward him. White-topped, the gray-backed swells, the ocean, endlessly rolled, all the way from China. He shuddered, touched the cool windowpane and turned back to his wife.

"I missed it," he said. It was the last day, and she couldn't reach him.

He had had one of his men bring a pickup truck for her luggage, not realizing that she had not brought it on the train. It deepened his anger that she hadn't told him. Behind the truck was the first of his black Cadillacs, a car exactly in its details and appointments like the ones that his mother, Queen Anne Burdette, had been chauffeured around the town in. Without touching her, without having spoken at all—beyond the few words tossed above Jacey's head—he herded his wife and son into the blistering car.

All the windows were down; he opened the door for her, wondered if she would mind the smell of cigar smoke, thought as she slid in beside him how smooth her arms were, hairless, brown as berries, was, for a moment, transfixed by the simple slender curve of her thumb as she raised her hand to press lightly the slight beads of sweat at her temples. As her legs shifted under her skirt he realized the awkwardness of his dreaming; his penis rose to the quick birdwing sound of her stockings, and she said, "Whoo, boy, this is a hot car you have put me in," and smiled showing all of her sparkling teeth. The boy fumbled, instinctively, into the back.

J.C. grasped the wheel and pushed himself back against the seat so that his forearms bulged. In the hot car it was as if an even hotter fire burned beside him. He pressed his forehead against the wheel, feeling slightly faint. He sat up.

"I don't know," he said.

"You will," Elizabeth said, handing him a handkerchief from her purse.

He took the piece of cloth and wiped his sweating face. The perfume will kill me, he thought, drive me mad.

He started the car and drove down the short row of cotton bales to the street.

Two blocks up the Burdette houses began. First was his brother Franken's place, a red brick three-story Georgian mass, winged on both sides by two-story sections trimmed in white wood. Then came the main house, the house he had wrenched from his father, a white Greek Revival mansion, porches around three sides, square widow's walk cupola on top, broad slate roof that hung heavy and menacing, like the edge of a cliff, over square columns. The house was surrounded by masses of supplicant bushes, the yard populated by massive, mossy oaks. Beyond the main house was Bryce's place, a clapboard affair painted bright red with a wraparound porch.

As they reached the edge of Bryce's yard she asked him to drive her around the Courthouse Square. Inside the Square itself, in the middle of a wide green lawn, was the courthouse, built before the Civil War in imitation of the Capitol building in Washington. A four-faced clock on the spire above the dome told the time. In the yard below, county work farm trustees wearing white uniforms with blue stripes down the arms and legs watered the grass.

J.C. swung left around the courthouse, past the downtown businesses. Two banks, department stores, a drugstore on each corner, benches with their backs painted with advertisements for funeral parlors and feed stores, a wide concrete slab sidewalk. On the back side of the courthouse was a small bandstand. An old man in prison fatigues pushed a flat broom across its green floor.

Jacey, sitting first carefully and silently in the backseat, then as they came into the town feeling his excitement swell until he was unable to resist it, pulled himself up by the seat back and looked around at the stores and the courthouse.

"Are those the clowns?" he said, pointing at the trustees on the lawn.

"Are they what?" his father said.

"Clowns; are they the clowns?"

"They're convicts, Primo," his mother said. She touched his face, brushed a spot away.

Jacey stared hard at the men working on the lawn, amazed. "Convicts," he said slowly. "Convicts." He stood up and leaned over the front seat, looking past his mother at the men.

"I want to be a convict," he said.

"We'll put in an application," his father said.

"You would make a fine prisoner," his mother said.

They rounded the Square and made the turn through the iron gate into the main house driveway. J.C. slowed for the cattle guard, three steel rails laid over a shallow ditch. The open gate was permanently tied back by a mass of Cherokee rose. Laggard white flowers hung in the tumbled greenery.

Through the backyard Elizabeth could see the cotton fields rolling away to a horizon of pines. It's like the Big Island, she thought, the way the fields begin in the backyard. She smiled at the thought, at the connection. This would be the time of their togetherness, a conversion she was submitting to. She aimed now at something, she felt, something huge and bright at the edge of her life. As she got out of the car, under a large magnolia whose limbs had been lopped off ten feet up the trunk, she realized suddenly that this was part of it. The house was so white it seemed to glow, ricocheting sunlight. A black woman in a clean white dress stood on the porch steps holding a bouquet of daisies. Someone had watered the boxwoods next to the house; the leaves gleamed, full of crystals. Elizabeth leaned against the car door to catch her breath. The place seemed to have reared up suddenly in front of her, like a beautiful wild horse. J.C., washing his hands, came around the car and dragged her bags out of the backseat. He caught the surprise on her face, the dash of fear—fear, he figured—and was delighted. He wanted her to be hit hard, tumbled by more than she could stand.

"It's all gorgeous," Elizabeth said, shading her eyes to look at the house, the wide backyard, the fields where dust hung like a thin cloud over the cotton. She walked away from the car, ignoring for the moment the woman on the steps, and craned her neck to look up at the cupola.

"It's as if you're at the edge of an ocean," she said, thinking of Charleston and the widow's walks, grief and spy houses at the edge of the battering Atlantic.

"We are." J.C. came around the car to her. He nearly touched her, came close enough to smell her perfume, faint sweat. "All this used to be part of the southern sea." His arm swept outward. "All these lands are an ocean."

"You *do* say." She laughed, pushed lightly off him and ran up the steps to take the flowers from the black woman.

Jacey had wandered into the azaleas by the drive, where he stood dreamily inhaling their wild oak smell, hearing for the first time the keening of cicadas, the droning that soared high, stopped, then began again.

"This is Matilda," Elizabeth cried back to them from the porch. "She has flowers for me."

"Mr. J.C. found those," Matilda said, nodding at her employer.

"Mr. Jackson Coleridge Burdette III," J.C. said, delighted at the sight of the two women on the steps, his wife—wife!—taking the white flowers from the maid Matilda.

"I'm the Fourth," his son cried, almost out of sight in the azaleas.

"That you are," J.C. said, "Mr. Four."

"I want to go upstairs," Elizabeth said. "Could you all get that." Her hand waved at the luggage.

She handed the flowers back to Matilda and entered the kitchen, leaving them all outside. As if she had been there before she crossed without hesitation the polished brick floor, went through the breakfast room past a blue china bowl of chrysanthemums centered upon the glass-topped wrought-iron table, crossed the front hall that was lined with portraits of redheaded men and fair-haired, handsome women and climbed the wide, uncarpeted stairs. She paused only briefly in the up-stairs hall before the tall glass-fronted armoire to glance at the deeds, de-crees and diplomas propped on its shelves, climbed the narrow stairs to the attic floor, made her way across the blue-painted boards and climbed the circular varnished pine stairway into the square glass-sided cupola that overlooked the lands.

Breathless, she leaned against the rail. Eastward was the town, dominated—so close that it filled a third of the clear sky—by the courthouse and its green copper dome. Off to its left a thread of yellow smoke curled above the wide peaked roofs of the Burdette fertilizer plants. She did not yet know that the roofs belonged to her husband, but her attention was caught momentarily by the smoke, pale nearly as winter sunlight, yellow and thin. North, beyond the tops of live oaks, were the buildings of the town; south, beyond more treetops, were the roofs of other Burdette houses, darkened as if by rain. In the fourth quadrant, due west, over cedars and pines, were the lands themselves, the sweep of cotton fields that from that height were endless, rising and falling along the massive contours of the land to a wavering blue horizon of pines.

She looked a long time at the fields. A wasp skittered against the upper panes, but it didn't bother her. It *is* a sea, she thought, and it's enough to drive you crazy. Taking the fluted hem of her dress in both hands, she whirled on the narrow balcony past the four windows, passing town, homes and trees to again look out at the fields. The rows began beyond a line of bushes and chokecherries at the back fence and sprang away, curved like sea swells toward the horizon. In Hawaii she had climbed with her native lover to the top of the windward range and at the very edge of the cliffs that broke downward from their feet like rippling green waterfalls had looked out at the gray-backed Pacific climbing its mountains to a horizon of whitened sky. There, in the presence of a limitlessness she had never encountered before, Kaui's brown hand clasped in hers, she had felt the wildness in herself that seemed to spurt out of her body into the unbroken air. She had wanted to jump from the cliff and fly away into the unhindering sky. Her lover, sensing this, or himself enraptured by the closeness of this beautiful *haole* woman, had grabbed her in his arms, held her harshly, squeezing her until she thought her bones would break. He had brought her back to the pitted rocks they stood upon.

"You are too much a bird," he had told her, and there was fear in his black eyes when he said it. She had laughed.

At the top of her father's house in Charleston, on a squared-off space on the roof accessible by a trapdoor, was an open balcony, a

39

widow's walk. From it she could look over the roofs of the two houses between her father's mansion and the Battery to the bay. As a child she had been taken there by her father to watch the ships entering the harbor. He had told her the history of Charleston as he held her on the high balcony. Far out in the bay the low brick walls of Fort Sumter were black against the horizon. Eleven years ago—eleven, or was it twelve? yes, twelve—she had entered an exile from that place, Charleston. If she returned there, everything would be different. Her friends would be changed, her father older, new leaves on the trees. She flapped her hand in front of her face as if to sweep away the thought. Charleston was still an anchor, her stone of Scone, kept under an old chair. If she never returned, there was no way to remove it. She could circle its absent, unchangeable face forever.

She raised the window overlooking the drive and leaned out. Her husband came out from under the porch roof, crossed the drive and looked into the car.

"I didn't bring much," she ventured to him. "The rest comes by boat." Teak bed, the blue curtains, the white wicker porch furniture.

"Come down," J.C. called back. "I want to show you something."

"Where is Jacey?"

"He's in the house locating cookies."

"Wait," she cried, fearful suddenly that her husband would run away.

She laughed to herself as she descended the three flights of stairs. She glanced at the portraits in the main hall, looked for a moment at the tall vertical windows on either side of the front door. The panes were streaked with wash lines. This is mine now, she thought, a little awed. She rubbed her arms as if she were cold.

But when she came into the kitchen and saw her son perched at an enamel-topped table in the middle of the floor, wearing an old felt hat pushed down over his ears, eating cookies from a plate in front of him, she was not afraid anymore.

"Cookies, Mama," he said with a seriousness that made her laugh.

She ran up and kissed him, took his small perfect face between her hands.

"You're settling right in," she said and smiled at the maid, Matilda, who leaned against the counter beaming at the child.

"I like it here," Jacey said and offered her a cookie.

40

She waved no. "I'll be back in a minute," she said and went outside to her husband, who waited by the car, holding the bouquet of daisies.

"I meant to take those with me," she said, retrieving the flowers from him.

"Ugm." Bounding into his life again.

"You have wasps in your attic."

"Snakes, too, sometimes." Your attic.

"Whoo."

"Last month Matilda found a skin under some old clothes, and now she won't go back up there."

"I don't blame her."

He played with the flowers, separating the stems.

"I was going to make you ride in the truck," he said.

"I wouldn't have minded."

Handing him the flowers, she unpinned her hat, then her hair, which she shook loose as he watched her.

His penis rose again, insistent, defying his mind, which wanted wounds: he imagined her running long-legged on the beach at Waikiki, absent from Canaan.

"I remember what you looked like," he said, as if the thought were a picture they both could see.

"You're the same."

"Hardly."

"This is a beautiful place," she said, retreating to an easier perception: the house reminded her of a tomb or a museum; she chose, in contrast, the bustling yard, the cotton fields beyond full of long distances.

"I want to go out there," she said and walked away from him toward the back of the house.

He laid the flowers on the car hood and followed.

She crossed the yard to the fence that was pressed with wild, country vegetation: chokecherries, a ragged chinaberry tree, masses of blackberry bushes.

"I like how you kept this," she said as he came up behind her.

"The bushes."

"Yes. Wild. Do you have horses?"

"Yes."

"I'll ride out there."

He told her about the old trail to the swamp. She could see it, meandering through the rows. It was the old Burdette trail that Rooley had beaten out on his way back and forth to the river.

"We've always kept it clear," he said. "You can follow it all the way to the swamp."

"I will," she said. "What is that?"

"Yellow Spring."

Behind the encircling band of cedars shimmered the fifty-foot pool of clear water. She walked briskly toward it, J.C. following.

"It's the spring the town is named for," he said as he caught her. He hesitated to take her arm, dropped his raised hand.

"And you have it." She bent to get under the cedars. The spring was ringed with rectangular slabs of rough-hewn unmortared granite. The water edges of the stone were clear. At the far side, a narrow stream flowed out through a shallow troughlike, stone-lined aqueduct. It passed through the cedars on that side and disappeared among bushes behind the red house across the way.

She knelt over the water.

"It's so clear it's hardly there," she said. "How deep is it?"

"Ninety feet."

"It doesn't look ten."

But then it could be a thousand, she thought. Craggy outcroppings of white stone descended, narrowing to a blue, steady-held core.

"What's at the bottom?"

"A tunnel. A hole really."

"It goes on deep?"

"Nobody knows."

"Let me see."

She stood up and began to take off her clothes.

"Elizabeth," he said, but he made no move to stop her.

She was brown all over except for a narrow rim of white around her pubic hair. The thought of her breasts exposed—in Hawaii, to whom?—made him ache. He said nothing, watched fascinated, while a burning, like shame, ran through him.

She looked around again, ran her hands smoothly up her body, brushing it, as if there were fine dust on her.

"Come in," she said.

He was afraid to, and the fear stuttered into anger. *"No."*

"You wish you could." She looked down at the water, stretched upward on her toes and dived, cleanly, into the pool.

He would remember this. Her long legs sweeping in scissor kicks, toes pointed, the crescent of black hair, the whiteness of her buttocks. As if he held her by a cord, he pulled back from the water, his hands reaching out to her. She couldn't see that, falling downward into the clarity of the pool. He thought she would turn around and come back up, but she did not. He had an impulse to drop to his knees and push his face into the water, but he held himself upright, watching her. She passed the twenty-foot ledge, a rim of stone jutting into the pool, the mark of his earliest triumph over his brothers, and continued downward. The pure element, he thought, marveling again at the clearness of the water; nothing could live there. She swam boldly, diminishing as she fell in the unblurred water. She passed the thirty-foot mark, a pile of red field rocks he had wedged one by one into a crack in the wall when he was fifteen. "Elizabeth," he cried, speaking her name out loud for the first time. "Elizabeth." She passed the final mark of his own adventuring, a single tenpenny nail jammed into the rock, stroking deeper. Her body grew smaller, a brown stain falling downward. He dropped to his knees, passing his opened hands instinctively over the water, as if to clear a space. Still she descended, sixty, seventy feet. Just as she seemed to merge with the blue haze at the bottom she turned, rolled over and kicked hard upward. She came up fast, scissor-kicking, streaming a cape of bubbles. Halfway up he could see her face, eyes and mouth open, her arms stretching upward. She veered to the wall, paused a moment to expel air, then shoved off with feet and hands. As she rose, wide-eyed and straining, her long hair swept back, he saw in her face, for an instant, the girl she had been, the pure lines of bone and skin that made the child, the blue eyes wide with triumph and fright, and his heart hurt and something gave way in him so that he stretched his arms into the water to grasp her, caught her as she rose and pulled her, still swimming, from the water onto the stones.

She fell back from him out of his arms across the granite. She turned her body away from him, gasping and coughing, her arms over her face, her mouth against the stone. He sat back on his knees and looked at her. Water-sleek, she gleamed. She rolled over onto her back and looked up into the patch of sky between the tops of the cedars. Defenseless before him, he stayed his hand that reached hesitantly for her. She looked at him.

"I knew I could do that," she said.

Desire punched him, the old desire, born of the wonder at her beauty, her boldness. He brushed the water off her skin—off her breasts, her stomach, his open hand moving across her pubis, touching at the same time—heel and fingertips—her thighs. She turned one leg slightly outward, deepening the slim concavity of her inner thigh. He ran his hand along it, feeling the muscles, the smooth skin, the dryness under the wet. Her hand fluttered over his, grasped fingers, slid them upward to moist hair—he probed, for an instant with almost clinical objectivity: what is here in this sliced body?—bent over her and with his fingers spread the lips of her sex and kissed her there. She moaned and lifted her body; he touched his tongue to the raised crescent of candlewax scar just below the hair, slid upward again to the pale, scentless lips, thrust between them, began, licking upward, the rising rhythm they neither had forgotten. Eyes open, he watched the flush spread down her face and neck, seeping across her collarbones; she blinked, looked away, back, her hand fell open across her belly, fingers curled, her body lifted to his mouth; the bone of his chin stabbed the bone of her pelvis, bobbed against her; she gasped: "Ah, ah," then, "In me, get in me." Raising herself—from a place deeper than the spring beside them—she grasped his shirt, wrenched his clothes; he followed, in awe now, the quick tugs at his garments; helped as he could, feeling a madness rushing through him, tore at his own clothes, broke them off him, trousers jamming at his knees, shirt split, until, the center of him opened to air—what eyes?—he punched back onto and into her lifted body, took her, as he was taken, quickly, hard and unstoppable.

For moments he was blind and deaf, a conqueror surely, but oblivious—for seconds, at least—of that: blown out of time, ringed around only by the cries that came from her—and once, from him—lost: to the four years almost five, the empty bed, the misery of his fetid reconstructions of her, the hidden photographs, almost lost . . . until . . . until, moments later as they lay beside each other breathing the moistness of the cedars, feeling on their skins the slight coolness of the spring-cooled air, listening to the murmur of the spring, her hand brushed up his chest, she raised herself, looked at him and said, "The clock's back in your eyes."

"It wasn't ever gone," he answered, turning away.

"You don't have to be like that." She wanted to pull his flesh, his thoughts back to her, but she sensed she could not. She had given already what she wanted to give, with ease. Anything else was hard—she wouldn't try.

"This is a terrible thing," he said.

She laughed. "This?"

"God almighty."

He got up, jerked on clothes, looking all the time away from her. Beyond the cedars the wide back lawn was empty. Cicadas sawed up the light. She still lay, naked, one leg bent at the knee, looking also out at the lawn. The back of the house, a flat white tongue-and-groove wall, reared, she thought, like the side of a ship. Matilda came out a door at the end of the porch carrying a flat tub. She walked to the top of the steps, glanced briefly in their direction and tossed an arc of water onto the gardenia bushes below her. The water made a rainbow as it fell.

J.C. gathered her clothes and dropped them beside her.

"Get dressed," he said.

"The winner," she answered and smiled.

"What?"

"Breaking her in, J.C."

"Finding the lost."

She pushed up on her elbows and grinned at him. "I wasn't lost."

"You were missing."

"Not that either."

"Jade," he said sharply.

She sat up, leaned back on straight extended arms. "Will you take me around the lands?"

"Only after *purdah.*"

"After what?"

"Isolation; after your quarantine."

"Am I carrying something?"

"My heart."

"Mr. Romance."

He intended to shut her in the house. *He* would dole out her liberty—now he would do that. He would break her down, like a horse or a bird dog, like the world that resisted him. She saw in his eyes what he intended and smiled.

"I have a motorcycle coming," she said.

"Not into Yellow Springs."

"Why do they call it yellow? It's blue."

"The pines."

"What pines?"

"All this"—he swept the air—"used to be yellow pines. You can get my father to tell you about them. He claims the sap of the virgin pines was so pure you could drink it. It was supposed to be yellow, like gold."

"And now gone."

"Everywhere but around the swamp."

"You told me—Lazarus Swamp, where your great-granddaddy built his house."

"The foundations are still there."

"I'll look at that, too."

"We'll see."

"Yes, we will."

He left her then, walked away from her, left her reclined naked on the warm granite, unable, or unwilling, to follow.

If he thought he had sealed her into place, he was to find he had not. Toward the gray-suited back that retreated across the lawn that day, she sent no anger—and no plea for forgiveness. Her senses had drifted already to the lands that lay beyond the bush-clotted fence, to her own wonderment, and to the delight she took in this new life. Another adventure had swum up, like a bright face breeching the spring. Though she had been told, letter by letter, of the history and ways of the Burdettes, she had not been able to imagine this place. She would have invented it though, she thought then, as, giving him time to disappear, she waited under the trees. She was to think that often, for a few years: this clear spring, clean as a miracle, the fussy cedars, the house, the land rolling westward: I could have made them up. If she was to be changed by this—by Burdettes, by their demands—it was a change—a destruction—that would come, that was only possible, as a hardly noticeable accretion of events, slight moments, as limewater dripping in a cave will build forms, unchanged in any given day, in dailiness always the same—only, over years, built into hardness, into stone. She was not afraid of Burdettes, then or ever.

She stood up and swung her clothes about her. She felt the air on every part of her naked skin, on each separate part at once. She crossed the stones and looked into the spring. The blue core wavered, far down. Hawaiian trochus divers had taught her to dive that deep; ninety feet was nothing to them. She knew she had bested her husband, in some way probably humiliated him, but she told herself the same thing she always did: they will have to fend for themselves.

She dropped to her knees, leaned down and took a mouthful of water. She held it, then swallowed slowly, a little at a time. It was sweet, with a faint taste of limestone. She leaned down and took another mouthful.

As she rose her son came up beside her, touched her naked shoulder. She turned, and widening her eyes in mock surprise, spit a long slow stream into his laughing face. He dropped to his knees, scooped a mouthful of water and spit at her. Half of it dribbled down his chin, but the rest splashed against her breasts. They both knelt together, scooped up water and kneeling in front of each other spit it out into each other's faces. Half a dozen times they knelt, cupped mouthfuls and spit at each other.

"We need to get you out of that suit," she said finally, clasping him to her, then pushing him out to arm's length. She stripped the splashed suit off him, pushing him down sitting to take off the shoes and socks. As soon as the last sock was off he sprang to his feet and ran away around the pool. He made the whole circuit, clambering into and out of the run-off stream, dodging her arms that reached for him as he fled by where she knelt on the stones watching him. She laughed to see him run, rose to her feet and jumped into the water. She went under and bobbed up, tossed her long hair out of her eyes, called to him to come in.

He ran on, to the exact spot of her entrance, and running still, feet kicking air, bashed overboard and in, kicked up into the short stroke he had mastered in the lagoon at Waikiki, and swam to where she treaded water, waiting. She gathered him into her arms.

"It's cold," he said, surprised at the shock, unlike the waters of Hawaii.

"It's a spring," she said. "The water comes out of the rocks."

"Is it cold down there?" he asked, pointing beneath them.

"Always."

His mind jumped with the thought of it—he peered down into the spring: the white descendant rocks, the blue light hovering over the bottom. He felt a thrill, a sudden almost wistful pull to plunge downward, touch the shimmering beneath him. Cold in the ground—he was always to know it, the temperature in caves: fifty-seven degrees, he was to learn in geography class—the temperature of life underground.

47

"What's down there?" he whispered.

She bent his head to her and whispered back: "White angels."

"Can I see them?"

"Only if you do your eyes like this." She closed her eyes until the lashes touched. "Just a little to look through," she said.

He did the same: through the lashes a stray shaft of sunlight across the water broke into rainbows.

"Now put your head down," she said.

He ducked his head as she did. Beneath him there was only whiteness, whiteness and then the blue heap of shadow far down. It moved in the crack of his eye. Far down, the water so clear that it seemed he was hung in space, nothing between him and the broken-backed rocks, between him and the blue shawl of quivering light . . . in which something moved—refraction of sunlight? ghosts?—he was too young to guess—he stared, until his chest hurt with trapped air, and unable to breath, he slashed his arms in the water, broke the surface: "I can see them," he cried.

Elizabeth laughed, delighted. She held his head back between her two hands, brushed with her thumbs the water out of his eyes. "You've got seeing eyes," she said, "angel-seeing eyes."

"Did you see them?" He kicked up against her, clung to her shoulders.

"I saw them, too."

"White angels."

"I went all the way down there," she said, plunging her arm down.

"To the bottom?"

"To the very bottom."

"Can I do that?" He wondered: at the whiteness that drew him on, the blue center.

"Maybe someday."

"Take me with you."

She looked into his eyes, blue into gray. "I would do it if I thought you could stand it."

"I know I can."

Her laugh came bright: "All right."

She showed him how to clear his ears, had him practice holding his nose. "When I blow my nose you do it. Like this."

A dreaminess came over him, already before his head was even under water. He fell back in her arms, his eyes closed.

48

"Hold around my neck," she said.

He clasped his arms around her, crouched his body against her breasts. She stroked to the side of the pool, swung her legs around, and with him cradled against her body, pushed strongly downward.

She held him with one arm across his body, swimming in wide strokes with the other. At eight feet she covered his nose and had him blow. His eyes widened, he struggled against her breasts—she swam downward. Ten feet farther she had him blow again—she covered his nose with her hand, sailing down. The surface no longer existed. She had a sudden wild mind-sight of the land above her, gray-backed, growing cotton, the white house craning above them. She had noticed through the trees the screened porch J.C. had told her the family met in to make their decisions. Their laws. She would be there, too, now that she had come; she would have a say in this enterprise. Her son squirmed against her— she knew they would not make it, had no intention of going all the way. She pushed him away from her, he scrabbled back: she wanted to see his face. She pulled up, twenty-five feet down, had him blow his ears one more time, quickly now, no time to linger. She looked upward: the sky was brighter than any blue light beneath them could be. For a second she saw herself crouched among the blued rocks, looking up at the ragged circle of light. She would live down there if she could—she had wanted to take her son there, break into and rest in the clean bottom room of Yellow Spring. She wouldn't be able to, she thought—not this place anyway, and she turned and kicked back upward—here was a limit, that for now she was unable to cross. He would have to dive alone; she realized her error in trying to take him with her, in trying to throw him ahead of her into the world: the boy, too, was on his own. Then the thought faded into the pain in her lungs and there was no thought at all, only the hard kick of her legs, the rustling, refracted surface above her, and the boy clawing at her breasts, the last enchained seconds and then the breaking through, into air and sunlight.

You wake up one morning and spring has come all of a sudden. You have missed the redbuds this year, even the forsythia and the scarlet flowers of the quince. It was only when the dogwoods bloomed, sparkling like the crests of waves, outside your bedroom window, that spring had come for you. You rise from your winter bed and go to the window. In the four-petaled blossoms of the dogwood is a mystery. It has been there all your life but each year you forget. Here it is again, outside your window this March, shimmering in the green heart of the flower. It drags you downward, your heart hammering, into the unknowable past. Your hand rises, reaches for a wand of blooms. The pane is there, clear and hard, impenetrable. You press your face against the glass and gaze a long time at the flowers trembling in breeze. There is something you must know, but cannot learn. Outside the whole world has broken into life. Your body is desire.

In the days to come, years from now, when she would rise from her rumpled bed, wrap the ripped rags of her gown around her and pace the room, in those days, just rising, unfathomable still, she would think of the first morning by this spring, of the absolution she must have been seeking there. Thinking, the course of her life would startle her suddenly, like a path turning. All the mornings she had swum here, rising early in the dawn light, crossing the dewy yard, slipping her robe and gown and entering the cold water of this spring—all the mornings came back to her. Later, on those same mornings she would take her breakfast on the brick terrace below the porch, sweet rolls and fruit juices, brought to her by the succession of maids her husband hired as she found, inevitably, that she could not get along with anyone who worked for her. Her son, who in the first days sat across from her at the white wrought-iron table, was soon gone, into the widening world of school and playmates. Her own world was unchanged, only accelerated. The lovers came and went: Haven in his tottering mansion on the banks of the Okeekee River thirty miles downstream from Canaan; Rooley, her painter cousin; zookeeper Delight; Marcel. They came and went, named and nameless. And in the final days when she paced the room in ragged clothes, her head splitting, they came back to her, came to her as the first morning by the spring, Yellow Spring of history and lore, came back to her, the two dives, her husband's muscular body, her son running in the grass. Empyrean solace they would seem as they flickered in her consciousness, the memory of her husband's long back leaning over her body, Jacey running toward the bushes as if he would throw himself in them. But then, behind the solace would arise the sense of menace that had grown larger as she grew older. It was a darkness in her that shadowed then eclipsed the sunny memories. As she paced she tried to throw it off, tried to hold on to the beauty, force it to stay. It would not stay. She crossed the room and stood before her dresser upon which were the artifacts which kept her sane: a photograph of her taken in Hawaii as she leaned out over a North Shore cliff, the spray of pheasant feathers given to her by Haven, a handful of Roman coins her son had sent to her, a patch of mauve silk from the gown she wore to her first cotillion. Between them in the glass surface of the dresser she could see her face, less clearly than it appeared in the ornate mirror in front of her. She bent and touched her lips to the clear glass, the image blurring and disappearing as she drew closer. She kissed the glass, swept the artifacts around her, pressed them, picture, feathers, coins, against her skin. She could not slip the knowledge that poured up from her insides. She raised her head and looked into the mirror. There was no longer any pretense. She was accomplished.

Jacey woke with his head throbbing and his mother's mouth over his. He coughed, oozed spit; she licked it from his face. He reached for her, crying, and she drew him up. He could not speak, had an image of hugeness, of light, of the horrible fear of not getting back to the surface. She caressed him, brushing the water off his body. "There, there," she said as he burrowed into her shoulder. He curled against her. She sat back on her heels and murmured into his ear soft sounds. He touched her face; his hand drifted downward to her breast and pulled the tip of it into his mouth. She let him suck, holding his head against her.

She looked down herself at him, remembering how it had been in the house in the hills above Pearl Harbor. When he was a baby she had suckled him, refusing to feed him from a bottle. She traced the line of his fine nose, straight and narrow as her own. She touched the half-cleft chin, the hardly formed line of the jaw, pressed lightly into the concavity of his sucking cheeks. His hair was golden, unlike her own black and J.C.'s red. Her father's hair was blond, but not crimped in curls as Jacey's was. Could she give milk again? She wished she could, wished her breasts would fill again and give now, whenever she wanted, sustenance to this child. If this suckling was already taboo, she could dream away beyond admonishment, she could, as always, slip restraints. She pressed her fingers into the breast, squeezed outward as she had done as a nursing mother to accelerate the flow. She squeezed the breast with her full hand. "Mama, Mama," he murmured, falling back with her into the dream of beginning, into her own early time, the mornings when he would come to her as she lay in the great teak bed in her white bedroom and she would take him in her arms and hold him as she ate her breakfast. There was a time in her life when she had lived as she wanted. She felt the stirrings of

51

something, something that was getting up inside her and moving away, a territory, a possibility, shifting. The sun scattered rags of light through the tops of the cedars. In Hawaii house plants were trees. She remembered her awe the first time she was taken up into the Koolau Range and shown the schefflera, the philodendron, the coleus, plants she had known as tame shrubs in brass pots under the windows in Charleston—here they were trees. She had once seen a schefflera as big as her cottage. She had walked up under it and stood among the rayed, otherworldly leaves. Things could burst loose into something greater than themselves. She understood what her husband was up to, what he had meant in his endless letters over the five years. They were letters of plans and of accomplishments. This plant I am building, this machine that will transform acid into fertilizer, this warehouse that I have now triple-decked with five thousand bales of my neighbors' cotton. You must help me make and do, the letters cried. Such a simple, obvious request. She had no desire to do that, she knew: to protect, to nurture, to sustain. There was so much else. You must help me to look and live, she could have written, though she did not. There will be many days when all I want to do is sit by this spring and look out at the fields. I will not be seeing the accomplishment of cotton, I will be seeing only a sweep of green under a wide blue sky. It won't *mean* anything.

The child was asleep. With one hand she pushed his hair back and with the forefinger of the other traced the line of his forehead. She remembered the fit of his head in her palm, remembered the nights when she had lifted him from the crib and held him in her arms, for no other reason than to feel the fit of him. There had been nothing in her life that fit her so well as this child held against her breast. She laughed now, softly, at the wonder of it. Her husband's body, the strong slice of loins driving into her, had brought something else, a splitting into atoms that broke being itself loose, but that was different. She felt no remorse at having taken Jacey into the spring. The water shimmered before her, containing its own light. She could protect her son—she believed that always. She was strong enough for that, every day of her life she would be.

She rose with the boy in her arms; he stirred, his eyes opened, he kicked against her, and she put him down. He rubbed his eyes, wiped his mouth with his open hand.

"Did we go to the bottom?" he asked.

"Near enough."

"It was too far." He was crying again, in the soft soundless way he had taken on in the last year. She ran her fingers through his hair, pushing his head back. He smiled up at her.

"It was majestic," he said.

"It was? All you did was kick and fight."

"My ears hurt."

"Maybe you're too little to dive in a spring."

"I want to do it. I think I can do it."

"Someday you will. Now," she said, brushing water off him, "run to the house and get towels."

"Okay." He sped off, naked, across the lawn.

She walked around the spring to the trough where a patch of sunlight lay on its back on the granite and lay down beside it. On her back she spread her arms and looked up into the tops of the cedars. A mockingbird, out of sight, meowed like a cat. Her father had once told her that she was too wild to stay in a house. "Every time you come in," he had said, "you have to walk around for half an hour until your soul comes back into your body." She had no idea what he meant. There was often a restlessness in her. Something that made her move on. She wondered if she would leave her husband. The thought didn't scare her. There was always another world. In college, her roommate had been appalled at the way she spent money. "There's always money somewhere," she had told her, and she believed it. Life was endless—the problem was never too little to do, only too little time. If she wanted only to *see*, she wanted to see many things. When, by the spring, J.C. had pulled back from her body she had seen the fear in his eyes, underneath the fierceness. It had always been there—it had drawn her to him, the boy's fear he tried to conceal. He would push himself always hard against it; he would deny it always, she knew that. She wanted to watch him. "What do *you* want me to do?" he had once asked her, and she had replied that she would be happy to watch him sitting in a chair on the lawn. "Just that?" he had said. Yes, just that.

A white butterfly fluttered vagrantly above her head. She lifted a hand to it; it was too high to reach.

She thought of her mother's quietness, that had seemed, all those years of her childhood, inviolable. Her mother had drifted through the rooms of the big yellow house like spirit. Everything in the house was immaculate, though she never seemed to touch anything. Elizabeth had seen her father rise when her mother entered a room. She had seen him do it when no one else was there. When her mother died—in the April she was fourteen—her father had stood over the coffin, among the day lilies in front of the library fireplace, and gazed into her still face. He had been so silent that finally she had reached to touch him. As her hand moved he had cried out, "I loved you so," in a voice more passionate than she had ever heard in her life.

She clasped herself in her arms. Old moon, she thought, trailing down the sky. Old father, resting in a chair in Charleston. He had hated her wild ways. Always, he raved against her. She never minded. She loved him and understood that he could not accept her. Haven—whom now she must go see—had asked her once, as they lay in the nighttime dunes above Sunset Beach, why nothing ever seemed to bother her. "This, for instance," he said. "You don't seem to mind at all that I'm your husband's best friend." She didn't know. And it was true he was her husband's best friend: was that *supposed* to matter? She never counted their friendship in any sort of balance. Haven, at that moment, was the one who held her—out of need, and desire, she presumed—she lived there where he was, desire meeting desire.

She pushed up on her elbows to watch Jacey as he came through the cedars carrying a pile of towels half as big as himself. She marveled still, as always, at the sway of his small body, the excellence of movement in the perfectly formed legs and hips. The charm and mystery of him thrilled her. She could look back the whole length of his life, threading into any present moment all the pictures of the past. She knew him running, she knew him sleeping, crying, singing. She knew that he was carrying just as many towels as he could possibly lift. How could her husband fool her—subvert and antagonize her—when she had before her always the breathing definition of him. Their son was a spy, or no, not a spy, a mime, a mimetic genius who recreated in each breath, each gesture, the whole of their lives. She knew her husband knew this. It was why he had swept breathlessly the small boy into his arms. His eyes had been wet, with tears of knowledge.

She took a towel from Jacey and without speaking, wanting to preserve the picture of him, unrearranged by speech, silently dried herself. Jacey, in his intuition, knowing what she was doing, said nothing. He was already dry. The whole world—sun-spanked grass; a bird calling in trees; the Negro cook in her starched white brilliant cotton; the gleaming kitchen; the smells: of simmering greens, frying chicken, the grease on the garage floor, cotton poison; the spring, that from the house steps was blue, not crystal; the shaggy cedars—thrilled him, set off in him a series of charges that had propelled him, laboring under towels, across the lawn. He watched her, an eagerness in his eyes, a fascination, that brought a smile to her lips. Unconsciously, the towels dropped at his feet, he dried himself again, following her movements, with bare hands. He loved the hugeness of her body, the great blackness between her thighs, the relentless curve of her breasts, the solid swell of belly. Dreamily, he touched himself in the places she touched: shoulders, breasts, loins, bowed his legs to reach between them, hauled the invisible towel upward over his sex.

Their eyes met and they both laughed, aware. She flicked him with the towel. He ducked away laughing and ran out of her reach. She followed him, walking at first, then running as he sped away around the pool. At the trough he veered away across the stones, just eluding her grasp, and dashed through an opening in the cedars onto the lawn. She ran after him swinging the towel. He dodged, but she gained on him. At the fence, just before he spilled into the arms of a scruffed camellia, she caught him; her hand grasped his shoulder, she spun him away from leaves, and they fell together onto the grass.

She held him down and kissed his laughing mouth over and over. He squealed and wiped the kisses away as she gave him more. Holding him down with both hands, she rose above him.

"You can't get away from me, little boy," she said.

"Oh yes I can," he cried as he struggled.

"Never, never, never."

"Yes, yes, yes."

She pressed her mouth against his cheek and blew noises onto his skin. He squirmed loose and bit her lightly high on her right breast. She bit him back on the shoulders, nipping him, on the chest, the stomach, and then lightly took his small penis into her mouth and pulled it out from his body like elastic, and let it go. He squealed and pushed her away.

She fell back on her side, breathing hard. He climbed up her body and sat in the curve of her hip, his feet splayed in the grass. They looked at each other.

"You're too rough for me," she said, "too big a boy for me."

"Will Rufino come here?" he wanted to know.

"No, not here. He'll stay in Hawaii."

"I wish I could see him."

"You'll have new friends here."

"Not Rufino though."

"Someone else."

"Someone else," he repeated slowly. She caressed his face.

"We'll get the grass itch," she said. "Let's get dressed."

They rose and hand in hand walked back to the spring.

4   Jack Burdette walked through the fields toward the main house. Land master, he said to himself, master of the lands. He flicked the end of his burlap sack at the cotton plants, which were defoliated and scrawny, shaggy-headed with burst-open boles, awaiting picking. Every so often he stopped to gather handfuls of the rusty pebbles that had collected in the rows and dropped them in the sack. The pebbles, smaller than the end of his little finger and round, were a sign of good land, as gallberry bushes were a sign of good land, but he wasn't grading ground tonight, September night, he was on the way to batter the side of a house, and he wished the pebbles were larger. The moon over his shoulder was a sliver of light.

He came through the back gate, pausing at the spring to scoop a mouthful of water, and crossed the yard to his regular throwing stand beside a ragged pyracantha bush. He stood there awhile, checking the range. A semi passed out on the street, changing gears. The house, under the slight moon and the cottony stars, seemed again to have grown—as it had now on these nights for the last four years—all the proportions stretched, so that if he thought about it, he could imagine the ceilings soaring up into haze and the rooms widened out, needing shouts to be crossed with voices.

In the thousand rooms where I have been, he thought, remembering something he had written down after his wife died. If he counted them up, how many times would he have been in each of the rooms of that house? He had been born there, sixty years ago. In those days the house was lit with coal-oil lamps. On the other side of where the garage was now, attached to it by a short passageway, had been the privy, a small hexagonal building made of brick. A Japanese plum tree grew on the spot now. In the evenings they had walked the horses in the backyard. There was no fence between the fields and the yard; his mother had complained about the plow mules' making their turnaround on the grass.

He had brought Annie to this house, thirty-six years ago. Though she had been dead now for nearly twenty years there were still times when he had to catch himself to keep from calling Mattie by her name. Queen Anne. Queenie. Queen Anne Cattridge Burdette. She came back, came back. Dead woman, so blond. The first time he loosened the bodice of her gown he had touched nipples that were so pink they were nearly transparent. He was the only man on earth who knew that.

Their bedroom was in the corner, facing south and west. Now his son's bedroom. He shook his sack of pebbles, opened it and took out a handful. I got you right where I want you, he thought, bucking himself up. He hadn't realized when he began this ritual four years ago that something like this could become a job, too. He was getting tired of it, but what else was there to do? He believed in finding things to live for, and he would have come back anyway, he knew, to this high house. Regardless of whether or not his unruly son was a menace. Mattie laughed at him because she thought it was only an old man's anger that drove him, and the anger, to her, was silly. It wasn't only anger, and anger or not, Mattie would have come with him if he'd let her. She would have held the sack for him. He weighed the pebbles in his hand. He had scuffed up a million of them in the cotton rows. He was the only man he ever knew who had found a use for them, another Burdette first. The house lights were all out. He flexed his arm. Wake up, you arrogant prick. He flung the pebbles as hard as he could against the side of the house.

Jacey woke right up. He had no idea what the noise was, but it shot him off the edge of sleep. He lay in bed and listened to the pebbles hitting the house. Maybe it was Rufino, he thought, dazed. I want to go swimming. It was his first night at Canaan. Another handful went *prAAAt* against the house. He slid out of bed and went to the window. An old man in shorts stood by a bush in the middle of the yard. Jacey didn't know what to think, but he was delighted. He waved. The old man paused and squinted up at him, took a step back, then forward. He waved and then with a huge, full-armed gesture motioned for Jacey to come

57

down. Jacey, naked, stopped only to tie his sneakers. He had only just learned how, and it thrilled him now to tie everything he could find two ends to. He figured that when he grew up he'd like to get a job tying things. As he left his room a light came on and went off under the door of his parents' bedroom across the hall. He almost stopped to investigate but he decided to go on.

He descended the wide, polished-plank stairs to the first floor. A light burned on a table beside a long yellow sofa. He walked down the hall, turned left through the breakfast room, groped through the dark kitchen and opened the back door. The air smelled of flowers. The smell came from a tea olive bush—he didn't know the name of it—beside the steps. The scent was so thick that as he ran down the steps he seemed to pass through an invisible bush made entirely of perfume.

The old man waited beside the pyracantha, jiggling pebbles. He grinned at Jacey.

"How 'bout you, sport?" he said.

"What are you doing?" Jacey asked.

"Stoning this house."

"What does that mean?"

"Watch this."

The old man pushed hair out of his eyes with the back of his wrist, reared back and threw a handful of pebbles high against the wall. They spattered against boards.

"We save the windows for last," he said. "Here." He cupped three or four pebbles into Jacey's hand. "You try it."

Jacey threw. The pebbles hit the bushes under the back windows.

"You got to get closer—it's all right."

The old man scooped out more pebbles and handed a few to Jacey. "They're kind of light individually," he said, "but in a handful they do all right." He whipped the rocks elastically at the house. *PrAAAt* they went against the wall.

"It's a good feeling," he said. "I come up here four or five times a year for the good feeling that's in it." He brushed his hands together and stuck his right out to Jacey.

"I'm your Granddaddy Jack," he said, pumping Jacey's hand.

"Oh," Jacey said. "I'm Jacey Burdette." It was the first time he had shaken hands with anyone.

"Pleased to meet you," his grandfather said.

"Won't we get in trouble?" Jacey asked.

"Who's going to get us?"

"Well, my daddy."

"Your daddy can't do a thing about this. It's one thing he can't do anything about. Did you see that light come on?"

"Uh huh."

"We're getting his attention."

He held the sack up to his chest, scooped rocks out and threw three handfuls in quick succession. "Bam, bam, bam," he cried, "Hot tamale!"

"Whew," Jacey said. He reached for the sack, which his grandfather opened for him, grabbed pebbles and threw as hard as he could. He was scared and delighted at the same time.

Jack threw several more quick handfuls. *PrAAAT, prAAAt, prAAAt,* went the rocks.

He dropped his arm and murmured, "Delightful; this is just delightful, umm, umm, yes sir."

"Umm, umm, yes sir," Jacey echoed, throwing his own rocks.

He stripped off a sprig of pyracantha berries and threw those. They didn't get the distance the rocks did.

"You know what we ought to have?" his grandfather said. "Paint bombs. That's what I'm going to get. The next time I come up here I'm going to get paint bombs."

"I've seen a bomb," Jacey said.

"You have?"

"Uh huh. In Hawaii. They have a big bomb at the Navy base."

"I bet they do. Which reminds me that your daddy was off in the war for three years and only sent me four letters. Not that he should have done different. We had already busted up by then, or we were on the way to it, and I am sure he was embarrassed to be in touch with the man he was about to draw and quarter, seeing as it was his father and all. They were cold communications for sure."

"He sent us a lot of letters. I saw them." Jacey thought of the bundles wrapped in ribbon in his mother's dresser.

"He's a strange man," his grandfather said, pausing to push his hair out of his eyes. "I don't recognize me in him at all." He pressed his thumb against one nostril and blew snot onto the grass. "I recognize his mother," he continued. "I recognize her all right." He cleared the other nostril in the same manner. "My wife was strange, too." He wiped his hands on his shorts. He was wearing suspenders. "Everybody loved her—you never saw such a funeral as that woman had. Folks came from everywhere." He pulled at his bottom lip and then spit into the grass. "I guess a lot of it was simply because she was a Burdette. We get a lot of mileage out of that—you'll catch on to it after a while."

He stripped berries off a branch, carefully avoiding the thorns. "It's on my mind a lot these days," he continued, shaking the berries in his closed fist. "I think about what we've been in this country and what we're supposed to become. Your daddy wants us to be tycoons."

"What are they?"

"Big-shot businessmen." He sniffed at the berries. "Hell, I can understand it," he continued. "That's not the problem. Thirty years ago I wrenched this farm into tobacco and peanuts. My daddy threw a fit. Cotton, cotton, cotton—that was all he wanted, just like his daddy wanted it before him. But it was time to change. Tobacco made money and so did peanuts. I convinced him. I got him to let me plant ten acres of tobacco. It turned a hundred and twenty-five percent profit. Daddy came right around. 'You want to plant tobacco,' he said to me, 'you plant tobacco.' And I did it—we did it together. This damn bombardier"—he tossed the berries at the house—"doesn't need any partners. He's a one-man band."

He reached into the sack, drew out a handful of the round, rusty pebbles. "And I can't get over it," he whispered as if to himself, "I can't get over it."

"I can't get over it," Jacey whispered in refrain and stroked his grandfather's arm.

"Yeah boy," his grandfather said and whipped the pebbles at the wall.

They threw until the sack was empty. Jack shook the dust out of the bottom, folded the burlap and tucked it under his arm.

"What now?" Jacey said.

"Head on back home."

"Can I go?"

"You got to go in to bed."

"I'm not sleepy."

He took the child by the shoulders and pressed him against his body. He remembered the energy he once had, what he had done with it on this land, in this house. The porch door opened and a woman in a white nightgown came out. His heart jumped; he started, but did not move toward her, held the boy's small head against him. The woman came to the edge of the steps, bent down and plucked a sprig of tea olive. They were close enough to speak, but neither of them said anything.

"You want to come with me?" Jack said to Jacey.

"Yes sir."

He picked Jacey up and holding him like a long bundle in his arms looked over his body at the woman.

"I guess it will be all right," Jack said. He felt a warmth in him.

"Umm, umm, yes sir," Jacey said, linking his arms around the old man's neck. Jack felt the touch of the small warm hands pulling his head down and he kissed the boy's hair, looking all the time at the woman on the steps. She held the tea olive toward him, the tiny white flowers faint in the dark leaves. Then she waved the sprig at him, a slight motion of her wrist, and smiled. Ghost, he thought. He drew the boy against him close, turned and made his way across the yard, through the bush-tangled gate and out into the whited fields.

So Jacey's first awakening at Canaan was in his grandfather's house. And it was a dog that waked him, a black-and-white-spotted bird dog that licked his face as he lay in bed under a single tall window overlooking a fish pond and his grandfather's garden. He pulled the dog's head to him, and the dog put both front legs on the bed, kicked with a hind one trying to get up. Jacey sat up laughing; the dog scrambled into the sheets. He pulled the covers over them both and was snuggling in under the dog's ricocheting muzzle when a voice said, "You are certainly the something or other dickens."

He poked his head out to see a squat, round-faced woman looking at him. She wore a blue bandanna on her head and grinned out of a face full of creases.

"You're funny," Jacey said.

"I don't take dogs to bed," the woman said and handed him a glass of orange juice.

Jacey sat up. The dog bounded out of the bed and wagged to the woman. She thrust his muzzle away, roughly and affectionately.

"Where is this?" Jacey asked.

"Your granddaddy's house: the Hall of the Cotton King."

The room had high white walls, a rubbed pine desk pushed against one of them, and a whitewashed plank floor covered with a big multicolored rug. Books were stacked in random columns in corners and around the edges of the rug. The whole place was full of light.

"We threw rocks," Jacey said and gulped the orange juice.

"I know *all* about it," the old woman said.

"We're going to get bombs."

"I don't doubt it."

Jacey jumped out of the bed.

"You always sleep naked?" the woman asked.

"Uh huh."

"Like a field nigger. I'm going to have to get you something."

"I don't want it." He struck a pose, belly out.

"Whoo, you're something, ain't ye. Just look."

Jacey strutted around the room, pushing his body and his small pecker as far out as he could.

"Mr. Sashay."

"I can do this, too," he said, angling back to a spot in front of her. He stuck his arms out and rolled his hips.

"Hoochie-coochie," the woman said.

"The hula dance. From Hawaii."

"Hu-la-la."

Through the open window he saw his grandfather in a large straw hat stooping in a field of flowers beyond the fish pond. The old man looked up and waved. As he did so a flock of yellow butterflies rose out of the flowers. It was as if his grandfather had thrown them into the air. Jacey clapped his hands and stopped, amazed.

"Some more," Jacey cried.

"You're crazy," his grandfather shouted, cutting flowers.

Jacey raced out of the room, down a short hallway and out onto the back porch. The old woman followed, saying, "Slow down, slow down, child," as he ran ahead. The dog bounded after them.

"You just run around butt-naked all the time?" his grandfather said as he made his way out of the flowers onto a pinestraw path. The path was one of several that ran through the garden.

"Let's have some breakfast, Mattie," he said as he passed the round fish pond and came up the back steps.

"At your service, maestro," the woman said and went back into the house.

His grandfather set a bundle of flowers into a chair at a white wrought-iron table. The flowers, red, yellow, orange, purple, filled the chair to the top of the table.

The old man rubbed his hands. "Now for the eats," he said. "You hungry?"

"A little."

"When we get through," the old man said, pulling chairs up for himself and Jacey, "we'll take the tour. Your mama called to say she'd be over to get you after a while, but I reckon we have time for a little tour."

The old woman came out of the door carrying a tray. She set bowls of oatmeal in front of them. The oatmeal was sprinkled with raisins and cinnamon sugar.

"This is Mattie," his grandfather said. "We run around together."

Jacey didn't know what he meant. The old woman smiled at him with big, cracked teeth.

"His ponkypoon," she said and went back into the house.

The old man leaned toward him. "She and I have been friends now for nearly the whole twenty years since your grandmother died. It's a pleasant habituation."

In a minute Mattie came back carrying bowls of cut fruit and glasses of orange juice. She set the food down and slid into a chair between Jacey and his grandfather.

"Let's bow," the old man said. Jacey looked to see what he meant—he'd never done that before. His grandfather bowed his head low over the oatmeal; Mattie bowed her head, too. Jacey sank his head, keeping his eyes open; the oatmeal smelled delicious.

"Lord, here we are again," his grandfather said. "We got this little naked boy here who's come to us like one of your miracles. Take care of him. Take care of me and Mattie, too, and all Burdettes and their kin even that son of a bitch J.C. Bless this food Amen."

The old man put his hat back on and dug into his oatmeal. "Mighty fine," he said and beamed at them both.

Beyond the flower garden, off to the right, were the woods, all pine. Through the trees, Jacey could see the cotton fields bright with sunshine. Off to the left, beyond a grassy space, was the pond. Its black water curved away past the edge of the house into a bank of tangled bushes beyond which the cotton fields rose evenly toward the top of a low hill. Just beyond the hill ridge Jacey could see the slate roof of another house.

"Who lives over there?" he said pointing with his spoon.

"Your cousin Rooley and his wife Alsace," his grandfather said. "They're about as wild as the rest of us."

"Are we a lot of people?"

Mattie laughed. "The Burdettes think they're *all* the people," she said.

"Ain't it true," his grandfather said. He paused with a spoonful of oatmeal in front of him. "There was a time when the Burdettes *were* all the people. Everybody we knew we either owned or were kin to. I used to see that in my daddy. He used to look at folks sometimes like they were speaking a foreign language to him. I wanted to shake him awake. Your daddy's like that, punching around in a dream. You would have thought that the war, and Harvard, would have changed him, but they didn't."

"Who else?" Jacey asked.

"Well, we're two-sided"—"At least that," Mattie put in, laughing—"We've got the Land Functional Burdettes and we've got the Queer Burdettes. The Land Burdettes—the ones who run the place—come down oldest son to oldest son from Langston, who careened into this territory out of South Carolina after the Revolution; to Rooley; to Wheeler; to my father, Jackson; to me, and so on. You're one of them. The Queer Burdettes are the ones you might call the adjunct side. They either helped with the running of the land, like Eustace, or they took off, or if they stayed, they came up with their own special projects. Rooley's from the queer side; so are his brothers Bernard and Delight. Their father was my brother Ransome. Ransome worked with me, but his sons have drifted off into other worlds. Rooley's a painter and Bernard and Dee run a zoo down the road from here."

He paused and looked out at the garden, which lay open in its bright dress to the early sunshine, and sighed. "It looks like I've joined them," he said.

"Me, too," Jacey said.

His grandfather dropped his spoon back into the bowl. "Music," he said brightly, got up and went into the house. In a moment a loud aria boomed out of the open windows. His grandfather came out washing his hands and twitching a little as he walked. He resettled into his place. "Breakfast is the best time for the opera," he said.

Jacey cocked his head to listen to the male voice soaring high in a complicated despair.

64

"That's *Adriana Lecouvreur,*" his grandfather said, nodding at him. "Old Michonnet."

"O sadness," Mattie said drolly.

"Whoo," Jacey said.

They ate under the frothy bower of the music, his grandfather pausing regularly to raise his head to it as if it were sunshine he was taking full on the face. Jacey remembered how it had been in Hawaii, that he had been away from now no more than a week, when he and his mother ate breakfast out on the porch. The wind made the coconut fronds jump, as if animals were swinging in them. Years from now on the fire escape of their apartment in New York, Jacey would tell Martha of the first meal at his grandfather's, of the music and the bowls of bright fruit and the smell of cinnamon, and he would try to recreate for her what it had been like. There would be by that time, nearly fifteen years later, something in the memory he could never recover: a smell, the actuality of his grandfather's rufous, music-dreamy face; Mattie's eroded knuckles, hard as hickory nuts; the sound of the dog under the table gnawing fleas—something that was essential, that he missed, that he couldn't rediscover.

As Adriana and Michonnet dragged their despair through the theaters and ballrooms of Paris, Jack told Jacey of the early days at Canaan when the Burdettes had carved the land into a receptacle that would support them.

"That field up there," he said, pointing across the pond, "was the first cotton field on the lands. It's sandy ground; the old soft-tipped plows they used in those days could cut it. There's a branch that runs in through there, and the ground's rich. Your great-great-great-granddaddy Rooley had it cleared. They say he used to drive the mules himself, hauling out the timber. He was redheaded like the rest of us and mad at everybody all the time."

With his fingers he plucked cantaloupe wedges from the blue china serving bowl. "His son Wheeler," he continued, "my granddaddy, was the man who made the land. Rooley beat it up, but Wheeler seduced it. He was a tall man with a face like a heron—there's a painting of him up at the main house—he petted and stroked this ground until it rolled over on its back wagging its tail. He was the cotton man."

He stood up and walked to the edge of the porch and balanced there on the edge of the gnawed boards. He waved an arm at the woods. "These pines have always been here, or pines like them. But out over yonder"—he pointed past the pond—"the fields have been there for more than a hundred years. Wheeler grew the cotton that put coats on the backs of half a dozen Georgia regiments. Joe Brown, who was governor during the War, called him the Butternut King."

"Butternut," Jacey said.

"Yes. It was the dye they used on the uniforms. Brown, cinnamon-colored."

Mattie laughed and winked at Jacey. "Any minute now he's liable to fall on his knees and start kissing the ground. Watch out when Jack Burdette gets to singing of the earth."

Jacey was drawing on the table with a blueberry. He drew a face and poked eyes and a nose into the center of it. A mockingbird whistled and clucked in an oak tree by the fish pond.

"I want to go swimming again," he said, looking up at his grandfather.

"Cleanliness is next to godliness," his grandfather said, still gazing out toward the pond. He turned around. "We might as well do a little natural exercising. Here go, girl."

He came back to the table and began to clear the dishes off.

"We need to shell those beans," Mattie said. "I want to put them up today."

"That's what we'll do," Jack said, "but first we want to take a little dip in the pond."

After the breakfast dishes were cleared away, Jacey walked with his grandfather through the flower garden to the pond. The whole house, he saw, was surrounded with flowers that grew higher than his head.

"These are zinnias," his grandfather said, touching the stalks as they passed. "And the little one in yonder are marigolds and cosmos. I wanted more than a garden; I wanted a forest of flowers."

The soil underfoot was dark gray, the same color as rain clouds, and Jacey scuffed his feet in it as they walked. Beyond the garden was the grassy verge that gave into the pond. The ground was clear around the house side of the pond, except for masses of cattails that grew against the low banks. The pond was half a mile across; halfway to the other side a sagging fence crossed from one bank to the other.

"That fence," Jack said, pointing, "was the invention of my grand-daddy. He went through a period where he wanted to divide everything up, even though it was against the old will. He strung fences all over this

66

property cutting himself loose from his brother. It was a feud that didn't get settled till the last year of my granddaddy's life."

"A feud," Jacey said, "a feud, a feud, a feud."

He ran ahead to the edge of the pond. Fingerling bream darted away from the shallows.

"This is where we used to do a lot of our swimming when we were kids," his grandfather said as he came up beside him. "When we weren't dipping in the spring. Now your goddang father uses this pond for his irrigating and it gets too messy. He'll drain it right down to the mud before he'll stop."

He scratched in the center of his chest. "But we've had rain this summer," he said, "so your daddy hadn't been able to do that much damage."

He shucked his suspenders, unbuttoned and dropped his shorts. Underneath he wore a pair of green BVDs that snapped up the front. He pulled his undershirt up over his head. He'd left the hat at the house.

Jacey, who was still naked, watched for a second his grandfather peer into the dark water before springing past him into it. He ran as far as he could before the depth of it keeled him over on his face. He went under and came up laughing, a strand of fuzzy green algae in his hair.

"Hey, boy," his grandfather said, wading in after him, "I'm giving instructions here. You got to follow along."

"*You* got to follow along," Jacey said, splashing. His eye caught a glimmer of silver off to his right and he dived at it. He opened his eyes underwater into a coffee-colored, mote-filled light. He felt his grandfather next to him and came up.

"Can you swim?" his grandfather asked.

"Sure."

Jacey swam away, almost dog paddling, his head out of the water like a turtle's. Something ahead of him moved in the water, cut three short curves and disappeared, and Jacey swam toward it. Then he saw the curves again, like smiles drawn on the water, and then a flat fist of a head, black and wet, and the body behind it, four feet long, that the curves were made of. Behind him his grandfather made a whooping noise and he heard him thrashing toward him, becoming articulate as he came, shouting, "No, boy, no!" But Jacey, who had never seen any kind of snake before, swam on toward the undulant form creasing the water ahead of him. The snake, which could have dived or could have swum away from

67

a boy, did not. The small hatchet head turned in his direction as he swam up to it, flicked at him, a space of six inches or so between them, missed, and then the whole snake, as Jacey tried to turn away, swam under his outstretched arm, grazing his side, pressing him just hard enough with the ungiving leverage of muscle for Jacey to feel a sudden terrifying awareness of its power, so that as he shoveled himself around in time to see his grandfather falling backward with the cottonmouth grasped in both hands, the snake attached to his upper chest like an unusual, fugitive tail, the shock in his eyes reflected not only his grandfather's horrified screeching face, or the sight of the snake suddenly spinning through the air, but his own revealed and personal knowledge of menace.

He would never forget it. The snake would always be mixed into the delight of this day. His grandfather, who had jerked the snake's head so violently away from his chest that the fangs, curved like stitching needles, were still hooked in the skin, fell back into the water thrashing. He went under and came up yelling, "Oh, God, oh, God, oh, God," rose, and high-stepped toward the bank. He stumbled to his knees in the shore mud, pedaled back up grasping tufts of grass, came upright, jerked into a run and then, for a moment, seemed to recollect himself; he stopped and, turning back to Jacey with a face that was drained of color, said, "Come out of there, boy. Come out of that water and help me here." Jacey looked back once to find the snake, but it was gone under, and he came out of the pond.

"Gather my clothes," his grandfather said, calm now, and as Jacey picked up undershirt and shorts, the old man, with thumb and forefinger, pinched the two slivers of bone from the skin below his collarbone and threw them into the water. He touched Jacey on the head and said, "Let's go. We got to take care of this business." They headed toward the house, his grandfather picking up speed as they walked so that by the time they reached the garden path Jacey was having to run to keep up.

Mattie rose from the porch table where she was shelling beans. To Jacey, trotting behind his grandfather, she looked bored, unconcerned. Jack stopped below her on the steps and dropping his hands said, "I've been bit by a goddamn cottonmouth, Mattie."

She wiped her hands in her apron and came down the steps. "Sit down on the bottom step and be quiet," she said calmly. "You're going to be all right."

She eased him down, straightened up and went back into the house, humming to herself as she went. His grandfather slumped down on the steps, pressing his left hand against the bite. Jacey pushed his chest against his grandfather's bony knees and looked into his face. There were deep vertical lines running down his cheeks and the old man had his eyes closed. Jacey leaned into his grandfather's lap trying to see under his hand. The area around the bite was turning green and the old man's chest was beginning to swell. Mattie came out of the house carrying a straight razor and a handful of white towels. She knelt on the step by his grandfather and gently pried his hand away from his chest. The old man moaned and laid his head on her shoulder. "This damn thing hurts like fire," he said through clenched teeth.

"It'll stop," Mattie said. "Turn your head away."

Grasping the blade like a pencil, she cut crosses into the small puckered hole of each fang mark. Blood oozed out of the old man's chest, and she held the towels as a dam below the left nipple to catch it before placing her mouth over the cuts and sucking. His grandfather looked away into the garden. Mattie spit a mouthful of blood onto the ground. She stroked the old man's cheek and said, "You're going to be all right, baby, you're going to be all right."

He looked at Jacey. "Did you see that snake fly?" he said and made a sound that was halfway between a laugh and a cough. Jacey rubbed small round circles on his grandfather's knee. Mattie dipped her head and sucked at the bite. When she raised her head to spit the area around the cuts was first white, except for the crisscrossed punctures, then it reddened again, was dark red, purpling, by the time her lips closed on it again.

Mattie sucked and spit for fifteen minutes. As she tired she pressed the towels for longer periods against the cuts, sitting back on her heels and looking Jack in the face. Her mouth was rimmed red. The old man was turned away; as the session went on he had slid down on the steps until he was nearly lying across them, his feet sprawled out into the yard.

He picked a strand of hair away from Mattie's forehead and said, "You're about tired out, aren't you."

"I wouldn't do this for just anybody," she said.

As she leaned in again a pickup truck came around the side of the house, skidded to a halt and two men got out. They were both big and stocky and redheaded, and one of them carried a small paper sack which he fumbled open as he came up the walk between the zinnias.

Mattie looked up. "You got it?" she said to the man carrying the sack.

"I got it," he answered.

Jacey moved over on the step so the man could get to his grandfather. He wondered who he was, didn't like him rushing up. The man knelt and withdrew from the sack a syringe and a small bottle of amber fluid.

"Bad place for a tourniquet," he said, glancing at the wound. He poked the needle through the rubber bottle top.

"You could try one around his neck," the other man said, hanging back.

"Argh," his grandfather said and spit on the ground.

The man held the needle up and squeezed a drop out. "This won't hurt a bit, Uncle Jack." Then he smiled at Mattie and Jacey. "I always wanted to say that," said. He turned to his companion. "Give me that flask, Dee." The other man took a scuffed silver flask out of his back pocket and handed it over. He unscrewed the top and poured a little on the old man's bare left arm. "Want a sip?" he said brightly.

"Shore," his grandfather said, and leaned his head over and took a little.

"Okay," the man said and plunged the needle into the old man's arm.

His grandfather winced. "You putting that stuff in the right place?"

"The next one's in your ass—between the cheeks." The man winked at Mattie, who blushed and ducked her head to the old man's chest.

The man—Bernard—sat back. He had a big round head and a forehead that because of his receded hair took up half his face. He refilled the syringe and plunged it into the right arm.

"There," he said as he pulled the needle out. "I think we got it surrounded."

"Oh," Jack said, wrenched up and vomited between his feet.

"He's sick," Jacey said, remembering feverish nights in Hawaii when his mother had held his head over a basin. On those nights he could feel the wind as if it were blowing in the room and the air was always full of creatures.

"I think he'll live," Bernard said. "Go ahead and get that shit out, Uncle Jack."

70

"At your service," his grandfather said weakly, retched and spit green bile onto the ground.

The other man—his somebody uncle or cousin: Dee—who was also big and stocky, but who, except for a wispy fringe over his ears, was completely bald, stood a couple of yards off with his hands in his pockets, looking on.

"We better get him in the house," he said, rocking on his heels. Then he began whistling a fast little tune and looking around as if there were others who might help.

"You ready to be carried, old man?" Bernard asked.

"I been waiting for it all my life."

They all got up and the two men lifted the old man by the shoulders and legs and carried him into the house. "Be careful with this valuable merchandise," Jack said, but Jacey could see that he was having trouble holding his head up. The two men were serious, the bald one more serious than the other—he looked intently at the old man's chest, as if there were a message scrawled there.

They carried him down the hall and put him in a big bed in the front bedroom. A slight breeze lifted filmy curtains over the front window. Mattie went into the bathroom. Jacey could hear her gargling. She came out wiping her mouth with a towel and went to the closet, where from an upper shelf she pulled a quilt and two blankets. She tossed them open and laid them on top of his grandfather.

Jacey had followed behind the men, imitating the slightly spraddled walk of the bald man. He stood in the bedroom door watching Mattie cover his grandfather.

"Good thing," the old man said as the blankets floated down on top of him. Mattie flung the second one up and it settled open over Jack's head. "Good, good," Jack said. "Bury me deep."

"That serum'll make you drunk, Uncle Jack," Bernard said. He tucked Jack in, pulling the covers back from his face.

"I'm freezing," Jack said, "and I hurt all over." He spied Jacey standing in the doorway. "Better tend to that boy," he said. The others turned briefly, all of them at once, to look at Jacey, who was still naked, though he was covered head to foot with greenish pond muck.

"You are a sight, young'un," Mattie said.

Jacey, shy before strangers, said nothing. Said nothing, then broke the shyness and the freeze of emotional bewilderment by darting across the room and kissing his grandfather solidly on the cheek.

"Sweet, sweet," his grandfather said, "little jay bird." He raised one sinewy arm and caressed the boy. Mattie put her arms around him from behind and lifted him up, turning his head against her ample breast. "Good as gold," she said.

A car drove up outside. Jacey, sure of who it must be, squirmed loose from Mattie's grasp and ran out of the room, down the hall to the back porch. He was in time to see his mother in jeans and a T-shirt getting out of a pale blue Buick. She wore a sunhat that was bigger than his grandfather's and flopped down over her face. Jacey ran up to her crying, "Granddaddy got bit by a *snake*."

"My, my," his mother said. She carried a bundle of clothes.

"It was a *goddamn* snake; the teeth were stuck in him. We went swimming. Mattie sucked the juice out." Jacey spit a couple of times to show her the technique, then grabbed her hand.

"Come on," he said. "Granddaddy's in bed."

Elizabeth allowed herself to be pulled up the steps. At the end of the hallway she saw a stocky man leaning against the wall drinking from a flask. The sunlight from the front door made him hard to see. He lowered the bottle as they came up the hall.

"Is he all right?" Elizabeth said to the man.

"He will be," he said and stuck out his hand. "I'm Delight Burdette," he said. "Who are you?"

"I'm delighted . . . to be Elizabeth. J.C.'s wife." Close up she could see how blue his eyes were. His big head looked like something axed out of a stump.

"May I go in?" Elizabeth asked. The man took another drink, wiped his lips with the back of his hand and said, sure, go right on.

"Come on, Mama," Jacey said, pulling on her. They went in.

The old man lay under a mound of blankets, his faded-out red hair swirled on the pillow. The hair seemed as long as a woman's. His eyes were closed, but he opened them when she came up beside the bed. He raised a hand and said, "Where you been, girl?"

He looked straight into her eyes and she felt again what she had felt the night before when she watched him from the porch. He had understood her as she said, All right, yes, with a sprig of tea olive. You can take my boy. His eyes were a gold-flecked green, dulled now by his pain. You can take my boy, or anything. She had descended the darkened stairs from her husband's bedroom. His bedroom, not yet hers. Earlier, she had refused to make love to him, had said, Maybe tomorrow, now I want to sleep. He had lain beside her, tensing. When the first rocks hit the wall, she had wakened, snapped on the light and looked, frightened a moment, into the strange room that appeared around her. "It's my father," J.C. had said and turned the light back off. She heard her son get up and go down the stairs. As her husband began to tell of his relationship with his father—in a dry, controlled voice, as if the information were being forced out of him—she pictured Jacey stepping out into the dewy night to meet an old man who threw rocks. She felt a surge of delight.

She had touched her husband's lips. "I'll be right back," she said, got up and in her nightgown went out, leaving J.C. wreathed and angry in his sullen sentences.

She leaned down and kissed the old man, squeezed his hand hard enough to feel the comfort of his bones.

"I've been working my way to you," she said and felt a compassion and a sudden dense love stir in her. She brushed his hair back from his forehead. A short, plump woman stood at her elbow watching.

"He's bad to be a boy," the woman said, touching Elizabeth on the shoulder. The woman's hand was twisted with arthritis.

"Always will be, sweetheart," the old man murmured. He closed his eyes. Elizabeth stepped back. Another man, almost a copy of the man in the hall, sat in a rocker by the window paring his nails with a pocket knife. He nodded when she looked at him.

"What do you need?" Elizabeth said to the plump woman.

"We've just about got it," the woman said, "but if you want, you can come out to the kitchen and help me make coffee."

"I will," Elizabeth said, "and get this one cleaned up." She laughed her clear, stainless laugh.

As his mother had done, Jacey leaned over his grandfather and stroked his hair. He could smell his grandfather's breath, which was sweet, as if he had been eating nuts. The old man opened his eyes and looked into Jacey's face that was only inches above his own.

"You get into everything, don't you, boy?" he said. His grandfather's presence was huge to him, benign, easy to take.

Jacey kissed him again, on the mouth this time. The old man closed his eyes.

"Come along," Elizabeth said.

She took him by the hand and led him from the room. Delight Bur-

73

dette still stood in the hall, leaning against the wall, his feet crossed at the ankles. "Is he going to be all right?" Elizabeth asked again. Delight had several rings on his fingers that caught the light as he waved a hand in answering.

"He'll be as good as he ever is," he said and held the flask out to her. She nodded it away.

"How ever good is he?"

"Full of spit and high kindness." He bared his teeth as if at something inside himself. "It was just a cottonmouth," he said, half absently. "Cottonmouth's don't kill."

"Occasionally they maim," the plump woman, who had followed them out, said. "I'm Mattie Bates," she said. "Come on in the kitchen, honey." She extended her hand as if she would shake hands but instead she reached out past Elizabeth's receiving palm and stroked her arm, bare below the T-shirt. "You're another one of the fine ones," she said, though not unkindly.

Elizabeth thought that the woman didn't know *what* she was. Last night's spattering pebbles had wakened her out of a dream. In it she saw Hawaii, the high green cliffs, streaming mist. She was walking in a foggy meadow with a man. The man was familiar to her, her lover, she thought, but she didn't know him. Down the slope a small brown animal darted behind a bush of yellow flowers. Instinctively she had run after the animal, across wet lank grass, into the woods behind the bush. The man had called to her to stop, to wait, but she had run on, all her mind fixed on the small animal, vanished in the woods and mist.

"Does he often throw rocks at the house?" she said as they entered the kitchen, a long high-windowed room with a floor whose planks were stained the color of chestnuts.

"Oh, surely," Mattie said. "He does that real regular."

"Rocks, berries, stumps, plow parts—if he can lift it, Uncle Jack will throw it," Delight Burdette, who had followed them in, said. "He was going to get a cannon."

The room smelled of fresh fruit and the light from the window was the whitest yellow. On a pine table in the middle of the floor was a pile of fresh green beans.

"A cannon," Elizabeth said.

"Yeah. There actually was one," Delight said, "belonged to our great-granddaddy. Jack was going to fix it up and blast out J.C.'s wall. He never got to it though."

74

"Like most else," Mattie said. "You'll want to clean that boy," she said. "Maybe outside would be best. There's a hose at the end of the porch."

"I'll take care of it," Delight said. "I been hosing cages all morning anyway."

"Cages?" Elizabeth asked.

"Yeah. We got this ruffy little zoo down the road. Bernard and I started it when we were kids and since we've gotten grown we've kept on. Any kind of animal walking around south Georgia we've got at least one of. Snakes, too. That's how come we had the antivenom on hand."

"And you make a living with your zoo?"

"More or less."

"A little less than more," Mattie said and laughed.

Delight scratched the fringe above his right ear. "It's terrible, terrible," he said. "You'd think people would pay money to see wild animals."

"Do they?" Elizabeth said.

"Sometimes. It's out on the Florida road, so we get what tourist traffic there is. The rest comes from the filling station—H.C. Sinclair, finest gasoline in the world—and the little bit we make from selling animals to other zoos and to the fools who think they can make pets out of wild creatures. We slide by."

He took another sip from the flask and turned to Jacey. "How about a little dance in the fountain?" he said.

Jacey was all for it. He ran out of the room leaving little pale flecks of pond goo on the hall boards, on the porch, the steps.

The yard was dirt and pebble, trodded down smooth as a floor. Patches of pine straw became paths that led in various curves into and through the horse-high zinnias. Jacey dashed down a path as Delight came down the steps, his flask flashing in the sun like a big medal.

"Here we go, boy," he cried and ran after Jacey, caught him at the far garden edge that gave into the grass before the pond. He swept him into huge red hairy arms, laughing whiskey into his face. "Toilet seat!" he cried from huge brown-streaked teeth. "Water fountain! I got you."

Jacey squirmed, frightened, then glad, pushing against the man's chest.

Delight carried him back to the porch askew in his arms like a sack with neither top nor bottom, put him down next to a green coil of hose. Jacey jumped away, but Delight caught him, held him and spun the

75

spigot on. The hose uncoiled on its own like a snake, first slowly, then quicker, the nozzle jumping on the ground. Jacey reached for the rummaging tip and thought of the snake, the strong muscle of it flexing against his side, and pulled his hand back, frightened. He began to cry, cried without any understanding of the tears, the tears just welling out and a hurt in him aching, spontaneously—he would always remember this: the tears, how they hurt, the sudden bursting forth from no thought, the aftermath—he sobbed, wanting none of this: water wash, this hulked-up man, his grandfather, south Georgia. He strained in the man's grasp, crying, "No, I don't want to, I don't want to," humiliated at his tears but unable to stop, wanting to flee, back to Hawaii with his mother, to pick hibiscus flowers for his mother's breakfast tray, play under the breadfruit trees with Rufino.

"You're just a baby," Delight said and reached for the hose. Jacey, instinctively, reached for it, too—snakehead—to protect himself, grabbed the hose six feet down from the nozzle. Delight lurched forward, losing his grip on him, as Jacey grabbed the hose with both hands and dragged it toward the flowers. Reaching, Delight stumbled and fell across the coil, the flask still tight in one hand. As he did, Jacey, pulling the hose, turned back, caught by Delight's body on the coil. As the man got up on all fours, Jacey swung the hose two-handed at him; the nozzle struck him in his open mouth as he leaned forward, cracking off half of both front teeth. Blood jumped in Delight's mouth and he covered it with his hand. "Oh, shit, you damn devil," he cried.

Jacey, horrified, dropped the hose and ran into the flowers. He didn't know where to go, ran through the sleek high stalks that smelled green, full of earth and no perfume, bright-petaled crowns bobbing around him, ran through them all to the grass and kept running along the edge of the pond where cattails shifted in breeze, the pond back twitched by the same breeze, somewhere in there the snake, growing new teeth, swimming.

He was halfway around the pond when his mother caught him. He turned before she reached him, saw her loping after him, her hair flowing back as she ran, and though he didn't slacken his pace he knew she would catch him and was glad of it.

5 They drove back to the main house in a car full of flowers. Jacey would remember all his life the great heap of zinnias, cosmos and marigolds Bernard had piled into the back seat. He rode on top of them, swimming in color, in the perfumeless, woody scent of them. His mother laughed when he threw handfuls of flowers into the front seat; she threw them back and made faces at him through the rear-view mirror. His terror subsided in her laughter.

They hauled the flowers into the house by the armload. They made half a dozen trips and by the time they were finished, the flowers had found places in every room of the house.

"This is a colossal silliness," his father said when he came home at lunch and found zinnias stuck in the chandeliers. Elizabeth filled vases and bowls with blossoms.

Jacey, chastened by his battle with Delight, and vaguely though persistently disturbed by the memory of the snake, its strength and heaviness, had to be cajoled by his father to speak of the experience. When he did he became so excited, dancing around the bedroom flinging his arms, that his father shushed him, seemed even, oddly, to the boy, to resent his exuberance, and so he fell into silence and the adventure passed into his memory and into the nighttime journeys of his dreams.

The flowers kept for a week. They were still bright the next Sunday when Jacey came out with his father on the way to church and found Elizabeth reclining on the terrace in a lounge chair rubbing her brown arms with olive oil. She wore a twist of three yellow marigolds in her hair. She was going riding, she said, west.

"You'll hit the swamp," his father said.

"I'll turn in time."

His father pressed his sides with his wrists and spat into a gardenia bush that was covered with drooping brown blossoms. "Why don't you come with us to church?" he asked.

"I don't think so. It's too pretty a day."

"Agh . . ." He turned and looked at Jacey, seemed to recognize him, turned back to Elizabeth. "There's a trail out there," he said, giving in. "You follow the river south for twenty miles and you come to Haven's house." Jacey could see that in the brief moment of his pique there was still pleasure in giving directions.

She looked at him, shading her eyes with her hand. "I wondered where Haven was—in relation to this, I mean."

"He's not anyplace at all in relation to this."

"He was your best friend."

"He was."

"But you don't like him now?"

He tore leaves from the gardenia and crumpled them in his hands. "My father used to chop wood every morning," he said, "way back, when he was a kid. His father used to take care of the mules among many other chores. Haven's people have had servants brushing off the seats of their britches for them for six generations. The only way he knows he's dirty is when somebody's cleaning him off."

Elizabeth stretched and turned on the lounge, pulling her legs up as if it were a bed. "What does he do?" she asked. "Does he do anything for his money?"

"He's turned his land into a quail preserve. Yankees come down and hunt on it."

"Let's do that," she said, sitting up.

"Turn Canaan into a preserve?"

"No. Go to Haven's and hunt."

"I don't have the time."

"Clock-eye man."

"Surely—come on, Jacey."

Jacey, who had been making handprints in the dew on the patio table, came quickly to his father's side. His mother reclined in riding boots, fawn jodhpurs and a black silk shirt knotted at the waist. Her hair was tied back with a bright red ribbon. She stroked his arm, languidly, touching him with just the tips of her fingers. Her boots were so shiny that he could see the movement of her arm reflected in them. "You go on," she said. "I have things to do."

They walked the block and a half to the sprawling brick church. It nestled among pines that were taller than its black cast-iron steeple. As they walked his father shot his cuffs and twitched at the pants of his blue seersucker suit. "You can get into trouble where you live," he said mysteriously, tipping his hat ferociously at other bedecked townspeople on their way to church. "Your great-grandfather, for example," he said as they crossed under the light at the courthouse corner.

He stopped and pointed back the way they had come. "The old

church was back there," his father said, "in the Quarter." Among trees at the edge of their house Jacey saw a flash of silver that might, he thought, be his mother. "Your great-grandfather built it for the Negroes and it was the only church any south Georgia Burdette, up till then, ever attended. But he got mad at a fellow who wanted to put up a store down here where we're headed and he bought the land and built another church on it."

"Why did he build a church?" Jacey asked.

"Because that way he could deed the property to itself and nobody, no matter what happened to Burdettes, could get the land back. It was a clever idea, but he got no satisfaction from it because he spent the rest of his life fighting with the people in the church. He couldn't get along with anybody but Burdettes, and since there were more townfolk than Burdettes, they voted things around the way they wanted them. Hello, Demott," he said to a man in a white panama hat. They had reached the church walk, and his father stopped. "The resistance made your great-grandfather so mad that one time, during a Sunday service, he stormed the church on his horse." He rubbed his hands together laughing. "He did that," he said, a softer tone coming into his voice.

"What did he do?" Jacey asked. He wondered how many of the people gathered on the steps were his relatives.

"He rode his horse into the sanctuary, drove everybody out and padlocked the front doors. He told them that come Monday morning he was going to have his horses stabled in there. 'I gave them the church and I can take it away' was what he said about it. What happened, though, was that the board of deacons voted out his membership and had the chief of police put an armed guard at the front door. Granddaddy never went back. Whatever eternal qualification attendance would have given him he was willing to forgo to make his point."

His father brushed his sleeves. Jacey saw that a light-gold pollen had collected on the cloth. "Goldenrod," his father said. He put his hand on Jacey's shoulder and they walked toward the church. "It makes me wonder that I would think of that story now," he said, his voice soft again. "I think of your mother and stories like that come to mind."

The story had seemed to relieve his father, but by the time the service was over he was angry again. They swept out into sunlight and a crowd of relatives. What Jacey remembered later was color: his Aunt Lois' pink, the lime-green dress of his Aunt Louise, Ethel's bridal white,

Alsace in a thin dress stitched with rows of rainbow beads. Franken's son Burleigh, a boy three years older than Jacey, stared at him from under a froth of chocolate curls, murderous maybe. Everyone else was delighted to see him.

They all bent and touched him, kissed him. Stout Lois, his Uncle Bryce's wife, black-headed and wearing a faint peppery mustache, swept down to him singing his name, "Jacey, Jacey," in a way he'd never heard it before. He shied into the arms of Louise, Uncle Franken's wife, a spindly woman, also black-headed, who pecked him on the cheek with her thin and rigid lips. His rickety Great-Great-Aunt Ethel, pale as the ash of a hickory fire, gray eyes flashing, clucked. Alsace, the youngest of the women, wrung her hands and looked as if she wanted to flee.

"Where's Elizabeth?" Bernard asked, and his father turned away, looked up the street that was filled with the cars of churchgoers and said, "I don't know."

"I would have thought she'd come on to church," Bernard continued, but he stopped short when J.C. swung around and glared at him. "She's probably still tired from her trip," he mumbled and punched his fist into his palm.

But his father had walked away. Jacey was afraid he had forgotten him and he ran after him calling Daddy, wait. He could feel the looks of his relatives as they followed them up the street. His father stopped at the light and waited for him. A flock of birds wheeled around the courthouse dome.

"She's been one week in Georgia and already I'm upset," he said. Then he looked at Jacey as if he had just seen him for the first time. "It's all right, son," he said. "Everything is going to work out."

They waited at the corner for the relatives to catch up, then in a group walked up the street to the hotel, where around three square tables by the front windows they had Sunday dinner.

Beyond the restaurant windows the yellowed stone wall of the bank gleamed in sunlight. His relatives chattered, everybody, it seemed, at once. Aunt Lois held a glass of water to the light and talked of elderberry wine; Alsace moved her knife and fork around and spoke to the tablecloth about Rooley's paintings, which she said were sad now, "dripping," she added, "with tears." Across two tables his father talked business with Bryce and Franken. They spoke of sulfur, which was a word Jacey had heard somewhere, and of alum and of Florida, of freight hauling, of this year's cotton crop. Jacey thought of his mother reclining on the lounge at home. They had not stayed long enough to see her leave. Once on a trip to the big island they had ridden horses. His mother had galloped in the surf while Jacey and Kaui watched from the dunes. He imagined her now riding up church steps, standing in the saddle shouting.

He wanted to run find her. He turned around and looked out at the street as if she could suddenly appear there. Bernard stroked the back of his head with a large, rough hand.

"You have to come see the animals," he said.

Jacey didn't hear him, shied from his touch.

"You ever seen an armadillo?" Bernard continued. "Or an otter?"

"No," Jacey said.

"No, *sir,*" his father said, adjusting his collar.

"No, sir."

"Well, you're bound for a treat. If you come out to the animal farm I might even show you a skunk. You know what a skunk is?"

"Polecat," his Uncle Franken put in from the other table.

"Will Delight be there?"

"He's scared of Delight," Bernard said. "Delight spooked him."

"He's capable of that," his father said.

"He chased me," Jacey said. His mother was riding a horse across the cottonfields, descending the bank of a river.

"But he sure didn't catch you," Bernard said, and everybody at all three tables laughed.

"Did the county get in touch with you?" his father said to Bernard.

Bernard straightened up a little and looked at his father. "About what?"

"I don't know for sure. Ansel Purdy said something about the sanitation."

"The sanitation?"

"The smell, Bernard," his Aunt Lois said as she arranged the heavy gold crenellated chain she wore around her neck. Her voice—she didn't look up from the gold—rose and fell among the syllables. She turned to Louise, who with stiff fingers was ticking her son Burleigh's hair into place. "Recently you can smell the zoo for a mile before you get to it," she said.

"I know, I know," Louise said, her eyes hard on Burleigh, who twitched under her hands.

"What y'all got over there now?" Franken said, loudly snapping a breadstick.

"Nothing new, except for a couple of diamondbacks Delight picked up in the road."

"I don't want to hear it," Louise said shrilly. "Not snakes at the table."

"They stink like garbage," Bernard continued, ignoring her. "One of them's six and a half feet long." He lowered his voice over Jacey's head. "He's got testicles on him the size of a twelve-year-old boy's. Aside from the snake," he said loudly, "nothing new."

Franken tapped his thin neck with two fingers, as if checking for the hollow spot, and said, "It's twenty years since y'all been collecting those animals. You ought to be able to keep the place cleaned up."

"It's Delight who needs the cleaning," Louise put in. She smiled a thin, riveting smile at Jacey, who shrank in his chair.

He was to hear about the zoo, find his way there under the scaly sycamores above the reeking refuse pond, wander joyful along the pine-straw paths among the otters and possums, the whitetail deer and ring-neck ducks; Delight would offer him a raccoon cub of his own, which his father wouldn't let him accept, and he would take his first Canaan animal ride on the mottled back of an Angolan goat, which bucked him off as cleanly as any horse; he would hear the stories, the ones about Delight's remarkable way with wild things, about his drifted life that excused him from high school and college, from marriage and any other responsibility to family process and the hardworking world, about Bernard's protection and attempted absolution of his brother—from the alcoholism that dragged him down—about his devotion and his own rigid bachelorhood, but not today, not this sunshiny afternoon when his mother, as black-headed and far more beautiful than any of these strange aunties, had ridden away into wilderness and left him.

"I want to go," Jacey said to his father, who looked at him with speculative, amused eyes. "I want to go," he said again and rose from his chair.

"We'll go then," his father said, touching his face.

The party broke up then, the relatives shooing each other away from soiled dessert plates and emptied coffee cups.

"Can I walk home?" Jacey asked his father as he paid the bill.

"Don't you want one of these?" his father asked him, handing him a peppermint.

"Yes. Can I walk home now?"

"What's your hurry?"

"Maybe Mama's there."

His father's face clouded. "We'll walk together," he said. "I want to show you something."

Bernard passed, holding his suit coat in one hand while he rolled his sleeve up with the other. "Come out to the zoo," he said. "Delight won't get you. He hasn't been able to catch a little boy for six or seven years now." His big ragged head bobbed as he spoke, the white sleeve rising up his brawny forearm.

"Yes, sir," Jacey said, pressing back against his father's legs.

They walked home, hand in hand, a little apart from the crowd of relatives. Townspeople passing spoke to them, to his father first always. A farmer in a pickup truck tipped his hat and called hello.

When they got home his father told him to go upstairs and change his clothes. He wanted to show him something. Jacey ran to his room, glancing through the open doorway of his parents' room as he passed at his mother's clothes, which were tossed around as if she had tried on dozens of outfits before selecting her riding clothes. On the bed her nightgown swirled across the pillow.

In his room, under the high ceiling with its filigree of worked plaster around the edges, Jacey changed into shorts and T-shirt and bare feet. When he emerged his father was standing at the window at the end of the hall looking out over the backyard at the cotton fields.

"Those fields go on nearly forever," he said as Jacey came up beside him. He ruffled his hair. "People think that. When you get up above about a thousand acres, people can't picture how much land there is."

"*Does* it go on forever?" Jacey asked. Maybe this was what his father wanted to show him.

"No, it stops—at the swamp."

"Can we go there?"

"That's where we'll wind up. That's what I want to show you."

"Mama went there."

"Through there."

"When will she come back?"

"I don't know." And his father drew him in, enclosed him in the strong arms that until last week he had no memory of ever feeling.

"High land is always pines," his father said as they got out of the car on the low bluff overlooking the river. The road turned south here and became a trail running along the riverbank, past Haven's house, across the Florida line, fifty miles to the Gulf of Mexico at St. Luke's.

"Where are we now?" Jacey asked. He walked to the edge of the bluff and looked down at the stream. It was as dark as coffee.

"Lazarus Swamp. This is where our land ends. The swamp goes on through the next county for miles."

"Is this where Mama came?" He squatted, pulled tufts of yellow grass and tossed them into the water.

"She said she was headed this way."

"We could follow her," Jacey said, thinking of hoofprints. "We could track her down."

"We might." His father had changed to khakis and a white shirt with the sleeves rolled up. The bottom of the trousers were tucked into muddy riding boots.

"In Hawaii, Rufino and I used to go on adventures in the woods."

"Adventures, huh?"

"Yes sir. We would go looking for papayas and breadfruit. Rufino would take them home to Lee May. She made doughnuts."

"Out of papayas?"

"And breadfruit."

"What did your Mama do?"

"She went swimming."

"Every day?"

"A lot."

His father squatted beside him. "That's a live oak," he said, pointing at the thick branches above their heads, "and that thing that looks like a tree house is a deer stand."

"What is that?"

"Where the hunters stay when they're waiting for the deer."

"Could we stay up there and wait for Mama?"

"We could, but we'd probably miss her."

Jacey felt his father tense, felt the tightening. "Mama had a good time in Hawaii," he said. "We always had a good time. I used to go with her to the beach."

"Who all went?"

"Everybody—Mr. Willis and Roberta, and Antonia and Kaui. Mama could ride a surfboard because Kaui taught her."

"Who was he?"

"He was Mama's friend. He showed her how to stand up on a surfboard, at the beach."

"Could you do it?"

"A little. They wouldn't let me go out far."

His father swiveled around to face him, but he looked past him downstream. Jacey could see his sex bulged against the khaki at his crotch. His father looked down at the river. The shredded tops of cypress knees poked from the water.

"Did Kaui come to visit you?"

Jacey felt a catch in him and a vague oppressive movement in his stomach. "Sometimes," he said.

"Goddamn," his father said, so softly that Jacey could still hear the rustle of breeze through the woods.

"He just came to say hello," Jacey said.

"Not goodbye."

"Goodbye, too."

"Ha," his father said, "ha" with his mouth wide open. He stood up and lurched a few steps down the trail and came back. His breathing quickened and he looked quickly around as if he might run away. He walked to the crumbled edge of the bluff and stood looking down at the water. The edge, tufted with grass, curled out slightly, like an extended lip. He leaned out, so far that Jacey thought he might dive. Just above his head, two green dragonflies hovered. His father raised a hand, as if, Jacey thought, he might try to catch the glossy flies, and then the bank gave way and he fell out of sight into the river. For a moment the dragonflies hung where they were, at the edge of empty space, then one then the other flickered away into the trees.

Jacey ran to the edge of the bank. His father was pushing himself to his knees in the shallow water. He was soaked, the white shirt gone tea-colored, his boots cleaner. He started to get up, pushed up on his hands, but stopped and sat back on his haunches in two feet of water.

"Are you going swimming, Daddy?" Jacey asked.

His father wiped a strand of root moss from his face and laughed. "I near about did," he said.

Jacey laughed, to stem the fright that had struck him when his father fell. Something in him was struck, too, by the sight of his father on his knees in the stream—he didn't want to see him that way, fallen and muddy.

"I was just thinking about how often I've come down here to get a little relief from my problems," his father said. "But this is the first time I've fallen in."

"I thought you were diving," Jacey said. He wanted to reach down to his father, even as he was repelled by the sight of him on his knees, the dark water purling slowly into his crotch, his large bony hands rerolling the sagging sleeves. Years later, on his own knees in the stiff sand of a Caribbean beach, his wife doved against him, he remembered his father falling into the swamp, remembered the whiteness of his arms as he slicked silt off his skin, and he thought then what maybe he had thought without awareness years before, that no matter how dark the water, a body always comes up cleaner, a body that he had seen in its muscularity and power for the first time as he knelt on the riverbank at the western edge of Burdette Canaan. The flesh under the cloth was firm and powerful. He saw it when his father stood up, the water draining almost in clots off him. The wide planes of his chest stood out from the clinging shirt, the nipples hardened by the cold water. Through the shirt Jacey could see the hair on his father's stomach and lower down, the full outline of his penis and testicles, the ridged muscles of his legs. It was different from seeing Kaui, bounding down Sunset Beach, or Rufino, who often came to work in rolled-up shorts; it was different from that, this man, taller it seemed than anybody he knew, the crimped red hair flattened on the wide skull, the nose large and bony, humped a little on the bridge, the wide cheekbones prominent as welts, redder than the rest of his face, the shoulders winged straight, unsloped from the muscular neck. He pulled back, to save himself from the force of his father's body and to see it better. Pushing backward, he stood up, watching his father as he carefully set his feet in the black river mud, reached forward, grasped root ends and pulled himself in a rush up the embankment onto his knees in the grass. Jacey thought of his grandfather high-stepping in his underwear out of the pond. The cottonmouth fangs had stuck in his chest. Grimacing, his grandfather had pulled them from his skin and thrown them into the pond. He thought of the snake, toothless, swimming in the dark underwater.

"Snake got Granddaddy," he said.

"Snake got him," his father answered as he began to strip off his clothes.

"Are you going to be naked?" Jacey said.

"Yes, naked. Or almost."

Stripped of shirt, boots, gray high-riser socks, the swamp-greasy khakis, his father stood before him in his shorts. Seeing him this way

86

now, the skin itself exposed, the ginger hair on legs, belly, chest, even, in slight tufts, on the shoulders, Jacey was amazed, thrilled, frightened. He felt as if his father might *do* something to him, he didn't know what. He backed away to the car, touched the door handle, wanting to get in but afraid to. Then he heard behind them, down the track road, the sound of another vehicle. He looked sharply at his father to warn him, but his father, who looked up at the sound, didn't seem to mind. He went on wringing out his shirt. The water that poured out of it was clear, not dark like the river.

"Somebody's going to be here," Jacey said, almost breathless.

"Sounds like it," his father said.

As Jacey turned to look a jeep came around a bank of young poplars that cut the road off from the main land. In it were his cousin Rooley and his wife Alsace. They both wore straw hats. Rooley was driving; Alsace held on with both hands to the top of the windshield. They came fast up the track, the wheels jumping on the ruts, came so fast that Jacey thought they might not stop at all, which they did all at once, Rooley whipping the wheel to the left, skidding suddenly dead into a bank of gallberries.

"Whoo, boy," Jacey said. He wanted to go, to ride. His father, who stood beside the car in his white BVDs, made no move to cover himself. Jacey felt a vague embarrassment, at the dark hair at his crotch showing through the cloth. Rooley and Alsace got out of the jeep, both on the driver's side, went around back and rooted in a pile of cluttered items, canvas, buckets, tackle boxes. Rooley came up with a large sketchbook and Alsace pulled a checkered umbrella out of the pile. The whole operation of stopping, jumping out and rooting around went so fast and they were so intent that they did not even seem to notice Jacey and his father until, their goods in their hands, they started toward them.

"How's business, J?" Rooley asked then, a big grin on his face.

"Fair to middling," his father answered as he rubbed his legs with the squeezed-out, rolled-up shirt.

"Hello, Jackson," Alsace said, as her eyes swept quickly past his father, sorting the woods. Her yellow hair was wild. She popped the umbrella open, lifted it over her and peered out at the sky.

"Expecting rain, dear?" his father asked.

"Too much light," she said. "We have to test the light."

"I'm working some new stuff out," Rooley said as he rolled sketch-book pages back. "I'm trying to figure out how to get daylight into dark." He strode energetically over to the bluff edge and looked down.

"This where you went in? Right here?"

"That's the place."

Jacey thought his father might put his clothes back on, but he made no move to.

"The light's good," Rooley said. "Bring that thing here," he said to Alsace. "Hold it over that way." He squatted down as Alsace shaded him with the umbrella. He sketched furiously for several seconds.

"This doesn't really do any good," he said.

"What?" his father asked.

"Sketching. You can't do it without color. What I want to do is cover this area with a tarp. I've got a bunch of cloth and I'm going to string up big patches of it to see how the light comes through. Move away, honey."

He stood up. All his movements were jerky, as if his bones didn't fit right.

"My mama paints pictures," Jacey said, turning away from the sight of his father, who, still in his underwear, was stepping back into his boots.

"She's probably terrific," Rooley said. His fingers were black with charcoal dust. "I wish you could put the trees on little wheels and move them around," he added. "Would you mind, Uncle J, if I dammed up this river?"

"It might not be the best thing," his father said.

Alsace, under her umbrella, was doing a little short-step shuffle dance. "All God's chillen got shoes," she sang nearly in a whisper. "Why did you go swimming, Uncle J?" she asked.

"I wasn't swimming, I was falling in."

Rooley swung around. "I think if I dammed up this river I could get a new kind of light under those trees. It's amazing: live oaks never lose their leaves. That means that whatever lives under them never gets out of the shade." He turned to Alsace. "What would that *do* to you, you reckon, living your whole life in the shade?"

"I do now," she said, "in many ways."

"Shoo. Let's go over this way." He scrambled down the bank with Alsace following, the umbrella jabbing the air.

"We'd better head on back," his father said, still half naked.

"Aren't you going to put your clothes on?" Jacey asked.

"No sense in it. I'd just get the car wet."

"Why don't we wait for Mama?"

"She's going to be gone awhile yet." His father thrust his fingers back through his hair, then patted it flat with both open palms. "You coming tonight?" he called down to Rooley, who was standing knee-deep in the stream sketching furiously; beside him, Alsace, her jeans rolled above her knees, tipped the light out of his way.

"I'll be there," Rooley called without looking up.

"Getting this crowd together is like trying to herd wild dogs," his father said. "Come on. Your mama will be back before you know it."

Jacey, crouched on his knees in the front seat, looked back at the man and woman. "Who are they?" he asked.

"Your cousins. Rooley's Uncle Ransome's son."

"Why is he drawing?"

"He's a painter. Alsace used to be, too, but I think she gave it up. They met when Rooley was in art school up in New York. She comes from St. Louis." His father glanced at the rearview mirror. "Her grandfather founded the first steel-fabricating company west of the Mississippi. I went out to see it year before last."

"I was in Hawaii."

"You were in Hawaii. Rooley's a good painter as far as I can tell. His mother had the artistic streak. She used to play the piano late at night. They lived where your Uncle Bryce does now, but she's gone, too."

"My mama's gone."

"She'll be back," his father said flatly. He held the wheel two-handed, tight at the top. "She might be back by the time we get home."

But she wasn't. At home they went their separate ways, like strangers, Jacey into the hands of Matilda, who made him take a bath as if he hadn't already had one that morning before church, and his father into the bedroom, where he closed and, Jacey discovered later, locked the door.

She wasn't back for supper. They ate together at the kitchen table. Matilda and the gardener, Hosea, served them a supper of sardines, Vienna sausage, saltine crackers and a fresh spinach and avocado salad. His father poured the oil from the sardines on his salad. For dessert they had slices of the lemon cake Matilda had baked for the fall meeting which was to be held that night. Jacey watched the door for his mother. His father, briefly, and without success, tried to teach him to whistle through his cupped hands.

She wasn't at the meeting either.

"Where is Mama, Daddy?" Jacey wanted to know as he followed his father upstairs to set up the porch. His father wouldn't answer him. On the porch, around a large straw rug, were a wicker sofa and several wicker chairs and three or four high-backed rockers. On a low table in front of the sofa Matilda had set out the cake, a stack of china plates, forks and napkins, iced tea and lemonade.

His face pressed against the screen, Jacey watched his kin arrive.

Rooley and Alsace came in their jeep. Rooley stamped his feet and threw his arm across his wife's shoulders as they climbed the steps. Jacey felt a misery creep into him as he watched them and he wanted to go look for his mother but he didn't know where to start. As his father crossed back and forth between his bedroom and the porch—through the empty bedroom on the other side of the hall—Jacey followed him, asking the same meek question.

"I don't know," his father answered him, fondly at first, then with increasing impatience. "She didn't tell me where she was going or when she would come back. I don't want to hear about her right now." He felt a panic rise in him, panic that drove him farther and farther from the jollity of his relatives. They all came: Bernard, shaggy-headed, waddling like a bear; Delight, who wore a narrow strip of adhesive tape across his upper lip like a new white mustache; his Great-Great-Uncle Eustace and Great-Uncle Ransome, one thin and twangy as fence wire, the other burly, a huge belly bound on either side by wide red suspenders; Bryce and Franken; Bryce's teenage son Carroll, who held his narrow head so rigidly straight atop a long cordy neck that to Jacey he looked as if he might be paralyzed; his cousin Burleigh, black-haired and blue-eyed like his mother, snapping a cap rifle at everybody within range. With them also was a single Negro man, David Welps, the overseer.

Jacey shrank from them all, first into his father's bedroom and then when he was rousted from there by Delight, who had brought him the skin of a squirrel he had stretched and tanned, to the living room, where he first paced in front of the ceiling-high walls of books, then hid—for a moment almost happy—under a large ficus behind a magazine rack in the corner, and finally, after Burleigh pumped him full of imaginary bullets, into the yard, where he wandered around in the moonlight near the back fence crying noiselessly to himself. The crickets sawed their bones and the owls called from the woods behind Franken's house. Without being able to name them he could smell the tart dog fennel wands growing among the brambles against the fence. The scent of tea olive drifted up from the edges of the fields, mingling with the faint musty scent of the opened cotton bolls. His mother had made Hosea cut brackets into the briars so she could see into the fields. Jacey slipped between the masses of bushes, head-high to him, and leaned against the fence. Next to him was a twist of gallberry shrub, and from above came the faint stench of chinaberries. For a moment he thought he saw movement out in the fields, but it was only the edge of cloud shadow. A wan breeze hesitated among the cotton rows and came on. He stretched his hand upward and, without looking, grasped a cluster of chinaberries and pulled them still attached to the branch down to his face. The berries stank of their life. He touched his tongue to them; they were bitter.

He held the berries to his face and looked at the field, hoping his mother would suddenly rise up among the cotton rows. After a while he let the berries go and came back into the yard to stand under the yellow light from the upstairs porch.

"What it means," he heard his father say, "is that we will have to borrow to finance the purchase of the sulfur wells."

"I'm flatly opposed, flatly," an older voice said, probably that of his Uncle Eustace.

"I want another slice of that lemon cake," Delight said. "Sure is . . ."

"There's no way around it, Eustace," his father continued. "This is the time for expansion. Support prices are going up. Farmers are going to increase acreage, not only here but all over the South and the Midwest. We get the wells and we have a straight run with our own processes to markets all the way to the Dakotas. Not only that—if we can increase production of sulfuric and superphosphate enough, Allied Chemical would be willing to distribute overseas."

There was a man lying on the porch. Where Jacey was, on the outboard side of boxwoods below the first-floor porch, he could see the bottoms of two feet, stuck up straight. The feet wore flipflops, just like he had worn in Hawaii. Jacey edged closer into the boxwoods.

"That sounds fine," he heard Eustace say, "but I am opposed, today, tomorrow, and the next day, to mortgaging this land for any purpose whatsoever."

"Good for goddamn you, Eustace," the man said and raised his hand along the wall.

"Granddaddy," Jacey said.

His grandfather sat up. He had one arm in a sling made from a checkered bandanna. "Jackson Coleridge Burdette IV," he said, grinned and lay back down.

Jacey ran around the porch, climbed the steps and sat down beside his grandfather. The old man lay flat on his back, his left arm in the sling across his chest. His right cradled the humped motor of a bell-tooth chain saw. Jacey snuggled down onto his side.

"Have you seen my mama?" he asked.

"I sure have. She rode down to visit Haven Laurens. Let's listen to this. Sit real still."

The voices went on above them, ringing out into the light-glossed live oak leaves across the driveway.

"It's a dilemma that has to be faced," his father was saying. "We've already made commitments."

"You can unmake them," Eustace said.

"Big business," Rooley put in. "Empire."

"Doodah, Doodah," Delight added.

"Shut up, Delight. This isn't the time to quit. Bryce has made arrangements with the Federal Land Bank for a six-million-dollar loan. We're anchoring that with the south lands."

"All the south lands?" That was Bernard.

"All but your place."

"My place goes," his grandfather whispered. "Goddamn it to hell."

"This isn't the risk you think it is," his father continued. "It's an augmentation that fits like a glove. We're built for it already."

"And whether we want to do it or not, we're going to do it," Eustace said.

"I had to show you with the warehouses. You wouldn't have gone along if I hadn't shown you first."

"I suppose."

"Look. It's the same road. We're not turning off. The only thing that makes it difficult is you can't see very far ahead of you right now. It'll work out, just like with the warehouses and the fertilizer plant and

92

the acid plant. We're following the same road, heading for the prize."

"Hot dog," Delight exclaimed, "Hot diggety dog!"

"Bryce'll give you the land figures and the new percentage arrangements and you'll see what I'm talking about. Then we can vote. Bryce."

"Bryce butthole," his grandfather said and pushed himself up with his good arm. "Help me up, boy."

Jacey stood still while his grandfather steadied himself into an upright position.

"What are you going to do?" he asked.

"Cut the legs out from under this little par-lay."

He bent down, freeing his left arm a little from the sling, grasped the chain saw by handle and cord and pulled back sharply with his right hand. The saw roared into life.

"Oo, Mama!" Jacey cried. He could feel the vibrations in his feet, so hard they itched.

"Good Lord," his father said from above, now faint.

His grandfather hoisted the saw, held the motor close in against his body and advanced on the square column that supported the porch roof. Jacey started to follow, but his grandfather yelled back for him to move off the porch.

"We'll have no voting tonight," he yelled and laid the big bow of teeth against the wood. The column shuddered as sawdust gushed out under the blade. Above their heads Jacey could just hear the commotion of feet and the yelling.

Jacey raced across the porch, down the steps and out among the parked cars. From the running board of Rooley's jeep he watched his grandfather. The saw bit cleverly into the wood, the old man driving and clearing, until it hit the heartpine core, where it snagged and skipped, bit on, roared so loud that Jacey felt the sound in the bones of his head.

"Go on!" his grandfather cried. "Bite through!" He bore down, cords standing in his forearms, sawdust shooting over his back. "God almighty, go!" he yelled.

Then there were women there, crowded in the kitchen doorway, all his aunts and cousins, and his grandfather, sweating, flicked a look at them and yelled, "It's coming down, the son of a bitch is coming down," bore down hard, until just at the moment when the men, led by his father, burst between the gathered women, the chain snagged, caught, and the saw roared and choked abruptly off.

His grandfather jerked back on the saw, twisted it, reached for the starter pull, but not before his father, rushing—bird, Jacey thought, like Wheeler, a heron-bird—caught the old man, snatched his unslung arm away and pushed him back. The saw hung in the column, the bow arced down under the weight of the motor.

"Get off, you," his father cried. "Get off!"

The old man gasped and stepped back, rubbed his free hand hard down his pants leg and drew himself up. His hair was the color of red clay in water, diluted.

"Shoo," he said. "What you going to do, pesthead?"

"I've had enough of this," his father said. He advanced on the old man, shaking his fist at him. His shoulders twitched. "You're insane!" he screamed into the old man's face.

His grandfather didn't say anything, just stood there beaming.

His father raised his fist and let it drop. He stood there in front of the old man and a current ran fast through him, a shuddering.

"Ah, Jesus," he said, "all you cowards, jerks."

Jacey was close enough to see the flicker of hesitation in his father's eyes, the misery and what he would only later call yearning, but it passed quickly and the younger man seemed to pull himself through bones into a sternness.

"Just leave me alone, Daddy," he said quietly. "If you won't come with me, just leave me alone."

"Find a place to go," his grandfather said, just as quietly.

The old man adjusted his arm in the sling and pressed the fingers of his free hand against his chest where the snake had bitten. Jacey wanted to take his grandfather's hand and place it on his father's face. He wanted his grandfather to touch his father, just touch him.

"Granddaddy," he called from the driveway, "you all quit."

But that wasn't what he wanted to say, not at all. His grandfather patted the bite, as if tapping it back into place. His father stood with his hands at his sides, opening and closing fists. Jacey ran to the porch and reached upward, to pull himself up to them. It was too high and the boards were slippery with dew. His grandfather reached down and pulled him by his arm—the way he might grab a shot rabbit out of the grass—onto the porch. Jacey laughed out loud at the sensation of his body rising. His grandfather set him on his feet; Jacey spurted between them, touching them both.

"It's all right, Granddaddy," he said. "It's all right."

The old man laughed and cupped the back of his head, drew him into the space between them. Jacey caught the faint scent of urine in his grandfather's trousers and the clean starch smell of his father's khakis. He ran his hands up their bodies.

In his father's eyes there was an impenetrable glitter, and Jacey felt again as he had that afternoon when his father stood nearly naked before him, felt the same vulnerability and loss, the same desire to turn away.

His father looked at his grandfather. "I've had enough of you," he said. He stepped over to the column, wrestled the saw loose and heaved it into the drive. It hit the side of Rooley's jeep. He stood for a moment looking after it and then turned and went into the house.

"I guess we can go home now," his grandfather said. He smiled, but his smile was false.

Jacey pushed through the departing relatives and went inside to look for his father. He found him sitting at the desk in the office off the second-floor hall. He was looking out the window. The moon had lain down in the fields.

"Daddy?" Jacey said, pushing past fear to his side.

"What is it?" his father said sharply, but then he caught himself and touched Jacey's face. "What is it?" he asked again.

"When is Mama coming home?"

His father looked into his eyes and very slowly pressed his index finger between Jacey's lips. Jacey began automatically to suck it. "I don't know," he said. "I've been thinking about it and I don't know."

Jacey pulled away. His father's hands hung in the air between them. "What did you want to show me?" he asked.

"I've forgotten," his father said. He smiled, a sweet, rueful smile. "If you stick around," he said, "I might remember."

6 Elizabeth woke early the next morning in Haven's bedroom under a billow of white muslin to the distant airplane whirr of an attic fan. The muslin, bellied down from four bedposts as if it contained a body made of air, vibrated faintly. Beside her, under the single sheet, Haven slept, his long elegant racer's legs crossed at the ankles and his sandy crew cut gleaming on the pillow as if he had brushed his hair in his sleep. "This is a woman's bed," she said out loud and then, "Somebody ought to turn off that fan."

Haven stirred, raised an arm straight above his head and let it drop back into the narrow space between them.

"It's my mama's bed," he said. "I told you."

She raised herself on an elbow and looked out through a fretwork of wisteria at the lawn, which sloped down to the river. A Negro in a khaki worksuit rode a mower at the bottom of the yard. The smell of cut grass delighted her, and she rolled over in bed and hugged first herself then Haven. "One more new damn perfect day," she said and laughed.

"They're always that way for you," he said.

"It pleases me that you see me like that."

"It's because you are."

"Yas, yas."

But she didn't mention the smell of the grass or the sharp spice scent of lantanam flowers mingled with it: she thought, burdock, plantain, pokeweed, highbush blackberry, wild sweet William, yes, yes, I had forgotten. "I want to go outside," she said. She sprang out of bed and began to gather her clothes.

"There's the way," Haven said, indicating the french doors.

Her canvas satchel, buff-colored with a long canvas loop for over the shoulder, lay tipped over on the floor, a lipstick, a package of tissues and a compass near its open mouth. Haven sat up and looked at it.

"Explorer," he said, got out of bed and picked up the compass. "You need this?" He turned the instrument in his hands. His naked body was amazingly narrow, as if it had been shaved off along the sides and the limbs stuck back on.

"J.C. sent it to me." She held her hair up with one hand as she rummaged around the room for her clothes.

"He figured you were lost."

"He was hoping."

"You're the most unlost woman I've ever seen."

"Tell it to the po-leece, baby—*where* are my panties?"

"Over there, by the palm tree."

He sat back on the bed holding the compass loosely in his open palm. "Don't you want to slide on back up here for a while?"

96

"I'd better go home. They'll miss me."

"Do they know where you are?"

"Yes. Of course."

"Well, stop a moment for breakfast. And I'll have to show you to my mother."

"Certainly you will."

Haven's mother lived in the opposite wing. In her former room Haven kept a few artifacts, tortoiseshell combs and a silver tray of perfumes and lipsticks on the white Florentine dresser which gave the room the faint lingering scent of a boudoir. On the wall between the french doors was a portrait of her painted when she was a young woman. The long ascetic nose and the wide-spaced gray eyes were the equivalent of Haven's.

They ate a light breakfast of grapefruit and raisin toast in the cheery breakfast room (lilac wallpaper, a polished brass chandelier) that overlooked the formal garden at the side of the house. Then Haven took her to his mother.

In a room the color of wheat, the old woman reigned, slumped in a brocade chair with two nurses fluttering like white pigeons around her. She wore a dress of pale blue vitreous silk, out of which poked two gnarled feet shod in dirty bedroom slippers. Her white hair was streaked with yellow, like smoke stains. She was staring at the floor as Elizabeth approached.

"Fucking, I see, the scion," she said without raising her head.

Elizabeth wasn't sure she had heard her right. She felt a flash of anger at Haven for subjecting her to this. "What?" she asked. One of the nurses brushed the air in front of the old woman's face as if her words were flies.

"Fucking, I said, the scion." The old woman raised her head. Her eyes were not the gray of the portrait but a sooted blue, overcast, deep in muddy sockets. Her face was seamed and creased like a piece of dried fruit. Elizabeth felt a sudden withering tenderness in her, a desire to touch the woman's blasted face. She bent in a deep curtsy, the first she had made since dance class when she was thirteen. Beyond the open windows a redbird sang its four notes.

"She hears words," the nurse said, "and they stick to her."

"Hello, Mrs. Laurens," Elizabeth said. "Your son and I have had a wonderful time."

Haven crossed from Elizabeth's side and bent down and kissed his mother's dry forehead.

"Don't, don't," the old woman said, shying. "It's too late to start that."

"Plenty of time yet, Mama," Haven answered. He turned to Elizabeth. "Mother will be eighty next month," he said, a rising note in his voice, as if this were a triumph he shared in.

"Congratulations," Elizabeth said, feeling, past the tenderness, the defiance she still encountered in herself, at thirty yet, in the presence of the old.

A phone rang somewhere back in the house. The black phone on the bedside table did not ring. Haven reached past his mother's drooping head and picked up the receiver: "Yes?"

He listened a moment, then held the receiver out to Elizabeth. "J.C.," he said.

"Where are you?" J.C. asked as if he were not the one calling. The mouthpiece smelled of old cheese.

"In Haven's mother's bedroom." Over the sound of birds she could hear the racket of the mower. The thin leaves of a plum tree lay against the screens.

"What are you doing?"

"The usual. Living with gay abandon."

"Why don't you abandon yourself to the homeward road."

"I was about to do that, but I stopped for a moment to speak to Mrs. Laurens." She twined her fingers in the cord, wanted for an instant to pat the old woman's gray head, ruffle her hair. "Haven lives right on the river," she said. "You could come down and throw him in."

"We all miss you," he said, and she knew then, a week after her arrival in Yellow Springs, that the imploring would continue. "Your son misses you," he said.

"Ah, Jay, that's not the tactic."

"What is?"

"You'll find out."

"Well, come on back up here so I can work on it. I've been putting a few things together."

She laughed. "I'll bet you have."

"Come on, Elizabeth."

"Yassuh, boss."

98

She handed the receiver back to Haven, who took it and spoke eagerly into it: "J.C."

"He's gone," he said and hung up. "Mother," he said, bending down to speak to the old woman who stared again at the floor. "This is Elizabeth Burdette. I was best man at their wedding, J.C.'s and Elizabeth's. The Burdettes of Canaan. The Burdettes."

"I don't know where it is anymore," the old woman said, shaking her head. "I just can't find it."

"Ah," Elizabeth said. "Ah." She was glad her own mother had not lived this long, and she hoped she would not.

"I don't think I could stand that," she said moments later as they walked down the brick path to the stables.

"What?" Haven asked. He flicked a riding crop against his pants leg.

"All that age on me. If my mind went I don't know what they would do to me."

"It's probably what you'd do to *them* that's got everybody worried."

"Shoot. I'll be gone before long."

"You'll always be gone before long."

Elizabeth looked back at the brick house, handsome under wisteria vines and a slate roof. The stables they approached were made of the same brick as the house. She heard the chittering of birds off to the right.

"What is that?"

"The quail."

"Let's go see."

He took her around to the pens, which were actually large boxes of narrow-mesh wire, upended on bare ground, and attached at one end to small low white houses. The runs were filled with quail chicks, black-and-white-streaked heads bobbing.

"Oh, my," Elizabeth said. "All the wild birds." Up close their backs were a speckle of black, brown and white.

"Camouflage," Haven said.

Elizabeth crouched down and stuck her fingers through the wire. The chicks surged away, in a mottled wave. "How do they learn to be wild?" she asked.

"They don't actually. You shoot near them and they die of heart attacks. I pick up birds all the time without a mark on them. It's good though for Yankee morale. It makes them think they're hunters."

99

"And you make a lot of money this way?"

"An extraordinary amount. I charge two hundred dollars a day per person, run half a dozen hunts at once and have to turn supplicants away at the door."

"Lor-dy."

"Money, money."

There had been no shyness between them, at least no shyness on her part. She had ridden up the path, which, when it reached Haven's land, had become a wheel track that swung away from the river a quarter mile into the pine woods. She had found him lounging in a straw hat against one of the cypress poles that supported the dock house.

"Are you fishing?" she had called with a casualness, as if she had left him only the day before, and she had seen how he gathered himself in his lanky body, how the sight of her seemed to kindle something in him, something that had not been there at all a moment before.

"Elizabeth!" he cried, emotion rushing up through the sound of her name. It was just the way she wanted it—the way she knew it would be, was why she came. Always, she understood that kind of welcome, where she could find it. Like lucky charms, like the small gifts she brought her son, she kept these refreshable intimacies alive in the pockets of her life. A blue heron rose from a patch of yellow reeds on the far side of the river, flapping into a dignified ascent. She dismounted and walked her horse to the land edge of the pond house. It was built on pilings over the tea-colored water. Haven came straight to her, as if he had been waiting full of hope. Her eyes, the tease in them, she thought, stopped him a moment. "Jacob," he called past her. A Negro came quickly, as if he had been waiting for the call, around the side of a long brick building.

"He'll take your horse. You've ridden from Canaan?"

"All the way."

"I should have figured on it."

"I'm sure you did."

He grinned through horsy, crowded teeth. "J.C. said . . ."

"What?"

"You were coming."

"I thought you didn't talk." She was surprised to hear they did.

"I talk to *him*. I called him. He said you were coming home."

"I am."

"You did."

He wore a white cotton sweater, through which she could see, faintly, the pale flesh. She thought of some proprietary image, dog on a leash, bird in a cage, something pinned down. As if glass between them shivered, cracked and fell, and he was released, he stepped to her and took her in his arms. She had ridden down through the viny woods for this, come all this way. She let him fold her in, hold her tightly, squeeze hard. Break my bones, she almost said out loud, I want to feel my spine crack. Dependable Haven, my ineffectual aristocrat.

"I love it," she said into his shoulder, "when you come off your elegance."

"I would say the same about you."

"I smell like horses and olive oil—that's not elegance."

"Enough for me."

"I have a cousin named Delight."

"Everybody does."

She pulled back laughing. "No, I mean actually, a redheaded drunken cousin named Delight. My little boy broke his teeth."

"I know Delight Burdette. That zoo has been there a long time. He's a strange man, Delight. All that drink and all that woodlore. He had the kind of gift that would let him catch a wild rabbit in his hands, but the drink's almost got him now. I remember once when we were young— Delight must have not been more than fifteen—he tried to fix a barn roof for his daddy. He was so drunk that he pried up a strip of tin, then, having forgotten that he had just done it, stepped into the hole he'd made. He must have fallen thirty feet. Broke his arm in three places. Bernard tries to take care of him, but he can't. Delight was bound to get his teeth broken."

"Like my bones," she said, moving away from him. "This horse has rearranged my bones." She shivered inside, something in her picking up speed. "I know what I want," she said.

"What?"

"You naked, prancing around the room. I want to strip you down."

"You shall, all my gifts exposed."

She wished for a moment that the ride had been longer, that she was not stopping but going on. She wanted to rush onward, as far as flight could take her.

"Have you eaten?" he asked.

She told him no. "Then come up. I'll feed you."

101

They walked hand in hand to the house, an angular Georgian structure fretted with wisteria vines. She felt, as they walked, the pleasure of their interlocking rhythm, the matching strides, even though her bones creaked, her legs gone wobbly as a sailor's.

In the long dining room, under crystal chandeliers, a servant in a white coat brought them a supper of broiled quail, wild rice and salad. They sat on either side of the corner of a long mahogany table. In the center of the table was an array of yellow chrysanthemums.

"You live alone," she said, speaking what looked true.

"My mother's here, but she's old."

The wine he poured her tasted smoky, woody.

Afterward, in fading light, they walked around the grounds, which generations of Haven's forebears had twisted into the elegant shapes of trimmed hedges and brick pathways, all the flowers arranged, heaped purposely on themselves, shocked into beauty, trained. As they walked he touched her lightly from time to time, with just his fingers, brushing her in places, increasingly intimate.

"As if you are reminding yourself," she said when he pulled her to him under a scuppernong arbor behind the house.

"I'm making it up again. I'm creating it right here." He was silent a moment. "I've never understood you," he said, then she could see him blush in the light that leaned under the triangular leaves and she forgave him the obvious remark and let herself go, gladly, against his bony body.

"Emporium, empire," she whispered as leaves brushed her face and she smelled the heavy sweetness of the grapes.

"What?"

"J.C. has an empire; you have an emporium."

"A sweetshop for the Yankees. They love it down here. Would you mind touching me?"

"I wouldn't mind it; I planned on it."

And she thought of the salvation of touch, the flesh ripening against flesh, becoming for a moment, for a night, something else entirely. "Give it," she said, "to me."

"You're strange," he answered and touched his pale lips, pulling back into the light. His wan face was whiter.

"You are the kind of man who has memories before they are memories," she said.

"Don't you have memories?"

102

"Not that way; not in my mind. I didn't know you until I had touched you. I had forgotten you."

"And now?"

"I've known you always, or for exactly this moment I know you. It's the same moment always."

"Not for me." He stepped away, and began to pace. "I think of you."

"While you're guiding Yankees?"

"Before, during and after."

She liked hearing that—she wanted to be in his mind, in all the minds that could manage her. The selfishness of the desire did not bother her, did not hinder her.

"I used to think you didn't give anything," he said. "You just didn't have that human kindness. Humaneness. Most women will serve a man, they love to, but you won't. You wouldn't pass me the wine if I didn't ask you to."

"I've been told that kind of thing before. . . ."

"And look at you—you've ridden all day—thirty miles—and you haven't even changed your clothes, you haven't even complained about feeling nasty."

"You want me to complain?"

"No. I love that you don't."

"You want me to be like a man?"

"Not at all."

"Like this, then," she said, knelt before him, unbuttoned the khakis and took him in her mouth. He spread his legs and leaned back against one of the posts supporting the arbor. All around her was the smell of grapes; they pulled the flimsy boughs down with their clustered weight. She had a fleeting feeling of enclosure, of the weight and surety of concealment; the vines above them were twisted, wrenched around themselves; for a moment, in entrapment, the swell of vines, the grapes, she felt something being offered her. The hair at his groin was golden, she knew that, she held him in both hands, cupping the whole of him, sucking the feverish flesh deeply into her mouth. She looked up his length, past the lank sweater hanging just below his navel, past his narrow forearms which flittered against his chest like broken bird wings, the throat, stretched, the chin straining upward, the mouth, gone slack and defenseless, to the eyes, which were screwed shut as if against a fierce, battering

103

light. She wanted that, that sight: the aristocratic face torn from its dignity, become brutish, vulnerable, penetrable. He moaned out loud, his hands rising spastically, the thumb knuckles beating lightly against his collarbones. And then she lost sight of him, gave herself in specific concentration to the centered heat of his body, grasping him hand and mouth as he began the weak sluicing rockery into her mouth, gave in to the heat, to the hard force of him, to the quickening impoundment of her senses, everything—grapes, the long ride, Canaan—diminishing, falling backward to a vanishing point of heat, of the knowledge of herself kneeled before this body, holding it, changing it, burning it.

Out of the thrashed light, a moon now, guttering in clouds, unmoored, she rose from her body. It was her turn and she lay underneath him, her teeth chattering, clots of heat breaking loose inside her. "Oh, no," she cried. "Oh, no." She couldn't stand it, not her body feeling this way, tearing like bread, like a peach split by hard thumbs. "Oh, no, no, no." She hugged him in the cradle of her knees, grappling his buttocks to her; her whole body, unclothed, mashed out the juice and fragrance of grapes, yellow-speckled grapes, the scent exploding in her nostrils as she heaved her body up against his, the sticky sweetness oozing across her shoulder blades, her whole back slimy with juice, with smell. His face was forced past hers, chin in dirt, in the split skins of grapes, no sound coming from him beyond the slurp of bodies pounding, the wet sucking sound of their enjambment, the measling sliming of treaded grapes.

"Ah, well, now," he said when he lay beside her, his long arms folded under his head, "now you may want to bathe."

"I'm all-over sticky," she answered. She felt her body slowly releasing the pulse of her lust—goodbye, goodbye.

She did not know then to what extent she would always be a girl, easy in the means of her senses. She could not see herself in a yellow dress leaning from the second-floor porch of a hotel in St. Guillaume calling to a boy winding a fishing net. She could not hear what she said to the boy then, what made him look at her with knowing, assessing eyes, and how the faint smile on her lips would broaden as she saw him understand, as she watched him carefully place the folded net into a faded canvas sack, stow it in the locker of his beached skiff and climb slowly up the rocky strand toward her. She could not know the words she would speak to him when he entered her room, tentative yet bold, how she would look past his shoulder at the wind-abraded Caribbean rippling with sunlight, could not see herself raise her naked polished arms to his face that was as smooth as if he had never shaved and pull him, by his face, by the bones of his skull, easily, murmuring words she made up as she said them, into the narrow bed in the corner of the room. There were already knots in the string of her life—she thought this—and she didn't know if the knots—the moment she decided to leave Charleston, her life in Hawaii, her marriage, her return, this act—were the handholds she used to pull herself along, or the stops that kept the line from running free.

"In daylight, this place must be full of bees," she had said to Haven as she watched him pull on trousers and slinky sweater.

"And now mosquitoes," he said, slapping his naked thigh.

The arbor leaked moonlight, and a streaked column of it lay diagonally across her body just off the centerline.

"Are you going to get dressed?" he asked.

"In a bit."

"I remember how you used to run around naked."

"And what else?"

"The smell of you, that olive oil."

He rubbed his close-cropped head with the knuckles of his right hand. "Why don't we move this circus to the bedroom?"

"You go on," she answered. "I'll find you in a minute."

"Okay." He hesitated, bent down and brushed the moonlight across her breasts. "It's down the porch, just past the wisteria bushes—you don't have to come through the house if you don't want to."

"Okay," she said but she was already gone, up through the leafy roof, up into the sky. She hardly noticed when he passed between her and the moon and his footsteps faded into the already dewy grass. She could see herself, lying down there, mosquito bait, under the swollen arbor. Once at Folly Beach, sitting on a blanket by herself below her family's cottage, she had watched a flock of brown pelicans—twenty or thirty—floating on the water just beyond the surf line. As she watched, half a dozen of the birds rose all together and from a height of twenty feet plunged headfirst into the water. They folded their wings and fell, headfirst. Later she watched the flock flying along the beach, strung out in a line, almost stationary in the wind. And she had seen a boy, a boy she knew, James Cantrell, plunge his closed fist down the mouth of a captured pelican. With one hand he held the bird's beak open and sank his fist down the bird's throat, all the way to his shoulder. The bird hadn't made a sound, no protest. She remembered the color of the bird's eyes, brown as a buckeye, and the way it didn't fight. Maybe Haven made her think of pelicans. Haven, so thin he was almost scrawny, so dignified and always armored with his relentless courtesy, but who carried, she could see, a misery in his memory of her. But she could float off, above Haven, above his arbor, his viny house.

She got up, pulled on her underwear and her shirt and, carrying trousers and boots, walked out on the lawn. Her husband would miss her even if Jack had given him the message that she was here. And Jacey would run around looking for her. She felt, as always, a curious distance from them, from their need. The river murmured faintly at the bottom of the lawn. She walked down to a group of white wooden chairs arranged in a semicircle at one side of the riverhouse and sat down. The chair was wet but it felt good against the fading fever in her skin. She would like, she thought, to ride off south tomorrow, to the Gulf. From here on, Haven had told her at supper, it was nothing but pines and swamp lakes, a wild tangle of wilderness.

"Panthers," he had said, his eyes widening as if to scare a child, "and bears, loops of snakes in the trees."

"Loops." She hadn't even known this was Haven's land. The trail, skirting pine woods and white-headed cotton fields and the stripped stalks of tobacco plants, had meandered through woods of a different order from the water growth. By the river grew trees that did not flourish in the gray soil away from the riverbank. Willows, tupelos, ashes as large as the oldest oaks, cypress, and more frequently as she penetrated south, the ragged crowns of cabbage palms. It was only now, as she thought about it, that the fields she had glimpsed through the trees, fields grown up in broom sedge and gallberry, must have been the fields of this plantation, Haven's place, arranged now for hunters' pleasure, plantation that she did not even know the name of. She would ask him, she thought—all these Georgia boys named their land and repeated the name of it to themselves to make them feel secure. Canaan—the Promised Land. What was old Langston Burdette running from that made him vision these raw pine woods as the land of milk and honey?

She got up and pulled the chair closer to the river so that when she sat down again she could stretch her feet out and touch the water. The grass ran right into the river, as if the stream had leaked out onto the lawn. Under her heels she felt grass stems, not mud. She got up and waded out to her knees. The river curved away through a gate of moonlight into dark trees. She would move like this always, she thought, thinking of the ride, her decision to come here. There was nothing yet in her life to hold her, nothing she could see. She could smell on her skin the sweet odor of crushed grapes. Scuppernongs—somebody had told her they were not even real grapes. But what else were they? She wished her husband would come for her; she had wished it in Hawaii. She wanted something to fight against, something huge that would not give in until it took from her what it wanted. J.C., she had known from the first time she had seen him in the lamplit ballroom on Oahu, was a man like that: he would never give in, never let her go.

She lifted her foot and stirred the water with her toes. Out in the stream a fish jumped and fell heavily back. It was all she could do to keep from diving in after it.

Her mind came back to her as she squatted by the pen looking at quail.

"Why don't y'all come down and hunt sometime?" Haven asked. He stood with his arms crossed over his chest, looking into the pens. She was grateful to him.

"I doubt J.C. wants to, but I'll come again."

"The sooner the better. For me."

"Do you mind if I don't say when?"

"Yes. But I can live with it." He touched her hair, slid his fingers along its silkiness. She remembered her father doing that, the way, when she was a child, he would lift her hair to the sunlight to see the gold in the black. "I have to be going," she said.

"I'll ride with you to the end of the land."

"No. I want to be by myself."

She stuck her fingers through the wire, pushed against the wall of it. The ruddy chicks hopped over each over, half rising in inarticulate flight. She pressed her mouth against the wire. "Fly," she whispered. "Fly."

He had climbed into the deer stand, a narrow floor of boards nailed into the middle branches of a young live oak on the Canaan side of the river, to watch for her. Fifty feet off the trail, thirty feet in the air, he sat with his back to the striated trunk watching the way she would come. He was quiet enough for the squirrels to slip eventually back into the oak. A mockingbird flickered through the branches, lighting here and there, dropping little patches of song. He could hear the drone of the cotton pickers far back in the fields, faint as the hum of wires.

He hugged his knees and stared down the trail, willing her out of bushes. He had mortgaged the south lands to invest in Texas sulfur wells. Six million dollars from the Federal Land Bank would do it, would make Burdettes a partner in a consortium that mined and processed sulfur. He had not even known they pumped it up through wells; he thought they tore it out of mines with jackhammers.

He slept and wakened in late afternoon to the sound of squirrels scolding in the branches above his head. Far down the tree-shaded avenue of the trail he could see Elizabeth moving slowly past a large maple whose branches hung down over the water like a willow's. She leaned down and seemed to speak to her horse; from this distance he could not tell if she made words. He scrambled quickly and as quietly as possible from his perch, anxious that she not see him, and mounted. He trotted his horse, a sorrel gelding with a white blaze, out onto the trail. A great swath of fox grapes hung suspended from the branches of a sycamore over the trail; he noticed as he walked his horse under them that the sweet odor remained though birds had made off with the grapes. She was dressed as she had been yesterday, in a black shirt and fawn jodhpurs, her bag slung like a picking sack over her shoulder. She saw him and rode toward him with her eyes widened in mock surprise.

"Why didn't you come back last night?" he asked. "Why didn't you call?"

"I didn't think to." She looked tired. The bun of her hair had slipped around her neck.

"I couldn't sleep," he said and dug his fingers into the red mane.

"I walk when I can't sleep."

"I remember."

As he spoke he walked his horse next to her. The vivid odor of her body came to him, of her sweat and olive oil, the perfume she wore blended with the other scents. "I don't know if I can stand you doing this."

"What?"

"Disappearing. I can't stand getting geared up and then no place to run."

"I didn't know you were racing."

"Don't mock me, Elizabeth."

"I'm sorry. I'm tired. I haven't ridden this far in a long time." She patted the neck of her horse. "Sister Maxine."

"What?"

"I'm going to call this horse Maxine."

"Her name is Startler."

"Not anymore." She looked up into the trees across the river. The descending sun caught in the tops of a stand of yellowing tulip poplars. "I'm glad you let me do this," she said. "I appreciate it."

Emotion caught in his throat. "I didn't . . ." he started and stopped. "My father tried to saw down the house."

Her laughter barked. "That's wonderf—oh. . ." She looked down into a smile, looked up at him, reached across the space that separated them and stroked his horse's neck. "I thought he was sick from the snakebite."

"Apparently he recovered enough to take a chain saw to one of the pillars."

"You stopped him?"

"Yes. We were all up on the porch at the meeting. He slipped in downstairs and tried to saw the pillar out from under us."

"Samson."

"I stopped him." He leaned down and pressed his face in the horse's mane. He looked up at her, feeling his heart accelerate. "Ah, Elizabeth," he said, "there's so much I want to talk to you about. Why won't you stay?"

"I'm here now."

"But I have to *depend* on your being here. Don't you know that's what I need?"

"What you need is something to wrestle with."

"I don't know about that." He reined the horse around. It side-stepped away from a driftwood log half buried in yellow grass. "Let's go home."

"I was headed that way."

As they rode side by side, up the swamp road that at the hill line became a sand track that passed through woods into the open spaces of the fields, he reached down and touched her bridle rein, let his fingers rest on it. He wanted to grab it, to ride away across the fields pulling her behind him, but he restrained himself, out of fear and out of the quiet pleasure he felt at riding across this land with her beside him. The blue sky was speckled with thin high clouds, running into the darkening east. In the fields light shone in the burst cotton boles. It was as if the fading day had collected itself there, or that the tide of light, sweeping back, had uncovered these gleams, like shells on a beach. "I don't know if I have . . ."

"What?" she asked.

"Nothing." He had been about to say that he didn't think he had the strength to endure this, her coming and going, but a sadness flooded him: there might be nothing he could do about it. "My life is just beginning," he said, "and already I'm thinking that it is so different from what I imagined it would be."

"Only with me," she said. "The rest is like you planned."

"No. Not even the rest. I'm not sure any of it is." He looked southward toward the pond and his father's house. A line of pines marked their location, out of sight now beyond the hill line. "He hasn't settled down the way I thought he would," he said.

"Your father?"

"Yes. It's gotten so for the last few years I could forget about him." He laughed. "I got to liking his throwing rocks at the house. When you were gone it would give me more time to think about you. He'd wake me up and I'd lie there wondering what you were doing, out there in the Pacific." He shook the reins. "I'm still wondering."

"You knew what I was doing. I was jollying, like always."

"But without *me.*"

"I knew where you were, I felt where you were. I loved you."

"Loved?"

"Do, did, done. I done loved you. I done loved you all the time. Everybody's so afraid of that."

"Of what?"

"That they won't get loved."

"Aren't you?"

"No. I never had cause to be."

"You were always loved, the way you wanted to be." He spurred his horse ahead, reined in and swung across her path, trotted a few yards into the leafless cotton. "You never had to miss it," he called back to her. "You always got it."

She spurred ahead of him on the road. Dust splashed up from her

110

horse's hooves. She pulled the mare's head around and stopped in the road facing him. "It's like that," she said, "but why shouldn't it be?"

He kicked his horse into a canter. The tall plants slapped against his boots. "Because everybody else has to suffer a little," he yelled as he passed her.

She spurred her horse and cantered along in the road, parallel to him. "You think it's your job to teach me."

"Somebody's got to, babe." Somewhere up ahead a cotton picker droned, running late. They passed a cotton shed, small square boards, empty. He had had it painted last year, before he bought the pickers and didn't need it anymore. "You can't seem to learn on your own."

"Ha," she cried, but he had spurred his horse into a run. He looked back to see her kick the mare hard and slash it once across the rump with her hat.

They ran, J.C. crashing through the splintered cotton, Elizabeth on the hard sand road beating a rhythm with her crushed hat. Across the lands, over the rise and fall of the fields, through descending day, they ran, J.C. keeping the lead, the advantage of his surprise, Elizabeth beating hard behind him to catch up. At first he held his mind in, thinking of the runs he had made in the other direction, toward the swamp, that he had made alone, then the speed, the hard action of the horse beneath him, swept thought from him and he ran, mindless.

No word passed between them until they came up the last long rise before the fields ended at the line of bushes before the backyard. Elizabeth had pulled next to him; she rode with her head down along the horse's withers, reaching behind her to hit. J.C. didn't slow down as they approached the bushes. He made for a low breastwork of blackberry scrub between two chinaberries. He looked across at her: she was not slowing either, but as he looked she turned her head and yelled words.

"All Burdette horses are jumpers," he yelled back.

She laughed and leaned farther over the strong tan neck. "Don't get self-righteous," and then they were—together—at the line of blackberries and he rose in the saddle as his horse went up and over the bushes, felt the unhindering flick of leaves pass underneath—Elizabeth rising beside him, marvel of the mares bent forelegs—and down, neither horse stumbling, running on until the buttress of the house was before them and they reined in clattering on the terrace bricks.

He grabbed her reins and pulled her horse's head around. "Jesus,"

PART

7 Her long hair, loosened for the night, fell across her shoulders. Her crossed feet were propped on the arm of the scrolled living-room sofa so that the light cloth of the gown held the shape of her legs. The blue silk pooled between her hips. He opened the Chinese box on the table under the portrait of Rooley. There was another lacquered lid under the first one. "I like blondes," he had told her when they first met, and she said, "No, you don't, you like brunettes, you like the way their hair stands out against the skin. It excites you." She was right, she was right. And she knew, too, that he was afraid of the power that drew him toward her.

This was one of many nights. The reorganization of Elizabeth, she called it, smiling at him. She had taken to reading late at night in the first-floor library. Waking to the empty bed, he would descend the stairs and find her there stretched out on the sofa under the high front windows, a single lamp illuminating her book. Books were opened and piled around her, in disarray. Two hundred years of Burdette books lined ceiling-high shelves on two sides of the room. The ceilings in the house were fourteen feet high, each with a sculpted rosette of plaster in its center. Elizabeth lay on her back, plucking books off the floor like chocolates, glancing up occasionally at the library rosette, which looked a little like a squashed chrysanthemum. How nice, she would think, how cozy, and return to her book. Her husband, in his maroon silk robe, barefooted, would find her. He brought his anger with him and his load of topical conversation.

She was not a joiner, he pointed out. She had refused membership in the Women's Missionary Union, the garden club and the March of Dimes. I understand, he told her, that as Burdettes we are not *required* to do anything, but it is better that we participate.

Better for whom, she wanted to know.

For you, he told her, for me.

For you.

And her hats—they were killing him.

My hats?

Why don't you wear hubcaps?

Ah, J.C.

And your cars, your goddamn cars.

In her first five years in Yellow Springs she wrecked four of them, one roadster after another. She drove whatever was fastest and prettiest, Mercedes-Benzes, Jaguars, an Austin Healey painted bright red. Each had been smashed. She had never been hurt.

Why do you buy those goddamn cars if you're just going to wreck them, he wanted to know.

She laughed. She no longer drove cars off bridges for the fun of it, but she still liked to run for speed. He couldn't stop her; it was her money, built solidly into a trust fund created by her father, an act which the old Charleston banker had long since regretted. Regretted because it gave her freedom to flee. She never came to see him. She rarely wrote. When she did, her letters were light and superficial, a slight recitation of insignificant events.

When J.C. asked her why she ignored her father, she told him she was too old for parents. As, apparently, are you, she added, reminding him of his own father tending marigolds at his house by the pond.

On her second day in Yellow Springs she had returned from his father's house in a car full of flowers. It was the day the old man had his encounter with the snake.

He's nuts, J.C. had cried, the guy is nuts.

Nobody is who makes a world with these in it, she said, handing him a bouquet of zinnias.

Their son had run around the house with marigolds sticking out of his clothes, singing a song his grandfather had taught him.

But that's not what I want to talk about, he told her as he paced the library floor.

"What do you want to talk about?"

Your lack of surrender, your feats of rejection.

"Oh, good."

She propped her book, open, on the sofa back.

"It's not just your father or Charleston, it's all the rest, too: here and there, Hawaii."

"What could you know about Hawaii, dear?" she said, allowing her long fingers to drift down her body.

"What did you do there?" he asked for the thousandth time.

"What I'm doing here."

"Playing and sleeping?"

"Lovely way to live."

"It's selfish."

"So what?"

"So, stop."

He stopped. Pacing energetically, he saw himself reflected in the windows, and remembered driving as a teenager around the Square marveling at himself in his first car reflected in the plate-glass store windows. "I'm forty years old," he said, "and I've come into my strength."

"I'm thirty-five," she said, "and fair."

"I can't get over you."

"I never thought you could."

He sat down in the middle of the floor. The rug felt cool beneath him. He wrapped his robe around him. "I've been reading," he said. "I wake up and you're not there and I read for a while. I'm studying the nature of love."

"Lovely topic."

"A specialty of yours, maybe?"

"An interest."

"My books say you have to give it to get it."

"I've always heard that."

"How come you never went along with it?"

She shifted her body toward him. The gown fell away from her thigh. In the woods an owl called, a melancholy, mewing sound. In the window beyond her head he could see the green dome of the courthouse lit by floodlights. She fingered the ebony rosary that she had begun wearing around her neck for jewelry.

"I never felt any need," she said.

With the fingers of his left hand he pushed at his cheek. "Love?" he said. "To give love?"

"Nor to get it."

"That's impossible. Nobody's like that."

She raised her arms slowly above her head, stroked the silk fabric of the sofa back. "Is it strange to you?"

"It's maddening. It drives me crazy day and night."

"When I was a girl," she said, "my father took me to the fair. In one of the sideshows they had a huge barrel, maybe thirty feet across. Inside the barrel they had little monkeys, chimps, riding motorcycles—have you ever seen it?"

"No."

"The monkeys wore little flight suits and those leather aviator helmets. They even had goggles. Around their necks they had chains attached to a pole in the center. What they did was ride the motorcycles around the sides of the barrel. They would climb all the way nearly to the top, going round and round. The centrifugal force kept them up."

"This was at the fair?"

"Yes. In Charleston, in 1930. The spectators stood on a kind of balcony around the barrel. The idea was to be amazed that a monkey could do such a thing, ride a motorcycle around the inside of a barrel. You could see their eyes, the monkeys', as they went around. They were full of pain."

He pushed open palms along the rug. "And that's why you don't care anything about love?"

"No."

"So what's the story about?"

"Nothing. It's just a story. I didn't care about the monkeys at all. I wanted a motorcycle."

He looked past her at his reflection. Apple trees, he thought, remembering the summer he was twelve when his parents had taken him and his brothers on a trip to the mountains. In orchards by the road the trees were full of apples the color of the leaves. He had told his father he wanted to be an apple picker.

If you want to pay the price, his father had said, that's what you can be.

He had wanted, then, to pay the price to climb in those trees. But he had not paid it; his attention had slipped on to other, brighter chances. He wanted sulfur wells and he had convinced his brothers that it was worth the price. He had convinced the Atlanta banks, too, and now he owned a sea of sulfur. That against this, he thought, a yellow hole in the stony Texas ground and this woman here, supine in the audacity of her own self-creation. Whatever he paid, there was more to pay tomorrow.

"I must have written you a thousand letters," he said.

"Two hundred and seventy-six."

118

"You counted?"

"Yes. And I have them all."

She slid off the sofa.

Snake, he thought, snake.

In the perpetuation of her touch he found strength. She made love to him anywhere, anytime, any way he wanted her to. Once he took photographs of her, spread-eagled on his parents' bed, one long leg propped straight against the bedpost. "You want to see the pink?" she had said and opened her sex with the fingers of both hands. He held the camera close, one of the first that developed its own pictures, the same camera, he thought as he wrenched himself, his head throbbing, around the pummeled bed, that he had used to take pictures of his son riding his first horse, diving into the spring, balancing on a fence post.

"Do you like this?" he asked her.

"Yes," she said, squeezing her breasts, trapping the nipples between her fingers.

She had overcome his shyness by her willingness to do whatever he wanted. "How about this?" she said, bridging up on her neck, so that her body became a slanted table, the bone of her pubis protruding.

"Touch yourself."

"Like this?" With the flat of both hands she pressed down on herself at the center, as if forcing back against the lift of her body.

Close, far, he ran on a pulley of desire taking shot after shot. The rug was littered with the black slimy trash of crumpled negatives.

"Put a finger in, two fingers." Three, four even, it did not matter—she attempted whatever he suggested, and when he faltered, she encouraged him.

She turned over, pushed up on her knees and with her face in the pillow, reached around and spread herself wide.

There were moments when he wanted to drive his whole body into hers. He knew them, had known them, even in the nights when she was in Hawaii and he had paced the floor conjuring her wild and crying into this room. "Do that," he said, "do that."

"My ass?"

"Yes, go ahead."

She did. Anything. There was nothing else in the world but the sight of her, the sound of her fingers sliding in and out.

119

"I want to walk around inside you," he told her. "I want to be completely inside your body; I want to wear you like my armor."

"Try."

So he came to the bed, the camera dangling on his chest, grasped her slim, muscular hips and climbed up behind her. He entered harshly, the lubricant of her sex resisting him momentarily, the flesh itself resisting, so that she moaned and twisted partially away, reached around for him, guided him, and he shoved himself blindly like a boy, into her.

He kept the photographs in a book of equine genealogies shoved under boxes of shotgun shells on the top shelf of his closet. Jacey found them there when he was fifteen on one of his forays into the mysterious possessions of his parents. J.C. never knew, but Elizabeth found out. Jacey took the photographs and hid them in a locked overnight bag he kept in his own closet. Elizabeth, who knew where her son's keys were hidden, opened the bag and found the pictures of herself. She was delighted at the thought of her son looking at her this way. She wanted to run find him, to tell him that she knew. But she did not. She replaced the pictures, all but one of them, a shot that showed her sprawled, open-legged, in the gold wing chair under the window, the window whose panes reflected his father half crouched behind the camera.

He would never tell her son what they had done, but she wanted to. She wanted him to see, just as her husband had seen. A way of knowing, an initiation. Not to fuck him, not any of the incestuous clemency that she had no experience or thought of. It was something else—a desire to split open the world for him, to show him the palest flowers hidden in the moss under the live oaks, to take him down into the spring, into the sparkling waters that depth made impenetrable. Here, here, look at this, she wanted to say, turning the leaves of her life, of every life, all of it, like the pages of a book. Here is how it feels to ride a horse all day, here is what you see when you round a bend of this river, the Okeekee, here, in this clear water under the willows, is a school of fish, gold-backed, thick as flies; you can catch them in your hands.

When her husband touched her, often surprising himself (by the suddenness of his desire, by the odd places where it overtook him—the old barn, a cut-over cane field, the upstairs hall of the Hotel Burdette—by the power of it), she responded, not to the intimacy—she had said, No, not love—not to his strength, the rushing undeniable urgency of his lust, but to the surprise of the moment itself, the seemingly indecipherable connection he made, intuitively, unconsciously, between her hand, raised maybe to stroke a rusted plow blade Rooley Burdette had embedded in a swamp oak a hundred years before, and the possibility of desire—responded, surrendered, to the way, for a moment, the world dodged away into mystery and to the exploding excitement of newness.

He thought she might break his body down, as she had nearly broken his mind. In his body he did not find the iron resistance that he continued to enforce against her in his mind. He knew no way to outthink her—beyond his steady aggressive disapproval—because she did not, apparently, he told himself, think.

"Do you ever piece it out to yourself?" he asked her, on one of the library nights. "Do you ever *think* about the meaning of what you do?"

"What do I do?" she responded, giving him a look that was both naive and cunning.

"Ricochet is about all."

"I have a *plan.*"

"Would you show it to me?"

"I do—every day."

"Somehow I've missed it."

"No you haven't. You get the benefit. You and anybody else in striking distance; but mostly you."

"You mean what?"

"If you can't see, you'd better just keep watching."

"I might get tired. I think I *am* getting tired."

"No you aren't. And you won't."

Maybe not, he thought as he looked at her sprawled negligently on the green silk sofa. The courthouse clock struck three, and he felt the night penetrate the room. A pine warbler called faintly from the woods; he wondered if the striking clock had roused it. The bird called again, its cry fainter, farther off. Something in him stirred, a connection frailer than birdsong slipping into place. He remembered her arrival in Yellow Springs, their lovemaking. Afterward he had returned to the office. He sat at his desk all afternoon and into the evening, afraid to go home, afraid to go back and look at her again. In the station courtyard, over his son's shoulder, he had watched her; her arms hung at her sides, her hands held straight down, fingers loosened as if she had just dropped something, the sunlight turning the ends of her hair red-gold, her face polished, it seemed, by the light, so open to him, he remembered, so amazingly open, that the feast of sentences, the complex briefs he had prepared in the long nights, in the days, became loose freight in his chest, became instead, *feeling:* unreportable, indefensible, ungatherable scraps. He had run away from her at the spring, taking first what he thought his pride demanded, but sure as he hurried from her that he had taken nothing she would not freely give. He stared out the window at the street where red cotton trailers trundled behind tractors and pickup trucks, the white heaped fiber flecked with leaves and sticks. John Dance, the gin manager, called to tell him they had broken down again, but J.C. had no recollection of what he answered. He remembered only that he had drifted into a silence that John had finally mumbled words into, before breaking, apologetically, the connection. His secretary came into the room, spoke to him, crossed to the filing cabinets and placed papers in a drawer—she was there for several minutes before he saw her, before he became suddenly aware of another presence and gave her a look of such otherworldly intensity that she dropped the invoices she had pulled from the files and fled the room.

He had a headache, and his bones hurt—that must be what he felt creaking and grinding in his body, his bones crawling with some new disease. What had washed out of him at the spring washed back in, and lodged. "Not this," he said, aloud, "not this way, not all of this." He didn't know what he meant, beyond the swell of feeling in him, that he wanted to beat back, fling back to wherever it came from. He had waited five years for his wife to return and now he couldn't face her. It was too much: let her evaporate, let the whole life fade.

His brother might understand, either of his brothers; they had both married into different versions of this. But he didn't want exposure. He thought of Bryce's wife, Lois, daughter of a wealthy tobacco farmer on the Panhandle, her large pretensions, her chitinous jewelry, her modulant, obtrusive voice. Bryce was a teenager, still nineteen, when he married her, and he had stuck it out no matter what. He kept his ways and laughed at Lois'. Franken was different. He'd married tiny black-headed Louise, captured her from the stagnant country aristocracy of a family that owned a bank and a small-town GM dealership, and she suited him just fine. To J.C. it looked as if Franken had bent his own ways to hers, but that wasn't true; his were ways that leaned in her direction already. Their deliberate and rigid formality, the tension—as of creatures who feared an approaching light—that radiated from them, hummed around

122

them, was the opposite of Bryce and Lois' compulsive, divisive heartiness, but they seemed content in some way to live at the center of it, protected behind their shield of natural disaffection, and made no attempt to break free. So his brothers had made their accommodations. So he had not.

He picked up the brass replica of a cotton boll that anchored papers on the glass desk top. In Hawaii, on a trip to the botanical gardens that, despite the war, were still maintained, the agricultural agent had shown him a cotton plant as large as a small house. "We have no winter here," the man said, "so the plant grows." And none at all here, he thought, in this affair.

He cried out and struck downward with the brass boll, shattering the glass top. It splintered into a puzzle of cracks, held down still by papers and books. He heard Bryce rise from his chair in the next office, heard a typewriter go silent in the outer room.

"J," his brother called, "you need any help?"

He would not have him come in, did not want his face observed. "No," he said. "I dropped a paperweight."

He got up and went to the window. Long shadows leaned away from the transformers at the city power station across the street. The sun was going down behind the dome of the courthouse; it peeled a rind of fire off the copper. At times in his life he had discovered a strength in him that he had not known was there. He had found it as a boy when he had dared the depth of the spring, as a teenager when he risked his first money buying tobacco, at Harvard that first leaf-strewn fall when he thought his loneliness would kill him. He had found it in the war, out of boredom and then out of the lurching rhythm of action, and he had found it, he remembered now, when his mother died, out of his helplessness and his hopeless grief. It was nearly twenty years since his mother had died, and he rarely thought of her now. They had buried her in the family ground beside the clear stream that ran from the spring through the woods behind Bryce's house. "A Burdette at last," his father had said and snickered and returned to the main house, where he drank punch and ate yellow cake and laughed with the robust kin. Appalled at his father, misunderstanding, J.C. had fled the house and hidden himself in the cedars by the spring. He sat on the granite flagstones watching a few thin cedar needles float on the light-bristling surface of the water. What comes after this? he thought, what could possibly come after this? No one had hurt, he thought, in that time as he had. He brandished his grief like a weapon, cutting whoever came near. But later, when he discovered that his father *did* grieve, when he heard in the night the footsteps as his father paced the upstairs hall, when he heard even, late, faint as birdsong, the muffled cries from the abandoned bedroom, he had been the one, the one of all the brothers and kin, to comfort him. He had written a series of letters to his father that he posted daily for two weeks at the box on the corner of the Square. He had written as if a great distance separated them, speaking of his love for his mother, Queen Anne, recounting the events of her life as he knew and imagined them, speaking finally of the future, of the passing of grief, of what they, father and son, would hold always between them. His father never spoke to him of the letters, but one day, a week after he had finished writing, his father had approached him as he sat on a bench in the stable hallway repairing a piece of harness, and in the half-light of the stall, had taken his face between both his hands, bent down and kissed him, gently, on the lips. That was all.

That was all, he thought now, that strange overcoming. But where would *his* help come from, this time? Each day, one way or another for the last five years, he had overcome his yearning for Elizabeth, or, at least, he had lived through it. On the horizon of his life he had set her image and traveled each day in its direction, strewing accomplishments as he passed. If only he could get there, arrive there, winded and worn, but still alive, still desiring. Now she had come back and she was more beautiful than ever, larger, more alive. Outside, a cotton trailer passed, pulled by a tractor, on its way to the gin. On top of the cotton a boy in faded overalls lay sprawled on his back. He was singing a song, one arm stabbing time. J.C. leaned out to hear the words, but he could not make them out—something tart and breathy—above the noise of the tractor. He closed the window and turned back to the room. Just when you figure it's over, he thought, is when it's barely begun.

8 Elizabeth lived fourteen years, more or less, in Yellow Springs, dawn to dusk, dusk to dawn. She spent time away on jaunts and excursions, escapes; once, when she was in her late thirties, she lived for six months on an island in the Caribbean. She slipped away, to Atlanta, to the woods, to the sawgrass beaches on the Panhandle.

Since she joined no clubs and did not become a woman pillar of the church, she had time on her hands. "Lazy time," J.C. called it, among other things, but it was never lazy time to Elizabeth. She rose late, as she had in Hawaii, and in fine weather took her breakfast outside on the terrace made of bricks taken from the old Burdette house in Charleston. Next to an unpruned Japanese plum tree that reminded her of the islands, under a blue-and-white striped beach umbrella, she enjoyed her fruit juices and sweet rolls. She had Hosea, the gardener and house servant, cut the bushes back from the fence so that she could see the fields. She loved her view of the fields, bold and harkening like a sea, but all her life she missed the actual ocean. "Until now," she reminded herself, "I have spent my whole life in sight of the ocean." It was a fact that had never meant anything to her until she moved inland.

She took the spring as her partner, blue pool, clear like a window into another world. And she learned to love the fields, their sealike qualities, and the ground itself. The soil of Canaan in the main was gray, the color of thunderclouds, rich with humus, sand and limestone, but in places, along the margins of fields where the ground dipped in creaselike runs all depending toward the swamp and the river Okeekee, before J.C. planted them in coastal Bermuda, the runoff streams cut down into soil that was startling in its beauty. Below the topsoil was a layer of white sand, as fine and loose—when it dried—as flour. In the sunlight the sand glittered like diamonds from the quartz in it. Topping a rise on her horse, she would stop and look down at a white sparkling river of sand and something would stir in her, some quickening response to the loveliness of it. Underneath the sand, in veins like ore in rock, was the red clay underlayment. The clay was not all red; in places it was orange, in others white, and occasionally it was blue, in pockets and streaks, the color of veins under skin. Her new cousin Rooley, thrashing among paints and canvases in the attic studio of his tall Victorian manse beyond the pond, told her that he got his inspiration from the land, from the bands and streaks of color that ran under the green and gold of the fields. She could believe it. She often stopped to walk along the sun-hardened watercourses, knelt in a clay bed and pried out chunks of the dense vivid earth. Toward the swamp the soil darkened, from gray to brown to black, until at the riverbank it was the same color as the river itself. She did not love that ground as much, it did not have the cleanness and the long endlessness of the tilled land. It didn't collect light the way the fields did.

Her life, she thought, was a trip without a destination. Which suited her fine. The pleasure of it was in seeing something new. A hobo, she thought, looking at the world from a boxcar door. She visited the families of the black men who worked on the farm because they reminded her of the islanders she had known in Hawaii. She learned how to scrape the innards of pigs and cows for chitterlings and tripe and to prepare and eat blackbirds and robins and how to string a trout line and how to call a coon hound out of the woods. The Negro families were frightened of her at first—mistress of Canaan—but her manner won them over. She knew not to bring them any gifts beyond her presence and her willingness to listen to them and her interest in their lives. She charmed them as she charmed everyone she met. The relationships contained, as all such relationships did, the hesitancy and self-protection of the Negroes, but she did not mind, she countered reserve with kindness, with the willingness to help their children, which was a secret of a kind, that she had learned from her father: help the thing a person loves and that person will love you. She did not help them paint or furnish the clapboard shotgun houses they inhabited in the small community grown up along the town street on the north side of the lands, and she didn't help with car payments or water bills, and she did not interfere with her husband's methods of managing his work crews, but when a child was sick she was willing to tend him, to drive him to the health center or to sit up with him; she took children with her on excursions, to the county fair, to the beach fifty miles away in Florida, to the river, to the spring.

She had no interest in reform, no enlightened heart that told her that equality was necessary; she had only her interest, her delight in entering a world that was different from her own. An old man named Ramsey taught her to make baskets out of white oak, how to split the strips of sour wood and soak them until they were pliable and how to weave them into the sturdy baskets he sold from a stand by the north road. When his wife came down with pneumonia after a fishing trip in the rain, Elizabeth tended her, brought soup and fresh rolls and even once cooked supper for Ramsey. The old man had not enjoyed her cooking, and Elizabeth had not done it again, but she did not mind his displeasure.

Her husband—curiously to her—objected to her spending time at the cabins, but she didn't mind. "You just watch what I'm doing," she told him, "and you'll learn something." He argued with her or attempted to (she would rarely argue back), but she went her own way nonetheless.

He never reconciled himself to her doings, but eventually he stopped speaking of them, went on to other things.

As she grew older she continued to wear her hair long, her only concession to maturity a loose, nested bun that she wore low on her neck and that was liable to shake free when she rode. Her clothes were fashionable, skirts of silk or cotton or wool, depending on the season, with a tendency toward blouses of silk or long-staple cotton, dresses of the same materials, few suits. Throughout the fifties she was famous locally for her hats. They were of all shapes and sizes and colors, round and big as wagon wheels, small as a hand, of floppy straw, soft felt, hard and resiny-looking like carved wood, glittering. It was a time of hats—all the women wore them—but hers were so unusual, blooming with veils and scarves of rich hue, fashioned of canvas or peaked patches of raw silk, adornments so audacious and contrary that many of the women were intimidated by the sight of her and the men were stirred, often displeased, always attracted.

She had her hats and her rich clothes, but she was most often dressed in the simpler garments of her pleasure: the briefest of bathing suits for swimming, jodhpurs and a silk blouse, tall boots for riding. The spring taught her that the country was old and her trips on her horse taught her that even after two hundred years of farming, it was hardly tamed. Paved around with granite slabs hauled before the Civil War from quarries in north Georgia, surrounded by red cedars the wood of which paneled the attic, the spring was a moment of timelessness to her, a still point in the change around her. The stream that exited from it and ran fifteen miles to the swamp river Okeekee had once held the ceremonial houses of Creeks and Choctaws on its banks. In the cut of earth along the banks, among the roots of elderberries and willows, she found shards of pottery, old tools and cutting stones, occasional bones. The stream, unbridged at any point and narrow enough for a good horse to jump across, was clear as tapwater. It was just deep enough to swim in, and she liked to float over the rim of the spring and down its length, occasionally for a mile or more. Yellow Spring Course, it was called. It ran through the woods past the family graveyard behind Bryce's house and on along the edge of pines bordering the fields to the pond beside Jack's house. On the other side of the pond the Course exited into a branch that was dense with swamp trees and bushes.

In the Course and on her rides across the lands and in her afternoons in a johnboat on the river and in her drives around the rolling south Georgia countryside she was amazed at how much she lived in the past. She woke up in the morning fresh from sleep, her mind turned toward the living world, some new frame of it, but by ten, by eleven, by one, she was drifting in a dream of the past. She didn't get along with cooks or housemaids, she cleaned behind them and cooked behind them and when they objected—if they did—she fired them. Others came, usually young women from the houses on the north lands. She did not mind their work, or what they thought of her; she minded having her train of thought broken.

She had once kissed a stranger on a street corner in Honolulu. She had come out of the Royal Hawaiian Hotel at four in the morning on Haven Lauren's arm—they had been to an officers' party—and on the street corner under a clump of coconut palms beyond the taxi stand an old man in a tattered raincoat stood alone in the rain. As they waited for the car to be brought around, Elizabeth had watched the man, who stood still as a sentry on the blacked-out corner. From the distance of half a block she could not tell he was old, but from the way he stood so motionless, so contained, the coat pulled around him, she could tell he was standing, not waiting. She left Haven and walked to him. He turned as she approached. He had a singe of white beard and his eyes were wet as if they had been rained in. She stopped in front of him and looked in his face. He smiled a weak, apologetic smile and touched his bottom lip, which was cracked and bulbous. One of the wanderers, she thought, one of the Pacific hoboes who had washed up here and was stranded now by the war. He brushed a film of rain off his face and looked at the ground. Elizabeth touched his face and kissed him on the lips. The man leaned into her without raising his arms and she caught him with her hands against his chest. She pushed him back upright and he looked up at her with frightened imploring eyes. "Remember me," she said. "Don't forget me." Then she turned and walked back to Haven, who waited for her beside the idling car.

In Hawaii she had told J.C. the story of the fallen man and she told him again in the bed late at night after lovemaking. He was not interested anymore. She had always been able to break him out of whatever obsession ruled him; she knew that he valued her for her ability to do that, but here at Canaan she found herself less and less able to turn his mind from what held him. She was, she saw, not what he had wanted her to be,

128

but there was nothing, she told herself, that she could do about it. She told him the story because she wanted him to know what she was capable of. "That old man, wherever he is, will have the memory of a beautiful woman kissing him," she said.

"You must think pretty highly of yourself," he answered.

"Of course I do. I'd be a fool to pretend I'm not beautiful."

"You *are* that." He sighed and fell silent. His hand moved across her and gripped lightly the swell of her belly.

"It's a strange thing," he said. "I get to know you twice."

"Isn't that fine," she answered. "I'll go away again, and you can know me three times, or four or five."

But not twice or more, only once. Only once, he thought. If he held her money, he told himself, he could change her. But she held her money herself. Her father had seen to that. How could the old man be so stupid. It amazed him that she wasn't interested in returning to Charleston. Even he, estranged from his father, felt occasional twinges of desire for reunion. If he slapped them away, it was no reason for her, who had not broken with her people, not to want to return to them. But she never said anything about it. And here, in Yellow Springs, he could tell that no one meant anything to her.

Often, coming in for lunch, he found her in the library talking to three or four women from the town. The women sat in chairs while Elizabeth lay on the sofa, following with her eyes the smoke of cigarettes to the ceiling. The women chattered while Elizabeth listened. Afterward when J.C. asked her what they talked about, she could never say. Perhaps she didn't want to tell him, but he believed that she really paid no attention. "What do you do?" he asked, meaning what went on in the library.

"I watch them move," she told him. "I look at their faces."

She could never tell him what they said, but once when he had commented that Angela Dobbins, the wife of the owner of the meat-packing plant, looked especially cheerful, she had told him that no she wasn't cheerful, she was frightened to death. "Her husband wants to have another baby," she told him, "and she's terrified." He hadn't seen that at all, and the next time he saw Angela he tried to pick up the fear Elizabeth had told him was there but he could not. She looked happy and peaceful to him.

"I don't think she's upset," he said as they sat in the kitchen on a Sunday night eating tunafish sandwiches.

"You just have to look at her," she said. "You can tell by the way she squints her eyes."

He supposed so, but as Elizabeth got up to put the empty tuna can in the trash, he wondered at her, at her confidence and at the mystery of her and that he needed to know what she told him.

He wanted her to tell him about Hawaii, but she would not, beyond superficialities and light moments, unconnected things. She didn't describe what her heart was like there, what her fears were, what she wanted. She told him of the places she had seen, the people, how she spent her mornings, how the island changed after the war, but she would not tell him what she needed there. He wanted loyalty from her, and the askew thing she offered was not enough.

"I have to know," he told her as they lay in bed at night. "I have to know what was going on."

They listened to the rain rustle on the porch. "You have to understand," he said, "that I need to know what you were up to—all that time is a blank to me, as far as you're concerned." This time, time at Canaan, was a blank, too.

"Certainly not a blank," she said.

"I can't figure it out. I mean, you tell me the details but I still don't know anything. What did you *say* to your friends?"

"Nothing much. We joked a lot."

"About what?" He wanted to know if she made love to them.

"About you—always."

"Aggh."

She touched him, got out of bed and went out on the porch. Through the sheers he could see her form silhouetted by the glow of far-off lightning. In a moment she came back and slid in beside him, wet all over. He shied from her.

"What are you doing?" he asked.

"I wanted to get wet." She touched him. "Don't you want to make soaking love?"

Yes he did, Jesus, yes he did. "You're crazy," he said.

But he was the crazy one, he thought as he pulled off his pajamas. I am getting something—this sweet body, for instance—that I have known now—for years! interrupted years!—that I don't want to live without, but I am cheated still, always cheated.

"We'll have to change the sheets," he said, but as he took her, slippery and cold in his arms, he didn't care, for the moment didn't care if they had to change the sheets every night of the week.

Years later, after the end, sitting with his wife, Martha, on the same Caribbean beach that Elizabeth fled to, Jacey remembered that during his grade-school years his mother often waited for him across the street from the schoolyard in one or another of her sleek, dangerous cars. Parked always under the same oak tree, whose branches swept so low over the street that she could stand in the seat to pick moss, she waited for him, in a Jaguar, in a Mercedes roadster, for six months of afternoons in 1955 in a cherry-red Thunderbird, in an Austin Healey with a black canvas top she let him fold down for her. From the top of worn steps of the same school his father had attended, through the cinnamon branches of the crepe myrtles lining the street, he would see her across the long distance of the grassless yard. If the weather was warm she would have the top down; often she wore one of her wild, alien hats; she would have leaned back in the seat and propped her feet on the dashboard; she would be reading a book, or talking to a passing child or singing one of the fey songs he would remember all his life, or doing nothing, simply staring up into the heavy, fern-covered branches of the live oak. She brought him gifts: seashells whorled and spiraled, pieces of Indian pottery the color of bones, bones the color of pottery, flowers with the deep unguent scents of the swamp, garnets and quartz stars, hard little balls of blue clay, a handful of red berries. She told him stories about the gifts that by the time he was eight he knew were made up. She told the stories anyway and laughed when he pointed out her incongruities.

On the beach in St. Guillaume, capital of the French Antilles, Leeward Islands, he remembered the gifts and the stories and missed them, but he missed most the smell of her, a scent concocted of sweat and olive oil and a perfume called Chartreuse. He missed her smell and couldn't bring it back. Once in a while he would smell it, always out of nowhere it seemed, and he would be flooded with the sense of her presence. It was in the box of letters he inherited from her, in a pair of gray gloves he found in the glove compartment of her last car, in a scarf she wore riding. It was an aura glowing around her, and when he slid in beside her he felt it envelop him so that as they tore through the country on the speeding trips she took him on, he felt a part of her, more even than just a part: in her, inside, captured and secure.

He was good at school, a fair winning child, well liked by teachers and students, but he was most at home with Elizabeth, though he sensed, even as a child, that she was not so much joining him, connecting with him, as playing out something in front of him, creating an elaborate, fantastical role, and that their union was expressed most fully in the depth of his appreciation of her playing, in his belief and acceptance of her gifted and sustained acting.

He didn't mind, just as he didn't mind the strangeness of Burdettes. Delight's mouth healed, though he bore for the rest of his life a scar like a cat scratch across his upper lip and the porcelain caps he had fitted over the stumps of his front teeth stayed white while the enamel around them yellowed. Bernard and Delight liked to sit in rockers on the porch of their filling station, under the steep blue roof that had the words ANIMAL FREAKS painted on both sides in large white letters, and watch the tourists spin by on their way to Florida. Occasionally Delight, primed on still-run whiskey, would step out to the road and try to flag one down. Occasionally some kid, riding in the back of a station wagon, would get his parents to stop for a tour of the zoo. Mostly the brothers pumped gas for farmers and sold fishing and hunting supplies to the sportsmen.

Rooley and Alsace lived in a tall, narrow Victorian house in the cotton fields across the pond from Jack. Rooley painted brisk, abstract canvases that were charged with conflict. "It's the tension between what I am and what I know," he told Jacey on the afternoon he found the place, solitary as a birdhouse in the center of cotton rows, on one of his jaunts across the lands. Rooley had led him through attic rooms whose walls were hung with paintings. There was even paint under the paintings, on the walls themselves. "I paint everything," Rooley explained, lifting a canvas to show him swirls of yellow and green on the plaster wall. "I can't get enough of it." His wife, Alsace, a mild woman with a shock of yellow hair like splintered wheat, gave him bacon and orange juice in the living room. "You go down there and get her to feed you," Rooley had said, leaving him at the top of the stairs. In the living room, with the plate of bacon in his lap, Alsace sitting across from him on a ripped leather sofa, a famished look in her eyes, he listened to Rooley's footsteps cracking across the floor above their heads. The footsteps were punctuated by shouts and cries.

At every shout Alsace flinched and her eyes widened a little. They sat without speaking for a long time until Jacey caught sight of a redbird flitting through a bush outside the window and went out to look for it.

"They're a wonderment," Jacey gravely told his mother that night as she shucked him of his clothes.

She asked him where he'd heard *that* word, but he couldn't remember. Maybe, he thought, it was from his Uncle Bryce, who was an empire partner now and who occupied an office next door to his father's in the warehouse off the Square. Jacey had been there, too; his father had taken him with him to the office shortly after he arrived in Yellow Springs. His uncle, a burly, rufous man with the same rattled red hair as his father and grandfather, had burst out of his office to greet him.

"Aloha, boy!" he had exclaimed and swept Jacey into his arms.

Bryce took him on a tour of the warehouse. They ambled down the close lanes of cotton bales, hand in hand, as his uncle told him the story of how cotton made its journey from the fields to the warehouse.

"First you defoliate it," his uncle said, waving a hand as if it were happening in front of them. "You have to get the leaves off now, which is something new since your father went out to Mississippi and met the Rust brothers. They make cotton pickers, the Rust brothers do, and now we have four of them. Used to be nigras picked the cotton. You didn't have to defoliate then—a human being can tell the difference between a boll and a leaf. A cotton picker can't—if it's on the bush it'll get it, leaf or boll—you follow me?"

Jacey didn't follow at all, but he was delighted by his uncle's bouncy, wandering chatter. He couldn't remember what else his uncle told him about cotton, couldn't catch how it was hauled from the field to the gin, what happened there inside the monstrous machinery, how it got to the warehouse to be stacked in rows three bales high, strapped in metal bands so tight that when Jacey thrust his fist against a bale it felt as hard as the floor they walked on.

"I'm proud you're here," his uncle told him, and maybe it was then that he said the word "wonderment" which Jacey applied with pondering gravity to his cousin Rooley of the yips and colors.

Jacey met his Uncle Franken, who was tall and lean like a poplar tree, and who wore his red hair in a bristling crew cut, at the first family meeting. Franken, after J.C. had come back from the war, had become comptroller of the company. It was his job to shuttle the funds between the lands and the businesses and his job to assist in the negotiations J.C. accomplished and planned for the aggrandizement of their holdings.

133

There were also his Great-Great-Uncle Eustace and Great-Uncle Ransome and his Great-Great-Aunt Ethel. Eustace lived on the Florida road behind a forest of camellia bushes. He collected paintings, though he would never buy one of Rooley's. "There's no use buying what you can walk across a cotton field and see," he explained, an explanation that angered Rooley. Jack's brother Ransome was fat and the only Burdette of his generation to have black hair, and he drove an immaculate white pickup truck with every accessory the Ford Company offered. He ran the farming crews, as he had done for forty years, and spent his life in the fields. Ethel, sister to Jackson and Eustace, youngest of her generation, lived alone in a white house a block south of Bryce and kept to herself. She was a spinster who at seventy-five still talked of getting married.

He didn't know if his mother recognized them, these Burdettes. Maybe each time she saw one she had to be reintroduced. Hello, hello, I'm Elizabeth your cousin, niece, granddaughter-in-law. She rode her horse, pounding down a cotton row toward the swamp. She ran the roads in her dangerous cars. She did what she wanted.

But she came to know Burdettes, passing by. She came to know them all, and as she drifted through the early years, the fifties, measuring time as if by the feel and look of the skin on her wrists, by the growth of trees, by the cut of the Okeekee into a certain willow bend, by the number of books she read on the first-floor library, by the maids who came and went, by her lovers, the faces of Burdettes, cousins and kin, became dear to her, her entertainment and her audience.

The main house, which on the day of her arrival had dazzled and frightened her, remained mysterious to her, edifice and museum in which, by J.C.'s pleasure, she was a visitor, nothing more. He would not let her make changes. When she attempted to replace the heavy bedroom draperies with fairer ones, he stopped her, because, he said, his mother had hung them and they were still satisfactory. The paintings on the downstairs walls, of Burdettes and of sailing ships and huge Bierstadt trees soaring lonely in webbed and misty forests, were satisfactory too, as were the colors of the walls and the sofas and tables and the worn, unraveling carpets on the polished wooden floors. She created for herself an imaginary house eventually, and as she walked through the main house rooms, eight downstairs and up, plus baths, fireplaces in every room, she redecorated in her mind, hanging paintings that were full of colors of the world around her, the clay of the fields, the changeling sky, the spring with its blue bole of light far down. In her mind she painted all the walls white and she threw the furniture out, except for a reef of green silk pillows from the main living-room sofa, and she pulled the rugs up and put down mats woven of pandanus and rice fiber.

He let her bring in plants. She borrowed Bernard's truck and went around to the nurseries and bought every plant she could find that reminded her of Hawaii. Areca palms and ficus trees and schefferas and philodendrons of all sorts filled the rooms. J.C. objected to so many, but she reminded him of the trees in Hawaii and he let her do what she wanted. In the islands the bushes that here were house plants had been untamed, wild and unruly trees, and she was saddened to have to settle for so little, here. Numbers could only do so much, but she tried. "Oxygen," she said when he complained, "we need the oxygen," and bought more plants. He let her fix the kitchen as she wanted, bought her a new stove and filled the laundry room with apparatus. She thanked him and patted the new dryer and went riding.

On her rides, and in her drives in the fantastical sports cars, she met the Burdettes that her son feared she would never come to know. She met Delight of the raddled aspect, who became her lover in 1952, and Rooley, raging among his bright and divisive paints, who in 1955 became her lover too.

Eustace, because he told her stories of the old times, became one of her favorites. The old man, gallant and excitable, still liked to cruise the land visiting the arenas of memory. He drove his black Oldsmobile, washed and waxed once a week, as if it were a jeep, into the roughest and least accessible places on the farm. He was forever having to find someone to pull him out of whatever bog or hole he'd gotten himself stuck in. The first time Elizabeth met him was on one of the downhill roads into the swamp where in an attempt to avoid a slough he had rammed the car into a stand of young pines. While she tried first to pry him out then with a hatchet she found in the backseat to hack him out, he stood in the road with his thumbs hooked in his belt telling stories of his old-time feud with his brother Jackson. "I would have killed him," he told her, "but I probably wouldn't have been able to live with it. So it was best I didn't—watch out for that bee!" As he talked he stamped his feet and twisted his wiry torso as if it were all he could do to keep from dancing. The car was stuck, and she had to ride her horse back to the farm office, where she

135

borrowed a jeep from the manager, came back and winched him out. The next morning she received a bouquet of yellow roses containing a card on which he had written in his spidery Victorian hand the words "Angel of Mercy" and the hours when she might expect to find him at home. She often visited him in his big white house on the Florida road, where they sat on the front porch drinking orange juice and eating strips of the thick fatback bacon he would fry up for her.

Jack and Mattie became her friends, and, along with Delight and the Negroes, her teachers. As a child of twelve she had spent a summer in a girls' camp in the North Carolina mountains, and she discovered that she was less interested in hiking and lanyard-making than she was in helping out in the kitchen of the big open-air dining hall. After meals she would drift back into the kitchen area to help the college boys who served the tables do their chores. She became a pet of the cooks, who gave her extra desserts, and of the boys, who told her stories of college adventures and promised to take her with them on their trips to Asheville. She discovered in Mattie and Jack a similar affinity. They were willing to allow her to help them in their simple round of chores and tasks they had built for themselves out on the south lands. She hoed in the garden and planted the marigolds and zinnias and cosmos Jack tended. She worked the kitchen garden with Mattie and learned the needs of the country vegetables she grew. Elizabeth could tell the difference between the flowers of butterbeans and black-eyed peas, she discovered that radishes were the first vegetables to make fruit, that broccoli and peas could take cold but not a hard frost, that tomatoes fared better if they were staked but made more fruit if left unpruned, that yellow squash must be picked when very young but that the other squashes, gourd, acorn, turk's cap, were better if left to ripen. She was delighted to learn that sweet corn if planted in single rows only would not make ears. "The leaves have to touch for them to pollinate," Mattie told her, and the fact and the picture of it in her mind, of corn swaying in the arms of corn, seemed to her completion and proof of an important eternal law.

Mattie taught her to can and freeze vegetables, to boil peanuts and to make pickles. She would have taught her to make a quilt and to tat and sew, but Elizabeth's fingers were impatient and she gave it up. "It's important for a person to learn quietness, and there is no better teacher than handwork," Mattie told her, but Elizabeth laughed and moved on. There was always music where Jack was—J.C. had allowed him to carry off his

136

player and record collection—and as they worked in the garden or in the kitchen they were surrounded always by the rise and fall of the creations of the musical masters. "It's one reason I'm grateful not to have to do field work anymore," Jack told her as they hoed butterbeans. "I couldn't have music out there. Now I've got my ground and these bodacious plants and my music everywhere. I believe opera keeps the bugs off."

The moccasin bite healed, but Jack lost some strength in his right arm. He kept it in a sling for six months, and when it came out he was not able to lift as he had been able to before. "The only thing that bothers me," he told her, "is that I've had to give up my dream of being a big-league pitcher." He had played a year of semipro ball in the teens, and he liked to remember it as they sat on the porch after supper sipping elderberry wine. "Wasn't there a one-handed player during the war," Elizabeth asked him, and he patted her head and said, "Yes, darling, there was, and I appreciate your thinking of it. If we ever go to war again I'll head for the tryouts."

Jack drove her around the lands and rebuilt them in his stories for her. He showed her the first fields and the oldest woods, tracing each as if it were the pedigree of a thoroughbred through its generational changes. The pond had once been a field of saw grass, and half of the first cotton field was now in its fifth stand of planted pines. He showed her which plants were native and which were imported and taught her what flowers came in each season. They would drive to the last ridge before the long woods fall into the swamp basin and park the truck and look out over the country. "Mattie would see it as a quilt she was making," he told her once as they sat, their feet propped on the dashboard on the shoulder of the sand road ridge passing a bottle of vin rosé between them. "She'd think of it built up in patches of cloth, but to me it's more like one of Rooley's paintings—all these planes of color fitting together, each one made on purpose and beautiful. Don't you think it's beautiful?"

She did at that. She had not expected to fall in love with territory, was, as she reminded herself, a sea woman, and ground had only been what you walked across to get to the water, or if anything more, only a kind of accent or filigree to the huge, bright beauty of the ocean. Ground was particularity, this chinaberry here, that twist of river driftwood there, this dewy grass, but on Canaan, as she rode alone or with Jack or Jacey, she began to know it in its great generalness, its fine expanse. It was the sky, full of weather, that made, if anything did, the

137

connection for her. The sky was as big as the sky in Hawaii, and it changed more frequently. The cold rains of winter were followed by the cloud-broken days of spring and early summer, which were followed by the hot, dry cotton-making days of July and August and then by the thunderstorms of fall. The changes were not only seasonal but daily. "This country will give you a lifetime's worth of weather in a day," Jack told her, and he was right. A fair morning sky could fill with clouds by ten, crack into storms and wild wind and be back to blue by noon, the only evidence of disturbance the leaves floating in puddles on the terrace. "There have never been two seasons exactly alike," Jack told her. "Each one is an individual and has its special little ways. One spring the cold will turn back and kill the azaleas, a mild winter will come and the peach trees won't get enough frost to set the fruit, a summer full of rain will drown the corn, fall will last into December."

It was the weather that started her on her list making, weather and the dream house that J.C. wouldn't let her make at home. She got free notebooks at the feed store and began to put down long notations of the changes in weather, by days and by seasons. From weather she went to plants, their order of appearance and their varieties. Looking over the lists, she learned that the flowers of early spring were mostly odorless and came in an order of increasing scent. First were crocus, then violets, then daffodils and narcissus, then dogwood and redbud, then azalea, then Japanese magnolia and the fruit trees, plum, pear, sweet apple and peach. The Japanese magnolia and the fruit trees had perfume, but it wasn't until the arrival of honeysuckle and magnolia in May that the air was filled with the smell of flowers. Wisteria and crepe myrtle came then too, in May, and though they did not carry the room-filling odor of the bolder flowers, they had a boldness of color (wisteria, purple; crepe myrtle, pink) that made up for the shallowness of scent.

She made lists of garden vegetables and kept a diary that described the growth of the plants, from the first fingerling shoots of radishes and sweet peas in early spring to the final yellow flowers of bolted turnips and mustard greens in the fall. She tabulated the farm machinery and the names of the Negro hands and their families. She clocked her husband on paper, scribbling a record of his daily routines, his early rising, his two over medium eggs for breakfast, his baths, his after-lunch naps, his workout on the exercycle in the garage three times a week. One of her favorite lists was of railroad companies. Parked by the tracks that cut through the northern quadrant of the lands she wrote down the names on the sides of the boxcars. Georgia Northern, Burlington Northern, Seaboard, Canadian Pacific, Santa Fe and Topeka, the Rock Island Line—she took them all down. She never asked herself why she made lists, but she knew that she drew comfort from them. Holding the little notebooks with their picture of three ears of corn and the words "Dekalb Seed Corn" on the cover, turning the pages to her list of native animals, or to the shoe sizes of all the Burdettes, or the names of the rivers in south Georgia and the towns they passed, she felt a security that she was startled to discover she craved. She had been bold all her life, known for her fearlessness and her wayward zeal, but she found now, in the naming and ordering of the territory she had settled in, a new sustenance. She showed the lists to no one, only referred to them occasionally to Jack and Mattie. When J.C. saw her once, on one of his impulsive rides to the river, writing in one of the notebooks and asked her what she was doing she did not try to conceal her act but only brushed it aside, telling him that he would not be interested.

She wondered if it was not the righteous eccentricity of the Burdettes themselves that drove her to list making. Righteous, she thought, because each one was so sure that he was on the track, in whatever aberrant way he lived, of something grand. She had visited Alsace and Rooley, had sat in the paint-speckled attic as Rooley Burdette II dashed to and fro jamming color onto canvas. On the lawn behind their house Rooley had set up a series of tents each made of a different color of cotton fabric, and he moved from tent to tent to paint. "I want to see how the quality of the different light affects the paintings," he told her, and she agreed that was a good idea. Alsace strode through the rooms of her brick house as if something far away were permanently on her mind.

She added them to her rounds, as she added Delight and Bernard and the other Burdettes. The animal zoo was on the southeast road, a mile up from Jack's. She stopped there regularly, at first to see the animals, then later to see Delight. The brothers had extended childhood hobby into adult vocation. The yard behind the station was filled with wire cages of different sizes in which the native animals of south Georgia were gathered. They had raccoons, squirrels, otters, skunks, a beaver that was so old the tips of its glossy fur had turned gray, an armadillo, a small herd of whitetail deer, snakes both poisonous and non-, guineas and quail, half a dozen goats, a pair of possums that hung head down from a stripped oak branch and never opened their eyes during the day, and a small black bear with the mange.

The bear was the prize. Delight told her it was the last—"and only," Bernard added—black bear caught in Burdette County. They had caught it in a loghouse trap on the river. "We used to see tracks running up in the fields," Bernard told her, "so Dee and I built a trap and caught her. It's a she." They fed the bear on fish and elderberries and fruits and the trimmings from Mattie's garden. "You'd be surprised what a bear will eat," Bernard told her. "It's about as careless as a human being."

The zoo was enclosed by a ten-foot-high board fence painted across the front with silhouette pictures of animals. Some of the pictures were of animals the Burdette brothers didn't keep, camels and a tiger and two elephants walking tail to trunk. "We show what we got and what we plan to get," Delight told her.

She was the same way, she figured, living on what she had and what was to come. She was not as scrupulous as her husband pretended to be about sticking to the facts of the moment. She laughed when he told her what she could and could not do. "You keep on making rules," she told him. "I think you've got a talent for it."

He laid down laws, that he denied he was laying down. I want you to start going to church, he told her, I want you to cook supper and make sure the maid gets the laundry done. Yes sir, yes sir, she said and went her own way. Once when she came back late from the river he had locked her out of the house. She tried the doors and when she found them shut against her (he was there: she saw his shadow against upstairs curtains) she drove to the zoo and walked among the pens. As she walked along the pinestraw paths between the cages she said the names of the islands in the upper Hawaiian chain to herself: Necker, French Frigate Shoal, Gardner Pinnacles, Layson, Lisianski, all the way to Kure and Midway. Some of them were not even islands, only crested shoals in the middle of the Pacific. She had landed once on Midway and while the plane refueled had stood on the farthest public edge of land, a fenced space beyond a clump of ratty plumerias, and looked out over the flat white ground at the ocean that was empty from there onward, she realized, to Alaska. For a single moment, very fleeting, she had the sensation that she was falling into the ocean, that she could not keep herself from drowning, but the moment passed quickly; someone hailed her from the tin terminal house and she hurried back to reclaim her seat.

The bear, no larger than a calf, snuffled in its cage and bumped against the fence for attention. Bernard and Delight were gone to the mountains to trap skunks. She squatted in front of the cage and looked at the bear, who stuck her nose through the mesh. The nose was cracked and rimmed with mucus. Hair had fallen out in patches along the bear's back. The skin underneath was pink and as soft-looking as a child's. "Poor bear," she said and touched the streak of black skin above the nose. The bear shied at the touch; she jerked her hand back, frightened, but in a moment the bear pressed its face again against the wire and this time when she touched it, along the cheek, it did not move back. It swung around and shoved its flank against the wire, and she stuck fingers through and touched its hair, which was so smooth that she rubbed her fingers together to see if they were oily. "Good bear," she said. "Good bear."

The bear turned again, pressed its expressionless face against the pen, raised a paw and laid it against the wire. The yellowish-gray claws were nearly as long as her fingers. They were blunter at the tips than she imagined a bear's claws would be. She thought of it ripping logs and ant-hills, tearing bee hives out of dead trees. "Why have you come here?" she said, making conversation. The bear snorted and swung its head to and fro. The head seemed too heavy for the neck. The hair at the base of the neck stood up in a fringe; the individual hairs she saw were not black, but a deep brown that shaded lighter toward the ends. "Dam bear, dam bear, what do you know?"

She looked hard into the bear's chestnut, irisless eyes. She didn't believe she would learn anything by talking to a bear, but she couldn't keep herself from speaking. She had read that bears were close to human beings in their habits. They eat the same foods we do, Delight had told her, and the way the dam lowered her head and swung it to the side reminded her of people she had seen. But it was not human knowledge she wanted as much as the relief of company. She had been locked out because she had stayed at the river past suppertime. Like a child, she had been denied the security of human companionship. Her father had done that to her when she was a teenager. His punishments had never been switches or straps, only the simple expedient of shutting her out. You can come around us if you do as we tell you, he said, and she accepted him at his word; she skidded out into the wide world and was gone.

If the world were not such a new thing to her, continuously unfolding, she would have missed Charleston too much to stay away. Her memories were precise and eccentric. She remembered the exact working and the shape of the letters stamped by the foundry that had made the iron gates leading into the garden: Hawthorn Forge, Cincinnati, Ohio, they said curved above a medallion depicting a bull snorting steam. She remembered the blue birdhouse swung on a wire in the branches of the holly by the gate. In December they strung colored lights in the holly and turned them on each year, by her father's orders, precisely one week before Christmas. Her mother had an organdy dressing gown that smelled of the perfume she had spilled on it during a trip to New York when Elizabeth was four. Her mother had a gap between her front teeth, and once, to Elizabeth's surprise and delight, she had whistled through the gap, a high piercing sound, completely unladylike. Elizabeth could never get her to do it again. But she had not been driven back; the world was too interesting for that.

"But you, bear, are in a worse fix," she said, shaking the cage. The bear shuffled a step backward and looked at her from the side of her eyes. "You're penned up, dear, and don't know how to work the latch." A couple of cowbirds hopped around the dirt floor of the pen shaking their glossy brown tails. The sun was going down beyond a small pond Bernard and Dee used as a catchment for the zoo refuse. A pale orange reflection had seeped across the pond surface as she played with the bear. "Maybe you need to learn from me," she said. She heard a car drive up outside the fence. In a moment she heard J.C. calling her.

"I'm in here," she called back. "Talking to a bear," she said to herself.

"How do you get in?"

"There's an opening in the fence around back—here," and she ran to show him. She was surprised that he didn't know the way.

"What are you doing?" he asked her as she bent a coil of untacked wire back to let him in.

"Talking to the bear."

"I should have known."

"She's a very wise bear. Come on, I'll show you."

She ran ahead of him up the neat straw path. "Come, bear," she called to the dam, which had retreated to a large doghouse-like structure in the far corner. The cowbirds hopped on the roof, fluttered around each other.

"Where's Bernard?" J.C. asked as he came up beside her.

"They're gone to the mountains. To trap skunks."

"Polecats."

"Why do they call them that?"

"I don't know. Because they'll send you up a pole, I guess."

She took his hand and drew it to her neck. "Have you gotten over your tantrum?"

He pulled away. "It wasn't a tantrum. I worry about you, and it makes me angry when you don't show up when you're supposed to."

"I show up eventually. And why am I supposed to?"

"It's the accommodation we make to reality—if we accept certain responsibilities then we'll have a life with a little satisfaction in it."

"I see."

The bear sat on its haunches stretching with one paw in the dirt between her feet. "Look," Elizabeth said. "She's playing in the sandbox."

"Curious," J.C. said flatly.

"Boy, you boy," she said gently and tugged his sleeve. She smiled. "Let's do it," she said.

"What?"

"Fuck. Fuck here with the bear watching."

"Right now?"

"This very minute." She began to unbutton her blouse.

"Ah, Elizabeth."

But he did not retreat. She placed her hand inside her blouse and bringing it slowly down popped the buttons free with her wrist. She pushed the bra aside and cupped her left breast. "Here," she said. "Here." He lowered his head and took the proffered nipple in his mouth. For several moments he sucked her. He took as much of the breast into his mouth as he could and she arched her back, helping him. She wished he could swallow her; the whole breast was sensitized and seemed connected with cords of heat to the center of her body. He raised his head; she pulled the bra aside for him to sup at the other breast; his mouth widened and his cheeks bulged with the fruit of her. For a moment she thought of Haven, whom she had made love to in his mother's bed the first fall she was at Canaan: the excitement she felt as lust stripped his reticence from him. She lowered her head and kissed his hair, thrust the fingers through the red springiness of it. She touched something hard on his scalp and brushing hair aside saw a tick, half gorged, fastened to the skin

143

just forward of the crown. She started to pull it loose but didn't, thought she would take care of it later: the heat ran all through her. She could feel it, she was sure, in her toes, the pain there was caused by this, and she was grateful when he knelt and tugged her off her feet to the strawy ground. She could smell the high odor of the bear as J.C. efficiently stripped her jodhpurs down. She could tell that if there had been a way to take her with the riding boots still on he would have, but she could not spread her legs wide enough; she sat up and helped him pull the boots off, thought, Here we work together, and wondered if he realized it too, then didn't care as his face descended into her groin and she lifted her hips to meet him, saw the bear over her right shoulder leaning forward off her haunches, swinging her heavy head from side to side, in approbation or approval she could not tell, or if any such idea applied to a bear, animal cousin, and she called out, "Look, look," so that J.C. raised his head, though she was not speaking to him—"What?—oh"—"Carrying on," she gasped, "a conversation . . . with myself," and laughed out loud— "Come on, Elizabeth, oh"—and she did, gladly, her body accepting the full weight of him, maximum load; she thought, pound me into the ground if you can. Her hands drummed a loose rain against his still-shirted back. "You're gaining," she said out loud, and then she did not speak again, beyond the articulate cries of her passion.

9

"What will you have? quoth God; pay for it and take it." Love like this, lovers: like a hobo loitering in a shady lane; like a bright bird flushed suddenly into sunlight from the ligustrum hedge, like a chip of blue mica turned up sparkling in the streambed, like the smell of sassafras in the bushy wood on a cool fall day.

Haven, Delight, Rooley—she found them, touched them, cajoled them, gave herself to them like pure rainwater raised to the lips, offered under clear sky after storm.

Under the water oaks whose heavy horizontal branches seemed to carry the strain of some arboreal Atlas holding up the weight of the river sky she would ride onto the terraced rising lawn of Haven's outpost on the Okeekee. She might find him lying on his back in one of his narrow bateaus, an old straw hat pulled down over his eyes and a cane pole propped against his legs. She would dismount and wade out to him and

144

they would paddle down to the park his father had carved out of the cypress woods as a resting place for hunters. There she would give in, there for a moment the teasing would stop and she would lay her body alongside his, and there, under the tall wind-run crowns of the old cypresses, time would fray and fade.

She offered him nothing more than her occasional visits, always unannounced, always brief, and he asked for nothing more than she would give him.

Delight, drunken pathfinder of the pine barrens, took her into the woods and showed her how to live there. She was a little frightened of him at first, of his size, of his shyness, of the sudden turnings of his mind: clouds blown into a clear sky. He came to visit her in his rusted pickup with the animal cages clattering loose in the back, showed up in the early mornings as she ate her light breakfast on the back terrace. He wore khaki, the rumpled, unpressed clothes of a soldier, though he had been in no army, and he sat with his long heavy legs crossed at the ankles looking out at the fields as she sipped her fruit juice. He would sit in silence until she spoke and then he would turn his wide, hewn face to her and look at her straight in the eyes, holding her gaze, not by force of maleness or even desire, but, it seemed to her, by a kind of remembrance, as if she were a creature he knew well and had watched long, all his life perhaps. She was too bold to be more than briefly unsettled, though when she reached the first time across the glass-topped table and stroked his coarse wrist, it was for the simple erasure of touch, obliteration of thought. She said, "Can you teach me about the woods?"

He took his silver flask from his pocket, uncapped it and drank; his large Adam's apple bobbed once. "I live in the woods," he said. "That's where my home is."

"Then you ought to know what goes on there."

"It's not a city or a house, but the creatures have their routines."

"Show them to me. I want to see everything they do."

"Everything they do."

"Yes."

And so he took her with him. In early mornings when the dew was still on the grass and in the late afternoons when the shadows flooded the fields they drove into the swamp, as far as the truck would go, and then they walked, along the deer tracks and animal runs deep into the unharvested woods.

You can eat anything that lives in fresh water, he told her, and any plant that isn't bitter and doesn't have a milky substance can be used for food, though, he added, some of them aren't tasty.

She accompanied him foraging and trapping. He taught her to snare rabbits, raccoons and possums. Together they dug up and transplanted ferns and wildflowers from the woods. From Delight she learned that a full-grown coon could kill a dog and that foxes, animals that were naturally lonely, called to themselves at night. She learned to tell the difference between the lost-child cry of a screech owl and the lonely, interrogative who-o of a horned owl. They floated down the river in a johnboat, and Delight taught her to build duck blinds out of palmetto and alder branches.

She would have let him touch her, but he did not. And it pleased her to delay her own caress. If Delight Burdette, lone ranger of the river marshes and mossy woods, dreamed of her in the night, if he carried her image with him on the one-man drunks he disappeared into for days, occasionally weeks, at a time, rousted by Bernard out of woods, or out of roadhouses fifty miles down the highway, out of the big purple hotel in Appalachicola or off the wilderness beach beyond St. Luke's, or out of a log-cabin motel in the Cattaloochee Valley in north Georgia, if he lay in a greasy bed in one of those places, or on the ground or in the reeking marsh, if he lay there dreaming a long dream of her body, of her radiant Charleston voice, of kisses and everything else, when he had risen, when he had finished his cold-water shaking and puking, when he arrived back at Canaan huddled beside Bernard, when he reeled choking and staggering from the truck to his bachelor bed, when he had finally slept it off and gotten up wan and shrunken, he did not then rush to Elizabeth, beg her or con her—as if he could—or romance her into flinging herself wild into his arms; he kept his peace, gave her his knowledge, did not pursue.

He taught her to lash sticks for tripods and Adirondacks, to weave rope, to start a fire in the rain. He could build a lean-to out of evergreen branches that would stay dry for a season. With his deer-bone horn he could call a turkey out of a gallberry thicket, and he could whistle a bird out of the sky. He told her that once when he was a teenager he had run a deer for half a day, wrestling it finally to the ground at the edge of a cornfield it hesitated in its exhaustion to cross.

He thought Daniel Boone was the greatest American. "His parents let him quit school when he was ten," he told her, "because they could see he was born for the woods only. The first time he went out into Kentucky, which was all wilderness then, he wound up staying there, by himself, for a year. He'd gone on an expedition with his brother and two other men for furs and hides, and when the others returned—after the Indians had stolen their whole catch from them—he stayed on, running alone. He slept in trees and in laurel slicks and he said that though he saw Indians nearly every day, they never got a glimpse of him. What that country must have been like, my God! Great meadows full of wildflowers, oaks and hickories and poplars as big around as bulldozers, the streams so sweet you could live off the water alone. You didn't even have to know how to do it to snare birds or shoot a deer; the animals were hardly man-shy at all. And think of it: a whole state that wasn't even a state yet, hardly even a country, and no white man in the world but you. You could get up when you wanted to, pee into any bush you wanted to, lie out looking at the stars all night if you wanted to and nobody would say a thing. . . ."

Walking beside him one November afternoon through the pecan orchard bordering the headwater branch of the river, carrying Coke bottles wound with trout lines, she said, "Isn't your life like that now; don't you just run loose in the woods?"

He snorted, squatted down, picked up a pecan and cracked it between thumb and first two fingers. "Not quite hardly," he said, picking the meat out with his fingernail. Breeze fluttered the scraps of red hair over his ears. She wanted to run her hand over the smoothness of his bald head, but she restrained herself, aware that if she touched him she would break the train of his thought.

"I quit school early," he said, "when I was sixteen—but I didn't exactly run off to the woods. Bernard and I had had that zoo going for a while. Bernard, he's strange in his own way, too. Daddy expected him to take his place as second in command—after he could see I was of no account in that world—but it wasn't possible what with J.C. bringing Bryce and Franken along, and anyway Bernard had that feeling for me that you see in a younger brother sometimes, like he *knew* I was something special, and so, after he'd gone up here to Old Dominion college for a semester or two, he came along back, to help me. He takes care of everything at the filling station and the zoo, but mainly his job is to see that I don't get in too much trouble."

He held his right hand out and spread the fingers. "See them tremble?" he said. She nodded. "That's from drinking. I'm a drunkard; bad, like they say, to follow the whiskey. I don't see a turning away from it, and what it does to you is take away that happy thing inside you that made it so you could stand to be alone with yourself. I can't get out in the woods anymore for long without being drunk. I can't take it. And drunk is no way to be in the woods."

"Our eyes are the same color," she said.

"I know. I saw that right off."

He rose and they walked on toward the branch. "Bernard's little prissy caution galls me," he said, "but I don't expect I could live without it. Nothing keeps me in line, but at least Bernard keeps letting me know where the line is."

The blue November sky was streaked with long streamers of pale cloud blowing out of the north; like chevrons, she thought, marks of endurance. They had hardly touched, beyond the work-touch when their hands met as they pulled in a mullet net or set a snare. She was two years past Hawaii, two years past that jolly life that she had never intended to live without. She thought about Kaui, laughing now with somebody else, and about Rufino and his Chinese wife. Maybe Rufino got back to the Marianas after all. She hoped he wasn't too surprised when he discovered they had become American, too.

"There's a different kind of air here," she said, "a different kind of light."

"From where—Hawaii?"

"Yes. It's got a kind of anticipatory quality. Smells and colors that take me back to the islands jump out of it sometimes. There're more of them here than anyplace I've been to in this country."

"There's always a place to remember," he said, stooping to gather a handful of nuts. He cracked a couple of them in his palm and passed them to her.

"Where is it for you?" she asked.

"The marsh out from St. Luke's."

"Why?"

"Because it's never changed. The original Spanish came up that way, through that marsh, and since then it's been just as clean and beautiful and pure as anything ever was. You can stand on the point and look out at exactly the same terrain that De Soto saw, the yellow grass, the pines behind. It just takes my heart."

"Sweet Delight."

148

"Have to have something," he said, and then his face clouded and he fell silent, as a drunk will when he remembers the failure at the center of his life. It is a failure that he has tried for years daily to wrestle down, but has found that sober he cannot; only under the anesthetic of the drink will the black claws rest and he find peace.

He moved away from her as if he might walk on and leave her, and she lengthened her stride to catch up, passing under the pines that led down to the river hardwoods in the branch. She had seen this veer in him before and it did not disturb her; she carried no one else's baggage, and would not. And as she walked she thought that the late-afternoon light falling through the pines was like the light in cathedrals, one of the old Romanesque churches where worshipers moved from pool to pool of light. I know very little as yet, she thought, but this is part of what I want to find out, this light, the feeling it gives me. She smelled the scent of pine needles and the wry anise odor of dog fennel and the bitter earth smell of the gallberry bushes. The tree trunks were streaked with the burn marks of last year's clearing fire. Burned down to the dirt each year, the bushes and ferns revived in the spring, bursting up from the ashes. Like blueberries in the fired fields up north, she thought, and she started to mention this to Delight, but his fierce frown made her laugh instead.

"What?" he said, not slackening his stride.

"You. Your mad face."

"I was just thinking about how I've never been able to do what I wanted to."

"And you can see it getting all over you."

She grasped his hand, and though she meant the touch only as diversion from his immuring thought, when he turned to her she let her hand slide up his arm to touch his face. She stroked the stubble beard that was redder than the hair on his head, pressed her fingers against his colorless lips. "This will do fine," she said. "Sweet bed of pine needles."

He had not had a drink that day so was shy and scrupulous, his light eyes full of the fearful future, but she cajoled him, placed his wide hand flat on her breast and made him touch her. "Here," she said, "here, like this." She drew the fingers closed over her nipple, drew his head down like a child's. He dropped to his knees before her and clasped his arms around her waist. "I love you," he said miserably. "I can't get you out of my mind."

"Don't worry about that. That's some other life's business." And with both hands she pressed his head to her sex. Certain magic in my power, she thought; I will never get enough of being able to do this. It was something she could do, and give—that, too—and she let herself down, loosening her clothes.

She had to lead him, unbuttoning shirt, unzipping and shucking pants, untying boot laces. She pressed her face against his bare skin, breathing his odor, which was hot and feral, like the smell of a shot bird. He whimpered; nearly, she thought, cried; his hands rose, the fingers feeble and blind, to stroke her skin. "Like that," she said, "yes," and washed herself with his palms.

She had to do it all. Eyes closed as he lay on top of her, he slid into her body groping, unpracticed fingers that she had to guide and teach. "This way," she said. "It's all right." He went at it finally, sprawled between her legs, his heavy body twitching—like a man stumbling, she thought, down a flight of stairs, hitting the risers, bam . . . bam . . . bam—until he gave it up, finally, in sweat and misery, without coming close to release.

She let him tell her that he was a virgin, that alcohol had done him in. "It's okay with me," she said. "I'm having a fine time."

He looked at her out of eyes that had been penetrated years ago by misery and guilt, and she felt compassion swim up in her and she touched him, stroked his thick body that was, she thought, maybe the whitest body she had ever seen, the freckles across his back and shoulders bright as burns. "Sometimes it takes time," she said, "and that's what we have plenty of," thinking, That can't be so, I'm moving on like always, but I will say it anyway. If she had any idea of what was to come for her, what was winging in like a white bird pushed by storm, she was not a woman to be deterred by the threat, or the surety, of future fall. Let's see what will happen, she thought, as she helped him to his feet. Let's just see.

"It's not a thing like living in the woods," he said, and he was right, it wasn't.

So began their ten years. Whether it was the alcohol or simply his own native fear, their lovemaking never became the central feature of their experience together. Only once in a while—once after more than a year's hiatus—did they, on an especially sweet-scented night or after a particularly difficult day working in the woods, slide into each other's arms and she let him fumble again toward completion of the act that always, as long as she knew him, baffled and eluded him. The failure, if it

150

was that, gave them, they believed, a freedom they would not otherwise have had: they had no secret to keep. Elizabeth continued to think of Delight as virginal in his woodlore and reticence; and he paid her court, dogeman and scout, simple before her will.

Rooley was more dangerous. Hardly a week after she met him, on an afternoon when the cotton fields around his island house drooped with the ragged white clusters of burst boles, when she had followed him up the narrow attic stairs to his studio, when as she stood behind him he struck again and again like a snake at the six-by-seven-foot canvas reared in front of him, on an afternoon which was the first they were together alone, he turned to her and said, ferociously, as if he dared her to disagree: "This is a life-and-death business with me." She would have teased him out of such grandiosity but that she saw he meant it, that he had been too long alone with his own thoughts and ways, and she said nothing. He gulped his work night and day like a man going under. She visited him in the afternoon and sat quietly in the alcove under the eaves watching him. The square west window behind her let in a narrow rhomboid of light along the painted floor that crept toward him as he worked, fading out, as time passed, into the boards before it reached his heels.

He was another kind of animal, she thought: tiger monkey that would scream and bare fangs. Once he stabbed a canvas to pieces with his brush. He would often sit in an old lawn chair for hours staring into the field of color brimming in front of him. The aluminum arms of the chair were colored by the paint he kneaded from his hands. Other days he was joyous, prancing around the littered, reeking studio crying out talisman words, Jericho, Roshashana, Pericles, Mary Mother of God, Marcel Duchamp shit goddamn; "This is the way to Jordan," he cried. "I have it now; I am on the goddamn road." Then the moment would pass and his fierce brooding would take over and he would withdraw from her until moments—hours—later he would look up startled to find her still in the room.

Alsace treated her husband generously, with a frightful tenderness that made Elizabeth wonder if she had not lost her mind. She would not comment on his ways, but Elizabeth saw her tremble when Rooley's shouts penetrated the living room as they sat on the leopard-spotted sofa drinking tea. "The Archangel," she called him with a bitterness that dissolved into a restrained and diffident compliance when he came into the room. It was only the bitterness, like a lingering smell, that made Elizabeth feel that the woman had any chance at all of surviving what she had gotten herself into.

Over the years Rooley gradually began to talk to her. He often spoke of himself in the third person. "He wants to sing with the angels," he said, "but he's marooned on this goddamn planet. He's afraid he'll never get free."

"Free of what?" she asked, thinking as he spoke of how she loved the odor of turpentine and the muddled dazzle of paints on his palette.

"Of the historical perspective," he said. "What else?"

"Your history?"

"Mine and every goddamn body else's."

"What does history have to do with it?"

"I don't know; it's there. I wake up in the morning thinking about history. I come up here and beat it to a frazzle on these canvases."

"Why don't you just let it go?"

He shot her a withering glance that she gathered in smiling. "There are some things you can't get away from, Beauty," he said. "Sometimes your only hope is to damage them enough so they can't get at you."

"What?"

"He doesn't know, he doesn't know." He paused, the brush held upright, its tip flaming red cadmium. "We come from a culture that gets the proof of its spirit through history. Christian or Jew, the only way to the heart of things is through historical time, through events. We count back through the days of memory, like kids on a nature trail marking flowers in a book. But there always used to be . . . greater significance. The flowers, the sights, whatever they were, used to change us, they used to fill us up with something, something sweet and supposedly everlasting. Now they're just monuments, cold and obdurate and senseless. Broken idols. And we don't know how to fix them, or find a better way."

He shook the brush. "So this is my meditation," he said. "This is my practice."

"It sounds like you ought to go to church."

"He doesn't go to church, no Burdette harpie church. He paints instead."

"Paints what?"

"The broken dream, the hope of hell, love on a cold day."

He never left the farm, hardly left the house, and he saw no one except his kin, and then only on meeting nights and at Christmas. She thought, I could live this isolated, but not today, not yet.

One day she said, "You people never notice each other."

He understood, but asked anyway, "Who?"

"Burdettes. None of you seem to mind how eccentric you are. Did anyone ever try to stop you from being a painter?"

"Of course not. There's only one Burdette job and it's always spoken for. The rest of us are on our own."

"Free."

"No. Money and blood—very powerful."

"Shoot. They don't have to be."

"The Burdettes are too far back in the country to get out of thralldom. We know too much about ourselves. That's what has Uncle Jack stirred up about J."

"Knowing too much?"

"Yeah. There's a taint. There's a taint that adds up to a smell, a smell that adds up to a spot, a spot that adds up to . . ."

"You sound like J.C. now."

"I sound like what I am: Burdette of the ratatatat generation, end of the line."

He moved about the long room as he spoke, touching objects lightly with the tips of his fingers. Along one wall was a line of tables. On the tables were coffee cans containing congealed paint. The plank floor was streaked with colors. Near one corner, painted on the planks, was a half-finished scene of sun rising over the shoulder of a man draped in a blue robe. As he spoke, Rooley walked over the man's body. Rolls of canvas, and finished paintings, their backs turned, leaned against the opposite wall. Sketches on curling strips of linen paper were tacked to the wall studs.

She let his bristly talk drift over her, content to be in the midst of jabber. She remembered attending the circus when she was five and being so frightened by the grotesquely painted clowns that her maid had to take her out. The painted faces, the loose, vivid clothes, the shocking hair had pierced her with a terror that set her screaming. Outside, under her maid's imperious, disapproving eye, the fear subsided, turned on itself into glee when, among the cars and boxes at the back of the tent, she discovered the monkeys bounding about their portable cages. She had made her maid, who before the svelte galvanic beasts had shrunk back in terror of her own, take her right up to the cage, where, before the woman snatched her away, she thrust her hand through the bars and stroked, for a second, one coarse, nut-brown back.

And she thought, Is my passion always this way: unexpected, come on me wild with teeth bared? Then she laughed, feeling her strength, feeling too the blankness in her, as if, as her father would put it, her soul had taken the day off, and she looked around, coming back to the cold room, March now, to this small slender blond man who paced before her, punctuating his vivid talk with swipes of his paint-clotted brush, and she thought, How did I get here, what choice did I make that brought me here?

Hawaii seemed so long ago; the hurtling motorcycle rides with Kaui under the North Shore cliffs seemed a dream; a dream of the brawling thunder of waves crashing the steep yellow sand of Sunset Beach. She had waded into the storm waves and let them beat her down to the cloudy bottom, tumbled so that she lost all sense of the upright world, and in that moment, a moment she had come back to over and over, she had felt her freedom, felt the strings and juices of her body dissolve into a residue of light, something, something: weightless, conscious, alive—so alive!— and joyous.

She said, "I know why you do this."

He stopped his pacing. "Do what?"

"Your painting. It's how you let the waves take you."

He wiped his brush with an oily rag. "No," he said. "It's not just that. It's not like falling off a cliff."

"What then?"

"I'm making something. . . ." He flung his arm at the easel. The painting there was a variegated field of blues, shot through with a rising yellow line. "This is an object," he said, "just like a bale of cotton or a can of cane syrup is an object. Rooley Burdette he doesn't want to make a mystery, he wants to make a thing."

"You're, I guess, doing it."

"You don't believe it's so?"

"I do, but it's hardly different from what J.C.'s up to. Is it different? If it is, I wish you'd tell me how."

"They don't pay this painter much."

"Money."

"So Rooley Francis Burdette does it for himself."

"It's still the same. J.C. gets the same sure pleasure looking at his cotton fields."

"You don't understand."

"I think I do."

He turned on her, his face gone white with anger. "You don't, you shit bitch. You don't. Why don't you just understand yourself out of here."

"Of here? This room?"

"This exact place. Right goddamn now."

"Okay."

She left then, slipping down the darkened stairs, through the sunlit rooms of the immaculate house and out into the fields, but she came back, not often—Rooley wouldn't allow that, and she had other trails to follow—but often enough to eventually find her way through the cousin's self-protective maze.

Delight told her that animals never thought of making love, and so it was with her; she didn't burn or pine, but the twitch came, out of nowhere it seemed, like all the other twitches that drove her, and when it came she acted on it.

One afternoon in late winter—it was 1955—as Rooley raised the cane pole he used to adjust the skylight, she noticed how the veins in his long forearms ran unbroken from wrist to elbow, and she was struck by lust. Nothing more was needed. She crossed the room to him, he turned, and as if he had been thinking of nothing else, took her into his arms. They bore each other down into a scramble of rags and wadded tissue. It was Rooley who cried out, Rooley who moaned and hid his face in her body.

They wrestled, generating heat in the cold room that made them sweat and gasp; they clawed at each other's body, raking skin; he dragged at her breasts so that she cried out; she bit him in the soft flesh above his hips, thinking that she wanted blood in her mouth, that she wanted to rise up from a carcass dripping blood, screaming like a hawk; he wrenched her head back and bit her neck, pressed his open hand hard flat against the bifurcate bone below her throat so that it seemed her chest would crack; she reached beneath him, between his legs, and pressed with her wrist upward, trying to lift him, as one would try to throw off a beast dropped from the trees. She could hear them, hear the slithering gurgle of wet flesh, hear his panting breath, hear the thud of

155

their bodies on the uncarpeted floor and, just before her mind went, before she was thrashed down as in the clear green wave of the islands, she felt herself possessed for a moment of an enormous strength, a strength that could move the house off its foundations, that could sweep the sky clear of storms, that could pull trees up and crack them between her fingers, felt the strength rise and merge into one great distended, penetrating cry, as she came, four breaths, before she felt, as her own orgasm rolled and rolled, the lash of his seed, universal solvent, roaring like a rose fire into the tissues of her body.

But she came back, came back. Somewhere in the house she heard a radio playing softly. Resting music. She thought of Alsace lying on the bed staring at the ceiling. Sprawled amid the stink of paint and turpentine, she touched his thin face that looked pale and shrunken to her, diminished. Why is it, she thought, that sex does such different things to men? Some crowed, some rested, some accused, some cowered, some fled. This one looked as if he had seen a ghost.

There were tears on his face, but she made him wipe them off, and though he began a miserable retreat into what the preachers might call morality, which she knew was only weakness, saying, No no we can't go on with this, she made him dress and follow her downstairs and outside into the light.

Alsace was back in the house somewhere; she did not come away from the soothing radio to speak to them. They left the house, crossed the narrow Victorian porch and walked down the steps into the bright cold sunshine of early March. There was nothing around the house but fields, the long sweep of ground down to the pond, a rising low ridge line off to the right upon which a stand of young sycamores mingled their white trunks. Around the house grew hedge bushes: boxwood, ligustrum, azaleas, a heap of Confederate jasmine piling up a trellis at the corner.

She walked away from him and stood alone at the edge of the grass, near the precise, delicate furrows of the new plowing. She gathered her gray dress around her and looked up into the sky, which was as pale as wash water.

He said from behind her, "This is an interruption that can't go on. I can't afford it."

"How do you know?" she asked, not turning around.

"It'll get between me and the paint. Not to speak of between me and Alsace. And J.C.—Lord."

156

She smiled at that. "Nothing can get between J.C. and what he wants. You don't have to worry about him."

"Me, not him."

She turned around laughing. "That's your lookout, sweetheart. You'll have to figure out how to stand it."

Above them a mockingbird swooped and cried, dipping low between them and fleeing back into the air above the corner of the house. Rooley looked up at the bird. "She's got a nest," he said.

"Where?"

"It must be in that jasmine bush."

She walked over to the bush and peered in among the evergreen leaves. She saw a twig nest containing three fledgling chicks. She plunged her hand in and drew the birds out. Their beaks were open and gasping and they made a feeble, mewling sound. They were as small as big toes, barely furred. The mother bird wheeled about her head screeching panic.

Rooley came up beside her and looked into her hand. "She won't come back to them now," he said.

"Because I've touched them?"

"She'll leave them to starve."

"Poor birds," she said and felt a grief surge up in her that brought tears to her eyes.

She held the birds up, as high as she could reach, into the air. The gray-and-white wings swooped around her, diving, rising, crying. "I'm sorry," she said, and then she threw the birds down and ground them under the heel of her boot to a mess of bone and blood.

Rooley was silent, looking at her. Then he said, "You frighten me."

She patted his cheek. "Try to get used to it," she said and then she walked off down the narrow track that wound its green way through the frail and orderly rows.

So it came upon her, the pulse of lust, love's other side. Like sudden summer rain bursting against the windowpanes. Like a piece of colored cloth blown across the lawn. Like a light switched on in a house at the end of a dark street. Rooley would resist, but her sweet flesh would hold him in thrall. Delight would follow always. We get what we pay for, she thought. And for this I'm willing.

157

10 His grandfather recovered from the cottonmouth bite and built a tower. It seemed to Jacey that he spent his childhood there, watching the country. His grandfather did not exactly build the tower; he reassembled it. He purchased the one-hundred-twenty-foot strip-metal tower from the state game and fish department, had it disassembled, loaded on a flatbed truck and hauled to his house, where he reerected it, strip by strip, at the pond edge of his garden. Mattie wanted to know what he expected to see from up there, but she, along with Jacey and his grandfather, was one of the first to climb to the small wood-and-tin house at the top. The little house, screened on all sides and furnished with a desk, a sofa, two rocking chairs, a straw rug painted with a scene of carousing naked maenads and the record player his cousin Bernard hauled up after the electric wires were connected, became the refuge and meeting place for the disenfranchised Burdettes.

Disenfranchised was his grandfather's word, and the truth of it was that it fitted only him. Jack was, in the years after his attempt to saw down the main house, not excluded from the quarterly meetings but if he attended, to beat on the furniture and shout, which he did, he was ignored. Even Bryce and Franken—"Those sluts," his grandfather called them—were wary of him, speaking lightly or hesitantly to him, inquiring about his health or his garden, but venturing no further into his affairs. If occasionally he left a string of bream or a mason jar stuffed with zinnias at their back steps (as was his custom with all his kin except J.C.) they did not reciprocate. The purchase of the sulfur wells—and the later take-overs of plants in Norfolk, Savannah and Mobile—brought with it the realization of their exposure to the dance of the world, and if it widened their eyes with something like fright, it incited in them a new sense of responsibility and a drive, second only to J.C.'s, to make their enterprises work. They were, in those years—his father included—men with little time for children, which Jacey sensed in his visits to their offices in the warehouse off the Square. Bryce continued to shower him with alohas and to crunch him in bear hugs, and Franken, of the austere aspect, continued to break the frame of his austerity with grins that contorted his bony face, but the greetings, the grins and the hugs were perfunctory and they were no longer accompanied by tours of the warehouses and plants. On Sundays after church he and his father rattled across the lands on their drives, but there were few weekday moments for extended exchanges between them, and the drives themselves became increasingly serious inspection tours, punctuated frequently by stops for sessions with the farm manager and with the manager of the fertilizer plants.

The strange Burdettes: Eustace and the brothers Delight, Bernard and Rooley were less affected by Jack's disfavor. Eustace, reigning in his breezy, antebellum rooms at the south end of Main Street, disapproved, but Jack was his favorite and he forgave him. Delight and Bernard came by; if they were a little closer to J.C.'s whip, they were also, tamed perhaps by their animals, more natively cordial, and so drifted through. Rooley, alive only in his paint, visited no one.

In the zone of his grandfather's suzerainty there was neither austerity nor any encroachment by obligations to the complicated world. "We are emblems," his grandfather told him, "of actual freedom, citizens of the World-Worth-Having. Here," he added with a sweep of his arm that lassoed the four corners of the tower house, "above the gnat line." Not only were they above the gnats (and the flies and the dragonflies), they were above the tops of even the tallest pines. "They have to raise these things up high," his grandfather told him, "so they can see where the fires start. You can think of us as watchmen." It was fine with Jacey to be a watchman. He was fascinated by the sight of so much country spread out at his feet. In Hawaii, from the cliffs, he had looked out at the Pacific that seemed to go on forever, and from the hills near their cottage he had been able to look out over other hills and over the harbor at Pearl, but here, with or without the binoculars that hung from a nail in the corner, he could see lands that were not only bewitching in their interplay of fields and woods, but were occupied by people he was kin to, people whose lives were threaded with his own. Without the binoculars he could see, four miles up the lands, the roof and cupola of the main house, and beyond them and just to the right, the dome of the courthouse. On the other side of the pond, trapped in cotton, Rooley and Alsace's house looked lonelier than ever. To the west, the trees of Lazarus Swamp knitted their darkness. To the south was the white-lettered roof of Delight and Bernard's animal fiefdom.

His grandfather rigged a pulley outside the window and drew supplies in a peach basket up to the eyrie. He tried to get Mattie to handle the job of loading the basket. "How about some apples?" he would holler

159

down and wait while Mattie, fulminating in the kitchen, ignored him. "I don't understand her," Jack would say and holler down again: "Mattie, Miss Mattie Bates." Then his grandfather would drop objects on the roof of the house until Mattie stuck her head out. "Can't you hear me?" Jack would yell down, jiggling the rope for her edification. Mattie would snort and go back into the house. That was how it became Jacey's job to descend the metal stairs, collect whatever it was his grandfather needed, place it in the wooden box and climb back up the tower, always arriving before the box, to help his grandfather haul the booty up.

"It reminds me of hauling well water," his grandfather told him, a pleased look on his face. "But you don't have to train water to fill a bucket." And, "Mattie, Mattie," he would cry, just for good measure, just to rile her. Then he would settle back, separating the halves of a peach with his horny thumbs, or with his pocketknife creating a pigtail of red skin from the hide of an apple, or pouring a glass of cane juice or eating a sandwich, and he would begin to tell Jacey what he called "the Truth of the Burdettes."

"The Truth" was Jack's version of what the Burdettes were and what they would become. Except for the ending, the story was very like the story his father told him of their occupation here. It was a story of struggle and of triumph and of endurance. "The regulation stuff," Jacey was to tell Martha years later when they talked on the beach in St. Guillaume. "They both wanted to create a myth that would hold them up, that would justify the way they were now."

The difference in the stories was that his grandfather wanted no expansion of the success already obtained. "There doesn't need to be any more conquering," he told his grandson. "We've covered enough ground." His father, driving the farm Chevy, his wide-brimmed charcoal fedora pulled low over his eyes like a gangster, painted for him a picture of endlessly opening opportunity. "You'll have all this," he would tell his son. "Someday you will make the decisions here and they will be decisions that affect not only all the kin, but all the world around you, a world you can't even imagine yet."

"I thought he meant people in Hawaii and all the big buildings in Atlanta and the Froster Beach cottages where we used to go when Daddy could get time off and tie Mama down long enough to get her in the car," he told Martha. As they drove across the lands of Sunday afternoons, his father would speak of the dominion that would someday pass to him. "But you have to make yourself worthy," he would say, and

160

Jacey would have no idea what he meant. "I couldn't figure it out and he never told me," he said to Martha, "so I made up ordeals of my own. I joined the church," he told her, "and I tried to be like Jesus—at least for a couple of days." He was the youngest Burdette ever to become a member of Berea Baptist Church. "I mean, it was *our* church," he said, "but no Burdette had ever thought of becoming a member. I not only thought of it but I went to the preacher by myself and did it—gave my soul to the Lord. Mama thought it was hilarious, but Daddy was very favorably impressed."

His father had tears in his eyes that morning. When the call came—the preacher as usual interrupting the final hymn to ask in his florid, high-stepping voice if there were any souls "called this morning to the light of Jesus"—Jacey had risen and pushed past the moment of panic when he found his way blocked first in one direction by the pink wool bulk of his Aunt Lois and then in the other by his father's seersucker knees. Stumbling through apologies, he reeled into the aisle and stumbled down the green carpet alone into the outstretched arms of the preacher. His father's tears had been in his eyes when, after the service, the congregation passed in line before him to shake hands and welcome him into the church. His Aunt Lois, creaking down in her manacling wools, whispered powder into his ear ("Sweetie, I didn't realize you wanted to get out") and recoiled from the sternness in her nephew's eyes, a new sternness, anger already at the procedure's not going right. Then behind her, his father, wiping lightly his hands on his trousers, took his small hand in both of his, looked him in the eyes and said, "Son, this means the world to me," words and tone he had never heard before, sudden new solemn acceptance.

"I thought I had found the way," he told Martha. "I forced myself to believe it because I was a boy with a hole in the inside of him and the church promised to fill up the hole."

With seven other children, all older than he, he had been baptized two weeks later at a Sunday-night service.

"Dr. Carruthers wore fishing waders under his robe," he told Martha. "The water was light green, the same color as in Mama's swimming pool in Charleston, and it was warm as bathwater. We lined up in the little anteroom where the choir dressed—their robes were hung around the walls, hymnals piled in corners—oldest first, three boys and four girls, me the last, youngest and smallest by far."

The pool, a four-by-ten concrete trough, four feet deep, behind a chest-high glass wall above the choir loft, could be seen by the congregation. Dr. Carruthers, wearing a dark green robe, stood hip-deep in the pool and raised dripping arms to the small crowd of Sunday-night relatives and friends as the organist played "Softly, I Come." One by one the children shuffled carefully down the five steps into the water. They floated away, buoyed by salt, Jacey discovered—into the minister's arms. "Once I shot a quail that fell in the river," he told Martha. "It lay on the water with its wings spread, looking around—that was the way we were, floating out so smoothly in those gaseous robes.

"I was afraid of drowning—the procedure, *you* remember, was for the preacher to tip your head back and dip you under—that was the act of faith, that letting go in his arms; his hand covered our mouths and noses—one girl I remember, Teena Wallace, panicked, she started kicking and sputtering; the preacher tightened up on her—I saw his arms tense—and thrust her down and then held her under the arms while she coughed it out; she was sobbing—I let go, the water was so buoyant— they'd put some kind of salts in it—and so deep that I had to swim to him; he put his hand behind my head, placed his open palm over my mouth and nose and tipped me back; I let go, for a moment it was as if I didn't have a body—I couldn't hear the hymn and I forgot my father and my aunts and uncles sitting out there—I didn't have a body, but it was only physical, the immersion I mean"—and here he reached to touch Martha, sought again their physical communion—"I was going physically, not spiritually, limp, and right there, in the middle of it, in that pool, laid out in the act of finding a place for myself in the pantheon of Burdette heroes, I felt myself still stuck between them."

"Between them?" Martha asked, shaking her blond head. This was on the beach in front of his mother's old refuge hotel in St. Guillaume.

"Between my mother and my father. If my mother had ever done that—get baptized—she would have tried to see how long she could stay under. She would have gone for the record. Just the feel of that dense water on her skin would have thrilled her. And my father, he would have been more pious than the preacher; he would have come up quoting scripture. But for me, another door was supposed to open: I wanted to slide out between them, I wanted to mean it when I went under, to come up filled with the Spirit, a new light like a tonic in my blood."

"What happened?"

"Nothing in particular. I was proud to make it in and out without gagging. I was awed by the event, the strangeness of it, but at the same

162

time I could see the underpants of the girl in front of me and I noticed that Dr. Carruthers' breath smelled of spearmint. At the time, without my being able to say it, it was important for me to be transformed; I wanted to be elevated in some way. I believed that Jesus and God were real, but it was the way kids believe elephants can talk and that the wind sings a song. I didn't believe in them the same way I believed in my father and my mother. . . ."

"You were only twelve."

"Twelve going on ninety, I think, if at ninety you're still calculating advantages."

His mother had not attended, but she had been there to get him when the service was over. Washed by the water, he changed his wet underwear in the basement bathroom and came upstairs to find his mother waiting at the side door. She had come for him on her motorcycle, a black Harley Davidson police bike with a stick shift. In those days there was no helmet law, and she wore her long hair tied back in a series of ribbons, yellow, green and red, crisscrossed in the long rope of black hair like the pattern on a snake's back. His father, he knew, waited for him in the sanctuary; he was talking with the preacher, building, Jacey knew—already at twelve—his intricate network of supply and demand, leaning over the preacher's well-fed frame, to assure him that the give and take of this particular enterprise—I hand you my son's soul, soon I will require payment from you—operated smoothly. But just as Jacey knew the game, game that was a life, he knew too that the tears that had been in his father's eyes when he waited, humble for a moment, in the receiving line to welcome him into this particular fold were real tears, the tears of a man who was, against almost his heart's deepest wish, releasing his child into the strange orders of the world, letting him—for a moment—go, and he hesitated in the stairwell between the outside and the inside door, looked back as the sanctuary door opened with a soft *koosh* sound at the gleam of light along the polished wood of the emptying pews, at the sound of laughter from one of his aunts.

His mother waited for him—this all took place in a second—gleeful in the sleek apparatus of her beauty: the mauve silk shirt, the tall brown boots, her hair violent with scarves. "Primo," she said, calling him by the island name of his childhood, "let's go."

"Christ," he said to Martha, "it was like she was some kind of juvenile delinquent. She wore a wide leather belt studded with rhinestones—a kidney belt, the bikers used to call it—and she had, of all things, a rosary

163

in her hands. She got it, I think, from Kaui, her lover in Hawaii; it was carved out of some kind of black wood that grows there. You remember how she used to smile, happy to see you and happy that there was blood in her veins—that bright red lipstick—she would smile and something in you would say, Here by God is life: I have to have it. She was smiling like that, laughing at the whole world, at that brick church our family had bought and paid for, at the preacher, at baptism, at my father, even at herself, decked out in her circus duds, and she saw me hesitate—I *did* want to go back in and have my father make a fuss over me—and as I stood there, my hair still wet from the baptism, my underwear wadded up under my arm, she crossed the stairwell and put the rosary around my neck.

" 'Mar-vel, mar-vel,' she said in the fake country accent she used sometimes; she was laughing at me, but behind the laughter was something else, a very dense and strong imploring; I could see for a moment how my mother was not connected to anything that other people were connected to, the church could have been a random pile of bricks, the baptism a swim in a tank, the preacher a ghost, and for a moment I was overwhelmed—at twelve years old—with a desire to protect her, to protect this woman who, I thought then and for years afterward, had never needed protection from anyone or anything, and just like that, as she bent down to put the rosary on me, I threw myself into her arms and when she had pried me loose and taken my hand, went with her and got on that crazy bike behind her and rode away, happy as a goddamn lark, Daddy and the church, and Jesus Christ himself, forgotten."

They rode through the spring night down Main Street, past the well-to-do houses of the south side. The yards were cloudy with blossoming dogwoods; the scent of Japanese magnolias, sweet nearly as honeysuckle, filled the air. Beyond the hospital the street became the Florida road and the land again was part of Canaan. The white brick house off to the right among oaks and camellias belonged to his great-uncle. Beyond the house, the fields and the pine woods belonged to all Burdettes. When they didn't pull in at the zoo, dark and shuttered like a place closed down for good, he knew that they were on the way to his grandfather's. A mile farther on the road forked, the left branch heading on through newly plowed fields to Florida, the right curving west through pines. They took the right fork.

They rode in silence, his mother leaned over the body of the bike, racing; the long scarves flapped back along Jacey's face. He held his mother by the waist, pressed his chest against her back. She had taught him not to lean away from the turns ("It throws my balance off; just sit still," she had said) and he had found that under that dictum the only way he could feel safe—feet pulled up like a jockey's —was to get his body as close to hers as possible. When she leaned into one of the long country curves, he leaned too, but only as part of her, papoose. He was not tall enough to see over her shoulder, but with his face turned to the side he watched the land stream by. In the ditches and along the fence rows plum trees and blackberry bushes were in flower. They passed a caved-in ten-ant house snugged back among flowering chinaberries. Beyond the house, at the edge of the woods, a large billboard reared up, white letter-ing on black: Burdette One Hundred Fertilizer, and underneath it in script the new slogan: "The Land Deserves the Best." His mother throt-tled up as they passed it—the road dipping beyond it into the first of the Lazarus branches—as if something in the sign were a goad. The land rose evenly beyond the branch, a final upsurge before the falling away into the swamp, and it was at the top of the longest rise, among pines, sweet gums and a few leafing hickories, that they came to his grandfa-ther's house.

The house floated above the freshly turned ground and the young plants of its surrounding garden. White, strung with gingerbread along every eave, it stood in the middle of the garden, so close to the road that the driveway was only a cleared space between garden and asphalt. His mother downshifted smoothly, her hand working the gearshift, foot rhythmically pumping the clutch. They eased to a stop at the edge of the crumbled earth of the flower beds.

"Hop off," his mother said. She held the bike upright as he dis-mounted then settled it down on the kick stand. He ran up the pinestraw path toward the house.

His grandfather sat on the porch in his wicker rocker in the dark listening to opera. He raised a hand in greeting and restraint as Jacey came up the steps. Jacey sat down on the top step and leaned against the porch post to listen. The opera was *La Bohème,* one he had listened to with his grandfather many times. It was the last scene, Mimi laid out, dying of tuberculosis. As he watched his mother follow him up the path, bending down twice to touch the frondy zinnia seedlings, the last strains of the opera floated in the air between them. Jacey felt a long way from the church, from the baptismal font.

"It had vanished," he told Martha as they lay wrapped in a sheet on the Caribbean beach. "I was back to being a pagan." High above him, the moonlight caught the edge of the tower, brushing it with a soft blue that was not there in daylight. His mother, keeping her peace, climbed the steps and went into the house, touching his grandfather lightly on the shoulder as she passed.

"The music stopped," he told Martha, "and we sat on the porch without talking. Right behind the music, as if they had been waiting politely for it to end, the whippoorwills started up. I could hear Mother talking to Mattie inside. It was very peaceful there on the porch, Granddaddy stretched out in his rocker, the spring night all around us. My grandfather liked to let music soak into him; it was like a warm bath for him, and I had learned not to talk when he was in his opera mood. As I sat there, waiting for him to come to, I felt some of the feeling I had at the baptism come back. It had been blown away by the ride, but it started to catch up with me in the quiet. When you're twelve, I guess, something like giving yourself to the church can either seem monstrous or like nothing at all. It had been nothing on the ride out; I had forgotten it. But now it began to crawl up on me like a big animal and as I sat there I started to get scared. God, I thought, might be coming to get me, some singing bear of a god who didn't have my best interests at heart. I looked up at my grandfather, but his eyes were closed. I got up and walked out into the garden. The ground smelled fresh, still rumpled from the last tilling. I walked down the pond path to the tower and climbed the stairs. It was warm enough for crickets, but the only thing I heard was a single mosquito, buzzing around ahead of his time. I pushed up the trapdoor and climbed in. Delight was up there, sitting in a chair next to the window, drinking. Delight always liked to go off by himself and drink. He had his corners, he said, that he liked to crawl into. He held the bottle up to me in greeting and turned back to the window. The lights were off, but there was light from the moon which made all the furniture bony. The dancing women on the rug looked stark and mean. I lay down on the sofa and picked up one of my grandfather's art magazines and thumbed through it, as if I could read it in the dark. Neither of us said anything until the music started up again down below. Then Delight pushed back in his chair, took a sip of wine and asked me what I was up to.

"I had never really talked to him much, never really gotten over my fear of him and my guilt, I guess, from the time I hit him in the mouth. I'd been out to the zoo plenty of times, it was one of my favorite places, but only when Bernard was there. Delight was a drinker, and you could never trust him. Trust his moods, I mean. Sometimes he was gay and sometimes he was angry and sometimes he was sad—you could never tell which mood was going to be on him. But this time there was something more fearful on the inside of me than anything Delight could bring to bear.

" 'I got baptized,' I told him, and the importance of it flooded over me, and the fear and the emergency thought that I had run out on my father. That last thought was it, I guess. I felt, young as twelve, the loss of him. It was the first time in my life I ever felt that, that some grip between us might get broken. I was scared to death, and I wanted to call out. I might have, except that I knew who I wanted to call out to. It was my mother, the motorcycle queen downstairs. But she was in the house and the music—a spiritual this time, Marian Anderson singing 'Deep River'—was too loud; she wouldn't hear me.

" 'I've been dreaming,' Delight said and leaned forward in his chair. He was sitting in front of me in granddaddy's rocker with his elbows on his knees. His bald head gleamed in the moonlight; the bones of his skull shone under the skin. 'I was just sitting here thinking,' he said, 'and the most curious dream came to me.' He scratched his forehead. 'I was riding in the swamp, along the path by the river. I came around a bend, that place where there's a big bank of willows hanging over the stream, and as I came up to them a woman stepped out into the path. She stepped right out of the branches as if she had been perched there in the leaves.' He looked at me to impress on me the truth of what he was saying and continued, 'She was dressed in white from head to foot and she wore some kind of white shawl on her head. She had her back toward me. I knew she'd stepped out to stop me, but it was strange that she faced the other way. I pulled my horse up and waited, I think I called to her—I knew her, though I can't tell you now who she was—and she turned around. She didn't have a face. Nothing at all but a kind of white light where a face would be. I wasn't scared, just fascinated. She stood in the path, looking at me, if you could call it that, and then she beckoned to me. When she raised her arm I felt a chill in me like ice. I couldn't move. Then she just faded away.' He raised his head and smiled, fey as a boy. 'Poof, she was gone,' he said. He took a long pull on his bottle and wiped his mouth with the back of his wrist. 'What do you think of that?'

" 'I don't know,' I said. I was terrified. I wrapped my arms around my knees and hugged myself. 'Was it a dream?'

" 'I was just thinking about that when you came up. I mean, I dreamed it, it couldn't have been a minute before you got here, but I don't know, maybe I did see it.'

"Delight was easy to push away, the way some drunks are: you just say, Look at the birdie, and they get lost looking, but that night I was vulnerable. On my skin I could feel the faint crystalline dust of the baptismal salt and I could remember the strength in the preacher's hand as he held it over my face. But more important, at that moment, was the picture I had of my father, leaning over the preacher, his hand on his shoulder and the look on his face of happiness. He had been happy and I had made him happy, by letting myself be dunked in a tub in the family church.

"I got up and went to the window. I could see my grandfather's feet sticking out on the porch under the eave. I thought of the rides we took around the lands, on horseback usually, and how they were different from the Sunday drives with my father. And I thought, out of a resistance I realized, of my mother. This place, gingerbread farmhouse on the south lands, had become a haven for her, too. But then what place wasn't? I had seen her once standing stark naked in the cupola of the main house. I had been up in the tower alone one afternoon after school looking at the country through the binocs. I used to do that all the time. I saw curious things. I once saw Alsace beating a dog with a switch in her front yard. When they put in the airport on the land Daddy sold between the zoo and town, I used to watch the planes take off. I once saw an engine catch on fire. All kinds of things I saw. This afternoon—it was late spring, the wisteria was just starting to bloom—I was eleven—I was looking north toward town at a flock of birds flying around the courthouse dome. The dome is right behind the top of the main house and I was wondering what would make birds do like that—they were wheeling and diving over the dome, blackbirds I guess, but I imagined they were martins flown in from their winter roosts, when my mother came up the cupola stairs. She climbed to the landing and stood in front of the window facing me. She didn't have any clothes on. The sight of her nakedness hit me like a hammer in the chest. The cupola windows are six feet high, so I could see all of her. Through the binoculars she was plain and close as a hand. When I was younger I saw my mother naked all the time; it was like a fetish with her. In Hawaii we took baths together. Later, too. But I had never seen her naked without her wanting me to. She stood there without moving and then she raised her arms to her hair, unpinned it and let it fall. I remember how the blackness of it fell suddenly down her skin. Then she began to touch herself, running her hands very slowly down her body. She covered her breasts with her open palms and even through the binoculars at that distance, I could see her squeezing them. It was like looking at hell's fire: I knew I should turn away, but I couldn't. She let her hands fall down her chest, her stomach, to her hair. Then she pushed down hard into the hair, like her fingers were digging inside a waistband. As she pushed she crouched and turned away, I thought, in pain. Below me my grandfather hoed in the garden, transplanting tomatoes. I wanted to call him and I remember thinking how odd it was that he could be down there hoeing oblivious and my mother, in my plain sight, buck-naked in a window four miles away. There was very little more, only one thing. She rose from the crouch, her hands still stabbed into her groin, and straightened up until she was standing at her full height facing the window again. She relaxed her hands, letting them drop to her sides, and then the right one came up and she kissed the tips of her fingers and pressed them against the windowpane, and looked directly at me. I know it wasn't me she was seeing, but through the binoculars it *was* me and I dropped the glasses and fell to the floor, as if the look were bullets. When I got up she was gone.

"This happened before Delight told me his story of the woman in white, but when he told me, that picture of my mother came back to me. I don't know if Delight was sleeping with Mama then, maybe he was, maybe I sensed it and was frightened, but I didn't tell him about seeing her. What I thought was that the story was some kind of missing link, not the story exactly, but the vision itself of a faceless woman in white standing under the willow tree, just as I was the link between my naked mother and my oblivious grandfather planting tomatoes. It was in the swamp she was standing, on the south trail. Somehow, what had gotten torn loose by my escape from my father at the church was mended, par-tially at least, by the story of that ghost woman. I was still scared to death, still pumped up with what seemed to me the possibility of having committed an enormous crime against my father, this choice, if that was what it was, and I crossed the floor and pulled the trapdoor open and looked down at the house to see if my mother was outside.

"I'm not saying exactly what I mean, but I looked down the silver-painted stairs that had little round bumps on them for treads and saw my grandfather's feet sticking out from under the eave. He had on his garden galoshes, the black ones that buckle up. Marian Anderson boomed out a hymn, not even a spiritual, called "Love Lifted Me"—if I was older than twelve I would have said yes, yes, and laughed at the irony—I was about to call my mother—after hearing the ghost story and remembering her in the window I wanted to *see* what she looked like (I didn't know yet that this would be the last year for a long time that I was in love with her)—but before I could get the word out my father roared off the highway in his Cadillac, barreling out of nowhere around the piny curve like a beast from behind a door. He ran right over Mama's motorcycle. He would say he hadn't seen it, but I never believed that. The bike was parked at the edge of the path, the front wheel tucked back, and he hit it in what seemed like the moment of his braking. It reminded me of the way you run over a snake in the road in that country, the way it works best to hit the brakes just as you go over the snake, so that not only will you crush it, you'll shred it as well. The front wheels went over the bike, rising over the body of it so that the whole front end of the Cadillac lifted for a moment off the ground; sparks blew out of the undercarriage and there was a ripping sound and the bike seemed to writhe like something alive. The car slewed to the left dragging the bike with it and came to a rest in the garden, hub-deep in freshly turned ground.

"I came down the steps, glancing back at Delight, who knelt on the floor looking over the windowsill, and crouched down on the first landing to see what would happen. Daddy jumped out of the car and ran up the pine path to the house. Smoke flooded out from under the car, but I didn't see any flames. My grandfather had jumped up, and before Daddy could get halfway up the path he was throwing things at him, apples, a glass of tea—the ice cubes caught the moonlight as they flew through the air, shined like little stars—a plate and something else I couldn't see. The barrage didn't stop my father, he rushed up the path, up the steps and past my grandfather—pausing only long enough to knock him down with a single punch to the side of the head—and into the house. I heard Mattie cry out, "Get away from here, J. C. Burdette," and then the sound of scuffling and my father came out dragging my mother by the arm. You didn't have to worry about my father trying to get his own back. He pulled my mother across the porch and then flung her by the arm down the steps. He kept hold of her hand so that she was jerked back and off her feet by the corner of the step, and she cried out. With his other hand my father unbuckled his belt and whipped it off. It popped in the air he pulled it so hard, like a whip will crack, and he began to beat my mother with it, with the buckle end; I could see the brass buckle flash in the moonlight. I started down the steps, scared to death, but crazy to prevent this, when I felt Delight catch me by the back of the shirt. I yelled at him, but he held on, and there was no water hose to hit him with this time. He pulled me back down and held me, his arms were around me, I could smell the rotten alcohol in his mouth; I was yelling, had been, suddenly heard myself crying: 'I don't want it, I don't want it,' but it made no difference to my father (then, or I realized later when I said the same words to him in a totally different context). What made the difference wasn't anything I did or could have done, it was my grandfather, old live-by-the-sword-die-by-the-sword Jack, who came out of the house carrying a shotgun, the same gun he carried when we hunted quail in the scrub fields east of the swamp, crossed the porch and placed the barrel against my father's head just behind the ear, snugging it in like there was a socket there, and said, in the hoarse way he had of speaking when he was excited: 'Stop, or I will blow you to kingdom come.'

"My father froze. The belt, which was at that moment at the top of its arc, fell back across his own head and shoulders. My mother lay half across his lap, her arms drawn in like a butterfly's legs when the chrysalis opens. Her purple shirt was pulled up so that one breast in its white brassiere was exposed. Very slowly, she pulled the shirt back down, covering herself, and then, as part of the same motion, she reached up to my father's head, which was rigid under the imperative of my grandfather's twelve-gauge, made a claw and tore, infinitely slowly it seemed to me, four bright gashes down his cheek. She bared her teeth then and hissed, a long suspiration that seemed to go on and on. My father hadn't moved, had only winced slightly at the gashing. She unfolded herself from his lap, and saying nothing to anyone—to any of us; I felt *us*—she got up, brushed her clothes straight and walked off down the pond path."

Between the moon-silvered struts of the fire tower he watched her walk away, along the pond toward the fields. Her stride was steady and she didn't look back. The pines cast shadows along the pond that fell short of the grass where she walked. A breeze blew across his face, flicking a coolness against him, as if it had brushed against cool water before

171

reaching him. "When nothing else would help, love lifted me," Marian Anderson sang, and then he could hear, above the music, the call of a whippoorwill, melancholy thing, across the pond. His mother walked toward the call as if that were exactly where she was headed. Below him his father put his head into his hands and began to cry. "Mama," he called, "Mama," tore himself loose from Delight's grasp and ran down the stairs. But even as he ran, he knew that he could not catch her, for even as he had pushed away from his grasping cousin he had seen her narrow, unbent body disappear into the heaped shadows of the dense woods beyond the pond and he knew he could not catch her.

11 "It began as a fantasy," Elizabeth said, "a dream in which I was dancing on a lawn full of camellia bushes. The camellias were in bloom—it was winter then—and the blooms were pink and white and peppermint and the sky was blue from top to bottom. Yes, it was winter: I remember how cool my clothes felt against my skin—did you know my husband's grandfather once had a man shot for threatening him?"

She said this on television, on a Sunday-evening talk show hosted by a woman she had grown up with. The woman, Lacey Pinkney, a former Charleston belle, had bought the UHF time with her husband's money. Her husband was a state senator from Tallahassee and Lacey was a local actress, model and lady sport. She carried a handbag with the message "Take What You Want" lettered across the side in blue thread. In the bag she carried at all times a portfolio of seminude photographs taken of her by the best of the Florida art photographers. She modeled for local trunk shows, and she was the woman in a sleek pink sheath draped across the hood of a Thunderbird in the local Ford commercial. She was the first woman in north Florida to have silicone implanted in her breasts, and though the operation left her without feeling in her nipples ("dough," she confided to the women at her spa, "they're just lumps of dough") she reveled in the increased attention the augmentation brought her. At thirty-seven, after three children, she still had a waist that was only twenty-two inches around, a fact which she rarely mentioned but which secretly delighted her; at sixty, she would still be working to keep it. Her husband chose to indulge her. He would wear the Navy crew cut that had excited her when she was twenty-one into middle and old age.

Elizabeth ran into Lacey at the Tallahassee airport on the night J.C. beat her. She had crossed the fields with a huge singing in her. As always there was nothing in her mind but the single voice that spoke to her as it had always done, that spoke out of a silence, out of nothing, saying walk this way, turn here, do this now. It was a voice as vivid as a face seen close up, but it was a voice without a face, simple, uninflected and undeniable. The furrows were ankle-high, heaped by the breaker plows. She was careful not to stumble as she crossed the field to the swamp track and made her way toward the house. The sky looked clear until she saw the moon, which was smudged with haze. The haze was the sign of the coming of the first hot days. She stopped only once, to take off her boots, and walked on carrying them, delighting in the feel of the fresh cool soil under her feet. It was the voice that told her to avoid the furrow ridges, something in her that she had always accepted as a voice, like the sudden cry on the bridge when at sixteen she had driven her father's car into the Ashley River. Then the voice went silent and her whole body was filled with the singing. Something in her seemed to accelerate, something that made the smell of the ground, dampened by dewfall, strong in her nostrils, that made the fair ambivalent breeze into caresses. Something in her clenched and tightened, grew strong and became the singing. She would turn away, turn away forever, yet she would come back. There was no principle of endurance in her, no bright light either, that she strived to reach. She was not, then or ever, holding on to anything, she was not interested in valor or nobility or integrity or the hope of a better world. World, world—the singing swelled in her like the sound of animals in the night. Once, driving home, she had seen a raccoon cross in front of the headlights. It had paused at the far side of the road and looked back at her out of its black mask with eyes that seemed to hold a human indifference. The eyes had refused her out of what seemed an intelligence as strong as her own. So she refused, so she did not make a choice of delight or despair, only refused, as evenly and as inevitably as the small animal in its solitary passing had looked her back into her loneliness. Once, cutting squash in her father-in-law's kitchen, she had asked Mattie if she still felt the girl in her. "Oh, yes," Mattie had answered with an eagerness that made Elizabeth wonder if the old woman did not carry the knowledge of her unbreakable youth in her always. "Oh, yes." Oh yes. Oh yes. Give it to me always, let it come. This right fright, too. Something plain and big as a sky. And then the veer: and then the turning away. And then the huge singing in her and the colors in her body, the inside of her turning gold, then blue, then red, then gold again. Green. And the listening, always the listening. The song she never told. The song her husband could not hear unless she held him close. What he would have, always would have, the monstrous giving-in which was not her giving-in, she knew, but his own. Go, go, go into the sparkling night. Give against it all, the fences and the stiles of her care, the gorgeous, magnifying, expanding circles of color. Like something in one of Rooley's paintings, she thought, Rooley who was a man who knew what she knew, who was a being like her.

She hesitated in her stride and almost turned back toward his house. Over her shoulder she could see the slate roof, glimmering a little wetly, just the peak of it showing behind her past the rise before the pond. But no, not now. The voice rose again, a murmur, and she continued down the road, walking in the center of it so she could feel the new sand spurs and the billygoat grass and the spiderwort brushing against her bare ankles, so she could feel the ache that rose now, ache that went deeper than any welts could go, and she thought, not the voice now, thought, There is somewhere else to go, and turned all the way around so that she was walking backward down the sand road, turned to fetch a look at Rooley's peaked roof, but it was gone, out of sight beyond the field ridge, a scarf of cloud hanging in the night sky above where it had been, like smoke. And at that moment, the roof vanished, the loss of it seemed to hurt her more than the beating she had just been given. Her legs felt weak; she stumbled and turned around again and broke into a run, a run that began a steady loping stride that carried her across the four miles of rising and falling fields to the back gate of Canaan.

If she had never been able to look straight on at her life, she had never been disturbed by that inability. There had been no need to see beyond what unfolded before her oblique glance. And it had never seemed to *her* that she looked away from what was directly in front of her, looked through it occasionally, but not away. So that when she entered the house, descended the laundry-room stairs to the servants' quarters, roused Hosea and Angela from their radios and sent them away, she did not think it necessary to ask herself what she was doing or to tell them.

Hosea, who endured the whimsical ways of his mistress for the money and for the ambivalent tenderness he felt for J.C. and because his family had for generations ministered to Burdettes, protested, but she cut him off with a glance that was harder than he had seen in her eyes before. Angela was new, the seventh or eighth maid Elizabeth had hired in the seven years she had lived at Canaan, and she was too young and too frightened of Mrs. Burdette to protest. Elizabeth stood in the basement hallway, so silent in herself that the girl, just nineteen, instinctively crossed her arms, hugging herself as she passed hurriedly under her mistress's firm stare up the stairs. Her crisp hair, which she wore always tied back with colored string behind her head, had been loosened, and Elizabeth was momentarily delighted to see that it sprang away from her head in a kind of shock, just as she had wondered if it would when she watched the girl work in the kitchen.

She remained in the basement until she heard the back door close and then the sound of Hosea's car starting up. She liked the house silent around her. It had always reminded her of Sunday afternoons in Charleston when from her third-floor bedroom windows she would look out over the slate roofs of her neighbors' houses and imagine the whole world empty of people. A cricket chirped behind her, and she looked around surprised. She did not see it at first but then she did in the corner next to a bucket that held an upended mop. She crossed the hall, bent down and caught the insect in her cupped hands. You must have been here all winter, she thought, hiding out from the cold. She climbed the basement stairs with the cricket in one hand, gone silent for now. She walked through the downstairs rooms jiggling it in her palm, thinking, Yes, this, this painting here, this flood of yellow curtain, these books will go. She climbed the stairs, entered her bedroom and, placing the cricket in the breast pocket of her shirt, packed a single suitcase. Of her personal treasures she took only her notebooks and the small wooden box covered in dark blue velvet that held the few small objects she felt she must always have: the pheasant feathers, the teehee seed necklace, the small carved silver gun, the patch of silk from her cotillion gown. J.C.'s letters she left in the bottom drawer of her dresser. In the bathroom she collected shampoo and soap and the silver razor she used to shave her legs all the way to the tops. The single bathroom window, eight by four like all the other windows on the second floor, had mirror panes in its bottom half. She saw herself as she bent to retrieve the shampoo. She had given her rosary to Jacey. She fingered her shirt where it had been, wished for a moment she still had it, her talisman for this particular moment in her life. Maybe a cricket will do now, she thought, and swept back her hair with one hand. She thought of women pressing back their hair before men. She had always taken it as a sign of surrender, the poor woman pushing back her hair with both hands, armpits exposed, eyes going wide for a second to admit the male. Seven years later, the women of Yellow Springs were still only passing faces to her, though many would think they meant much more. Her generosity—maybe not generosity exactly because there was nothing she needed to keep—and her bright talk and her willingness to pay attention to their stories drew them to her. She would not say to them that she never thought of them when they were not near her, that their lives passed her like a day's weather, were enjoyed and forgotten. Mrs. Nellie Johnson, who told jokes about her husband's bald head and skinny legs and who clung to the church like a life raft; Herva Walker, who could not lose weight no matter which diet she tried and took it out on her husband and son by browbeating them both beyond whatever limited potential either of them might have; Sonnie McKinnon, whose husband was the Burdette family doctor but who was carrying on a ten-year-old love affair with Tommy Pope, a spectacularly handsome life insurance agent and afternoon golfer—all of them were her friends, were what she could call friends; if she were brought to trial and put on the witness stand she could prove it: there was Nellie's cake tin on the counter downstairs and the Electrolux vacuum cleaner in the kitchen closet had been bought on Nellie's approval; Herva confided that she was embarrassed by her husband's country accent, and each time Tommy Pope decided to let Sonnie go, Elizabeth was the first to find out. But she didn't know them and they certainly didn't know her. When her husband made trips to Savannah and Texas and she slept on a pallet on the bedroom porch, lying near the railing so she could see the stars, she did not tell her friends, did not mention that she slept there or that as she lay on her back waiting for sleep she strung white ropes between the stars, weaving a net of small lights. She did not say that she heard voices from the spring, that she had seen the ghost of her mother wearing a pale blue dress rise through the cedars, her hands filled with golden grain and her hair wound about with knotted moss roses. She did not mention that on spring and summer nights she had lain down naked in Yellow Spring Course and let it carry her, feet first, to the Burdette graveyard, where she could climb out and walk dripping among the stones. The oldest graves were surrounded by low iron-railed fences, no larger than a child's playpen: Langston and his wife, Draycis; Rooley and Henrietta; Wheeler and his blondhaired consort, Felicia, each pair in its own spear-fenced pen. She walked there, under a lightning-scarred live oak, and in her mind saw her father salting an egg at the breakfast table, watched her mother leaning over the sink to water a Christmas fern. She would open the creaking gate of one of the pens—Langston's usually, he had been there longest—and lie on the gravestone and feel the last heat of the day come up through the stone into her bare body. There she would sing her frail songs, the mountain ballads her mother had sung, flitting across the gaps of her memory with words of her own devising: "I gave my love a cherry that had no stone . . . no stone . . . Down by the banks . . . of the Ohio . . ." "Come again," she would cry, spread-eagled on the grainy stone without a clue as to what she cried for, cry, until her mind fetched the memory of her husband standing on the porch in Hawaii, his thumbs hooked in his belt loops, his eyes hardened by tropic sunlight, the creases at their edges grown deeper from strain not laughter, and she would res-urrect the curious numbing desire she had felt then, that day or any day, to reach across the space that separated them, not for love, but for de-light and curiosity, to touch his face, to feel under her fingers the human breath, the kinked blood at the temples, the fine hairs at the base of his neck. That life, life, life, that she marveled still to find laid up against her own, preserved for her pleasure like fruit in a jar, the top twisted off and the rare, bold smell of it rising around her. In the graveyard she thought of her son and knew why she touched him so, why she came into his room at night, sat on the edge of his bed and took his sleeping head be-tween her hands, turning it gently from side to side, the way a child's head and body can be turned and held in sleep, the poor being gone, so drowned he could not be roused with pinches, with the nipping bites she trailed across his skin. She touched him for the life that was in him, touched him, flung unprotected in his jockey shorts across the big crisp bed pushed under the front windows of Canaan and holding him in her arms, all lights off, she would look out over the front yard of her house, so high up here on the second floor that her eyes were level with the crowns of the live oaks in which even now the small birds, cedar wax-wings, English sparrows, the solitary mockingbird, rocked in untroubled sleep. Connection, was what it was.

Kneeling on the white tile floor of her bathroom, her mind came back to her from the graveyard, from her son's white skin. Once, sitting with Sonnie at the glass table on the terrace, in the middle of Sonnie's anguished explanation of how Tommy had discarded her once and for all, Elizabeth had reached across the glass table and stroked the blond woman's face and touched the tears she shed. On impulse she drew the woman into her arms, and as she held her, her lips pressed into the blond crown of her head, she slipped her hand into the neckline of her green summer frock and touched the top of her breast. Sonnie, far into tears, had only sunk closer and drawn her shoulders in, allowing the bodice of her dress to fall open and Elizabeth's hand to sink deeper. Elizabeth pressed the woman's breast flat against her ribs so that she could slip her hand in, plunging downward until she felt the stern little nipple between her fingers. She touched the nipple, tugged it slightly outward, released it and withdrew her hand. Sonnie raised her tanned face and Elizabeth kissed her once firmly on the mouth and rose and taking her by the hand led her through the house, upstairs to her bedroom, where silently they undressed, Elizabeth helping Sonnie, brushing away the trivial tears, kissing her on the neck and touching her with the tips of her fingers everywhere. Sonnie cried all the time, and as the green dress slipped off her shoulders she began to count, "One, two, three four . . ." all the way to forty-six before Elizabeth had dress and underclothes off, and slipped her own yellow skirt and white blouse, knelt in the bed and drawn the woman into her arms. She remembered the way Sonnie cried out as she pressed her face into her sex, saying, "No, no, I haven't washed," as at the same time she pulled Elizabeth's head hard into her groin. Afterward, they talked in a brisk temperate way of other things, of their children and of a shop in Atlanta they both went to to buy shoes, the matronly details, Elizabeth thought, that were arrayed for their sustenance. Sonnie didn't look her in the eye again for nearly two years.

She thought of these things and rose from the scoured tiles, walked back through the bedroom and down the stairs. She would have to hurry, she thought, if she was to do what she planned. At the bottom of the stairs, in the curve of the hallway where until Jack's exit the portrait of J.C.'s mother had hung, she paused and looked at an Indian feather cape her husband had hung in its place. The feathers were dyed red and yellow and blue and had small green fluff tucked into the gaps between them; they made a pattern that was all color, a geometry of color that had no relation to the articulate world, beyond exuberance. I can't look at these things, Elizabeth thought, if I am to do this, but she looked anyway, until she could not bear it, and took the cape from its two brass hooks and wrapped it around her shoulders. She took the cricket from her pocket and held it to her nose. "For the life that is in you," she said out loud, "little life." There was only one more thing she wanted to do and to the voice that rose again in her head she said *Wait* and went down the hall to the library, where first she opened the tall front windows and then began pulling books from the shelves and throwing them out onto the lawn. Little by little in the seven years she had created for herself a library of her own, transferring it book by book onto the shelves closest to the windows. These books she retrieved now and tossed out into the dark, their white pages fluttering open like bird wings. Quickly, quickly, she thought, even if her husband had no car now to get him home. Jack would leave him to walk, she supposed, but she still must hurry.

It took her a long time anyway to throw the books out; she tried to be careful with them, but they all had to go and she had to throw them hard to get them beyond the porch. Then she raced back through the house, turning off lights as she went, descended the back steps to the garage, where she found the can of lawnmower gasoline in the corner next to a peach basket filled with pine cones. She had never burned a house before and wasn't quite sure how to go about it. Heat rises, she thought, and went back up on the porch and poured a trail of gas along the bottom of the walls around the three sides. She had to go back into the kitchen for matches. She did not turn on a light so that she would not see these life artifacts anymore; she did not want to lose her resolution before she lit the fire. She took a box of kitchen matches from the drawer by the sink and went back out. Standing on the top step, she lit matches and threw them at the pool of gas collected around the door. She had to strike several before she got one that worked. She raked it along the box and in the same motion tossed it in the pool of gas. The flame hit the liquid and there was a sound like a cough and then an explosion that scorched her face. She stumbled backward terrified, pulling at her clothes, pulling the pocket where she kept the cricket into a pouch between her fingers, poor cricket, she thought, and my God, how beautiful the fire is, and how hot. The flames jumped high up the windows and the whole wall was suddenly fronted with fire so that it seemed as if the flames had always been there, invisible until now, just coming into light. She wanted to stay and see the place burn, but there was no time for delay.

Her car started easily—a dark blue Jaguar this year—and she wheeled it around; even inside it she could feel the heat and smell the gas and the paint burning. A flock of birds burst from the magnolia by the drive, black flickering shapes rising frantically. As she accelerated down the drive, she watched the birds fly up into the clearing sky. She glanced over at the lawn, lit now with firelight; the tumbled books lay in the soaked grass, white and defenseless as birds that couldn't fly.

When, just beyond the church, she passed her husband, hunched up against the dashboard of Delight's pickup, she was glad. The voice had faded and the singing that had carried her across the fields was gone. She was glad to see him, and the feeling amazed her. She thought of turning back, but she knew that there would be no time now for talk; the fire would be fought, maybe beaten—she hoped suddenly that it would—the fierce surge of energy faded inside her, the relief and ease of this accomplishment taking its place, and she wanted to lie down, by the spring, let her hand trail in the crystal water, feel its endless coolness on her skin; she wanted to stand in the graveyard, risen on a stone, and feel the gusting wind take her hair, take her body up into the sky; she wanted to see her son running across the lawn with a slice of orange in his mouth, to hear her husband laugh with his whole face and body as he had in Hawaii; she wanted to be the final end and accomplishment of all the women who had gone before her, the chaste and constrained Bonnets of Charleston and the harebrained, defeated Burdettes. She wanted to weep tears into a dream, into a dream like a pool, like a hole in the earth, her body leaned out over the abyss, all the waters of her face falling into darkness, and then to fall herself after them.

She slowed down and drove past the lighted streets, past the kempt and polished houses each lit by lamps of the owner's devising, past the hospital that reared up under its white roof like a ship under sail, past old Eustace's house, past the last lamps of the town into the wet and freshly sown fields. She took the Florida road and beyond the last Burdette lands her mind seemed to shut down and she drove on toward Florida as if in sleep, no thoughts disturbing the easeful quiet that had descended on her.

12 When she stepped out of the car onto the asphalt pavement of the Tallahassee airport's long-term parking lot she was thinking of the time she saw a truck loaded with oranges turn over at the corner of Church and Tradd streets in Charleston. The truck had rounded the corner too fast into the path of another car and tipped over, spilling the bright fruit into the street. As she stood thirty feet away under a green awning before her mother's dress shop she had watched the great heap of oranges surge outward from the racked bed of the truck in a wave that broke into a million round parts scattering gold across the street bricks. Some joy had leaped in her then, and she had run into the street, four years old and dressed in white, and danced among the cascaded fruit.

She wrapped the feathered cape around her and patted the pocket where the cricket slept, pulled the single bag from the back seat and started across the parking lot. She was almost to the terminal when she saw Lacey coming out. She would have avoided her, but Lacey saw her at the same time and threw up her arms and ran up and hugged her. "Elizabeth Bonnet, you beauty," she cried, so loudly that people nearby turned to look.

Lacey hugged her three quick times, as if, Elizabeth thought, it were regulation, and stepped back beaming. "You are more beautiful than ever," she said, leaned in again and kissed her cheek.

"You are such a jerk, Lacey," Elizabeth said, pulling away.

"I know," Lacey laughed, "but now I'm successful at it." She wore her hair in a stiff blond tease that looked like a helmet, and her arms clanked with bracelets. She kept fluttering her hands to make the bracelets fall down over her wrists on which the thick hair was dyed blond, the same shade as her coiffure. She was dressed all in purple, and a long purple feather boa coiled around her neck. She mentioned her television program within the first three minutes, and if she had not Elizabeth would have escaped her and gone on into the terminal and bought her ticket for St. Guillaume.

"You have to come on my TV show," Lacey said, exposing her perfect teeth in an eager dog's grin.

"Your TV show?" Elizabeth imagined something with horses and plumes.

"My television show. I *have* a television show. It's part of what I do to keep entertained in this sad place."

"This sad place," Elizabeth said. "Yes," and laughed. "All right."

"And you come home with me, because we don't go on until tomorrow—it's live—and we can stay up late and talk about the good days when we were girls."

I was never a girl with you, Elizabeth started to say, but she held her tongue because she understood how some people's memories worked and she *had* known Lacey Pinkney all her life and just now she wanted to let that stand for something. She did not say yes to her husband because there was something in her that, like it or not, could not be taken over—could not be *taken*—and if she had not learned that it is only in the giving of that something, that little packet of self-love that hugs the heart, she knew that it could not be given on demand, better to offer it along with your change to the cabdriver or to the man who leans across the car bodice to wash your windows, or to this tinkling, sleek woman who grasped her hand and led her across the wet street to her car than to surrender it to robbers.

"Abandon everything and come with me," Lacey said as she hustled her across the parking lot.

"I was on the way . . ." Elizabeth said and stopped: she didn't want to tell Lacey where she was going.

"Wherever it is, you can go there tomorrow," Lacey said, pushing her bag into the backseat of a Cadillac Eldorado.

The sky had clouded over and a light, wintry rain blew out of the north. Elizabeth folded the cloak and laid it on top of her suitcase. The cricket had escaped. "I don't mind riding with you," she said, getting into the car. "I'd like to be on television."

They drove south and west through the hilly city, past oaks even more deeply stuffed with moss than the trees of Yellow Springs, past palm trees whose wet fronds gleamed with the rain's varnish. Under the streetlight at the corner of the ambitious new development Lacey lived in a large oleander was in bloom. The pink blossoms looked white in the misted light.

"You're a queer duck, Elizabeth," Lacey said as she pulled into the straw-covered driveway of a long and low brick ranch house set among pines on a low rise back from the street. "I think you are in trouble."

"No more than usual," Elizabeth said. The oleanders had reminded her of something, had stiffened something in her. She wondered if they had put the fire out before it burned the house. "I'm thinking of other things," she said.

"I know," Lacey said. "You won't tell me, but I'll get you drunk and then you'll say."

How bright and hot the fire had been, and how black the smoke, so black that she could see it against the night sky; it was darker, inky, billowing like clouds instead of smoke, rushing upward at tremendous speed, as if fueled by something inside itself, something more than fire. Lacey's house was lit by floodlights. When Elizabeth looked back from the front steps she could see nothing but a blackness beyond them; she had to turn away from the glare.

They had the house to themselves. "Randy's on a money mission," Lacey said, "pandering to the orange growers. I love it when he makes money." Lacey fed her hors d'oeuvres left over from a party the week before, mixed drinks for her—scotch and ice for Elizabeth, gin and tonic in a tall milky glass for Lacey—and chattered about her triumphs. Late in the evening she showed Elizabeth her new breasts. The nipples were as purple as the dress that held them.

Integrity is the first thing to go, Elizabeth thought as she lay on a paisley chaise longe in the glassed-in sunporch watching Lacey stride up and down. What is the second? Courage? Hope? She pulled her notebook from her back pocket and wrote: "Seven Deadly Virtues: Honesty, Hope, Faith, Charity, Courage, Integrity, Humility." On the Florida road, just north of the line, was a tenant house in the yard of which someone had heaped up mounds of broken glass. There were half a dozen piles of different-colored glass, clear, red, blue, the arsenical green of Coca-Cola bottles, each mound as high as a man's head. Often, passing by on afternoon trips to the beach, she had wondered what sense, or desire, had compelled the tenants of that house to pile up glass. Decoration surely: in sunlight the glass glittered like a treasure of jewels. But was it envy, of the finer plantation households such as Haven's with their dressed lawns and gardens, or contempt, or spite? The yard was bare except for the glass, a dirt yard. The mounds were a brutal decoration, of a primitive beauty—like a fire, she thought, like fire. "Show me your tits again," she said to Lacey, who strode up and down over straw floor mats sipping from her glass. Without modesty, Lacey released the bodice of her dress and exposed her turgid, pompous breasts.

"Would you mind if I touched them?"

"Not at all, dear. I let all the girls at the spa have a feel." She knelt in front of Elizabeth and arched her back toward her.

After initial softness the breasts were hard, dense as heaps of flour. Pressed, they compacted into an impenetrable roundness.

"Do you feel that?" Elizabeth asked.

"On the outside, but not in deep. They cut the cord."

Underneath each breast, like a thin smile, was the scar from the surgeon's knife.

"Augmentation," Lacey said, smiling her doggish smile. "Small, medium or large."

"Which are these?"

"Medium. If I got large I'd have to go to work as a stripper."

Elizabeth steepled her fingers over the purple nipples. "May I kiss them?" she asked.

"Oo, honey, what would the people think?" The smile crooked and Lacey began to raise the bodice.

"No," Elizabeth said, "let me."

"I don't know—all right, but then let's have another drink."

"Fine." She lowered her head and took the left nipple in her mouth. It was leathery and hard. She sucked, pinching the other nipple between all her fingers. After a moment Lacey raised one hand and began to half-caress, half-push her head away, but Elizabeth held on. It was not any kind of love, she thought, not even lust: these breasts were as unnatural as artificial fruit, though just as beautiful—no, it was instead the specific release of concentration, the narrowing down to a point—tough nipple—point upon which all her energy could be brought to bear, point, where for a moment, the reckless world fell silent. She would fly to an island and sit on a sun-washed beach and watch the ocean throw itself against a body it could not break.

"That's so sweet," Lacey said from above her in a cracked and slippery voice, "so sweet. But since the surgery, honey, I can't feel a thing."

The house survived. There was less gasoline than Elizabeth realized, and the fire trucks got there in time. The flames scorched the exterior around two sides, burning black marks all the way over the lip of the second-story porch. Inside, the dining-room and library walls cracked and the paint blistered and the room stank of smoke and the rugs and furniture bore new permanent watermarks, but nothing burned. There were long new seams in the kitchen counter, and for some reason the water pressure in the house was diminished for weeks afterward, but it finally cleared up, of its own accord. J.C. left the outside of the house as it was. He walked around the house touching the burn marks that were billowy at the top like the stain of thunderheads, if that were possible, and refused to have anything replaced. "I want her to see her work when she comes home," he said. He had no doubt about who had caused the fire. Elizabeth had disappeared; it was the sort of farewell gift she would leave. And besides, they heard her confess, heard it from her own lips.

Walking home the next night from after-supper chocolate malts at the Dairy Queen they saw her speaking from a television screen in the window of Kinnick's Appliance Store. Jacey, who was attempting to touch every pane of store glass in the three blocks between the Dairy Queen and the house, saw her first. He cried out to his father, who lagged half a block behind talking to a farmer. She sat rared back on a sofa with her booted feet planted flat, her arms stretched along the sofa back, talking to a woman in an evening gown. His father ran up the block.

"She looks like a damn longshoreman," he said, pressing his face against the window. The sound was off, but Jacey could read his mother's lips.

"I don't believe that families are so important," she said and dipped her head and turned her face toward the elegantly dressed woman at the other end of the sofa.

"Come on," his father cried, cuffed him on the shoulder and began to run toward the house.

They sprinted across the corner of the Square, past the huge camphor tree where a colony of blackbirds flitted around settling in for the night. The sky was pale as wash water, scoured clean by evening, though in the west, through trees beyond the house, Jacey could see the sun, burning fiercely, reluctantly on.

His father beat him to the gate, but Jacey got ahead of him by climbing the fence and running across the yard. The huge wing marks of the burn reared up the front wall. Jacey ran up the slanted cellar doors, across the porch and into the kitchen, where in a fever he snapped on the television set the maid watched while she cooked. It took a minute to find the channel; it was the first in that part of the world to transmit on UHF. His mother came in grainy and indistinct, nodding at her interlocutor, a broad grin on her interference-salted face. His father banged through the screen door and began to fiddle with the picture. "What's wrong with it?" he asked.

"It's channel thirty-six," Jacey explained and reached behind the set to switch the antenna wire.

"That's good," his father said and stepped back. He pulled up a chair and sat down, elbows on knees, kneading his hands between his

185

legs. Jacey scrambled up on the counter under a potted areca palm whose brown fronds were curled, clawed-up like the fingers of age, from the fire.

"My whole life has been a mortal mystery to me," his mother said. The camera drew close on her face and she smiled into it. "I've never been able to tell the difference between my life and my dreams"—"Lord, isn't that the truth," his father said—"but I know many people like that. The world is more full of people like us than you might imagine."

The camera dollied back so that both women were on the screen. Elizabeth stretched her legs out and crossed her pecan-colored riding boots at the ankles. Her hair was pulled severely back, held so tightly that the waves were flattened, and it looked oiled. The other woman leaned toward her, flouncing the light confection of her skirt.

"What exactly do you mean, dear?" she asked.

Elizabeth's hands rose as she answered, weaving the air in front of her words. "When I lived in Hawaii," she said, "with my little boy"— "That's me," Jacey said—"we had a gardener named Rufino. He had a victory garden in which he planted only Japanese vegetables. The year we left Hawaii, 1950, he was still counting ships in the harbor—in case the Japanese made a comeback and needed the information."

"Is that the sort of thing you do?"

"Of course not. But when I lived on Oahu I could never get the idea out of my head that I could go down the road, stick my thumb out and catch a ride to New York City. I dreamed it that way—the road was really there—and it seemed to be true."

"Oh, Elizabeth Bonnet . . ."

"Burdette . . ."

"Yes—you didn't really believe it?"

"Yes, I did. I knew a man who believed that the Hawaiian Islands got to be where they were because a Polynesian goddess swam two thousand miles towing them behind her on a pandanus rope."

"An old legend."

"I suppose, but he believed it."

"I'm sure. Now," the woman said, flouncing her skirt and pressing her blouse down at the waist so that her breasts stood out, "now we would all like to hear what life is like on a large plantation in the South." The woman turned to the camera: "As I mentioned, Elizabeth Bonnet Burdette is the wife of Jackson Coleridge Burdette, the owner and operator of Canaan, a fifty-thousand-acre plantation just north of the Georgia state line." She turned to Elizabeth. "All our viewers would be very interested to know, from the woman's perspective"—that was the name of the program—"what life is like there. Do you still live in the old ways?"

"Oh, yes: darkies and desire, dark desire."

"Ha, ha. You all grow cotton, I believe."

"Yes, I believe we do. It's white and fluffy and grows on a bush. I have burned my husband's house down."

His father made a coarse catarrhal sound in his throat and stood up. "She's going to ruin us all," he said. "God in heaven."

But the dressed-up woman seemed to take no notice of Elizabeth's admission. "And how did the Burdettes come to Canaan?" she asked.

"Out of the reputations they destroyed in Charleston, out of the dream. Sometimes you have to destroy the world around you before you can see the dream."

"Which was that?"

"For me, a dance among camellia bushes. . . ."

The house smelled of the fire, the sour piercing smell of wet ashes. The smell would linger long after any effects of the blaze. It was worse in the kitchen, which was the only room in the house in which heat had burst the windows. J.C. had had a man come immediately to replace the panes, and cleaners had worked all day to steam the front-room draperies and rugs. The house held the dense sweet riveting odor of their perfume, beneath which, like compost in a garden, the sharp odor of the dead flames lingered.

His father retreated to the sink, where he filled a jelly glass with water and drank it down in long shuddering gulps. "I've been thirsty ever since yesterday," he said and smiled weakly at Jacey.

"My mother's father once had a man shot for threatening him," Elizabeth said with a bright, wandering smile.

"We are all crazy," J.C. said and stabbed his crimped hair with the fingers of his right hand.

"Why are we crazy?" Jacey asked without taking his eyes off his mother. She was as beautiful as a movie star, even with the transmission interference. His longing caught in his throat, and he pressed his hands against his chest. He had never seen anyone he knew on television before. The medium cut her out of his life in the way a photograph or a painting could never do. Even as she moved, swaying back and forth on the sofa, reaching to pat the interviewer's hands, even as the rich, warbulous tones of the Charleston accent she had never lost—attenuated slightly by the TV speaker—flowed into the darkening kitchen, he felt the wideness of the gulf that separated him from her. He could not get her attention—this moving talking person—even if he threw himself on the floor screaming. "Mother," he whispered, "Mother," and her name: "Elizabeth . . . Bonnet . . . Burdette," the syllables an incantation for an unreachable idol. She had walked past the pond up the path that she had made for herself. For seven years, on Sister Maxine and then on the new mare Missa, she had worn new paths across the Canaan lands. He could follow her only if she let him, but usually, especially in the last year, she would not permit it. He knew Haven's telephone number by heart he had called it so often looking for her.

His father had not answered. He stood against the cracked counter, the empty glass loose in his hand, staring at the screen.

"We're a violent people," Elizabeth said and laughed. "At least the Burdettes are."

"It's her vengeance she's taking," his father said, but Jacey knew that was not it: she didn't know better than to say what came into her head.

"I understand your house is one of the oldest in that part of Georgia and that you have a spring in your backyard, or among the gardens."

"Yes, among the gardens to be sure, which are now beginning to bloom." Jacey glanced out the window, each pane of which carried the small square glue mark where the manufacturer's tag had been. At the corner of the garage a large forsythia was in full yellow bloom.

"We have a yard," Elizabeth said, "that piles up in springtime with flowers, and we have a spring, a round blue hole in the ground that my husband says is ninety feet deep. There're no fish in it, though."

"Not in a spring, I guess. . . ."

She didn't know the house was still intact. She was down there in a Tallahassee television studio, he realized, thinking she had left a pile of black rubble up in Georgia.

The flames had excited him. From the bed of the pickup truck he had watched them rise ahead of them, orange as pumpkins, topped by the black billows of petroleum smoke. He had heard his father in the cab gasp and cry out and Delight's facetious grimness as he yelled, "There's a murderer loose in the land," and then he felt the surge as Delight accelerated through stoplights toward the fire station. His father broke from the truck running in his bony lope toward half a dozen firemen eating oysters around a long bench at the back of the firehouse. "It's a fire," he cried. "Let's go, let's go," and the firemen threw down knives and shells and sprang to their jobs. It took less than five minutes for the trucks to reach the house and for the hoses to start. Jacey stood just inside the front fence with his father and Delight among the gathering crowd and watched the heavy streams of water pour against the house. Neighborhood dogs ran among the watchers barking and leaping in the light from the flames. "It's not going to go," Delight said with a grin, and his father glared at him so hard that Jacey was frightened—his feeling of natural lostness twisting in his stomach—just enough to set him free to run into the yard, where he squatted under a camellia bush. The heat made the skin on his face and arms feel thin and tight. He touched one of the hoses that lay rigid on the ground beside him and felt the hard muscle of water; he leaned down and pressed his ear against the gray canvas-coated tube and heard a dense humming sound and thought that the blood in his veins might sound like that. The water ate steadily into the body of the flames. Like Delight, he wanted the fire to win, wanted this on the same night— still—that he had been baptized, still on his skin the faint haze of salt from the green pool, his hair still untidy, and he was ashamed to think it, tried for a moment to push the thought/feeling away from him, but he could not, stood pressing his body back into the glossy camellia leaves marveling at the *need* of the flames punching up through the rolling ridge of black smoke. The lawn was littered with books. They were under bushes, open and closed, dew-wet. One of the dogs gnawed fiercely at a book in front of the azaleas by the drive. Jacey went over and began to collect them. He carried an armful back to his father, who stood talking with his brothers by the fence. The scent of newly blooming honeysuckle mingled with the stench of the fire.

"I found these," he said and held the pile out to his father.

His father was talking to Bryce. "I don't know," he said, rubbing his forearms as if he were cold. He still had on his tie, snugged tight under his neck. He took the books without looking at Jacey.

"These are our books," Jacey said, and then he saw recognition come into his father's eyes. J.C. looked at the books, hefted them, then swung them under his arm like a schoolboy. "Yes," he said, "I guess they are," and he put his whole hand open over Jacey's face, as the min-

189

ister had done, but he did not push him down, only held his hand over his face until Jacey squirmed away—"Daddy, don't"—and said, "You look just like your mother." Jacey felt something gust out of his father, something that he was too young to name but that when he thought about it again years later he would call grief. "I don't know where she is," his father said, turning back to Bryce. "She could be anywhere by now. . . ."

"Florida or Africa or down in the swamp," Jacey said.

"Florida," his father said absently, cradling the books against his chest.

Jacey felt some of the dignity of his new position—baptized—as he looked across the lawn at his cousin Burleigh, who was throwing a stick to see how close he could make his Labrador retriever go to the flames to fetch it. He started to call out to him, but his father touched him again, fumbling across his head and shoulder with blind-struck fingers. Jacey pulled away and ran toward the burning house. He veered past it, past Burleigh, calling, "Hey, boy!" and around the side. The black Labrador started after him, but Burleigh called him back.

It was quiet behind the house, the hazy moon casting a faint marblous light over everything. The darkness under the cedars was purple, but the spring collected light. The surface, as always, was disturbed slightly, as if a water bird had just paddled across it. Around the flag-stones were small humps of discarded towels: Elizabeth had begun to go in the water again, always the first to swim. Baptized already, he did not want to go into the water, but he knelt down and raised one of the damp towels to his face. It held the scent of her, like something made from her body. He looped it around his neck and looked into the pool, which seemed to glow with its own light. Something at the bottom burning, flinging light upward. His mother had told him there were angels down there; he was still too young to reach them. He could touch the next-to-the-last mark his father had established, the nail driven into the limestone wall. Along the walls the faint hairs of the cedar roots protruded; some days he found the spring clouded, like a glass of milk of magnesia, from the rock splitting of the roots. Tonight it was clear, faintly tremulous from the pumping muscle of the underground river. He was a boy still and something in him cried to stay one. When his father touched him he knew what it was he tried to shut out: the image of his mother and her untamable ways. He thrust his face into the water. It burned on his fired skin. He began to speak, words at first, then noises, he shouted into the water until the bones of his head hummed with ungovernable sound.

190

PART
THREE

13 She was gone for six months. Her postcards were re-turn-addressed Hotel Cecilia, St. Guillaume, A.F.—an island in the Caribbean, J.C. gathered from his atlas, 150 miles south of Cuba. "Saint Will is one of the Leeward Islands," she wrote, "and gets little rain. The breeze is often fresh with moisture, but it passes over us. I *think* it is one of the Leeward Islands."

His letters to her he wrote as if in a language he had never mastered. Propped in bed, a lapboard across his knees, he wrote, "I am all right," after ten minutes of staring at the page. He couldn't bear down in his thoughts. "The weather is fine though hot," he wrote, crossed that out and tried, "We've signed a contract with Allied Chemical," crossed that out and wrote, "Jacey is growing taller," crossed that out, scratched black ink through the letterhead, turned the sheet over and began again. Eventually he sent her envelopes containing one folded empty page, maybe a honeysuckle flower or a penny or a shirt button, or the brass stud from a bridle stuck into the crease.

She did not acknowledge his speechlessness nor his gifts. "It is a clear day," she said. "The sky is wide and plain. I got up early and walked on the beach. I found half a dozen sea urchin husks, each a differ-ent shade of purple. The lobsters here are just like the ones in the Pacific: spiny but without claws. How could that be?"

He didn't know. He carried the postcards around with him in his coat pockets. From time to time he would pull them out and read them again. "The hotel is a bright yellow two-story stucco building with twelve rooms on the second floor. I have a corner room in back that looks out over the bay. The town is built on a neck of land between two lagoons. The beaches of both lagoons are littered with old metal, tires, bottles, an occasional washing machine, and dead sea birds. Even under

193

the water there is debris, cans and bones of animals, rocks that don't belong there. Nonetheless, the water is clear."

He thought of showing the postcards to someone, his brothers maybe, or to John Dance, the plant manager, but he was afraid of their interpretation. Jacey saw the cards, but he had no comment. Since the fire and her flight his son had retreated into a silence that grew deeper day by day. He had begun riding his horse each afternoon, saddling up after school and galloping away down Rooley's path toward Lazarus Swamp, gone each day until sunset. He was late for supper always until J.C., who could not bring himself to remonstrate, had the cook move the meal to a later hour. Even then, Jacey would rarely appear at the table before J.C. was halfway through eating. J.C. felt the purposefulness of his son's askew rhythm and said nothing.

Once again his work became the exercise he built his strength on. He had bought plants in Savannah, Norfolk and Mobile and he drove to them regularly. In meetings he spoke of expanding into the Midwest, of operations they could buy in Iowa and Illinois, of the deep black topsoil there, of the farming that was *really* farming. The family had prospered, they were owners now of an empire that touched all the corners of the Old South, and if the construction of the empire meant that the ground they lived on was plowed through by the intricacies of a debt system that cost them millions each year in interest alone, they were sanguine about it, for the returns were steady and handsome. Eustace, whose white brick house roosted in a yard so dense with camellias that the grass wouldn't grow, relented; he used part of his profits to put in a swimming pool and made a down payment on a house at Sea Island, the resort for flush northerners that had been established on one of the Georgia barrier islands in the twenties. Eustace had an old man's love for Elizabeth, young and dashing, and he grieved for her presence, and blamed J.C., in his faltering way, for her absence, but he was Burdette enough to take the money that was coming to him. Rooley bought an airplane and enough paint one season to spray the tops of a field of planted pines silver, and he owned a truck, a semi that he drove himself, hauling his raucous paintings to shows that Alsace organized. Bernard and Delight expanded the zoo; they put concrete half floors in the cages and branched out into foreign animals: llamas and zebras, a long-nosed anteater from the Andes and even a tiger, a mangy, ten-year-old feline with muddled stripes bought for ten thousand dollars from a bankrupt circus in Waycross.

194

Only his father resisted, his relentless negative shining like a light in the woods.

The old man refused even his portion of the profits. The individual profits were issued quarterly in separate checks, one for the farm and one for the industries—each quarter Jack's earned sum remained an unsubtracted entry on the company books. The checks he tore unopened into pieces and tossed into the nearest wastebasket. "I don't even want to *see* what's going on," he said.

He still made his appearance at the family meetings, but more often than not these days, he was mute. He retired from stoning the house. He spent long days in his tower listening to music. On the sofa he propped himself on a bed pillow so that he could see only the sky. He listened to the wind blowing in the oaks and the sweet gums and followed the progress of clouds. Occasionally he imagined a different country below him, one covered in snow, or in the gorse and bracken he had seen in photographs of the Scottish Highlands in the picture book by his old bed, or in white sun-blistered rocks, or in water. But more often he left the ground as it was, the long-rolling terrain, earth the color of thunderheads, the disciplined rows of cotton and tobacco, the sprigged tops of pines, the swamp hardwoods. He had loved weather all his life, had raged in spring against the rains, endured the summer heat, stood on the back steps watching the wild storms of fall, shivered in the mists and frosts of winter. Weather had disciplined him though he had railed against it when it kept him from his work. It had disciplined, he supposed, all the Burdettes, maybe even the first Rooley, who had believed he could conquer anything. Weather united them all, he thought, first to last, at least all who had lived on this ground. Until now. Weather didn't affect a sulfuric acid plant, wouldn't stop business. But his mind shied from rancor. He was sixty-seven; time to change. The sky held his gaze. He had his garden, unfurled beneath him like the flag of a new boisterous country, and if spring rains kept him from the tilling, they did not keep him out forever; flowers could bear the delay, would leaf and bolt nonetheless.

His grandson, who, peering over the rim of his childhood into merciless adolescence, had been struck nearly dumb by what he saw, often joined him in the eyrie. Mattie, too, climbed the stairs and sat with them, all three propped comfortably on pillows listening to the vast music that poured from the small record player on the floor. A turbulence subsided

195

in Jack, though he could see in his grandson that one was building. It became harder for the boy to talk, and now when he did he wanted to know about the family. He asked if the story of Jack's father's shooting a man was true. Once it was, Jack told him, once it was true. Tell me, the boy said, and Jack told him, remembering as he spoke the cold fury of his father when Harley Cantrell, a white tenant, threatened to burn the cotton houses. A thousand dollars would keep him from it, Harley had said in a note slipped under the kitchen door. The money was to be left in an envelope on the front porch of an abandoned house on the south side of the lands. His father had sent Jake Epps, the fire chief, down to meet Harley. Jake had crouched under the porch with a twelve-gauge double-barrel shotgun across his lap, and when Harley showed up he had shot him in the knees. They carried him to the doctor and had him bandaged up—he would never be any good for walking again, the doctor said—put him on a train and sent him back to his kin in north Georgia. Jack didn't think his father had ever thought twice about it, any more than he would have thought twice about slapping a fly.

"He was that kind of man," he said, still as baffled as ever before his father's ways.

"Could you have a man shot?" Jacey wanted to know.

"Maybe," Jack answered. That was as close as they came to talking about the night J.C. beat Elizabeth.

At night the old snake wound twitched under the skin and he would wake and lie on his side staring at a patch of moonlight on the floor. "Shoo, shoo," he would say quietly, as if to the sleeping light, though that was not it.

"What?" Mattie would ask and touch his body.

He knew and he didn't know. A body could hold so many forces. He thought of the grip the land still had on him, the entrapment of place, and wondered what his life would have been had he not been rooted so deeply. But he did not treasure such thoughts, refused the false solace of what if and what might have been. Who he had become, who he was now disturbed him. "I'm sixty-seven years old," he said to Mattie, "and I don't know yet whether or not I'm a good man."

"You'll do," she told him and took him in her arms. She had held his body when it was coarse and hard from fieldwork and she held it now when it had become as soft as hers. Everywhere down his length the flesh had given in, dissolving into a new pliancy. Everywhere except in his

196

hands, which retained in their scarred palms the tough residue of a life-time of work. The lines that might have told his fortune were obscured by the lines his life had carved into the flesh. Even the fingerprints, the tenting arches and whorls of identity, were cut through with newer, deeper, just as permanent lines. They were hands still tough enough to catch a bee and hold it while it stung and they were hands that still, twenty years after he had first touched her, in a pine wood on a windy day in October, could excite her with their tenderness and restraint. She loved the contrast between the roughness of skin and the gentleness of his touch. And as she placed his hands on her breasts that seemed to have grown more sensitive with age, she would whisper into his ear, "No, you still couldn't hurt anyone, still couldn't."

Loving her, he let her beguile him, but he no longer believed there was any human act that was beyond him. Homicide, patricide, geno-cide—given the right circumstances, the right frame of mind, he was ca-pable of pulling any trigger. He could have blasted a man's knees into pulp; he could have shot his son. He thought of throwing his guns out of the house, but the grain of his culture ran too deep, and avoidance of temptation was not the answer, he realized. He had, in late years, lost his love of hunting birds—it was even hard to hook a fish—but he was still able to teach his grandson, still able to admire a perfect wing shot, still able to pop the head of a shot quail against his boot heel to stun the life out.

He prayed, Forgive me and make me better, but what he sought forgiveness for was vague, and he didn't know what it was he wanted to become. He began to learn to wait. In the ease of his music, in the comfort of long days in his tower, in the changing and changeless skies over Canaan he began to learn patience. It was another kind of discipline, he thought, and he was grateful for his music and the land that surrounded him, and for the gentling kin lounged on pillows on the floor.

J.C. found footholes in the expanding world of his work. In his mind the satellite plants had become oases, and he drove the few hundred miles to each of them with the hopefulness and deliberation of a thirsty man who expected to find a cool well at the end of the road. He drove be-cause flying made him queasy, and because he liked the anticipation that he strung out over the miles between Canaan and his plants. He regarded

197

the gradually changing terrain, the little towns with their grandiose courthouses, their meager rivers, their antique manses, with an almost amorous interest and delight. He took pleasure in the simple acquisition of a stranger's knowledge, in the fact that he had seen the water tower shaped and painted like a peach in Royce, that in Willette, South Carolina, the name of the town was spelled out in marigolds on the courthouse lawn, that in Gamblen, North Carolina, an old man in a crooked stovepipe hat drove a covered cart pulled by goats around the town square. On the way to Savannah he liked best the long miles of pine woods between Waycross and the coast, the even ranks of seeded trees and the wide lily-choked ditches running straight as a plumb into the withering distances.

His favorite drive was the one to Texas. He loved the miles of grassy fields in south Alabama, and the cobbled rank streets of Mobile—where he spent two days talking to his plant manager—and beyond, the vaporous coastal woods of Mississippi, where, just west of Biloxi, he often stopped at one of the houses that had been owned by Jefferson Davis. He liked to walk out on the wide oak-shaded lawn of the house that Davis had come to after the War, that looked across the now vigorously merchandised beach road into the bright Gulf, and imagine Davis there, imagine that bitter, phlegmatic man standing in his sandy yard staring into a distance of wave light from which he could not, not ever, expect relief.

Past New Orleans and the river he would swing west and south through the bayou country of southern Louisiana. The bayous, stained dark as the river at Canaan, surprised him in their narrowness and in their abrupt angular meanderings. Along grassy banks grew clumps of banana trees that reminded him of Hawaii, and he would pull off the road and reread the latest postcard from Elizabeth. Her fair, restless, light-hearted script filled the cards from corner to corner. There was hardly room for his address, and she was lucky, he thought, that the hotel—the cards were often views of the building or the grounds or the street in front—had printed its address in the upper left-hand corner, else she would have had no room for it. One postcard was little more than a list of the varieties of blue she saw in the ocean. Aquamarine, beryl, jouvance, sapphire, cyanic, pavonine, cobalt, turquoise, Yellow Spring-bottom-blue—"flits and shades and shining pockets," she wrote. "You wouldn't believe it. And what's amazing is that up close, no matter the blue in the distance, the water is always as clear as a swimming pool." He had flung the card against the windshield and stared out at the brief angle of bayou he could see between two ragged clumps of bananas. On the other side of the water, beyond the bushes, was a small farmhouse with a black rooster wind vane on the roof peak. Maybe I will be stunned all my life, he thought, maybe she will shock me into the grave. He pulled pen and paper from his briefcase, scribbled furiously for several minutes. "Why don't you send me pieces of your actual skin," he wrote—"it wouldn't be any more strange. What are you doing? What are you doing?" Would it be possible, he thought, to have a *conversation* with her? They had been married for twelve years and still they had no apparatus to build exchanges with. What kind of animal had he allowed into his house? "I'll go to Bernard's," he wrote, "and study the animals in the zoo. I'm sure there are pointers I can pick up there. Do you have any idea what it's like to come in the house and find these little blasters waiting for me? I'm afraid of my own mail. What are you doing? What, what?"

He tore the paper up and threw it out the window. He wished he had never hit her; he wished she had never gone away. "She wanders around at night," Hosea had told him, and the news had scalded him, as if he were being told that he could not satisfy her. He had wanted to question Hosea further, but he had been afraid to. It horrified him to speculate on what others might know. "What do you do when I am not here?" he had once asked her, and she had begun to tell him, but—as always—even in the face of his desire to know, he could not bear to hear. As she recounted an excursion in a johnboat down the swamp river, he had felt a clutching in his gut that drove him from his chair and out of the room. "If you would just stay put," she had called gaily after him, "you would be fine." But he couldn't stay, and she had not followed him.

He looked out the window. Several of the banana plants supported hanging stalks of fruit. Below each stalk hung the tree's single flower, a long purple tear. "Ah," he said, and pressed his palm hard against his face. He swung back out onto the highway and floored the car. He was miles down the road before the trooper caught him, but he was not surprised—he was almost relieved—when he did.

The family's sulfur interest was shares in a consortium that owned wells and the sifting mills that ground the congealed element into powder. He had bought a dozen low-bellied transport cars to ship the sulfur back to Alabama, Georgia and Virginia, and he dreamed of owning a railroad. His spirit would rise as he stood on the rail dock in Minot watching the sulfur being dumped into the cars. Once he had climbed to the top of one of the cars and, balanced on ladder and rail, had thrust his hands into the sunny powder. The plant manager had called for him to come down, but he had not heeded him. He wished the yellow filled the world.

It was that moment, or one like it, that moment, or the sudden stricture on the bayou roadside in Louisiana, that made him decide to bring Jacey with him on one of his Texas trips. Elizabeth had taken Jacey on one of *her* wistful journeys, downriver by canoe to Haven's, but this trip, J.C. decided, would be none of that—he would show his son the articulate creations of the responsible energy he brought to bear in the world, these long factories with their elephantine machinery pulverizing minerals into fertilizers—to make things grow, by God!—the sturdy derricks that pumped the liquefied sulfur out of the deep rock beds and the rail cars, filled to delicate peaks with the dense yellow powder.

But the boy wouldn't talk to him. He had not protested when J.C. sent a note to his teachers saying that Jacey would be absent from school a few days. He had not commented when his father described to him the sights they would see on the journey west. On the road the boy seemed content with whatever his father suggested, whatever motel or restaurant or brief side journey he came up with. He had shown him the chufa nut plantations in south Alabama, and Jeff Davis' house in Mississippi; they had spent the night in New Orleans, and J.C. had taken him to Pascal Manale's, where he introduced him to crawfish boiled in pepper and bay leaves; in south Louisiana he had described to him the salt domes that underlay the islands and swamps and shown him the fields of golden rice. The boy had cast vague, wandering glances at whatever sight J.C. pointed to and returned to the book he was reading. It was only in Texas as they crossed the dock in Minot and the boy saw the Gulf that was covered with the yellow powder of sulfur shining in the sun that his spirit seemed to rise out of its concentration on itself and he flung a hand outward and cried, "It's gold, Daddy, the water is gold."

J.C. would have given him anything he wanted at that moment. "Isn't it something," he said, "Come on"—meaning to show him the huge conveyers that transferred the sulfur into the cars, but the moment was too brief; by the time they rounded the corner of the warehouse the boy had sunk back into his silence, and when J.C. pointed to the row of cars each containing its load of sulfur, his son looked away and did not seem to hear him.

He began to badger the boy, to criticize him. He was appalled at his anger, but he couldn't stop himself. He made Jacey go to restaurant washrooms and comb his hair before he would let him order meals. He demanded long recitations of schoolwork the boy had finished weeks before. He kept him with him during the extended meetings with his managers. The boy did not fight; he hung his head and came along. As he prodded and picked, J.C. felt he was looking at himself from a great distance. From across restaurants and motel rooms, from the far side of greasy cobblestone streets in New Orleans and Mobile, he saw himself, a man of forty-three with thinning hair and the veined and brawny forearms of a wrestler, addressing this thin and small-for-his-age boy, boy who, he knew, was just now beginning his first tentative negotiations with the manhood that was to come. He saw himself, an angry and intolerant stranger whom he could not subvert nor delay, and he began to wonder, with an almost pleasant detachment, what he would do next.

Once at a wayside park in Louisiana he drove away from his son as he peed against an oak behind a picnic table. He was ten miles down the road, making up words to a tune he heard in his head, before he came to and could get himself to turn around and go back and pick up the boy. He propped a half-dozen of Elizabeth's postcards on the dashboard and made Jacey tell him everything he remembered of Hawaii, as if there were a solution back there in those islands. It bothered him that his son did not comment on the cards from the Caribbean. J.C. wanted to ask him what he thought, but here he drew the line, unwilling to admit directly that the messages disturbed him. He had noticed at Canaan how the boy's eyes brightened as he plucked the cards from the hall table where the maid had placed them, and how that brightness clouded over into painful concentration as he studied the pictures and the scant sentences they contained. Perhaps he memorized each card, picture and message, and rebuilt each for himself on his long rides in the swamp. Where did *he* go? Another wandering Burdette, just like his Bonnet mother.

"Maybe *I* should take a trip," he said out of a silence as they bumped across railroad tracks into a cotton town in Alabama. "Maybe I should just take off."

Jacey looked up from his book. "Why?" he asked.

"I don't know." It embarrassed him to talk this way to his son. "How about a chocolate malt?"

"Fine."

They found a Dairy Queen and J.C. bought his son a malt, retrieving again one of their oldest rituals, the end of their Sunday-afternoon drives when they would stop at the Yellow Springs Dairy Queen for refreshments. The boy, who in the past had been voluble and interested, drank the malt in silence, staring out the window at a group of teenagers sitting on the hood of a Chevrolet. "Don't spill it," J.C. had said, aware that his son no longer needed such directions, but, again, unable to stop himself from giving them. Without looking at him, Jacey had grasped the rim of the cup between two fingers and holding it like the wing of a dead fly dropped it out the window. J.C. slapped him hard on the back of the head. Jacey scrabbled with both hands at the windowsill as if he would flee, then dropped back into the seat, and staring straight ahead, began to cry. Anger, sharp and demanding, rose in J.C., and he would have struck again—resisting child!—but the teenagers across the lot were looking at him and they made him afraid. The image of his wife lying across his knees on his father's steps flashed in his mind, and he realized what he had not realized then: that he would not have stopped beating her if his father had not prevented him; he would have kept on, lashing her with the belt, then with fists, bone against bone, until he pummeled the life out of her. With trembling hands he gathered the postcards from the dashboard, tore them into halves, quarters, eighths, and dropped them out the window. He got out of the car and went into the store and bought another chocolate malt. Later he did not remember bringing it back to his son, remembered only thinking, Yes, I will buy a railroad, a railroad, but when four hours later they turned into the drive at Canaan—the streetlights turning the honeysuckle flowers along the fence yellow—he noticed that his son still held the drink, capped in plastic, untouched, between his thin legs, and he wondered if anything he could buy or own or subdue would ever help.

She had come to his room early and gotten him. This was last year when he had only been twelve a day, just beginning to be frightened by

202

the wide world. The sun, at seven-thirty, laid narrow yellow parallelo-grams on the floor, and she walked through them in a skirt the color of fertilizer sacks, held up with a long bunched and tied purple scarf, and shook him awake. He raised his arms like a lover and she came down to him, lay across him with her cool—almost damp, from the spring—face pressed against his. He listened to her breathe into the pillow and thought, O, my, wonderful, I dreamed I was flying over a big patch of bamboo. She kissed him, the kisses first noisy and wet then silent, trailing into faint pressure of softness, rose and said, Get up, we're going down the river. He bounded out of the bed and dressed, telling her of his dream, in which he had soared on gray wings so high he could see the sky between him and the feathery tops of bamboo far below. She smiled at him in the way she always did—a smile full of secret knowledge, delight in him—touched his face with fingers which always seemed to have just gone blind and hurried him down the stairs.

They drove in a farm jeep to the river. It was barely fall, the fiber was full on the cotton plants; along the road the goldenrod bloomed among the willowy wands of dog fennel. There was mist near the trees, and he wondered if this was what the ground looked like during the Civil War, tried to see the butternut soldiers cautiously stepping from the pine woods. Stonewall Jackson died on such a day, he thought, shot in the shoulder, drifting with fever. "Cross over the river," he said aloud, "and lie down in the shade of the trees," and he laughed at the connection as they bounced at forty miles an hour along the double-track farm road into the cool, dewy woods of Lazarus Swamp. A woodpecker hammered high up and the linked concussions drifted over the woods, leaving little concentric rings of sound behind.

The loaded canoe was pulled up below a clearing at the edge of Billy's Lake, a half-mile-long widened stretch of water that faded into cy-presses downstream. She hustled him into it, over a picnic basket that smelled of lemons, into the bow, quickly, shooing him with her hands, as if they were late. She took the stern and shoved them out into the faint current.

As she began her stroke she said, "The I is not I, the you is not you, the they is not they."

He said, "What—Mama, are you crazy?"

She said, "I've heard that you can drive a dog to ecstasy by saying its name to it over and over. Do you think that's true?"

He said, "I don't know."

She said his name, "Jacey Jacey Jacey Jacey Jacey."

"You think I'm a dog? Elizabeth, Elizabeth?"

"I want to drive you crazy with delight."

Patches of clear water alternated with stretches in which the woods bunched in on the river. They spent the morning paddling for a while, then getting out to haul the canoe around or over obstructions: downed oaks, lightning-crashed poplar tops, wayward alders. Kingfishers darted over the water in the open places, feinting and slipping over the surface, their dark blue backs catching light. Near the banks schools of minnows surged away from their silver shining bow.

He didn't wonder why they had come, luxuriated in the connective silence that held between them. When they crossed into Florida she raised her paddle and struck the sign (FLORIDA STATE LINE) that was tied into a sagging fence strung over the stream. The fence hummed and he could see the line of wire it angled off of on the bank catch the vibration, hump and buck, pass the blow into blackberry bushes. She had tied her skirt into a knot around her waist; looking back he saw the whole length of her tanned legs, the smooth white of her panties.

They stopped for lunch at the first of the chain of springs that hung like fobs along the river, medallions of crystal water that fed through brief outlet streams into the river. They pulled up on a sandbar backed by willows, got out and waded up the spring stream to a narrow shelf off a sandy beach under clay banks that were the color of a ripe orange. She fed him pineapple sandwiches, hunks of Stilton cheese and green seedless grapes. "I would rather have scuppernongs," she told him, "but it's too late for local grapes."

He ate the sandwiches, enjoying the tart sweetness of the pineapple. It was as if he had not come awake fully; the sun slipped rays along the bases of cypress trees, the leaves of a holly growing on the rim of the spring shook as if a bird had just flown out. She took off her clothes and swam in the clear water, diving deep over and over as if there were something on the bottom to retrieve. She came up smiling, not bothering to press the water out of her eyes, looking at him, her hair sleeked back flat and straight. He had seen her naked all his life, her boldness that he kidded her about now, didn't think twice about. Then she crawled out of the spring, crawled on her hands and knees and lay down beside him on the packed white sand. There were black bits of decayed moss on the sand,

and a few of last year's leaves, but she didn't brush them away. She lay on her side facing him. Her breasts, which were the size of a large man's cupped palms, sagged together, sinking downward. If he had been twenty he would have thought how our bodies drag us down into the earth. When he was twenty he would think this all the time, remembering her end, how she could not soar. Who knows when stillness comes into our life for the first time—stillness, not the sudden awe a child feels when at the circus twenty clowns explode from a tiny car, but stillness as if from our bedroom window late at night we see ourselves walking across the moonlit lawn crying. She said, "I want you to look at me."

"I've already seen you," he said and flicked a grape at her.

"I want you to look again."

She pushed up on her knees facing him and took her breasts in her hands. She squeezed them outward so that her saddle-colored nipples stuck out between circles of thumb and forefinger. They came erect, faint red appeared in the brown. Her stomach was as flat as a boy's, and her hipbones protruded like places where wings had been broken off. She pressed her breasts flat against her chest, then ran her hands hard down her body (her breasts jumped lightly upward as she released them) and plunged, wove, her fingers into the glistening, secret hair.

"I watched you playing with Sandra," she said. "You told her you wanted to fuck her. Do you know what that means?"

"Mama! I know what it means. They told me at camp."

She leaned back on her heels, cranked back until her shoulders touched the sand. Her fingers tugged at her pubic hair as if she would pluck it out. "Look," she said, watching him along the arch of her body as her fingers spread her sex. The outer lips were colorless and thin; inside was a rose. With spread fingers she held it open and plunged the middle finger of her other hand deeply in. "It goes in," she said, "comes out, goes in." She touched herself lightly at the top of the wound; her fingers stirred something there—quickly, quicker—with the loose wrist motion of beating an egg. Her head fell back, her neck stretched until he could see the shape of her Adam's apple, barely, like a lump under thick cloth. She said, "Oh, oh, oh—I *feel* it." He put his hands over his face, stared at her through spread fingers. I have seen this before, terrible god. He said, "I want to go home," and sprang to his feet as she began to moan, as she arched up, her buttocks leaving the ground, sprang up as she began to whinny, the finger moving faster in smaller, harder circles,

205

her eyes rolling back, spittle collecting at the corners of her mouth, crying sounds that were the sounds of nightmares, ripping at her body, body rising, straining off the dead, stinking leaves, both hands stabbing at once—sprang up into paralysis—stranded, O, help me!—as she sang out in one mad, indecipherable cry, her head snapping up behind staring monstrous eyes—sprang up screaming, "I want to go *now*, I want to go *now,* I want to go *now*"—screamed, fainted.

When he thought about it later, when he could think about it later, trenched in Martha's body while the lights of New York City held steady for miles uptown, what amazed him was not that when she shook him awake she was already fully clothed, the skirt long again down her legs, but that he so willingly got up and went with her, followed her back to the slim canoe, got in and paddled out onto the sleek, sun-cleansed river, paddled downstream, bowstroke, toward the rendezvous, she explained as he listened to the punctuating *chunk* of her paddle behind him, at Haven's.

Late in the afternoon as the sun was going down red as a peach behind pines, they rounded a wide bend and came to Haven's landing. Haven had taped a sign onto one of the boathouse posts which read: TRAVELERS EXIT HERE. They stopped paddling and let the canoe drift down toward the dock. The last rays of sunlight caught in the highest wisteria vines along the old brick walls of the house, and the slate roof shone as if it had been rained on. Two black Labradors chased each other on the lawn; when they saw the canoe they bounded down to the water and swam out to them. Perhaps Jacey decided then that he would never go back home: he would never go back home even if he went.

All this happened on the day after he turned twelve. The chinaberry leaves growing close to the country front porches in south Georgia had already turned bright yellow. The last cotton waited for the picker. Grief is a desperate hand, losing its grip little by little.

14 She could answer all his questions, she thought, gravely arranging J.C.'s slight treasures on her bureau. The morning sun streaked the room with a light that seemed to carry taste and smell with it. She had come here months ago—after a night at the expensive resort hotel on the north side of the island—and the room had by now become hers. It reminded her of her bedroom in Hawaii, though it was smaller and painted light blue. It was the light, she thought, the same light she remembered from the islands. A girlish light, she said to herself and laughed. She placed the last of his gifts—a button from his Navy pea jacket—on the bureau and went out through the jalousied doors onto the balcony. The sun was high already—here it seemed to leap into the midpoint of the sky—and she spread her arms to take it in. Always, she thought, no matter what, sunlight and water would save her. And the simplicity of this kind of life.

She gathered dried bathing suit and towels from the balcony rail, looked to see if Marcel was around—he was not—and turned back to the room. The way the light spilled across the floor made her stop. She loved where she was, she thought, loved it better than anything. It was her way to fill the momentary present with everything. Each moment that brought her pleasure seemed to be the greatest moment of her life. Skipping across the water in an open boat, climbing in the dry hills behind the town, talking late into the night with Marcel, picking the colorful flowers that grew along the shore road—each moment, in the moment of its happening, seemed to make her life into a feast of joy. Yes, feast, she said to herself, laughing—aren't you something?—and threw the suit and towels ahead of her into the room. The floor was covered with a straw mat, contained bed, bureau, desk and cane chair and a small table and lamp next to the bed. The floor was made of small ceramic tiles, fired dark blue. She followed the clothes in and sat down on the edge of the bed. What energy it took to live! She had begun to sleep later these days, waking only after the sun was full in the sky. All her life a tiredness had come over her from time to time. She chafed and strained against the life she lived and she had to run. It was the restlessness, she knew, as much as it was the need for rest. Such a need had brought her here. Seeking some new plunder maybe, some fresh ease. Marcel, eighteen-year-old son of the hotel proprietor, a conch fisherman, came to her in the night. She liked to listen to his earnest chatter. There was a time when she would have been impatient with his still-childish dreams, but she was able to tolerate them now. Maybe, she thought, she was changing into something else. Maybe she would calm down now. She had loved always to just look. As a child she had sat on the end of the public dock near her family's cottage at Folly Beach and, wrapped in towels and with a hat pulled down low, watched for hours as the gulls spun and fell in the clear blue sky. She hadn't even needed a book. She had sat as if in a trance, cocooned in heat, her eyes slowly blinking, watching gulls and the light on the water, perhaps a sailboat edging the horizon, watched, until the moment of impulse came and she rose and did something. Once, walking back up the dock, she had passed a young man fishing who had laid his catch—half a dozen striped bass—in a row along the boards beside his chair. She had never seen the man before—he was stocky and wore a green basketball shirt—but she stopped and without a thought in her head picked the six dead fish up one by one and tossed them over the rail into the water. The man stared at her with his mouth open, too shocked to speak. She remembered the anger in his eyes and the disbelieving face and that he hadn't challenged her. She had been fourteen and it had been a lesson in the possibilities of audacity, if she needed any such lesson. She had walked away down the sunny dock, free from reproach.

She scratched bug bites on her bare legs, got up and went into the bathroom to look for ointment. David McCracken, owner of the *Vestal Wind,* a sixty-foot trimaran, wanted to take her with him on his return sail to St. Thomas. He ran charter out of Charlotte Amalie and had fallen in love with her in the casino at the Wild Tern. David was a tall florid man in his mid-fifties who had been a bomber pilot in the war. A full chicken colonel, he told her, who had retired when he wasn't promoted to general. Black Widow bombers his planes were called, and she imagined spiders in the sky, red glowing bellies. He was another man who wanted her to do something. She had met him in the casino her first night on St. Guillaume. She had come in that afternoon on the plane from St. Thomas and taken a room in the big Wild Tern complex on the north side. The first thing she did was shake out all her clothes. Piece by piece she took them from the bag and shook them free of whatever dust and smoke she thought they might contain. She did it out on the balcony, which overlooked a crescent of yellow beach that was ringed by hotel cottages peeking out of thick stands of hibiscus and coconut palms. Her clothes couldn't have been touched by the fire and Lacey hadn't been in them, but she wanted to put them on with the feeling that they were soaked in the air and light of a place no one she knew had ever seen. She had bought a white cotton bikini in the hotel store and she put that on, something new entirely.

She stood before the long mirror wondering how many more years she could wear a bikini. Probably ten, she thought, looking down at her body, which was firm and tan. She had heard that as a woman became older her body became more like a man's: the waist thickened, the hips narrowed, shoulders broadened, a mustache appeared. She wondered if that was true and looked at her face in the mirror. The fine fuzz below her ears was still blond, no darker than it had ever been. She wondered at her wondering, thinking of the women she had known and their aging, their fear of slackened bodies, the loss they mourned. She had no fear of becoming old: her mother, dead in her forties, had not lived to see any diminishment of her beauty; Elizabeth believed that she would have been beautiful always, as her father still was, lean and erect, his face unmarked at sixty. She pressed her hands down her breasts and stomach, against the narrow bones of her hips to feel the resistance of her flesh. It was good to feel it, good to come back into her body. She gripped her thighs and re-garded the white marks her fingers left. Good, good, good. She wanted to live forever, still wanted that.

And then, standing in front of the ornate mirror, she felt tiredness fall over her, like a thin net. She grabbed towel and suntan lotion, her straw hat with the long pink silk scarf band, and ran out to the beach. In the soft sand behind the tideline she dropped the belongings, raced down the slope and into the green, clear water. Out on the horizon were other islands, small and misty, nearly blue. She swam for twenty minutes up and down the beach, driving herself through the frail waves of the la-goon-calmed surf before climbing out and lying down to sleep, ex-hausted, among her new belongings.

That night, in a fresh, loose blue dress, after a room-service dinner of rock lobster and spinach salad on her balcony, she descended the wide gold hotel stairs to the casino. The room, large as a warehouse, was nearly dark, lighted only by green-shaded copper lamps placed at the gaming tables. The carpet, which around the tables she saw was dark blue, faded to black in the spaces between them.

She signed for a drink at the bar and drifted among the tables. Arms in black satiny tuxedos reached into the light to gather cards and chips. She had never been in a casino before and she was delighted. The tired-ness that had threatened to overwhelm her—that had—was gone. She knew, as she moved among the tables, that she was being looked at and she held her eyes away long enough to let the glances become stares, and then looked. She had always enjoyed catching men looking at her.

One man, tall with short hair brushed harshly back, leaned against a blackjack table staring. She turned and stared back, but he did not look away, only grinned impishly and ran his eyes up and down her body. She liked him looking, and when he moved toward her she waited with expectancy and a fresh excitement. How simple it was, a lover like a new dress.

He bought her another drink and taught her how to play blackjack. His name, he said, was David McCracken, and he was a charter captain. He had strong, long-fingered hands that reminded her of Haven's and a way of jutting his chin when he talked, which Elizabeth could see he was not aware of, and which made him boyish and vulnerable and contrasted with the stiffness of his shoulders and his arrogant, martial manner. As they sat at a small table at the edge of the gaming room she had an urge to unbutton the bodice of her dress and expose herself to him. She knew when she thought it that she could frighten him, pierce easily the armor of self-possession and control he wore. And as she realized this she felt rise in her a familiar compassion and tenderness for the frailty behind the mask and she reached across the table and stroked his hand, looked into his eyes and said, "Won't you take me out into the air now. Won't you take me down to the beach."

He rose immediately, raised his hands as she turned as if he were placing a shawl upon her shoulders and guided her from the room. They walked out to the beach, where the moon had stirred up light in the raked sand. She let him take her hand and began to tell him of Canaan, of her walks at night in the fields and of the graveyard in the woods behind the house, of the way fall tracked leaves into the front hall. She would rather not have spoken of that place—though not for a wish to hide any-thing—just, she thought, because she would rather hear him speak of himself; she wanted to float in another world, devised by some-one else, and she felt, too, the eager girlishness come over her, the desire—momentary, incidental—to impress this man, to bend his interest toward her, and for a moment she was unsettled, unsure of herself. She stopped and let his hand go. They stood in front of the darkened beach bar. A light offshore wind rattled the dried-coconut-frond roof. She moved a step away from him, feeling the wind over her shoulder. She raised her hair to it and looked out to see where it seemed the wind chipped the tops of the phosphorescent waves, and she thought of the wind blowing up the spines of all these islands, touching them all at the same time, like a hand spread open, uniting them.

"I wish I could be everywhere at once," she said and leaned into him.

"What do you mean?" he asked and put his arm around her shoulder.

"I mean I would like to be here and over there, too"—she indicated the lights of the islands across the water—"and out at sea, and in Georgia and Charleston (which is where I'm from) and down there, lapping around in the waves."

"Lapping around," he repeated. "Yes, I've felt that way."

If he had not, she didn't mind. "You're a cordial man," she said a few moments later as they walked up the beach toward her cottage. They made their way along a sand path cut between moon-white coral beds. The rock had a roiled look as if it had been stirred and frozen. Large oleanders grew below the raised porch of her cottage, their opened flowers faded pink in the moonlight.

"I wish it would rain tonight," she said, picking a flower as they passed.

"It hasn't rained for a hundred and three days," he answered, "not on this island."

"On which island has it rained?"

"On all the Windward Islands."

"Maybe you will take me there."

"I would be delighted."

He was delighted when, in the light of the lamp by her bed, she stripped for him. She refused to let him touch her until all her clothes were off and then only after she had stood silent before him for minutes while he reclined on pillows on the bed, fully clothed, looking at her.

"I like you looking at me," she told him. "I like you with all your clothes on looking at me."

She turned to the mirror and stood a moment lost in her reflection. "Can you see me?" she asked.

"Yes. I can."

She pressed her hands over her breasts, flattening them. "Have you ever wondered how it is to be a woman?" she asked.

"No, never."

"I know what it's like to be a man. I watch my son and my husband and they teach me."

211

"How is it?"

"Like this."

From the table she took her hat, swept her hair up and put it on, squared her shoulders, slouched forward on one leg and cupped imaginary testicles. "Hey, baby," she said in her deepest voice, "you want some of this action?"

"Good Lord."

She slouched toward him rolling on her heels as she had seen the Hawaiian cowboys do. "I got eight inches of the best and it's all yours," she growled. "If you can take it."

"Your husband's like that?"

"Rougher. He likes to do it in the river, with the fish biting him." She threw herself on the bed beside him. "Does it embarrass you?" she asked.

"A little."

"I'll stop. Now you take your clothes off."

Curled up, the pillow between her legs, she watched him undress. He had a paunch, small and compact like a bowling ball; hair grew in a line from the tangle in his groin to another tangle on his chest. He was half erect.

It took her a long time to build his erection the rest of the way. With the sheets thrown back and all the lights on she worked over him, caressing and sucking, encouraging him with delicate fingers—carefully saying nothing, giving him the admiration of her delight in him until finally, groaning, he threw her back and took her, banging up hard into her.

He was grateful as she knew he would be, happy; he grinned at her like a boy as he dressed (she would not let him spend the night with her) and chattered of plans: he would take her on his boat to St. Thomas; maybe she would like to go with him tomorrow to the docks; he knew the islands well, there were many small islands that were uninhabited (no fresh water) and he would take her to them; she must see the way the sea changed color and how the flying fish flew over the bows.

She listened with slackening interest, thinking of how she had concealed herself from everyone simply by living openly, without restraint, going without apology for whatever brightness caught her fancy. It is such a life, she thought, such a life: not provisional, but permanent, a

212

way of being that would continue until she died. But then as she thought this, a shadow seemed to move over her mind and she remembered the fire and the beating that went before it. She shied, shifted in the bed, almost asked David, who sat at the dressing table tying his shoes, to stay the night. She pushed herself up (still naked) and touched his shoulder.

"Is there a town here?" she asked.

"Yes. On the south end of the island. My boat's there. I'll show you."

"Fine," she said. "I'll go there tomorrow."

She turned the lights off, kissed him and let him go, watched his shadow disappear beyond the cane window blinds, fell back on the bed. She could, she knew, make a life wherever she found herself. She would not make one, however, in this hotel. She wanted to smell different smells than this, taste different tastes. She had an impulse to get up and go walk on the beach, but as she rose she felt the tiredness that had overwhelmed her earlier come back, and she lay down again, pulled the roiled sheets around her and slipped, without hindrance, into sleep.

She got the tube of bug ointment out of the medicine cabinet and came back into the room. She had not been in the resort hotel when David McCracken came the next morning to fetch her. She had risen early, checked out and taken a taxi to the windy town on the south end of the island. The town was a dozen streets running like grooves down the arm of a peninsula that separated two mild lagoons. At its sea end the peninsula bloomed out and upward into a blocky headland called Goat's Head. The headland was covered with pine and myrtle scrub through which shone the white coral rocks that were the skeleton of the island. The town was a jumble of stucco-and-tin houses, painted in sun-bleached pastels. The government buildings had red tile roofs, and small brass plaques were set in the walls beside the front entrances. She arrived in the dry season, and the coconut palms were yellowed by heat and lack of rain. The wind blew always, vivid and steady; after a while she went long stretches without noticing it.

She took a room in the St. Cecilia Hotel overlooking the east lagoon. The hotel was across the street from the L'Azure restaurant and the white-fronted customs house. The street was paved in concrete and had curbs that were hewn from coral; in the rock beneath her feet as she waited to cross she could pick out the cells and carapaces of the animals that had built the island. David had followed her to the town, found her in the dim bar of L'Azure where she sat her first afternoon looking out the screened back door at children chasing a dog with sea grape whips. She allowed him to come up to her room, where they made love until dark in the narrow bed she had pushed under the south window to catch the cross breeze. He was not on a charter, had come down on the plane from Charlotte Amalie to solicit business, and he left the next morning after promising to take her on a voyage around the un-inhabited rock islands that nested along the outer reef in the mouth of the bay.

He had become by now a fixture, sailing or flying in every few weeks to spend an evening or a couple of days with her. She would not let him stay the night in her room ("I need to brush clean and get myself back," she told him) but, as with her husband, she made love to him with a fervor and dedication that thrilled him. He taught her to scuba-dive and to crew the trimaran, how to work a sextant and how to read the reefs and the shallow waters around the islands. He did not ask her about her home life and became agitated and resentful when she spoke of Canaan and her people there. His little primal quest, she realized, was to bend her so far away from Georgia that her former life slipped her mind and she tumbled defenseless and grateful, moistly into his. She did not particularly mind his determination to woo her—it left her free to think of things besides romance—and anyway she had Marcel to talk to.

She waited for Marcel now as she dabbed the yellow ointment onto the bites on her legs. They had gone out last night after coconut crabs. The crabs, which lived on land and looked like fierce, purple armored spi-ders, but which in fact were timid and vegetarian, were a delicacy of the islands and sold for five dollars apiece in the local market. There was also a small handicraft traffic in the crabs, which were occasionally injected with formaldehyde, shellacked and glued to a square of plywood, their tearing claws fixed in an upraised and menacing position. These were sold to tourists. The white meat of the claws was a delicacy, but even more was the gooey orange matter that filled the abdomens, which the islanders cooked over an open fire, split open and ate with spoons, like porridge.

Marcel had wanted the crabs for himself. They had gone out first in the afternoon, crossing the island in Marcel's old jeep to the western side, where there was a grove of coconut palms below a crumbling headland that had been the lead edge of the old French airstrip. Along the roads the African flame trees were in bloom, the horizontal branches burning with clusters of orange flowers. The trailing, viny bougainvillea piled its heaps of purple blossoms in bushes along the road, and there were the bell flowers of frangipani and the sweet yellow-and-white blossoms of plumeria. As in Hawaii, all the flowers were imported, brought in by colonizers who wished to strew a little color and scent among the rachitic, dusty green of pine and myrtle. Her sense of the recaptured past had fled quickly on this dry, windy island. St. Guillaume was not high as Hawaii had been; there were no misted mountains and the Caribbean was a sea that seemed built of patches and streaks of blue and white and green (she could see from a hilltop), unlike the blue-black fathomless Polynesian ocean. Even the froggy-leaved breadfruit trees were imported, as were the coconuts and all the other palms except for palmettos, which were native to Georgia, too. There were native flowering plants, passion vine and coral pea and the long runners of native sea grapes stretched latitudinally down the slope of beaches, but they were pale compared to her memory of the multitudinous paradise she remembered in Hawaii. Pawpaws and papayas grew in the yards of the islanders and banana trees shaded the privies in the back streets of the town. Pawpaws, she reminded herself, grew along the fence rows at Canaan, and Uncle Eustace had three or four banana trees that he religiously dug up each November and kept wrapped in burlap in the basement until they could be transplanted back into the yard in late March.

She was dissatisfied—peeved, she said to herself—and unhappy with her dissatisfaction. Wherever she had gone she had been able to delight herself with what she found. Her life in Canaan had taught her to love the ground she stood on, its variety of vegetation, its contours, and she was angry as much as anything at how her life in south Georgia in her seven years there had begun to take over her mind. I used to be a woman in love with the ocean, she reminded herself on her first climb up Goat's Head as she cursed a trailing bramble caught in her skirt. From the top of the headland the sea had looked dull and lifeless (it was a day of low dirty-cotton clouds) and she was not high enough up (she decided) to feel the endlessness of the Pacific. If some of this reaction came from something like guilt, or more probably from her displeasure at having her life interrupted by J.C.'s belt, she did not entertain such ideas. There were after all new measures to take, even on an island that seemed always about to veer into desert, and she would find them and take them as she could.

There was, after all, Marcel.

She fumbled the top on the ointment, stretched back on the bed, raised her legs and pointed her toes straight up at the ceiling. The yellow dabs of ointment shone on her skin. If her legs had been any shorter they would have been heavy, too meaty for men's dreams. The calves, like her father's, were full, maybe a shade too full, but the length of her legs—thirty-two inches crotch to ankle—and the slenderness of her thighs made men's heads turn. Marcel, careless in his bravado, secure in his animal possession of her, made her show him her legs in public, or almost public, places. He liked to stand in the hall within the sight of chattering tourists and have her, just out of others' sight inside the room, raise her skirt to her waist. "Show me your legs," he would say as they crossed the crushed coral parking lot at the Wild Tern, and without a thought, as they ambled between rented Fiats and Citroens, she would hoist the light skirt into a wad at her waist and step ahead of him to let him see her from the back. He liked to have her lie on the public beach with her top unfastened and rise up, as if forgetting herself, so that her breasts dangled free for an instant for the Negro children and the yam and beer vendors to see. She had been all her life more than willing to shuck her clothes (still swam naked in Yellow Spring) but she took delight in Marcel's insistent postadolescent randiness and so when on the secluded beaches of the west side he pulled her suit from her as they whooped in the lisping surf she pretended to be modest and frightened, exciting them both to a frenzy of desire as he led her by the hand dripping and naked to the blanket spread on the grass below the cliffs.

She had seen Marcel for the first time the morning after her arrival at the St. Cecilia when as she did her stretching exercises on the balcony she noticed a teenage boy tormenting a rooster on the terrace below. The boy was holding the small red-and-green rooster in both hands and spitting in its face. She called down for him to stop that, but he had only turned and, in complete possession of himself, as if he had been waiting for her to speak to him, grinned at her. He lifted the rooster as if to present it to her and then looking straight at her he slowly brought the bird to his face and took its head in his mouth. "You little dickens!" she cried and picked up a bottle of suntan lotion to throw at him. He held the rooster up by its feet and yelled, "Fighter!" She didn't understand what he meant, but she lowered the bottle. "You leave that thing alone," she said loudly and glared at him. "He's a fighting rooster," the boy called back, "in training." Then he thrust the bird under his arm and disappeared into the hotel.

She saw him again on other mornings—he was, she learned, the son of the hotel's fat and self-haranguing proprietor—but usually from a greater distance. He did not alter his training techniques, but he carried them on farther off—down on the beach where he leaned against the half-buried carcass of an old Buick and threatened and cuffed the quick little rooster into fighting fierceness. She met him when two weeks later he brought her first letters.

She had forgotten to expect mail (though she had, from the first day, sent postcards). She dreamed of Canaan at night, saw herself standing on the bedroom porch calling down to friends whose names she couldn't remember and who never seemed to heed her imperative cries. These persons, men and women in their thirties and forties, were dressed for a party and they crossed the lawn on the way to someplace she knew but couldn't call to mind. She seemed to view them with blinders on as they moved, like travelers hurrying to catch a train, across the sunny, freshly sprinkled lawn, unable to tell where they had come from or where they were going. Always (for she dreamed the dream or its equivalent many times) she sensed an urgency in their passage and in herself, but just as she could not say where they were headed, so she could not figure what it was she wanted to stop them for. The dreams left her with a hangover, a sense of otherworldliness and vague alarm that persisted well into the morning.

She learned to take the mornings slow, slower even than the leisurely breakfasts she enjoyed on the terrace at Canaan, and it was during this morning time, after her exercises and the breakfast of pineapple and native melon brought up to her room by the proprietor's wife, a thin, sallow woman with a lisp, that she wrote her postcards to her husband and the other Burdettes. The postcards, she knew, were acts of concealment; St. Guillaume did not have the air of lost wild paradise that she had found in Hawaii, and though the sea, washed with light like a Monet, was beautiful, it did not have the deep blue power of the Pacific that had strengthened her in her twenties. But she did not say this to her husband or to any other Burdette. Instead her cards were energetic recreations of the island sights, of towheaded children fishing with hand lines from the city docks, of the kinds and colors of fishes the sporting captains arrayed on their cleaning tables at the end of the day, of the old women in red and blue turbans selling flowers before the front gate of the Wild Tern. Writing the cards made her feel better and, not seeking sustenance from family missives, she did not expect replies. She was surprised when two weeks after her arrival Marcel appeared at her door bearing letters from her husband and her son.

The letters were not all he was holding. In his left hand, that he extended toward her, he held a crab that looked like some nightmare vision of a killer spider, dark purple, showing white in the joints, its pimply carapace so shiny it looked greased. She stumbled back gasping, feeling for the first time in her life that she might faint. He entered the room holding the beast out to her, and she saw that it was trussed in strips of what looked like inner-tube rubber. "For your pleasure," he said and held out crab and letters. She sat down on the bed, then jumped up and took the letters from him. She turned her back to regain her composure. "What is that thing?" she asked over her shoulder.

"Coconut crab. A delicacy."

She turned around and smiled at him. He was short and slender and had the darkest skin of any blond she had ever seen. He would have been beautiful except for his nose, which was large and hooked like a comic Arab's. It made his bright green eyes seem closer together. And he was posing like a body-builder. He had hooked the crab in the waistband of his shorts and stood (Mr. Statue, she thought) arms crooked up, biceps flexed, chest expanded. Through the strap-shouldered T-shirt his chest muscles were as round as the stones she had once seen in a creekbed in Maine. Through a full breath he looked at her with a fierce Comanche stare that—she was surprised—excited her. Then his upright fists began to quiver and she grinned and reached through the dare of his face and touched him on the forearm and felt the flesh ripple the way a horse's skin will and said, "That's beautiful—how old are you?"

He relaxed with a rush of expelled breath. "Eighteen, and I can open a coconut with my bare hands."

"It's the kind of thing I look for in a person."

"Wait here," he said and started to leave.

"Hold on—take your crab."

"That's for you."

"What could I do with it? I don't like spiders."

"It's a coconut crab. Five dollars American in the market."

She realized she would have to take it or risk offending him. "Okay."

He bolted out of the room and she heard him running down the hall, his hand, or fist, popping the wall, like a fighter working a speed bag, and then the sound of his hard heels hitting the steps as he descended the stairs.

He came back so quickly that she thought he must have had the coconut shelved somewhere for just such an occasion.

"You could try it on the crab," she said as he held the nut up balanced on his open palm like a shot put.

"What?"

"Just an idea. Show me what you can do."

It was a green coconut, just turning yellow at one end, and the plates of the husk had begun to buckle slightly. He went to work on it, balancing it on his chest so he could tear at it with both hands. It reminded her of Delight's bear tearing at a pork-and-beans can, and despite herself, perhaps, she thought, as a result of her strong dreams, she was struck with a wave of nostalgia. She looked at the two letters tossed on the bed and thought: In a few minutes I will be lying there reading them. The thought made her angry and she slapped the mattress beside the letters so they flipped over, obscuring the addresses. Marcel—that was his name: she had heard his mother calling him—tore at the fibrous nut. The slapping had rolled the crab on its back: its long antennae slowly tested the air around its upended legs. Marcel grunted, "Agh, agh, agh," and tore the coconut steadily down to its bald white core. He held it up.

"Bravo," she said and lightly clapped.

"I'm not finished."

He turned the nut so that the three yellowish eyes were uppermost and plunged his forefinger through each one. Juice spurted, dashing his shirt. He pushed two fingers through the holes, raised the nut and struck it against the heel of his left hand. It split with a mealy crack and juice spurted onto the floor and the bed. He held the torn fruit up. "See?"

"Quite nice," she said. "If you're lucky you can get a job at the fair."

219

He ripped the nut in two and handed the larger piece to her. He showed how with her fingernail to scoop out the pale, barely congealed meat. It was cool and sweet and dissolved on her tongue, and it reminded her of Hawaii when Rufino would bring her breakfast on a tray. Kaui had lopped off the tops of coconuts with a machete. The flesh was so loose in the nut that she could lap it out with her tongue. "This is the best time I've had," she said when she finished. "This is the first time I've gotten what I came here for."

"There is much more," the boy said, eyeing her over the rind of his half. She crossed the room, took a handkerchief from her dresser drawer and wiped his face and chest clean. "You are an audacious boy," she said.

"What is audacious?"

"Like me. You jump ahead without looking."

"That's good?"

"It's good enough for government work." She laughed. "I want you to go away now so I can read these letters, but if you come back this afternoon you can take me out to the beach and show me what this dry little island has to offer."

He went away then, first picking up the pieces of shattered fruit. He took the crab with him after she pointed out that she had no way to cook it. "My mother will prepare it for you," he said. "Are you afraid of it?"

"Not so much."

"It can't hurt you. *Regardez.*"

Grasping it by the gathered legs, like a bouquet, he held the crab up and touched its back to her throat. She held herself rigid as the hard, pimpled skin pressed against her. She did not look down but she could feel the eyestalks moving on her, the feeble brush of antennae. "See?" he said pulling the crab back. "It's safe."

She let her breath out and smiled weakly. "Maybe it takes practice."

"If you have the time."

"Possibly I do."

And she did, she would, she thought later as she lay on the bed crying the first tears she had cried since her mother died, holding her husband's letter, which was only two spare sentences: "The weather is dry. I saw a woman who looked like you," feeling that her tears were not for her husband or her son or for any life she had left behind, but simply tears of fatigue, tears of a general, ritual sadness, tears for the blue

220

booming sky out her window, tears for audacious, muscular boys, tears for all the travelers who would never arrive, for all those who must keep moving no matter what.

He came back in the afternoon and drove her in his Army surplus jeep to a deserted beach on the west side of the island where under a wind-drifting flame tree she fucked him until he cried like a child.

She sat up on the bed and picked her notebook off the table. The bug ointment didn't stop the bites' itching. The mosquitoes here were as bad as the ones at Canaan, but only if you were in places where the wind didn't reach. She uncapped her pen, turned the notebook to a clean page and wrote, "There's no birdsong on this island, but the air anyway is full of wings and cries. I was thinking this morning of how in the fall the leaves sneak into the house. I come downstairs and the front hall is strewn with them as if they've blown through cracks in the door. Isn't it amazing that you can see birds all your life and never once touch them, beyond a feather picked up in the grass? Maybe that's why men hunt them, to hold in their hands for a moment that winged life."

She blotted the words lightly with her fingertips, glanced out the window and wrote again, "Everywhere I go the gulls follow. I have even seen gulls at Canaan sailing high over the river like lost beings. Fifty miles—that's the distance from Canaan to the Gulf—must be a short flight for them, but it is far enough for the landbound to forget there ever was such a thing as an ocean. On a clear day I will look up startled at a cry and see the white wings sailing and I will feel a yearning so intense that it seems only some trick of fate or some little broken part keeps me from soaring up there with them."

It startled her to think this, and she put the notebook down. She had not acknowledged such feeling to herself, certainly to no one else. She had a reputation as an incorrigible, clever adventuress—at least she thought she did—not as a woman of deep feeling. There was though, now, a crack in her life. This flight was, she realized well into the fifth month of her stay, no short hop away from pressures at home. Had she come here to stay? No, that was not what she had done. She had secured herself, as she always did one way or another, with Marcel and David, with her notebook, which contained by now the names of native animals and plants, the islands of the Windward and Leeward chains, lists of the different businesses in St. Guillaume. She could cook a coconut crab now, in a pot filled with coconut milk and onions, or directly on a fire. Just as in Hawaii she knew the names of the reef fishes, which ones were poisonous always and which ones were poisonous only during certain seasons of the year. She even spoke a little French, which she practiced on Marcel and his parents and on the proprietor and patrons of L'Azure. Her money came by draft from her father's bank in Charleston. But she had not come to stay. When would she leave? She didn't know. Her son wanted to know, though her husband never mentioned it. He didn't mention anything anymore, only sent some article of memory or enticement folded in a sheet of white stationery. The small gifts were a kind of braille that only she could finger sense into. The button from his Navy pea jacket; a lock of hair from her horse, Missa; a scrap of ribbon that had wrapped the pair of binoculars she had given him for his birthday last January—all of them contained messages, questions and imperatives, for her. She had no answers for him—as she pretended—only the bustly postcards she sent off several times weekly from the brick-fronted post office down the street. The rainy season had come here but at Canaan they were picking the cotton under clear hot skies. She could picture Uncle Ransome raving from the window of his truck at a broken-down machine. And Jack and Mattie in the kitchen canning the last of the tomatoes. In a little over two months her son would be thirteen; why didn't she go back for his birthday? Why didn't she? She wrote him regularly, sending the letters care of Jack and Mattie to avoid her husband's prying eyes. And he wrote her back, speaking to her still in the guileless way of a prepubescent child. In the beginning—in Hawaii, she meant—she had not wondered what sort of mother she would be and she had not minded being the sort of mother she was. She had let Jacey run naked so often that he was eventually barred from entering certain stores because he was liable, without warning, to do his business on the floor. She had to housebreak him like a dog, leading him from whatever puddled spot he was relieving himself in to the bathroom.

She touched the green cloth cover of her notebook to draw her thoughts away. She had pasted a Matisse drawing of a clown on the cover, and the ribald, hatted face smiled at her. Rooley had given her the drawing, the afternoon she made love to him the first time in a litter of paint rags in the attic of his isolato brick house. Making love, as far as she was concerned, had come from no more than the impulse to feel Rooley's extraordinarily long arms around her. It was winter and the attic was cold; if the weather had been hot she probably would have denied him. Rooley had moaned and cried like a woman when she sucked him and she had felt, looking up the length of his limber body, that she was looking back down a long avenue of Burdettes at some original source of the raving gallant energy that had driven them to this ground. She wished for a second that she could dig old Langston up and have a go at him. As she lay back in the rags smelling the rich odors of turpentine and paint she had seen along an exposed roof beam a line of wasps paralyzed by cold clinging to the wood. As Rooley pumped between her legs, first one then another of the wasps fluttered off the beam away toward, she presumed, its nest in the eaves. She wondered if the rising heat from their bodies had been enough to bring a little life back to them.

"I've been cold all my life," she wrote. "I've been trying all my life to get warm."

There was a knock on the door and then the knob began to rattle—Marcel's characteristic procedure. "Come in," she called, though she knew he would stand out there until she got up and let him in. She wondered if this was some cultural holdover from his francine forefathers. She roused herself and opened the door. He held out a letter; she saw by the handwriting that it was from Jacey. "Are you prepared, Desirée?" he asked.

She took the letter from him and said, "David's in town."

"I saw his boat. What matter is that?" He was jealous and his jealousy made him arrogant and terse.

"He'll want to spend time with me. He's having a party on board for the passengers."

"At what time?"

"Seven o'clock."

"And you must go."

"I would like to." She stroked his arm, but he turned away and went out onto the balcony. David was on his last tour of the season. Next month the threat of hurricanes would shut down business until winter. She followed Marcel out and stood beside him looking down the beach. Children had piled up some of the litter—a few stumps, what looked like the frame of a washing machine, a slab of corrugated tin—into a fort. Down the beach, out of sight among a stand of windblown cedars, she could hear their laughter. "My little man in a shell," she said and kissed Marcel's bare brown shoulder. He squinted at her and shied. She raised

223

her hand to feel the wind. The sky was bright gray, the cloud cover so complete that it was hard to tell it was clouds and not just a change in the color of the sky.

"Storm by morning," he said.

"Let's drive up to Pont de la Cochon."

"If you wish."

"Marcel."

"If you wish."

"I actually do. I was just lying on the bed thinking about Canaan. Did you know that I am a member of a family large enough to populate a small town, anyway at least a couple of football teams, I think there would be enough. I am not part of them—I'm a Bonnet from Charleston—but whether I like it or not they consider me a part. I was wondering when I will go home."

"McCracken could take you on his boat."

"He only goes as far as Nassau. What did you do with the crabs?"

"I sold them in the market this morning."

"How much did you get?"

"Three hundred francs."

"*Magnifique.*"

"*C'est ça.*"

She asked him to teach her French because she wanted to try new words in bed. As she looked at him now, the hooked nose beakier than ever between the eyes that squinted out at the flat gray sea, his shoulders hunched together as if protecting him from a squall, she thought, Hold me, touch me, kiss my body, trying to remember the phrases. "*Enivre-moi,*" she said, "*enivre-moi toute suite.*"

He turned his head toward her.

"O-*Kay,*" he said bearing down on the last syllable to make sure she understood the difference between them. "O-*Kay.* I will make you drunk." Then they walked together to the bed and she drew him down on top of her. "*Mon oiselet,*" she whispered as his hard fingers broke her clothes loose, "*mon oiselet.*" My little bird.

"I feed Missa every afternoon," Jacey's letter said, "and I think she pines for you just as much as I do."

They drove past a green canal that the colonizing French had cut from the large freshwater pond in the center of the island to the fields

224

they had planned on the west side. Even with a supply of fresh water they found that the loose coral soil was too barren to support much beyond the myrtles, yaupons and blackjack pines that grew there already. The road side of the canal was fenced off; on the other side were the ghosts of the original fields, grown up now in yellowing weeds that were run through with the speckled lavender flowers of passion vines. The land rose toward the stolid hills which ringed and hid the pond. "My son has hair like yours," she said to Marcel. "All exploded-looking; blond. He's the only blond Burdette."

"I would like to meet him." Marcel always felt better after making love.

"Maybe you will, though I doubt it. You wouldn't want to get so far from home."

"Who knows?"

She returned to the letter. "When I come in the stables," he wrote, "she always has her head stuck out the window of her stall as if she is expecting you." She could picture the spotted gray head, her son reaching up. Where are you running to now, boy? "I give her a carrot or an apple, which she likes. I wondered how many fruits and vegetables a horse would eat so I tried giving her a selection. I have found that she will eat celery, cantaloupes, and even eggplant, but she doesn't like anything citrus. She just sniffs at oranges and grapefruits and turns away. She doesn't like greens much either, especially the sharp-flavored ones like turnip and mustard. She will eat collards, though. And sweet corn. Daddy told me that all the kudzu was brought to America from Japan in the thirties as cattle feed, but, he says, the cattle won't eat it, unless they are starving. Missa won't eat it either. Don't you think it is curious that no kudzu grows on Canaan? Granddaddy says it's because we are such good farmers. That's probably so, but I wish we had some. I like the jungly way it looks, so mysterious and green and the way it changes everything. It reminds me of Hawaii. . . ." She laughed.

"My son was five when we left Hawaii but he always acts as if he grew up there. Does it bother you for me to read this?"

"Of course not. I want you to love your son." He slowed the jeep to cross one of the outlet streams from the canal. White and red hibiscus grew in tall clumps along the far bank, and the coconut trees which overarched them were slender and nearly as tall as the palms in Hawaii. Through the cut of the stream she could see the Caribbean a quarter of a mile away, shining blue in the hazy sunlight. She smelled the scent of plumeria.

"Rooley has decided," she read, "to paint the trees in the Langston woods. I mean actually paint them. He's going to buy a crop duster to spray them yellow. He says that what he'd like to do is make a thousand-acre painting. Then we could all fly over in his airplane and look at it. I think that's a wonderful idea, don't you?" What am I doing here, she thought, my God what am I doing here? This Marcel boy, driving with the practiced insouciance of a born juvenile delinquent, was a stranger to her. His arm, laid across the top of the steering wheel, the hand dangling from the wrist as if it were broken, were to her at that moment such symbols of pointless arrogance that she was repelled. She wanted to jump out of the jeep and catch a plane to Canaan. She struck the pale blue sheets (her own stationery) across her bare leg. What are you doing, my little boyo. "Primo, Primo, Primo," she said out loud.

"What?"

"My son is in the seventh grade," she said. And she could see him now standing in the saddle picking fox grapes. What has come over me, she thought, and stood up to catch the wind. It whipped her long hair back until she felt she was being held by another being, trailing her.

"Sit back down," Marcel said.

She stayed where she was. "Have you ever wanted to travel?" she asked.

"Of course."

She couldn't hear him so she clambered back into her seat. "What did you say?"

"Of course, I would like to travel."

"I think I wanted to do that more than anything. More than anything besides screw little boys." She laughed and kissed his shoulder, trying to get back her place, a rightness here. He put his arm around her and drew her into the space between the seats. She remembered riding in Anthony Couchere's hunting jeep when she was sixteen. She had liked the uncomfortable space no better then. But she endured it, as she had then, because she liked the power in the arm that held her. The road rose slightly, then descended between pines to a shell-strewn beach backed by head-high myrtle thickets. A few coconut palms grew out of the myrtle, their shredded crowns clutching at the wind. A mile out, thin surf broke itself against the reef. Inside the reef the water was clear blue over pearly

226

sand. At the waterline and for fifty yards out, the inner reef extended it-self in a frozen rictus, a bed of dead coral. They parked by a massive breadfruit tree under whose shade deer flies flitted and bit. They walked through the yellow fingery leaves into the sunlight to a patch of floury sand above the band of broken seashells that ran along the tide margin, spread their blanket and settled in. Marcel was too restless to sit long, and he went into the water with spear and goggles to fish. Elizabeth lay back on the blanket to finish reading her son's letter.

"Rooley said he would teach me to paint," he said, "if I wouldn't be noisy. He hates for anybody to disturb him and sometimes he screams at Alsace when he hears her walking around downstairs. Sometimes she screams back and once she went through the house slamming every door one after the other. There are twenty-seven doors. I counted as she slammed them. Granddaddy has opened a flower stand on the Square and I think it is going to drive Daddy crazy. Last Sunday—which is when Granddaddy does his best business—on the way to church Daddy called him a white-assed nigger to his face. I didn't know what to think. I have never heard Daddy call anybody a nigger before, even colored people. Mattie said that was something a Burdette would never do. 'Even J. C. Burdette ought to know which side his bread is buttered on, and who does the buttering,' she said, but I guess Daddy's forgotten. Bernard and Delight have a tiger, the saddest old tiger you ever saw. They put it in a cage right next to the bear and they don't get along very well. Bears are actually stupid I think because I have seen this one, who has had the tiger beside her for two months, look up at him and draw back startled like she'd just seen a ghost. She keeps doing it, I mean, like you'd think she hadn't seen the tiger just a minute before. Delight says he feels the same way when he wakes up with a hangover wondering what damn planet he's on this time. Excuse the profanity, but you know how Delight talks . . . "

She put the letter down and looked out to sea. She could see Mar-cel's snorkel and the back of his head and then his feet shot up and he dived. He could stay down for more than two minutes and came up some-times brandishing an octopus on his spear. He had taught her how to tear the octopus' brains out with her teeth. The suckers left tiny white circles on her skin; she liked to feel the octopus clutching her; there was some-thing human in the desperation of those slender arms wrapping so tightly around the being that was about to kill it. And the black eyes looked steadily at her and, because the thing was not human, she was able to look hard back; sometimes she thought she saw another world and maybe a question and the same resignation, the same acceptance that was in the eyes of the pelican her pal had thrust his hand down the throat of on Folly Beach one afternoon in 1933.

She brought the letter to her face and smelled the faint sour odor of horses and it was for a moment as if the scent contained all the sad misery of humankind. She shook the letter and looked at it. Jacey's handwriting was changing, the meticulous looping script of childhood was just giving way to the cramped, vigorous strokes and curves of maturity. She wondered if a change in handwriting was the first sign of puberty, before even a cracked voice and the first faint hairs curling in his groin. "I want so many things," he wrote. "I want to paint like Rooley and farm like Granddaddy and catch animals like Bernard and Delight and drive a white truck like Uncle Eustace. I even want to shoot a gun like Burleigh, though you better not tell him. Daddy is very solemn and he's tired a lot of the time. Mattie says he needs a tonic, but she laughs when she says it. He's gone a lot, to Texas and to Savannah, and we don't talk much when he's here. We're going to New York, next month; I don't know how I feel about that. When are you coming home?"

How that life had crept up on her. She did not know when she was coming home. When she got tired, she assumed, which might not be in this lifetime. She got her notebook out of her straw bag and with her black pen wrote: "August 20, 1957; 11:30 A.M. In south Georgia goldenrod and black-eyed Susan are blossoming in the road ditches. The honeysuckle is already dying off as are the crepe myrtle flowers. In another few weeks the first asters will bloom. Fish can be caught only in the earliest morning or the latest afternoon, and usually only when there has been rain during the day. The first cotton is being picked and the next-to-last corn. Kudzu and chinaberry flowers are gone. I woke up this morning thinking of Charleston, of the old garden behind our house on the Lane of St. Louis. There was a quality to the mornings there that I miss, a softness, the light full of shadows and between the branches of the oaks the promise of a clear hot day. I would like to lie down under the forsythia hedge and think of the beach at Isle of Palms. . . . "

She had a habit of leaving notes behind her, like small trail blazes. She would write a word: sunflower or violet, destiny or fuck, and drop it as she passed. Sometimes she wrote sentences, sometimes brief stories,

228

often with obvious morals. She left the notes beside her plate in restaurants, along the river path, in restrooms, let them flutter from her car window as she drove. They were her connections, she believed, with a world full of strangers. Someone, she was sure, found them and read them.

She got up and walked down to the water. Marcel breached like a porpoise two hundred yards out and held up a zebra fish stabbed on his spear. He pushed it off the spear into the small fish boat he towed behind him. The boat, two by three feet and made of plywood, kept the sharks away. He towed it on a long string that he let go of to dive. When they fished together he made her pull the boat.

She unbuttoned her blouse and took it off. She thrust her shoulders back to take the breeze on her breasts. Once, one Sunday when she was fourteen, as she came down the steps of St. Michael's the wind blew her dress up over her face. She had been shocked and humiliated, and angry, so much so that she had broken off her conversation with Sally Baines, crossed the wide church court and walked home alone, not waiting for her father, furious, her head thrust back, terrified. She had stayed in her room during dinner writing steadily in her diary. But later that afternoon as she sat on a bench near the cannons in White Point Gardens wearing the yellow sun dress her mother had bought for her in New York, she had deliberately crossed her legs in such a way that the tourist sitting opposite her could see nearly to the tops of her thighs.

There was power in her body, surely, she thought, touching her nipples. Just as she had seen shock then cunning leap into the placid face of the tourist in White Point Gardens, so later she saw the same shock, the recognition, the furtive obsessive glances of filling-station attendants, waiters, store clerks and passersby. She had been known to cock her leg on the car dash to allow a grease monkey a clear view of her sex. With or without panties she had done this, her face set, her eyes boring in to catch the young man's vaulting expression.

She squatted in the water to feel its coolness between her legs. Then she walked back to the blanket, took the shorts off—she wore bikini bottoms underneath—and sat down again to finish Jacey's letter. "I will tell you something, Mama," he wrote, "and please don't be angry. I went into your dresser and read Daddy's letters to you. I didn't mean to exactly—I was looking for the hand mirror—but when I found the letters I read them."

It was like Jacey to do this, she thought, and like him to tell her, and like him to be evasive in the telling. He had never been able to keep a secret from her, had come to her all his life carrying tales that any other child would have kept to himself—at least, as a child, she had. "I read them," he said, "as much as I could of them"—he wanted to say he read them all, but he was afraid to lie to her—"and I was so sad and lonely when I got through." He was a boy who had never had a dog, or any other household pet—J.C. wouldn't allow it—only horses, which were diffident and awkward friends. "I took them down to the Course and sat by the water and read them, and I don't know why but I felt so bad. Daddy walks around like he's on fire on the inside, stalks around, I catch him sometimes upstairs on the porch staring out into the woods, just staring, and every once in a while he'll twitch his shoulders."

She had learned much about life from loving men. There so much of the mystery of life was, there in the look, the taste, the feel of men. But then as she thought about it, called to mind the thirty lovers she had had since her first one when she was fifteen, what came was not the knowledge of life's deeper meaning, no whiz of insight, but only details, the marks of a lover's manner and means, singly and representative. She thought of Rooley's anger when he noticed that her legs were longer than his, of Delight's habit of resettling his testicles as he walked. Haven had a way of shaking his hands as he moved about a room as if he had just touched something unpleasant. Her husband smelled often of fertilizer dust; kissing his back she would taste it, the sweet, crystalline chemistry of it, and it would set off a reaction in her, as if the chemical combined with her emotion, the foreign taste on the familiar skin, and something in her would leap up, glad and excited. She remembered dances with her first lover on the pier at Isle of Palms, and the slippery feel of their sweaty faces pressed together. One lover had taught her to make love in a hammock, and one had told her that she excited him most when he saw her naked underwater. Once, after a night bar-hopping in Washington (where she had fled after college), she went back to her hotel with a man who wanted only to sit between her spread-eagled legs and masturbate; she remembered his mournful, liquorish eyes as he stared between the parted lips of her sex and the way he tumbled into her arms as he came, and the false gratitude and perfunctory hugs he offered her when the act was over and his request to be allowed to come back and do it again. Kaui had wanted to make love only in the dark; the first time she touched his penis he had winced and thrust her hand away as if she had assaulted him. She had to coax him slowly into the kind of intimacy she sought, touching him so lightly that the pleasure finally outweighed his machismo fears.

She held the letter up so that it caught the breeze, giving against her hand like a thing with a little life in it. A cheekbone here, she thought, a hipbone there, the taste of sweat among the curling hairs at the base of the neck, someone's long eyelashes that years ago they had been told were an extraordinary feature for a boy—she collected all these, treasured them, as she did the letters J.C. sent her. "They made me see Daddy in a new way," her son wrote, "like somebody you thought was strong and you find out can be hurt. It scares me." As it had her when during a game of catch with her older brother she had seen her father fall, the knee given way, writhing and crying on the lawn. She flipped open her notebook and wrote: "Everybody has clay feet, everybody is vulnerable, everybody gets hurt. It isn't so much of a mystery—but why do I try to avoid it? I am in my own way J.C.'s equivalent: he refuses to acknowledge defeat from the world and I do too. Is it true that we are both willing to live without each other rather than admit we are wrong? Possibly. Probably."

She remembered her list of the Seven Deadly Virtues: courage, hope, faith, words like that. She flipped through looking for them but couldn't find them. They must be in another notebook. It is pride, she thought, in me just as in all the other desperate gangsters who won't give in. But how can I be thinking these things? I have come so far under my own wild steam. She hadn't gotten away, she realized, with living in Canaan. "She didn't get away with it," she said aloud and laughed. "That's what they will write on my tombstone, just like on the tombstones of all the other suckers." And then she felt a stab of fear, like panic: J.C. might get away with it, maybe he would ride to the grave in his chariot of realized self-will. Maybe he could bend the world down like a branch and bite off the fruit. But no, no, she had seen him crying with love for her, she had seen his eyes melt as she caressed him, she had seen him give in, even if later he denied it, even if he had to hurt her to prove it hadn't been so. She was his gift, his sweet hand of grace, the one light that kept out the madness of his mercantile obsession. Everybody has to learn to lose, she thought, maybe even me. I am very late in learning something like this, very late and reluctant.

He had beaten her simply because she teased him about some cherries. They had been in the kitchen waiting for Jacey to get dressed upstairs. While they waited J.C. sat at the kitchen table eating cherries out of a blue china bowl. She had been watering the plants, thinking that Angela the maid must be so slow that she could not learn to keep them from drying up. She had watered an areca palm under the window and turned back to the sink to refill her pitcher and the sight of J.C.'s mouth stained purple with cherry juice made her laugh. "You look like a New Orleans whore," she said and she pulled her kerchief out of her sleeve to wipe his mouth. But as she approached him he pushed back from the table grimacing in a face that seemed even funnier to her and screamed, "You goddamn egotistical bitch, you won't admit anything!" She had recoiled, stunned, the dark blue kerchief drifting in her hand between them. "You don't do anything but mock me." It wasn't so, she had done something entirely different, something that if there was error in it was an error of misattention, not meanness. And she came on toward him as if he had not spoken, as if he had just looked up like a small boy with a purple-stained mouth; she intended to wipe his face clean. But he rose and turned away from her as if he would flee, then turned back, his hands coming up in what she realized later was a preview of violence to come, fists shaking, and cried, "I don't want anything to do with you; you goddamn cunt, I'm through." Then he stormed from the room and she heard his heels striking the bare wood of the stairs as he ascended.

She had not thought *through* or *the end* or much of anything. She had dropped the handkerchief on the table as if marking his place and gone on watering the plants. When she finished she went out, before either of them came downstairs, got on her motorcycle and rode out into the country.

Her son was nearly done. "Come home," he wrote, "so I can show you what I am up to. I have something new to show you." She thought, he's in love. And she looked at the tallowy sea where the wind was building in the eaves of the sky. The gray plate of the heavens was beginning to break into pieces of heavy-footed cloud. She could not see Marcel for the light chop that had come up. She stood up and walked down to the water. A ghost crab, the color of honey stirred in milk, skittered backward along the bedded coral. At low tide the coral would be exposed. The bare rocks always had a look to her of something tortured and enduring. Occasionally at night she and Marcel came out fishing on the

232

reef. They used cane poles and fished the deep holes in the coral beds. He had told her that some of the holes led back to the sea, and she had told him about Yellow Spring and the blue light at the bottom of it. But she knew, as no Burdette did, that Yellow Spring had no outlet into open water. She had touched herself the coarse cold stream that poured out of the blanched rocks and she knew that beyond it there was only the darkness of the underground river.

She called to Marcel, but it was another name she spoke. "Kaui," she cried, "come out. Haven, Haven." How long Haven's fingers were, the tips rounded and the calcium moons filling half his fingernails. She would know her husband's cowlick, the swirl of hair beside the part, all her life. She was amazed at what her life brought her, at the baggage she carried willy-nilly through the days. You look out one morning and spring has come, for the first time in your life. The yellow wands of forsythia are shrugging off the wind for the first time in the world. And you begin to see the connections, you begin to see that the wind in the forsythia is the same wind blowing in your horse's mane, that the man you married is the man you have carried in your heart since you were a girl. You see that the house you walk through is the house you have lived in all your life, not because you were ever here before but because you built it, out of blocks and sticks, in the bare space under the holly tree when you were six. And even love with all its sweat and pain has been here all the time, running through your body like a summer fever, like a dream, like the memory of your mother's cool lips kissing your forehead when you were five. And the play of your heart is the play of a fish against the line, the rhythm of beats is the rhythm of water, is the play of waves against the bedded rocks, and you rise up on that first morning, clean as a dolphin, from the laundered bed and you go to the window and you say, Yes, this flowering tree, this althea, this cloudy dogwood, this wind, this green lawn that I have never before walked on, this love in my heart that is inevitable and infinite is mine, has been mine since before time began, since before the ocean beat on the unbreakable shore, since before there was sky or fish or men, or even the pulse of desire, since before light. And you are gifted, you are the chosen one of all because there are no others, there have never been others, there is only the whispering mystery of creation itself which is you of you from you in you, and you throw open the window and step out and the dew is the same dew you have felt on your legs all your life, the same sun, the same grass, the same frisking wind, and there is no difference, between you and the wind, between you and honeybees tumbling in the vines, between you and everything that flies and crawls and swims and sings, and you have known this always.

Marcel rose from the water not twenty feet from where she stood. She had not noticed the fish boat floating toward her. He rose and pushed his goggles up on his forehead. The point of his spear caught a vagrant ray of sunlight so that it shined like a diamond. His face was worried. "Hurricane coming," he said and threw his hand up at the lowering sky, as if to keep whatever was back there away a little longer.

15 You are a boy with crisp blond hair, rising from twelve to thirteen, in love for sure, and you go *pow, pow,* and your cousin falls down. Falls down, falls down. Jacey sneaked through the ligustrum hedge pulling off handfuls of hard purple berries. Twenty yards away Burleigh sat on the back steps talking to Martha Poitevent. As he crouched under the bushes he remembered stoning the main house with his grandfather. They had stopped doing that; his grandfather didn't want to fight anymore. "He's a lover, not a fighter," Mattie said, "and he's finally got grown up enough to admit it." Maybe so, but Jacey Burdette was still a fighter. That was what he was here for: to fight his cousin Burleigh Burdette. For the love of Martha Poitevent.

He shook the handful of berries, smelled them; they were scentless. Years ago he had tried to eat at least one of every berry and flower that grew in the yard at Canaan. He and Burleigh had done that: Italian cherries and Japanese plums were sweet, day-lily pods tasted like fresh string beans, quinces were sour, pyracantha berries were mealy and a little sour, magnolia seeds, holly, chinaberries and ligustrum were bitter. Burleigh leaned back on his elbows and looked up into the pines; Martha had her arms wrapped around her bare knees. Her blond hair which was the color of sourwood honey was set so that it curled under at her shoulders. Her eyes were as green as a holly leaf. Her skin was the color of almonds. "Sweet Hawaiian sunshine," Jacey silently sang, "you can hear the beachboys sigh as she goes by." He froze as Martha looked his way. To his left he could hear the murmur of Little Swearing Creek. If anybody had accosted him on the way over here he planned to say he was on his

234

way to build dams in the creek. Burleigh, three years his senior, had also taught him that. They had spent whole days when they were younger building dams out of boards, rocks and mud. Burleigh had been going with Martha for a year, ever since the church hayride last July. He didn't build dams anymore.

Jacey eased the cherry bomb and a book of matches from his pants pocket. He rubbed the rough red surface of the firecracker between his fingers, thumbed the stiff green twisted fuse. The cherry bomb was as big as a jawbreaker, and he had heard that half a dozen of them packed as much punch as a stick of dynamite. Burleigh lay on his back beside Martha looking up into the pines. He was talking with his hands the way all the Burdettes did; Martha rubbed her polished toenails. Jacey struck a match, lit the fuse and through an opening in the bushes tossed the bomb into the yard. It went off k-BLAT! in a yellow burst of light. Jacey jumped to his feet, beat the bushes back and walked out into smoke. Burleigh was on all fours below the steps. Martha lay on her back with her hand up as if she were warding off sunlight.

Jacey walked up to them through a cloud of purplish smoke the size of a tenant house. Burleigh pushed up on his knees; he wasn't hurt, only frightened. As he rose Jacey hit him with his fist on the side of the head. Burleigh went back down on one knee, shook his head and stared up at Jacey with a look of dumb surprise. As if I am Bernard's bear prancing up in long pants, Jacey thought and sliced another shot at Burleigh, catching him this time in the ear. Martha scrambled neatly up and stood watching them with her shoulders clasped in her hands. Burleigh shoved himself up like a man finishing pushups. Jacey let him rise, waited until he was standing, grinned hugely, and popped him hard in the sternum. Burleigh staggered back gasping, "You shit."

"Sweet Hawaiian sunshine," Jacey sang and smiled at Martha, who stared at them, somewhat dazedly.

Burleigh backed farther away, scuffing the ground with his heels. "You craphole," he said. "Have you gone completely crazy?"

"No," Jacey said and advanced on him with clenched fists. Burleigh feinted with his left and hit Jacey with a straight right hand in the forehead. The air went cold blue and Jacey woke up five seconds later, still on his feet wondering where he was. Burleigh popped him hard in the left eye and he felt the skin tear. "Oh, God," Jacey cried and rushed at Burleigh. His best fighting maneuver had always been to go for a choke hold.

235

He missed this one because Burleigh dropped to one knee and butted him in the groin. Jacey's whole body roared with pain, and he fell to the ground writhing. He hurt too much to think how embarrassed he was. Through a yellow film he heard Burleigh say, "This is my cousin Jacey. He's in love with you and hoped to make an impression."

"He has," Martha said and laughed a sweet jingling laugh that Jacey could feel like cool rain through his pain. He had his eyes closed, from pain and embarrassment both, but he sensed her when she came down the steps and knelt over him. She touched his forehead, smoothed the hair back. "Why don't you get him a glass of lemonade," she said. Jacey rolled away from her, kept his back to her. He heard the door slam. He hoped nobody else was looking. "It'll be all right," Martha said. "I already know who you are."

Jacey opened his eyes. "I'm sorry," he gasped, "if I scared you."

She squatted beside him. A couple of strands of pinestraw stuck to her knee. He wanted to brush them off, but he was too weak to raise his arm. "Why do you stare at me in church?" he asked.

"Because you're so pretty. I'm sorry."

He rolled over on his back and pushed up on his elbows. "Don't be sorry," he said. "I'm in love with you."

She touched his forehead with slender fingers on which the red nails were bitten back to the quick. "I know," she said. "It'll be all right." Flecks of gold in her holly eyes made them look old, and wise.

Burleigh came out carrying a glass of lemonade. Mrs. Poitevent, her hair pinned up under a tight scarf, looked out the kitchen window. Burleigh came down the steps and gave the glass to Jacey, who took it with both hands and sipped the tart juice. Burleigh rubbed the side of his head where Jacey had hit him. "I'm sorry," Jacey said over the rim of the glass.

"Well, nobody wants to be assaulted by their kin," Burleigh said peevishly, "but I guess I'll live. You've been like this since your mama went away, haven't you? Ever since she took off you've been acting stranger and stranger." He turned to Martha, who was absently brushing her hand over the tops of some clover plants that grew out of an old hay bale pulled up against the house. "He's started to pull disappearing acts, too, just like Aunt Elizabeth," he said. "He rides off on that horse of his and doesn't come home. One time he spent the night out in the swamp. Uncle Eustace found him the next day up in a deer stand by the river. He said he was talking out loud to himself, calling out like he saw somebody coming up the trail."

Jacey thought in a minute he might get up and hit Burleigh again. One thing he had picked up from his father was to keep his mouth shut around folks he wasn't related to. It embarrassed him for Martha to hear this; he had wanted to come into her life as a bold and remorseless man, not as a crazy mama's boy.

Martha looked at him over her knees. "I don't think there's anything wrong with that," she said. Jacey silently blessed her.

"You been hanging around Yellow Springs too long," Burleigh said to her. "You think because he's a Burdette anything goes. I get so tired of my family being crazy, especially Jacey's side of it. When are y'all going to straighten up?"

"About the time you stop being stupid, I suppose. . . ."

Burleigh picked at the skin under his ear as if there were bugs on it. "He goes out and hangs around Granddaddy's place," he said. "Another out-of-his-mind Burdette. You've seen my granddaddy—he's the fool selling flowers on the Square. When he makes a little money he'll probably branch out into boiled peanuts. I wouldn't be surprised if he cornered the market."

Jacey threw the half-full glass of lemonade at Burleigh. It hit him just below the neck. Burleigh took a step and kicked Jacey in the shoulder. Jacey rolled away and got to his feet. "You're crazy, Burleigh," he yelled. "You don't know anything." He charged his cousin and Burleigh knocked him down again. I want to be smart and strong, he thought as he went down, just once in my life I want to be smart and strong. He got up and if he had had his wits about him he probably would have waited for an opening, but his rhythm, such as it was, was long gone and he ran at Burleigh swinging his arms. Burleigh knocked him down again. This time when he got up his ears were ringing and there were long blue streamers hanging from the tops of the pines. Martha was either grinning or grimacing, he couldn't tell, and somebody, probably Mrs. Poitevent, was yelling at them from the back steps.

"Quit, Jacey," Burleigh said, but Jacey wasn't about to. He lowered his head and ran at his cousin, picking up a technique from him. Burleigh caught his shoulders and shoved him to the side and down. Jacey's face hit the grass, which he tasted—sour, and he thought suddenly of springtime and a cool morning breeze—before he pushed himself back up on his heels blinking his eyes, not quite sure where he was. Where he was was in Martha Poitevent's backyard within sight of her father's stables and Little Swearing Creek and a woman standing on the back steps in an apron and a headrag like a servant.

"You, Burleigh Burdette," the woman cried, "you leave that boy alone."

The last thing Jacey wanted was interference from adults—his plan was all askew now—and he waved his hand as a rejected lover will wave from the fantail of the ship that is carrying him away to a life of loneliness. Sidney Carton's speech came into his head and he said, "It is a far, far better thing I do than I have ever done. It is to a far, far better place I go than I have ever known," and then he keeled over into the grass that was so soft and sweet-smelling that he thought he might not ever want to get up again.

When he came to he was lying on a sofa in the Poitevent's sunporch. Martha sat on the floor beside him pressing a cool cloth to his forehead. On the mahogany wall opposite were painted portraits of the four Poitevent children. Each one of them, even the son Randolph, wore the same gray-blue velvet dress. Mrs. Poitevent sat at a grand piano under the portraits playing "Jesu, Joy of Man's Desiring." She still wore her headrag, though her apron was gone. Jacey blinked and touched his nose, which burned as if a bee had stung it. "I might have whipped him," he said, "if I had been able to get up again."

"Eventually he would have gotten tired," Martha said and laughed her jingly little laugh.

"Yeah, I was wearing him down. Did he run off?"

"He did. I told him to go home."

He pushed up on an elbow, but that made his head swim so he lay back down. "Does that mean . . ." He started to say does that mean you love me, but he was too dizzy to get the words out. There was a small cream-colored lizard on the ceiling. As he watched it chirped like a bird. "Gecko," he said. "You've got geckos in your house." Mrs. Poitevent looked up at the lizard, then she grabbed a black .45 from the music stand and shot a stream of water at it. A fine spray fell on Jacey, and he closed his eyes, enjoying the cool. "Actually," he said to Martha, "you want them around. They eat flies and all kinds of bugs. We had a house full of them in Hawaii. They'd sing all night, like little birds."

"Mama just likes to shoot her gun," Martha said. She refolded the cloth and pressed a cool side against his forehead. Mrs. Poitevent got up, came over and peered down at him. The wisps of hair that escaped her headrag were dyed lemony yellow. "How about some cookies," she said, "and a glass of cranberry juice. Then we'll have a talk about the Lord."

"Thank you," Jacey said, "that would be nice."

"What is your mother going to do?" he asked when she had left the room.

"She's a very famous local Christian." Her eyes were teasing.

"I've already been baptized. And since that happened I've been a little spooked about the church. Not so much because of the baptizing but because of the stuff that happened all around it."

"Mama hasn't been ordained, so you don't have to worry about the waters. I saw you get baptized. I also saw your mother. That was the night she went away, wasn't it?"

"That was the night." He hadn't talked about it to anyone, not even his grandfather, who would listen to anything. It was partially because he had the idea that no one saw his mother but him. Sometimes she seemed to be a vision only he could see. "I worry about her all the time," he said, "just like she was my child." What he didn't say was that if he thought about her too long he felt dead.

"I know what you mean. My mother's a ten-year-old, too."

"Who's a ten-year-old?" Mrs. Poitevent asked, coming back into the room. She carried a plate of tollhouse cookies and two glasses of cranberry juice on a tray.

"You are, Mother. A tiny child at heart."

"Suffer the little children," Mrs. Poitevent said. "How do you feel, Jacey Burdette?"

"Still a little dizzy, Mrs. Poitevent."

"What you need is a good dose of turpentine." The Poitevents were old lumber people. Mr. Poitevent's grandfather had made a huge amount of money chopping down and sawing up the great old virgin yellow pines, though Mr. Poitevent only went into the woods these days to hunt or to ride his horses. They still drew an income from the lumberyards, but they were owned by a northern corporation now. Mr. Poitevent was famous for breeding and training Tennessee walking horses. Jacey hoped she wouldn't really give him turpentine. "Thank you, Mrs. Poitevent," he said.

She patted his head and drew herself up. "When you feel a little

239

better we'll have a talk," she said. "Now I want to go out and bale some pinestraw. You send him on home when he feels a little better," she said to Martha. Then she went out the back door.

"I thought I was gone," Jacey said as he watched her through the window crossing the yard, fiddling with her headrag as she went.

"It's just a twitch," Martha said. "She rarely gives anybody turpentine these days."

"I'm glad to hear that. I'd probably have to stop being a sweet little boy for a minute if she shoved that on me."

"You're not a very sweet boy anyway."

"I'm not?"

"Sweet boys don't usually try to blow people up."

"I didn't try to blow you up. I was just trying to get your attention." He shoved himself around on the sofa so he was seated facing her.

"That worked out fine," she said and laughed. She took a cookie.

"Are you in love with Burleigh?" he asked. It was the question he had come over to ask.

"No."

"Then there's room for me."

"You're only twelve years old."

"I'll be thirteen in November."

"I'm three years older than that, almost four. My birthday's in February."

"The tenth."

"How do you know?"

"I looked it up in the church register."

"When you get to be sixteen you'll be able to see the difference between that and twelve."

"I've had girlfriends since I was four."

"There's still a difference."

"What?"

"It's a new kind of life. I don't expect I look like a twelve-year-old girl."

"You look like a woman."

"I guess I do to you—and that's the difference."

"That you're a woman? I just want you to be my girlfriend."

"We'll see about that. I think you feel well enough now to go home."

240

He fell back on the sofa. "I think I'm dying," he said. "I think Burleigh gave me a brain hemorrhage."

She laughed. "He hasn't got the punching power."

"He's got enough. You ought to fight him."

"Poor boy. Now pull yourself together. I have to work and you have to go home."

He wondered what her work was, wanted to volunteer, but he could tell by her tone that she meant what she said. "Okay."

They both stood up. "You're taller than me," he said.

"One of many reasons why you ought to forget about trying anything with me."

"I'm growing all the time."

"So am I."

"But you're stopping; I'm just starting."

"We'll see."

Years later, drunk in bed, he asked her if she remembered that first day. Yes she did but she didn't remember that as he went out the door she touched him across the back with fingers that felt to him as if they were dipped in fire. There's no way I could remember what *you* felt, she told him, but the sensation was so strong that he wondered why she had not beat her hands against the floor to put out the flames. You are incorrigibly romantic, she told him, and he agreed. And you think every experience that doesn't throw you into some kind of euphoria is compromised, she told him, and he agreed to that, too. You let me play it all the way, he told her. With you I could go just as far as I wanted. I liked to watch, she said, I liked to see what you would come up with.

He appeared at her window the next night and threw pebbles to wake her up. Just like his grandfather except his grandfather wasn't in love. Mr. Poitevent came to the front door in his bathrobe. Jacey came out of the boxwoods and hailed him as if Mr. Poitevent were a long-lost friend. Why don't you come around in the daylight, Mr. Poitevent said, and Jacey agreed that would probably be a good idea. That's not even her window, Mr. Poitevent said, that's my office. Oh, Jacey said, which one is her window. Mr. Poitevent, a slender man with straight black hair he slicked back like a gambler's, came out on the lawn and looked up at the second story. It's that one, he said, as if he had never figured it out before. Then Martha in a white nightgown came to the window and

Jacey and Mr. Poitevent stood looking up at her. The window was closed and Martha made no move to open it. That's it, Mr. Poitevent said, that's her window. Finally Martha smiled and waved. To Jacey she looked miles away, unreachable; his guts churned and he wanted to throw himself past Mr. Poitevent and run up the stairs to her. He knew then what it was like to not be able to put your hands on the thing you couldn't live without. It was a lesson that he would learn again, had had chances to learn already. She's your new friend, huh? Mr. Poitevent said, and Jacey nodded, struck dumb. Well, come over tomorrow and I'll let you both help me work the horses, he said. As he spoke Martha vanished from the window, like a ghost. Jacey was willing to stand in the yard all night, but he figured he had better go—he would be able to come back tomorrow; it was always easier to give in when he was sure there would be more tomorrow. Mr. Poitevent looked up at the house. That's her window, he said, now we know. Now we know, Jacey agreed and then he took his leave.

He rode his horse the mile across town and as he passed through the sleeping streets he thought, I will remember how the streetlight shines in the magnolia leaves and I'll remember the smell of the mock banana bush in Mrs. Doakes' yard and I'll remember exactly what Martha looked like in her white nightgown with her hair down and her hand raised waving at me. When the Bivins' fice ran out barking and his horse shied, he did not mind, though he did try to run the little dog over. It was the second time—counting the cherry-bomb morning—that he had forgotten that his mother had gone off and left him, that she might be coming back.

They would have a long life together, Jacey and Martha, and it was just beginning. At sixteen it is difficult to get away with loving someone three and a half years younger. Martha was frightened at first of what people would think—frightened of what she thought about herself—and it took a long time for her to admit she was in love, though she was the one who introduced sex into their affair, two years later at her family's beach house on the Panhandle. They became in the beginning, to the world, friends only, the kind of friends who rode horses together after school and shared dark and bumptious secrets. Martha's mother worried that she did not spend time with boys her own age. Her father was glad that he did not have suitors to contend with.

For Jacey, she was a well he could drink from endlessly. He came back the next day and Mr. Poitevent took them down to the barn, a dark green high-pitched building with a weathercock on top, and showed them his horses. The Burdettes were riders, but Mr. Poitevent was a horseman. The Burdettes knew their horses as they knew their servants: faithful and trusted retainers whom they used for pleasure and relief and depended on to make their lives bearable. To Mr. Poitevent horses were creations, beautiful objects that he molded the way a master potter molds beautiful bowls. He was not attached to their personalities and he did not treat them like children. "A horse is as stupid as a sheep nearly," he told them that afternoon. "He'll eat himself to death if you don't stop him." Jacey was just entering that stage of his life where everything an adult said seemed directed personally at him, and he winced at the image that came into his mind. He would probably do himself in through excess; Martha had already pointed out that it was a fairly outrageous maneuver to throw a cherry bomb at the feet of the girl you were in love with. And he was stunned with love. Every move he made, as they walked behind Mr. Poitevent to the barn, every gesture, struggled through agonizing ropes of self-consciousness. The boldness that had carried him twice across town to this house beside a stream had flown away, so far away that he couldn't remember ever having it. He stumbled over roots and when they passed Mrs. Poitevent's garden he couldn't remember the word for cucumbers. The horses with their chained feet and their arched broken tails frightened him as horses had never frightened him before. The sleek narrow heads seemed menacing, and when he went to the tack room for the tiny riding saddle he forgot the blanket and Mr. Poitevent had to send him back. His hands shook when he fastened the bridle on the chestnut stallion Mr. Poitevent was working with so that when the horse bit him on the shoulder in irritation he was not prepared. Mr. Poitevent seemed surprised that Jacey was such a fumbler and he took the horse out to the pacing track without telling them what to do next.

Jacey could think only of Martha, that she was beside him, smelling of lemons. She wore khaki shorts and a white oxford-cloth blouse and sandals. She was small, five two or three, and she was light-boned like her mother, though her legs were heavily muscled. She was very erect.

They followed Mr. Poitevent to the ring and stood side by side watching him work the horse. He rode, in the fashion of walking-horse riders, with his legs fully extended, angling forward from the hips, his back rigidly staight and his chin tucked slightly into his neck. At shows he would wear a small snap-brimmed hat and a three-quarter-length coat with a string tie, but at home he wore khakis, like a farmer.

The ring fence had a four-inch board along the top, and Jacey thought that if they were alone he would jump up on it and run around the ring. As they leaned against it, Martha's arm touched his and he felt the same ringing in his ears he had two days before when Burleigh hit him. Her arms were covered with thick silver hair, all lying one way as if she brushed it. For Jacey it was an image of her maturity; he thought of her as grown.

Later they walked by the stream and Jacey told her of his life. My mother is like this, he said, and my father is like this. My uncles are strange; they live together unmarried and one of them drinks a lot. My mother leaves home regularly and this time she has been gone for three months. Nobody knows when she is coming back. When they came to a tulip poplar log fallen across the stream, Jacey walked it to show her he was agile. He remembered giving a box of crayons to Eleanor Wilkes in the first grade and wondered what he could give Martha. He didn't know what sixteen-year-old girls wanted, and there was something in him besides straight love that was gratified a girl as old as she would be willing to talk to him.

Martha told him that she was a dancer. She went down to Tallahassee four times a week to take class. Jacey had never known anybody who wanted to be a ballet dancer and he was thrilled. She was going to New York, she said, but it looked like it would be over her father's dead body. Jacey's insides clutched when she told him and he wanted to beg her to stay, but he held his tongue.

I can do an Indian dance, he told her, and he showed her the dance he had picked up from a movie. You're not very good, she told him, but I don't mind. Good, good, Jacey said, I'm better at riding horses and fighting. This is pretty crazy, Martha said, and Jacey agreed that it was. I come from a crazy family, he said, and he told her about Rooleys one and two. Everybody's family is crazy, Martha told him, and he said he had never realized that.

They sat down under a huge sycamore that had bark scaling off in patches. You don't ever want to put sycamore wood on a fire, Jacey told her, and Martha asked why and he explained that sycamore wood pops so fiercely that it will throw itself out of the flames. You can do it for a joke, he told her; the fire will pop right out into the room. Why don't you have any brothers and sisters, she wanted to know, and Jacey couldn't tell her. I've always wanted them, Jacey said, especially a sister. She took his hand in her lap and told him that she would be a sister to him. That's a start, Jacey said, but I think I want more than that. Every girl to me has been a girlfriend, all except my mother. Isn't she your girlfriend? In a way she is, he said, we used to talk a lot, especially when we were in Hawaii. What was that like? Martha wanted to know. Hawaii or talking? Both. He told her about Rufino and the first drink of alcohol he had given him. It made me so drunk I fell down the steps of the Kaleakalui temple, he told her. During services? No. The temple is a ruin in the hills near where we lived. I jumped up because I thought I saw Daddy's ship down in the harbor and fell right down the steps. I landed in an old bucket that somebody had left at the bottom. I cut my hand and it swole up as big as a breadfruit. I had to get shots. I want to get out of Alexandria, she told him. I have had almost enough of it. I love it here, Jacey said, Canaan is so big and wild. My father wants to move to Tennessee, she told him, and buy a horse farm. Will he do that? No, he just likes to talk about it; he likes to scare my mother, it makes her come alive for him. I think my father would like to scare my mother, he told her, but I don't think he knows how to do it. Nothing that I know of scares my mother. I thought she was like that, Martha said, I see her driving around town and she always seems so purposeful, like she knows exactly what she is doing. That's the way she is, he said, she's just like that, even the time my father . . . And his voice trailed off as he remembered the beating and his mother walking away into the night. He didn't know Martha well enough to tell her about that, but the time would come.

He lay with his head in her lap and tried to let the nerves of his skull feel the muscular fullness of her thighs. Across the stream out of sight beyond the bushes he heard children singing. It was the hymn "Fairest Lord Jesus," and he thought he had never heard anything so beautiful. Do you hear them, he asked, and he was speaking out of a silence that he hadn't realized was there between them. Yes, she said, Mrs. Tillman is holding her Vacation Bible School class at her house. They listened to the children and the sweetness of their voices made Jacey feel tender and grown, as if he could remember long ago singing in a choir. My mother used to sing to me, he said, she knows all kinds of songs about people killing each other and dying for love and things like that. Do you know any? she asked, and he said yes he did and she asked him to sing one so he

245

did, a song about a young man taking his lover to the banks of a river and stabbing her there. You have a sweet voice, Martha said, but the song is frightening, and Jacey thought, Lord, she and I are here if not by a river at least by a stream and he sat up and began to apologize but she laughed and pulled his head back down, and then she kissed him full on the lips and he saw the blue streamers hanging from the trees and thought if he didn't want so much more of this good business he would be willing to die right here. He put his hands into her hair, touched the fine blond softness of it as some king would run his fingers through the first bright silks brought from the East. I am so happy, he said, I think I am the happiest twelve-rising-to-thirteen-year-old in Yellow Springs, in all of Burdette County, maybe this part of the South, and Martha said yes I know, I can tell by how you're squirming around, and he said it's pretty hard to be still and he jumped up and ran down the bank a ways, jerked half a dozen tea olive sprigs out of a bush, rushed back, knelt in front of her and presented them to her and began to tell even as she took them and thanked him smiling about his plans for the future which was a bounteous future including her and full of travel and wild carryings-on, elegant dinners in Italy and walks on African beaches, but which always came back to Canaan where they would swim in the spring and he would show her the white angels he just now remembered before they floated down the Course and down the river after that and wind up like Cortez or De Soto staring out at the wide waters of the Gulf that were full of promise and sunlight.

Their life together would be something like that and nothing like that, and as he looked at her noticing that her eyelashes were blue-black and that the clear fuzz on her cheeks grew in little white whirlpools just below her ears and that her nose was short and tilted slightly up and that her bottom lip was so full it looked pursed even when it wasn't, his insides began to cheer and he thought, Well, I could run a hundred miles, that is to the Gulf and back, and who cares that my mother is gone. There are so many things I want to show you, he said, and practical, she said, name one and he said, I know a man who lives in a big brick house right on the banks of the Okeekee River and he has pens that are full of quail. That's something, she said, but I want to go to New York City and live in a hotel in Greenwich Village. Maybe we will do that, he said, though he knew he was content now as a mockingbird began to whistle like a robin or was it a redbird and the gnats lighting at the corners of his eyes didn't even bother him, and how could he know that in a few years they would be in New York, not in a hotel in Greenwich Village but in a walk-up apartment on Tompkins Park three blocks up from the Hell's Angels and on this particular date they would be lying on a mattress out on the fire escape and he would be kicking the batik cloth he had dyed for her into the air and watching it settle over them like a passengerless parachute, spitting beer at pedestrians four floors below and laughing fit to burst? He didn't know and couldn't know just as he didn't know that he would grab her by the throat as they drove along the beach at Isla de Carmen a thousand miles down into Mexico because his endless despair had finally caught him in the form of a Mexican policeman in Ciudad de Carmen who escorted him to the stucco-fronted stationhouse where an officer in a uniform opened halfway down his chest demanded that he state why he had come there and what he was guilty of. I am dying, Egypt, dying, and not expecting pardon.

He was a gentle boy, so vulnerable and pampered that it made him arrogant. And he would struggle with his pride all his life.

I live in a house, he said, in which all the doorknobs are made of diamonds. In my house, she said, the faucets are pure gold.

I will one day swim the Atlantic Ocean, he said.

I will win the Nobel Prize for dance.

There's no Nobel Prize for dance.

There will be when they see me.

I can hold my breath for six minutes, he said.

I can make birds fly to me.

When I go to sleep angels carry me off to India.

My father is the greatest horseman in America.

My family is worth fifty million dollars.

They are not.

Yes, they are. I carried one of the quarterly checks up to Uncle Eustace one time and it was for seventy-six thousand dollars.

That's not millions.

It's still a lot. There're ten quarterly checks, and they're all pure profit. That's three million dollars profit a year.

I didn't know you were rich.

I didn't know it either. My granddaddy won't take his check. He just tears it up.

I've heard about your granddaddy.

I love him.

Then he must be a wonderful man.

She was pulling a piece of sycamore bark into strips as she talked. Then she scratched her ankles and stuck her feet out in a point.

"What is ballet dancing like?" he asked and she stood up and did a *plié* and then a *grand jeté en tournant* and a couple of other, more flamboyant maneuvers. "Oh," he said. For a moment her body became something better than a girl's. She stopped and stood with her hands on her hips looking across the stream.

"Can you do the soft shoe?" he asked.

"I can, yes, but I want to be a classical artist. I want to dance the great ballets."

"We had a maid once who could shuffle off to Buffalo."

She sat back down and took one of his hands in hers. "I will tell you and only you because I know that you love me," she said, "but I am going to New York very soon. I am already sixteen years old and that is old for a dancer to be without the training she needs. My teacher in Tallahassee is well-meaning but I need to be around other young dancers who are as committed as I am. My father had a dance room built in the attic and I work there every day, but it is not enough and he knows it. I will have to go even though he cries every time I mention it."

"I might cry, too," he said. "I don't want you to go." And he thought this is probably going to be my life with women: I love them and they bail out into the world. "I'll go to New York with you." He could hear the cries of the Bible children beyond the alder bushes.

"I wouldn't mind if you came. I would like to have someone from Yellow Springs with me. I want to leave here, but I don't want to forget where I come from."

"Well, you wouldn't forget if I was there. I mean, I'm a Burdette. We're all just big clumps of Yellow Springs earth raised up and walking."

"*That* is the verifiable truth," she said.

"Would you mind if we kissed again?"

"All right."

She put her arms around him and they kissed. Her tongue slid into his mouth and he thought he would pass out. Then they both opened their eyes and as their tongues played at the edges of each other's lips they looked at each other, their faces coming in and out of focus. He

248

wanted to live this close to her always and he felt the frightening desire to have all his skin pressed against all of hers. That was the thought: skin, not sex, and it frightened him because the stirring in his groin was new and was accompanied by a feeling of powerlessness like nothing he had ever felt before. But along with that was the realization of his loneliness, so incredible and so deep that he gasped into her open mouth. She pulled away, smiled and pressed in again, covering his face with small noiseless kisses. "I want . . ." he said, meaning I want to touch you, and though she stopped his mouth with her lips he raised his hands and ran them over her body, his fingers fluttering, skipping over breast and belly, legs, hips, the muscular curve of her buttocks, into the warmth between her thighs, his fingers prying at the cuffs of her shorts. She seemed to understand his need, because she did not try to prevent his wandering, only twisted in his arms so that he could reach more of her body. He thought, I must have been starving to death, or if he didn't think it, something in him that had nothing to do with thought knew it was true and he lapped at her as a hunting dog after a long day in the fields will lap at a cupped handful of water.

"You're licking me," she said.

"I know," he said. "I didn't mean to."

"I like it. Lick my face."

He did and she began to do the same thing to him until both their faces were wet and they pressed them together—"like two little frogs," she said—skin sliding on skin. He dropped his head and licked the bony space between her delicate and widely spaced breasts, undoing the top button of her chemise with his teeth, nipping at the lace edges of her bra, sucking the cloth into his mouth so that after a moment he saw the color of her nipples, pink as a tea rose through the cloth and hard as scars, and she said, What are you going to do if the children come through those bushes, and he said, Invite them to have a sup, and she said, Oh, I just wanted to know, I'm glad you feel at home enough to want to share the wealth. Which I don't really, he said, it's only that this kind of thing tends to make me feel cordial toward my neighbors. She shaved him off her with the flat of her hand and said, They're *my* neighbors and we have to keep in mind that we might want to do this some more—without interference; that noise you hear is my father coming this way: lie down. They squirreled down in the trough made by the sycamore roots and arm in arm listened to her father pound by on his horse. The hooves made a light, tripping sound full of the syncopation breeding and training had put there. Through the bushes Jacey caught a glimpse of the top of Mr. Poitevent's head; it was motionless along the line of the ride, the black hair gleaming. He thought, my life is changed now, I have taken a step that has changed everything for me.

"Is she a snake or a rose?" Mattie asked him as he sat on her kitchen table shelling butterbeans.

"She's a rose," Jacey answered, "and I don't know why you would even mention anything like that—it's not like you and it's not appropriate."

At the sink Mattie shook beans in a colander. "I mention it because you are a boy and can't always tell the difference."

"I think I can tell the difference between a snake and a rose. And who appointed you the keeper of the flame anyway?"

"Somebody has to say something to you. Your mama is living it up in the tropics and your daddy is inventing himself into a hole so deep that he'll need searchlights just to find his pants, and besides I've had your number since you were a little naked five-year-old."

"You haven't got anybody's number. You're just an old farm woman."

"I ought to slap you cross-eyed, boy. You have gotten so stony in the last few months that somebody's going to have to take you down a peg or two. You're like your daddy."

"Well, I'm bound to be. I wouldn't want to be like anybody else's daddy."

"Don't get smart with me. You might be looking at the cross end of a belt."

"Soo-wee. I'm sitting here trembling."

One step was all she needed to take, which she did, and backhanded him across the cheek. "You get out of my kitchen," she said, "and you stay out until you got all that smartness out of your mouth."

He fled crying and walked along the pond, tearing cattails out of the mud and flinging them into the water. Nobody was going to treat him like that. What business of Mattie's was it who he was in love with. "You're just a fieldhand cracker," he yelled back toward the house. "You're a fat old woman," but the house was too far away for Mattie to hear. "Goddamn it to hell," he said and felt a little better. He shouted all

250

the curses he could remember, all the words and phrases he had picked up from hanging around the cotton warehouses. "Shit, piss, fuck," he said over and over, like a fellaheen reciting prayers.

Martha was down in Tallahassee dancing. She was serious about her dancing and there wasn't anything for him to do but go along with it. She had taken him up to the attic and showed him her studio. It was a long barnlike room with a blond wood floor and mirrors around three sides. An upright piano was in a corner under the descending eaves, and beside it was a record player. "I practice here every day," Martha told him, "all by myself."

"I'll keep you company," he told her, and he did, sitting in a Morris chair under the windows that looked out over the front lawn where the hot summer was withering the dogwoods. On fair afternoons he could catch a glimpse of Mr. Poitevent passing on one of his horses.

At first he wanted to talk, but Martha shushed him and after a while he began to enjoy the silence between them. He was absent now from the afternoons in the tower with his grandfather, and the old man complained until Jacey told him what he was doing. "I can understand that with no trouble at all," his grandfather said. Besides, he said, he had his new flower business to take care of. It's very interesting, he told Jacey. I have spent so much of my life out in the fields that I have become used to not seeing folks. Now I'm learning to communicate with my fellow man again.

Jacey thought about how he was going in the opposite direction. As he watched Martha spin and leap in her tattered practice clothes he felt he had wandered into no-man's-land, the shot-up and abandoned territory where brothers separated by war might meet and embrace. You have to be careful about putting all your eggs in one basket, Mattie warned him, but he was angry with her and didn't listen. He wanted only to be with Martha all the time. Since it was summer and hot they had rigged a floor fan to make a breeze. Jacey lay on his back in front of it watching her as the mechanical wind roared over him. The fan was not enough, and by the end of the practice session Martha was soaked. The sight of her body outlined by the wet leotard drove him crazy. He was still young, still a few months away from the first indelible marks of adulthood, so his feelings were a mixture of an almost brotherly wonder and lust. Once he got up out of the chair and danced with her, imitating her maneuvers at the bar. She turned to face him and as he watched she kicked her leg high.

251

Behind her he could see their reflection in the mirror, the shape of her buttocks, the beads of sweat across her back. Her nipples were clearly outlined under the gray leotard and the bones of her slender hips protruded. They did not speak, and though he could not imitate her steps, she did not laugh at him. A grimness, concentration that obliterated everything but themselves and the music, came over them and they slowed, moving arms and legs in a rhythm that seemed to hold them like ropes. They stared directly into each other's eyes, dancing so close together that he could see his own image in her pupils. He began to unbutton his shirt and she followed him, slipping the shoulder straps of her garment. They undressed as they danced, following the music dipping and gliding along the waxed floor. What awkwardness there was disappeared in the attention they gave each other, the fine solitude of each other's eyes. They did not speak, nor, when their clothes were tossed aside, did they touch. Completely naked they danced in the great empty room under the eaves as the afternoon sunlight poured across the floor and the sound of her father speaking to one of his horses drifted from the yard. His penis, which was still a boy's utensil, was so stiff that it was no separate appendage at all, only a cocked trigger between rolling hips. When his glance flicked down her body she cried sharply, *No! only eyes,* and so they danced that way, stark naked, regarding only each other's faces. Later, when it was over, and she had made him turn his back to dress, when they sat against a mirror gulping water from a shared glass, he realized he still did not know what she looked like naked but he did not feel cheated—nothing lost—only felt the gain of her presence, the smell of her body rich and full in his nostrils and the slipperiness of her shoulder pressed against his and the coolness of her fingers as she passed the icy glass to him.

He rode back to Canaan that afternoon in a fever and when he found no one home except Angela, who was in the kitchen making a lemon pie, he climbed the stairs to his parents' bedroom, took the packets of his father's letters from the bottom drawer of Elizabeth's dresser and rode out along the Course where under a small grove of persimmons near the water he sat down and read them. He wanted to see what his father had to say about love; his hands shook as he undid the thin blue ribbons that held the packets, his mind running back to Martha's body, which was not tan at all, slickery with sweat. He had to turn through two dozen pages before he found what he was looking for.

"I love you like a fire," his father wrote, "like blisters, I hurt all over and I can't get away from it. Nobody has ever worked as hard as I have to so little purpose. There is no money no job in the world that can compensate for your not being in this hot south Georgia place. I am mad all the time, I get up in the night and go out on the porch and I try to call you out of the moon like a dog. When will you come home, when will I look across these fields and see you walking toward me? I have become the Dr. Frankenstein of my household creating you out of memory and misery. Elizabeth, I think I will lose my mind I miss you so much. If you are trying to teach me something believe that I have learned it, believe that whatever keeps you from my bed has died gone away to Ohio and won't come back. I rode out to Lazarus Swamp this afternoon and lay in the river wishing it would wash me down to the Gulf. I want to float away like a bottle. The message is still the same: I love you like a crazy man and I am going to die if you don't come home. . . ."

He flung the letter down in horror. A stray filament of breeze caught it and sailed it into the Course. He had to break through his shock to go after it; he was unable to catch it before it was soaked. The sky above the stream was clear except for a few long cirrus streaks, like skywriting. The Course was clear as a swimming pool, the spring water running over a hard clay bottom. Pickerel weed grew along the banks, nodding spearheads in the intermittent breeze. He shook the letter, trying to make it whole again. His father would beat him if he learned he had read this. What else could he do? Then his mind seemed to leave him and he lay down, in shorts and T-shirt, in the stream; the water so shallow that he had only to support himself on his elbows to keep his head out. His father had lain in the river, not this crystal stream, but flung out full length nonetheless. The orange clay underneath him was so hard that his body did not dislodge any silt. He turned over on his stomach and releasing the air in his lungs, let himself drift to the bottom. The current tugged at him but it was not strong enough to sweep him away. He turned on his side and lay on the clay with his arms stretched downstream. Above his head the light was vivid and streaked by the current. If he could stay there forever he would be happy, he thought, content. He didn't want a father anymore or a mother like the one he had. The letter had not augmented the surge of desire he felt for Martha. He had not looked at her body straight on, but he knew now that the hair in her groin was dark, and that she was so thin her ribs protruded, that her nipples were nearly colorless. I will either lie here forever, he thought, or I will get up and go away into the world. The thought made him laugh and he sat up, breaking the surface with a gasp. You make it so there is only one thing for you to do, he thought, and it was as if he heard his mother's voice speaking the words. So I reckon I know what I want to do, he said out loud. He still held the letter; it was a soaked illegible clump.

It would be years before he realized what drove him to lie down in Yellow Spring Course. The day would come when he saw himself wrapped in the shabby nets of sorrow and guilt, but he did not understand that now. He could not see the correspondences between himself and his parents, between himself and his mother's posturing artistry and his father's blinded drive toward domination. He sneaked the letters from his mother's dresser as one would grab messages from an accomplice, justifications that would erase isolation, only to discover his confreres revealed as the assassins who relentlessly tracked him. He could not say that, anywhere in his mind. Nor could he see that he was their merciless equivalent.

He got up, dried his hands in the grass and retied the bundles. The day was so hot that he began to sweat before he could dry off. He was still soaked when he arrived home after the half-mile ride up the Course.

16 Whatever current of guilt or fear ran under his actions, he wasn't deterred from his pursuit of Martha. When his father noticed lipstick on his collar after a Sunday-night date at the Dairy Queen, Jacey flinched at his laughter, but he did not explain. J.C. was glad to see the lipstick; if his son was interested in a girl he couldn't be too bad off. Maybe he would survive his mother's defection after all. The boy's interest in the world, at least in a girl, gave J.C. strength. He wanted to speak to him about it, to draw up energy from one who could find delight in life, but the boy wouldn't talk to him. He told him stories of his own past, in an effort to draw him out. He told Jacey of falling in love with an admiral's daughter in Australia when the ship spent a month in port in Sydney. Jacey watched him with his bright assessing eyes but he would not respond. The girl's father had objected to his seeing her and they both had realized anyway that when the month was up they would go their separate ways, forever. "It seemed to make us happy, in a way," J.C. said. "We had a limit, so for a while everything became possible. I don't think I ever enjoyed myself as much with anybody, until I met your mother." It was only then when, figment or reality, the memory of his mother glided into the airy room that his interest roused.

"How did you meet her?" Jacey asked, though it was against his will that he asked.

"I met her at an officers' ball in Pearl. She was going with Haven Laurens. Did you know that?"

"No."

"Haven was her fiancé actually, but once I saw your mother, I knew I had to have her. I don't know what it was about her except that she seemed to have so much more *life* than everybody around her. She was demonstrating a Hawaiian dance when I saw her—not the hula or some other tourist dance, but a dance done with sticks, a Kanaka dance. She had Haven standing out in the middle of the floor holding up a couple of bamboo sticks and she was prancing around him beating his sticks with her own. Haven was scared, she was hitting so hard, but she was laughing like crazy. There was a look in her eyes like everybody here can go straight to hell and it thrilled me. I danced with her—a regular dance—and tried to get her into a conversation, but I don't think she even noticed me; she left the dance with some native guy in a pickup truck, I remember that, I don't even think—I know—she didn't tell Haven she was going."

"What did you do?"

His father leaned forward in the wicker rocker (they were on the second-floor meeting porch) and looked out at the woods beyond the drive. Off to the left, beyond the garage, Jacey heard his mother's horse whinny in the stable. His father said, "I showed up the next morning at her cottage in a car full of flowers."

"A whole car?"

"A whole backseat. I got every kind of flower I could find: plumeria, hibiscus, frangipani, oleanders, some kind of little yellow flower that grew on bushes that I stopped by the road to pick—everything. When I got to her house I scooped them all into my arms, ran up to the front door and kicked on it till she let me in. Rufino—you remember him—came to the door—I thought at first he was the native she had driven off with"—Jacey laughed at that—"and told me she was sleeping. He didn't want to let me in, but I kept talking louder and louder until she

255

woke up. I remember she came to the door in a red silk kimono that had a picture of Fujiyama on the back. It didn't matter to her that we were at war with the Japanese. She told me to come in and help Rufino make coffee."

His voice trailed off and he hunched forward with his elbows on his knees looking out into the tangle of azalea and ligustrum in front of the live oaks. Ivy grew up the sides of the oaks. Jacey got up and lay down on the floor and began to hum a tune, some music, J.C. supposed, he had heard at his grandfather's. She had been naked under the robe; he could see the shape of her breasts. Her long hair was loosened and it fell in a black, rippling wave down her back, nearly to her waist. Underneath it, in blue and white, Fujiyama rose from the Japanese plain. She spoke to him in Chamorro—Rufino's native language, he found out later—and laughed when he didn't understand. Her teeth were white and there was a gap between the two front ones. Her eyes were as blue as the little starry asters that grew in the road ditches back home in the fall. He still held the flowers as she chattered to him in the strange lilting language full of vowels. Then she said in English, "Throw them down there," indicating the sofa. She plucked a hibiscus from the pile and set it behind her ear. "You have to be careful where you wear a flower," she said. "Above the right ear means you're single and above the left ear means you're married. Or vice versa, I can't ever remember which. Is this what you do for a living?" Her hand waved over the flowers. "Or is there some special occasion?"

"I met you last night at the dance."

"I remember. You were the fair lieutenant with the moo cow eyes, Haven's friend. Do you always stare at women like that?"

He cut his eyes away. "Only on special occasions," he said and bit himself inside for repeating her phrase.

"It must have been your birthday then," she said and laughed. "You go help Rufino while I put on some clothes, then you can tell me what a profound impression I've made on you." She whirled in the kimono so that he got a fleeting glimpse of her long tan legs and disappeared into the bedroom.

The cottage was small with low white ceilings in the corners of which whey-colored geckos chirped. He went out to the kitchen to help Rufino, who was angrily banging pots in the sink. "Too early," the old man muttered under his breath, "too early for visiting." He shot a quick fierce glance at J.C.'s silver collar bars. The old man wouldn't let him help, even took the blue china cups out of J.C.'s hand when he went to set them on the table. After a while Elizabeth came back. She was wearing a long pleated white tennis skirt and a white jersey. Through the jersey he could see the shape of her nipples. She sent Rufino out into the yard and sat down across from him at the table. The kitchen was filled with morning life, and he could smell her perfume and something else, a sharp bitter smell that he later learned was olives.

They drank the coffee and ate sweet rolls without talking. She looked at him all the time, as if, he thought, she might buy him. She had pushed the jersey sleeves up her arms and he saw that her wrists were delicate and there were fine silvery hairs on her forearms. Finally she wiped her lips with the tips of her fingers and said, "You've already decided that you can't live without me."

He choked on a swallow of coffee. "Does it show that much?"

"It shows like a lit-up Christmas tree. Did you know we used to have a tree in our front yard that we filled with lights every Christmas?"

"We did that, too."

"You did? In Charleston it was very unusual. I believe it's because people in Charleston are so afraid of giving their position away. A lighted tree would lead the rabble right up to the house."

"My people came from Charleston."

"Then you know exactly what I mean. But please don't start talking about all the people we mutually know."

"It was a long time ago. We left right after the Revolution."

She leaned forward on her elbows. "Tell me," she said, with a seriousness that he only barely realized was play, "have you been away long enough to get over it?"

She's a madwoman, he thought, but he looked back at her, fascinated. "My father still wakes up screaming," he said, "but the rest of us only wet the bed two or three times a year."

"That's good, that's good. I'm glad to hear you've made progress. I've only been away six years so I shouldn't lose hope."

"Definitely not. We can always get over something if we really want to. Time'll tell."

"*Ora, ora.*"

"What does that mean?"

"Time, time. It's one of Rufino's sayings. Actually not so much a saying as a mouthing. He's a Guamanian and a Japanese sympathizer. He still believes the rising sun will one day rise in Hawaii."

"It's getting late in the day."

"Oo. You don't talk like that all the time, do you? I don't want to jump into bed with somebody who's going to make jokes like that."

"I can keep it under control."

"Good." She stood up and stretched, rising on her toes. She dropped back to earth as if, it seemed to him, she had reached up to the sky. "You have to go away now," she said, "but if you come back tonight we'll go swimming on the North Shore."

"The North Shore beaches are off limits."

"Not to native Hawaiians."

He hesitated, thinking she would walk him to the door, but she only waved him away. "Run along," she said, "and thank you for the flowers. I've always wanted a carload."

He was through the house and climbing into his jeep when he realized he hadn't asked her what time to pick her up. He came back to the front steps. "What time . . . tonight?" he shouted through the screen door.

Her voiced drifted up from back in the house. "Eight thirty-six. Eight thirty-six sharp."

"Fine. I'll be here." He wondered as he got in the jeep if she meant it, that exactness, or if she was joking.

"We got married a month later," he said and leaned back in the rocker.

Jacey stopped his song and pushed up on his elbows. "I like that," he said.

"I do, too. I've always admired that part of your mother's and my romance."

"It's like a story, going so fast. I want to go that fast."

"Well, I can think now," J.C. said, passing his hand over his face, "of reasons to go slower." This will not do, he thought, this will not do at all. The disturbed memories chittered and stung like beautiful, angry, pecking birds.

A silence fell between them, and Jacey looked out at the descending night. He smelled the candy odor of chinaberry flowers and heard the crickets as their sawing rose and fell in the grass behind the house. Martha was walking in the attic studio, tapping her fingers along the bar.

His mother lay on a raft in a crystal sea. Sometimes they got mixed up in his mind. Sometimes he dreamed of talking all night to a woman he knew better than he knew anyone in the world, but when he woke up he could not tell who she was. Her name was just beyond his memory, just out of reach. Other times he dreamed that *he* was a woman. He would look down at himself, in the dream, and between his legs would be a tangled V of black hair, no appendage. The dreams frightened him but never enough to throw him out of sleep; he woke with a feeling of dismay and a desire to turn away, to forget. In another dream a shadowy form stood on the gallery just outside his window peering in. He lay on his back looking at the black shape and could not make it go away. In the dream for a long time he was frozen with fright, unable, and unwilling, to move. Finally, straining against harsh resistance, he rose, still in the dream, and threw himself at the window. He would wake in bed to the sound of the air conditioner shuddering and wheezing and the shadow gone.

He turned over on his stomach. The straw mat underneath him smelled faintly mildewy. "Sometimes I dream about Mama," he said.

"Sometimes I do, too. Lately I've been dreaming about her a lot." Shoo—fly, bird.

"Do you think she's going to come back?"

"She'll come back. There's no worry about that. We just don't know when, or what she'll be bringing."

"It seems like she's always gone away, even when she's here."

"I know what you mean. It's always been hard for me to get a fix on her, too."

Jacey kissed his finger and touched his own face. "What was it you saw in Mama?"

J.C. paused a long moment. "I don't know what it was," he said finally. "She had light in her eyes."

"Is she the most beautiful woman in the world, you think?"

"She was to me. I thought when I saw her that she was the most beautiful woman I had ever looked at, much less gotten close to." J.C. shifted in his chair, looked over his shoulder at his son sprawled on the mat. "She had a way of scaring people, men especially. A lot of it was her manner, but some of it was just the way she looked. That Indian nose and her smile, and those eyes—there wasn't anything soft about her, she wasn't one of those friendly neighbor types, she was a gunboat, fully armed."

He had watched a sailor take pictures of her as she sat on the hood of a car with her leg cocked up. She was turned so that her skirt concealed her legs, but her leg was up, bent at the knee—if the sailor came around in front he could look directly up her skirt. It drove the swabbie crazy, he could tell, her leg up like that; the grin on her face was nothing more than a sexual leer, full of the knowledge of her power. This happened in the parking lot of a restaurant in Waikiki and it made him so angry that he walked off and left her. She found him in the Royal Hawaiian coffee shop and for five minutes after she sat down he wouldn't speak to her. "You love it when I do that," she said finally. "That's what makes you so angry."

Leaning forward over the table with his head down, like a fighter coming up under a punch, he called her a slut and a whore. This was after Jacey was born, after she had told him she wasn't coming back to the States with him. "It gets you hot to see me do that," she said. "You wish I'd do it more often."

He fled the table and the town and drove back alone to the cottage under a full moon the color of a rotten orange. The wind had strewn oleander petals across the front steps; they looked like painted kisses tossed down. He went into the house and lay down on their bed. He knew she was right but he didn't want to hear about it. She has corrupted me, he thought, she has changed me from what I was. He got up and pulled open the top drawer of her dresser, which was filled with her underwear, silk panties that she was able to get when no other woman could find them in the stores. He grabbed a handful and raised them to his face. In the moonlit mirror he looked at himself with the panties pressed over his nose. "I can't stand it," he said, and began to tear them to pieces. He tore them (surprised at how tough silk was) until they were rags. Then he went out on the porch and threw the rags into the yard. "How you like them flowers," he shouted. "How you like them pretty little blossoms." He dropped to his knees and began to gather up the oleander petals off the steps. When he'd gathered up enough to fill his cupped hands he threw them onto the lawn, too. The breeze blew them back at him and he cursed and retreated into the house. He lay down again on the bed fully clothed and fell asleep. When he woke in the gray light before dawn Elizabeth was sleeping naked beside him.

Jacey got up and poured himself a glass of lemonade from the pitcher on the coffee table. "Do you think I could go to New York?" he asked. He remembered his manners and poured his father a glass.

"Why do you want to go there?"

"I think I want to go to school in New York."

His father studied his face. "What put that idea in your head?"

"I think I want to paint pictures, and Rooley said you have to go to New York if you want to be a painter."

"I haven't seen you doing much drawing."

"I do sometimes, and I like to watch Rooley work."

His father set his rocker in motion. His wide veiny hands clasped and unclasped the armrests. "I've thought of that for you myself," he said. "I was the first one of us not to go off to boarding school and I've always wondered what it would have been like. Your granddaddy went and his daddy before him. Bryce and Franken were at Woodbury Forest together for two or three years."

"Why didn't you go?"

"I was too busy making money." He looked at Jacey and laughed. "I found out all these crops we were planting could make you a profit and I refused to go. It made Granddaddy mad until I showed him how much I was making."

"I think I want to go away," Jacey said. "To New York."

"Why New York? You'd probably like Woodbury Forest better. Or even one of the schools in New England."

"The painting. You have to go to New York to paint."

"I don't know if that's strictly true, but it might be a good idea to visit New York. Would you like to take a trip up there?"

"If we could look for a school."

"We'll look for plenty of things."

That night Jacey called Martha and told her he was going to New York. "I'm going to prepare a place for us," he said. "We're going to leave this old land behind."

"That's good," she told him. "I'm so glad," but her voice was flat and sad.

"What's the matter?"

"I don't know. I don't think I'll ever get to New York. Daddy doesn't want me to go and I can't get Mama to stop listening to her gospel records long enough to help me."

"You're just worried about the auditions. Didn't you tell me the Drovena auditions are next month?"

"They'll never pick me. I'm too old."

"But you're great. They'll choose you in a minute."

"Oh, Jacey. To you I'm a star. To them I'll just be another little girl from the provinces, one more sweaty hopeful in tights."

"Don't say that. I come from very sensitive people. Burdettes are very good at the arts, we have a touch."

"So?"

"So I know talent when I see it. I know it naturally. I grew up listening to opera with my granddaddy and Rooley's told me all about painting—that's why I told Daddy I wanted to go to New York."

"To be a painter?"

"Sure. We're going up there just before school starts, to see the city and look at prep schools and all that. And you'll be there, too. They won't be able to keep you out. I wouldn't even think of going myself if you weren't."

"You sweet boy. I do love you. But I'm going to have to work like crazy for this audition."

"I'll help you."

"No. You'll just distract me. You can't keep away from me."

"I'll be quiet. I've got to practice drawing anyway if I'm going to be an artist."

"We'll see."

"Come on, Martha. We can help each other."

"We do help each other. But if I'm going to be a prima ballerina I have to concentrate. I can't look any other way."

"What does that mean?"

"Don't get scared. You're getting me where you want me. I'm not going to run away from you."

"I spent all afternoon thinking about your shoulders."

Her jingly laugh came over the phone. "My shoulders?"

"They're so rounded, like little hills. I could look at them all day."

"You can see them tomorrow night. I'll meet you at the Dairy Queen and we can go to the river and you can look at them to your heart's content."

"How will I stand it until I see you?"

"You just will."

"I'll pine."

"Only till I get there."

"Only till you get there," he said. He kissed the receiver. "Only till you get there," he said again.

262

. . .

J.C. descended the stairs to the deserted first floor. Into these polished proper rooms in which a mist of memory creeps over the fine
English furniture. We make up with our possessions for what we lack in
prehensile baggage. He made a quick circuit through the parlors—three
with brick-floored sunporch—drifted through the dining room where his
mother's fine crystal gleamed behind the glass-walled breakfront—crystal behind crystal—circled the dining-room table and stood before the
bay window. With the lights off, pressing his face against a pane, he
could see the mass of bushes under the live oaks. They had kept it wild
out there, breakwaters of growth between the family houses that all Burdettes had played lost-children games in. Just enough woods to keep an
owl, maybe a possum, a wandering raccoon. When he was a child he
thought even that narrow strip of woods was endless. There were unex-
plored places; he could get lost. But then he thought, There have been
nights when I got lost in my own house, when I woke up standing in a
room I didn't know how to get across. Save me from the darkness, let
there always be a light shining under the door.

He went through the swinging door into the breakfast room and
through to the kitchen, where he got a glass of water from the sink. As a
child he had carried water in a mason jar out to his father and uncles in
the fields. They had drunk with the cotton mule reins wrapped around
their wrists like gauntlets. His son was upstairs telephoning, the receiver
cord stretched full-length so he could lock himself in his room. Some important secrets being shared with Artis Poitevent's daughter.

Water glasses upside down on dish towels gleamed faintly, collecting light from the moon shining through the window over the sink. Old
folks believed that the moon shining on your sleep would drive you
crazy. A pregnant woman had to be careful because it could pull the child
from her body. His father believed the old superstitions, he planted by
the moon like an Indian. His mother, cosmopolitan riverport daughter,
had scoffed. But the rings of the moon told his father rain was coming—
sensible enough, but J.C. had always believed that his father saw more
than just rain in the faint blue circles. Elizabeth would know, she would
see into whatever farther dimension his father had peered into. His memories of her oppressed him, lay like heat on his mind. It doesn't matter
what two people do, he thought, it doesn't matter whether they get along
or not—all they have to do is rub against one another long enough for
absence to be appalling. His grandfather and his uncle had learned that

during the years their father had yoked them together running this farm. But when his grandfather died, Eustace had mooned like a lost boy. He had seen him lean out of the cab of his pickup to speak, catch himself and stop, and known that it was for his brother that the words were intended, choked off.

He sat down at the kitchen table and began to fold the napkins that were piled there from the washing machine. Elizabeth was probably right about Angela's incompetence. The girl was young and her mind wandered. But he wouldn't be the one to let her go. No Burdette had ever fired anybody, not directly anyway. Even Eustace, who was a tough old wheelhorse, let the manager fire the rough hands. The drinkers were the worst: they didn't show up and when they did they were liable to hurt themselves or somebody else. Ah, well. The napkins had come with Elizabeth; dailies, she called them. He couldn't get her to visit Charleston. When her father called, as he did only rarely now, she wouldn't speak to him beyond a few brief, patronizing sentences. If the truth were known he had loved her partly because she came from a place like Charleston. His people had lived on this land for two hundred years but they still didn't have the savoir faire of a member of the St. Cecilia Society from Charleston, South Carolina.

His mother had been DAR and UDC—she was an Augusta Colquitt and qualified for the old societies right down the line—but blood Burdettes were excluded. They were CDC—Children of the Confederacy—but just barely: one of their great-uncles had ridden with Gordon in Virginia. He had been captured at Chancellorsville and after the war had walked all the way home from a prisoner-of-war camp in Maryland. The story was that he had complained for the rest of his life about how hard the roads had been on his bare feet. He had been known as a fool even before he signed up, and certainly after. The Burdettes had resisted wars; they had resisted anything that might draw them away from their enterprises. They didn't qualify for the DAR or the Society of the Cincinnati because they hadn't fought in the Revolution. They had sided with the British, and their refusal had followed them down the years, had been the cause of their removal a generation after the war to the Canaan grant their former king had given them.

But Elizabeth qualified, she qualified for inclusion in society. The only way the Burdettes had ever qualified for anything was to make up their own. Yellow Springs was Burdetteville, as far as anybody in south

Georgia was concerned. His great-grandfather had once in a drunken fit ordered his overseers to rename every store Burdette. Tear the old signs down and put up new ones. Burdette Livery, Burdette Funeral Parlor, Burdette Saloon, Burdette Hotel. If the world would not have them, they would remake the world. The merchants had balked.

He leaned down and pressed his face in the napkins; they smelled of the cleanliness of their washing. He wanted to live by signs, too. Not just, as his father did, find the moments when the natural world whispered its secrets, but the true moments of turning, when life changed direction. Years ago walking on Massachusetts Avenue with his college roommate, above the heads of a festive crowd, a prostitute, shaking snow from her coat on the steps of a bar, had looked up into his eyes and asked him if he wanted her. Asked him with her eyes across the crowded, suddenly blurred space. Her face, cold white above her brindle coat, for that moment, had seemed as open as a child's, as vulnerable. He, callow and rich, afraid, answered with his lips, silently, so sure was he of her question, so quick with his response: No. But a second later, second in which, collar flipped up, she dropped away into the crowd, his heart reversed itself and he cried *Yes! Yes, of course,* out loud, so that his roommate, a fractious soccer star from Minneapolis, had barked a laugh at him, misunderstanding. He plunged into the crowd after her, sure that the sudden rope thrown between them—not a tug toward the rumble bed of lust, something else—would hold, but when he reached the steps where she had stood, he couldn't find her; she had vanished. His friend, catching up with him, grinning at his explanation, did not understand his agitation, reminded him that he had a history of only getting into the highest gear when the object he barreled toward was clearly unattainable. Angry, perhaps at too much truth, and at his own inability to explain what so brief and trivial a connection had meant to him, he had waved his friend into silence, cursed him and walked off in the direction of the river.

Under the rachitic elms where finally, later, the city hummed toward its approximation of silence, he walked, hands plunged deep into the pockets of his loden coat, he felt his intractable solitude draw around him again. If you make money they look at you and say Remarkable! Remarkable! Come home with me now, be my friend. He had been extraordinary all his life, the best student in Yellow Springs, Georgia, scion of the greatest family, lanky, swivel-hipped football star, handsome as a prince. He had been elected president of his class six straight years. And yet he came home on high school afternoons, climbed to the attic and in wrenching fevers of self-disgust banged his head against the red cedar wall of the clothes closet. Muffled by the fragrant boards he had cried out against his life. Mother dead, swimming in heaven seas, father whose hands opened only to reveal the compressed clods of Canaan gray earth, he could not bear to be only the little he was. Nothing was enough. He could have crossed the continent ravine by ravine, crawling through the dark spaces, through quarries and caves, through the dense woods of pine and oak, forcing his way through the remorseless, indifferent prairie grasses, across the cold mountains, down desert slopes—to what, to a cliff-shouldered sea, breaking so cold and lifelessly against the basalt rocks, to find what? Nothing that would ever be enough, no glance that settled like a homing bird into his heart. He could not catch that woman, no matter how good he was. She wouldn't look back a second time.

"Let that be a goddamn sign forever," he said, folding the last napkin. He used to go out in the woods and sing every song he knew. He had been doing it for years before he realized they were all songs of loss, irreducible defeat. His greatest-great Georgia grandmother, wife of Langston Burdette, had died of diphtheria tending to a sick woman. Somehow he must wrench himself up into such selflessness. Maybe tomorrow, maybe then. His mother had died in Yellow Spring; she had been found floating face down on a Sunday morning. He was sixteen and all he knew about it was that she was found floating there, dressed for a party at fifteen fathoms, a woman who never swam a stroke in her life. No one ever told him how she got there. The preacher, marshaling all details in his muscular will, said boldly, his eyes daring the congregation to disagree, that she had fallen, tripped in the dark. Like starving children, they wolfed that bread. His father after the funeral, silent on every other score, had roared over jokes Eustace told. And I who never roared with laughter again, until I met you, Elizabeth. What was so funny *then*? That half hour we spent trying to tie a bicycle into the trunk? An old man preaching hellfire on a street in Honolulu? Chasing a chipmunk in the little park we stopped in on the way to Hot Springs, Arkansas? The night we wore Chinese hats to bed? So long a history makes heavy weight.

He reared up, rose thinking, No, not here, not now, not again, and shouldered through the screen door into air. Up the length of the gallery, still blackened by Elizabeth's fire, he could see the courthouse. As he watched, the floodlights came on and the white facade burst into brightness. A police car passed, tapping its siren. A man and a woman stood against the front fence looking at the house. Tourists, he expected, sun seekers stopping to look at an authentic southern mansion. He walked up the porch and around the corner and hailed the couple from the front steps. They started to move away but he called for them to stop. He walked across the yard to where they stood, hesitating against the fence.

"We were admiring your house," the man said. He had straight white hair combed flat back. His wife was small and portly.

J.C. turned to look at the house and for a moment it was as if he had never seen it before. "Do you like it?" he said to the man.

"We think it's gorgeous," the woman said, "but it must be hard to keep up. Have you had a fire?"

"Yes. And it isn't really hard to keep, once you get a rhythm going. We're used to living there." What in the world am I going to do?

"There's a house up in Wrightsville like this," the man said, "except it has these other wings off to the side. The front looks the same, though."

"I've seen it," J.C. said. "It belongs to the Stamps family. Old Robert Stamps was a senator before the Civil War."

"Well, it's not any prettier than this place," the woman said, "not a bit prettier."

"Where're you from?" J.C. asked.

"From Shelbyville, Tennessee," the man said. "We're on the way to Daytona. We go down there every year."

"I've never been to Daytona, but I remember seeing pictures of people driving on the beach. Do they still do that?"

"They still do it. When we first went down there they were running races on the beach, that's where stock car racing got started, but now it's just the public cars, no racing."

"It's a pleasant thought," J.C. said, "driving a car along a beach."

"We enjoy it," the man said. "We look forward every year to getting down there."

They stopped talking and looked at the house. The dusk made the burn marks look like shadows. Shadows from another world, J.C. thought, from a light source that was undetectable through human means. A sign?

"We'd better be moving on, Mother," the man said.

"Won't you come inside?" J.C. asked. "I'd love to show you the interior. We have some very good old furniture."

"Thank you kindly," the man said, "but we always try to make Tallahassee the first night."

"Please," J.C. said, "please come inside."

"John doesn't like to drive after dark," the woman said.

"It sure is a pretty house," the man chimed in. "We hope you didn't mind us gawking at it."

"I'm delighted that you stopped. But won't you come in? I have cake and lemonade—I could fix you a drink." He reached over the fence and grabbed the man's sleeve, tugging it lightly between two fingers.

"No, no," the man said, unhooking the cloth from J.C.'s fingers with the alacrity and obliviousness of a hunter momentarily snagged by a bramble. "We've got to keep rolling on." The eyes of the wife, which were close-set and pale, narrowed for a moment, but she only repeated the man's thank-you and then they both moved off to their car, an old Chevy splashed with Tennessee.

"If you come back this way be sure to stop in," J.C. called to them as they pulled out into the evening empty street. The woman, safe now, thrust her arm out the window and waved broadly, as a girl would do.

He felt short of breath, threatened by the summery perfume of honeysuckle twining in the fence. Exhausted, but restless. He walked along the fence to the gate and crossed the street to the courthouse lawn. The descendant night had not diminished the day's heat, and he pulled at the top of his shirt to get air against his chest. He smelled the camphor tree at the corner, guileless, overweaning balm, full of unavoidable memory, Elizabeth arriving by train. He walked around the courthouse looking up at the rising tiers of masonry. When he reached the other side he started down the street that led to his office. He walked this way to work each morning. When he reached the office—gray, aluminum front pressed into brick walls—he crossed the street again, instead of going inside as he had planned, and made his way past the Pitkin tobacco warehouse down the block to the main east thoroughfare. At the corner he stopped and looked across at the Dairy Queen. Teenagers circled in their cars. A number of them sat on the hoods of automobiles behind the drive-in, laughing and talking. She had said, "It is worth your time to learn to confuse dream with reality," and he thought, Maybe I am better at that than you. The yellow grass he stood in smelled of piss, and the faint sweet dry odor of flue-cured tobacco. He would like to visit the places that were important to him in his youth, but they were all part of Canaan. And he would like to be a man who took action in his life, like all the heroes he read about when he was eight in the little blue biographies in the Carnegie Library off the Square. He was afraid to cross the street and go among the teenagers.

What I would like, he thought, starting off, is some place to break into. I want a past I have to return to secretly.

He walked a block east and turned north into Undertown, the neighborhood of warehouses and tenant cottages that had grown up around the fertilizer complex. When he reached the complex he stood in the dusty sweet-smelling street looking up at the high board facade of the original fertilizer plant. It had once been green with white letters that read BURDETTE FERTILIZER, but time and the years of chemical dust had changed the color to gray. He could barely make out the name. In places boards had buckled and a few hung down along the high front. It had always pleased him that he worked in an industry that did not have to concern itself with show. He could come here and plunge around in a tattered white cotton overcoat among the acids and the gases. He showed up for work on Sunday afternoons, a stack of mail under his arm. He had sacked fertilizer and pulled cotton with the crews.

He stepped through the wide gangway doors and stood in the dim electric light looking down the avenue that was fronted by huge open-sided bins in which the fertilizer was heaped in piles as high as three-story houses. Gray-faced Negroes on front-end loaders drove among the piles. They lunged against the heaps of gray, smashing a load into place, as if they were trying to break themselves and their machines against the squat mountains. She had said, "When I was a child I couldn't tell the difference between myself and the bees in the bushes. We were all part of the natural world." And he had said, "That makes no sense to me." He went back outside.

A quarter moon hung in the west with a single bright star beside it. From the far end of the building the night watchman with his round black clock slung over his shoulder waved to him and called, "Evening, Mr. Burdette." J.C. waved and moved on down the street in the opposite direction. He probably knew every one in Yellow Springs, at least through family. The night watchman came from a family of drunks and pistol-whippers who lived three blocks from the plant. He could picture

269

their house, a sagging shotgun cabin in a bare-dirt yard. Morning glory vines flowered on a string trellis hung from the eaves. The rooms smelled of peanut oil and sour sweat.

He walked east past the number two plant and the acid plant across the street. At the corner he turned north along the small, cloudy river that his plants steadily polluted. The people's river, he thought, and remembered when you could catch fish from its banks. Now it offered nothing, beyond a few elderberry bushes the fruit of which was occasionally used to make wine. The river veered away eastward and he came into a neighborhood of shotgun cabins. Huge oak trees arched over the street out of yards that were bare and packed from foot traffic, swept clean. In front of a pale house the size of his garage a small girl played jacks in the light from the porch under a large chinaberry tree. She wore a whitish shift and scampered on her knees like a little animal. She counted out loud to herself as she played. He stepped over a low chickenwire fence into the yard to watch her. He could hear a television threatening disaster from inside the house. Up the street a woman called to someone in a voice full of longing and resentment. I think my goddamn heart is going to break though I don't see how it can be possible after so much time. The girl, oblivious to him, crabbed on the ground gathering jacks as the tiny red ball bounced high. Stars on the ground, he thought. When the game was over she turned her small monkey face up to him and grinned; the grin made her pretty. He grinned back. She held the jacks and ball up to him as if it were the most natural thing in the world for him to play next.

"I've forgotten how," he said. "Can you show me?"

"You're pretty dumb," she said and screwed her face up.

"Sometimes I'm slow."

"Watch."

She tossed the jacks and began to play, scooping them up in the bounce one, bounce two, bounce three sequence of the game.

"I see," he said. "I think I see."

She gathered the jacks, handed them to him and sat back on her heels. He knelt and shook the small green and red stars in his hand. "I just throw them," he said and she nodded in corroboration; her thin yellow hair was pale as lemonade. He tossed the jacks onto the ground. They glittered faintly on the packed soil. He bounced the ball and scooped one up.

"You have to do it with the same hand you bounce the ball," she said.

"That's right."

He dropped the jacks and began again.

It didn't take long for him to get the hang of it, though he lost when he was unable to pick up four at once.

"Let me see you do it," he said and stood up. The girl took the jack stones from him, tossed them and began to play. Her concentration was fierce and steady, and for some reason it made him feel secure, carefree, to watch her. He could stay there all night if they let him, and the girl kept playing. He started to speak, easy enough in his means for the moment—"Listen, I haven't been . . ."—but the girl shushed him. And then a voice called from inside, sharp and adult, called her name—Jerry Jane—and she collected her toys, sprang up and whisked away up the steps. At the door she turned and gave him a look. The look was full of womanliness, something much older than her six or seven years. It startled him, not by its incongruity but because it was so recognizable. On the way to Sea Island, Elizabeth had taken the wheel and on the straight stretch through the pines east of Waycross—his traveling stretch—she had forced the speed to 110 miles an hour. He had screamed at her, his voice full of anger, behind it a world of fear. The door slammed and the girl was gone.

He started back and when he reached the river he crossed the street bridge to the other side, left the pavement and made his way through knee-high broom grass along the bank. The water was milky, variegated, like something just being mixed. Nothing could live in water like that, he thought. Playing with the girl had for a moment soothed him, but as he made his way through the bushes, stepping carefully in the gathered darkness over washed-out places where runoff had created holes and ditches, he felt the old familiar tensions rise in him. He had once been driven at a run to the banks of a river where in frenzy he had thrown himself in. He wouldn't throw himself in water like this, he thought, no matter how upset he got. He wanted to speak to someone; he had, he thought, necessary things to say, but he couldn't think who the confessor could be. He stopped at a pile of dry underbrush and began to break twigs off and toss them into the water. It is strange, he thought, how in a small town you can know people all your life and never speak seriously to them. On any day he could find a dozen men he had known for forty years, known in all kinds of situations, from ball games to dove hunts to high school classes. They had run around naked together when they were five years old. Never once after he was grown had he bared his heart to one of them. He knew their lives though, would know them on any dark planet. I never got over the war, he thought, and found that he was speaking out loud. "I met someone there," he said, "and now I am whipping along behind her like the tail of a kite."

He squatted in the grass, which smelled of fertilizer. He tossed a twig into the water. The current took it sluggishly as if it were reluctant to break away from its mixing. He said, "Why do you keep on with her?" and ducked his head, embarrassed to be asking himself questions, and out loud. He looked up and down the bank: no one else was about. "Why do you keep on with her?" he asked again.

"I don't know." He was silent for a moment. For a moment it was as if he could see the red roads running through the Oahu pineapple fields. "No, no," he cried. "No!" He sprang up and ran toward the bridge. When he reached the road he slowed down and trotted toward the complex. He crossed the road and went into the small shack beside the acid plant and asked the night manager if he could borrow his pickup. He would get it back to him.

He drove through town to Bryce's house. His brother was in the front yard watering the lawn. He turned as J.C. drove up and sprayed a stream of water over the truck, just missing the open window. "Oh, I didn't see you," he said in mock surprise. J.C. got out and walked over to him. "Why do you think I keep on with Elizabeth?" he asked.

Bryce twisted the hose nozzle shut. "Because you can't think of anything else to do," he said.

"No."

"Is this a test?"

"No, no. Why do I keep on?"

"I got it: you're in love with her."

"No."

"You're not in love with her?"

"I am in love with her, but that's not why."

"I give up."

J.C. squatted in the grass. "Here's why it is," he said. "She was the biggest risk I ever took."

Bryce hacked out a laugh that gave way to a short coughing spell. He squeezed his eyes shut with the tips of his fingers, making him for a moment, J.C. thought, look like a monster. "That's the reason, huh?" he said, getting his wind.

"Doesn't it make sense to you?"

"If you say it it does, but that's a strange reason to commit yourself to a woman. Did you just come up with it?"

"I've always known it, but I just now got conscious of it."

"I think you'll come up with a better one eventually. I think your big risk was the satellite expansion. Are you going to want another mortgage?"

"I guess so—can't we hold it?"

"Franken says no, but I think we can, one more time." J.C. knew that his younger brothers did not get along. Their wives were jealous of each other's position and that jealousy, parceled out steadily to each husband, inflamed, perhaps, an original rivalry between them. They practiced a wary jostling cordiality with each other, without boisterousness or physical affection, a smooth, nearly lubricious deference that failed to hide their entrenched and subtle grievances. "What you'll have to do to pay the loan off," Bryce continued, "will keep the tension high enough to drown out Elizabeth for a while."

J.C. looked into the woods that separated their yards. "Mebbe so," he said. Then he said, "Nothing drowns her out."

"She'll come back when she's ready to. This isn't the first time she's slipped away."

"No. But what about when *I'm* ready?"

"Seems like to me you would've learned by now that you're going to have to do things the way she wants them done if you want to be around her."

"I don't think I can do that."

His brother looked at him. "I don't know if you can either. I haven't seen much sign of your being able to do it up till now. Why don't you get yourself something going on the side?"

"Have an affair?"

"Sure. Something to take the pressure off."

"What about my reputation?"

"We're Burdettes. We don't have that kind of reputation."

"I do. I'm trying to do something different."

"You're always trying to do something different, make some farther mark. We're doing just fine. What we need to get'll come to us."

"You sound like Daddy."

"How could I not. I'm his son."

J.C. looked into the street. The camphor tree at the corner was a black mass of leaves. "How come you're watering the lawn at night?"

"I just needed to get out of the house. How come you're driving around in John's truck?"

"I was over at the plant and I needed transportation. I've been thinking about Mama."

"I thought you were thinking about Elizabeth."

"It's almost the same thing. Do you remember how it was that morning?"

"When she died?"

"Yes."

"I remember."

"Did Daddy come downstairs?"

"No. He stayed in his room. Eustace had to go in and get him. I don't think he saw Mama again until we were all at the funeral home."

"And by then he was joking, carrying on with all those Augusta kinfolk."

"They hadn't gotten here yet, but later, yeah."

J.C. ran his hand over his face. "There's something bad wrong with us," he said.

"Everybody knows that. We're just too powerful for anybody to do anything about it."

"Sometimes I just want to disappear. This is confidential, but sometimes I get this feeling that I just want to evaporate, become nothing."

"You're just tired."

"It's not fatigue."

"What is it?"

"I feel like I'm pushing against something I can't get through."

"You always get through."

"No, not this time. I remember when I had scarlet fever as a kid. Nobody had to tell me I was sick. I knew—it was an intuition or something—that I was sick, not like the flu or a cold, but really sick. My insides told me that something big was wrong, something I couldn't deal with. It's like that now. I don't even feel like trying to get through; I *know* I can't."

"Shoot. You're J. C. Burdette. We've always loved you because you would try anything. You always led the way. I used to watch you dive in

274

the spring when we were kids and I'd get a thrill at how far down you would go. Nobody else even wanted to go to the bottom, but you *only* wanted to do that. You just thought of it naturally, the way the rest of us would think of going to get a candy cane."

"I didn't think of those things either; I just moved and they came to me. They were next."

"Well, they weren't next for the rest of us. All the money you made in tobacco and going to war and getting married off on your own without any family there, starting this business." Bryce opened the nozzle and sprayed a stream of water at a drooping azalea. "We're not that unusual in a way," he said. "The country's full of entrepreneurial characters, all kinds of adventurers. But for us *you* were unusual. Families like ours, they stop producing after a generation or two. But not us. Look around you. The little towns around here are full of semi-Burdettes. There's always a cantankerous group that started the lumberyard or the cotton mill or the bank or the railroad; each one of them had some kind of spark that drove them harder than the folks around them. But you look a couple of generations later—it's usually the third—and the spark's gone: the grandchildren are living off interest, or they wind up employees of a company they used to own, or they're drunks or they've moved away where there's no pressure to be go-getters. That's the way it usually is, but not with us. I'm not saying Daddy didn't have it. It seems like with us there's always at least one in every generation who's got some kind of spirignum. Daddy got Granddaddy to try raising tobacco and we started making money again. We could have been in trouble without that. All Granddaddy did was feud with Eustace about who owned what. You remember those fences they built; they had the whole place carved up in parcels. Eustace told me that there was a time when he and Granddaddy carried guns—each of them was afraid the other was going to shoot him."

He sprayed an arc of water over the lawn and twisted the nozzle shut. "You know how the Russians are always talking about how they invented stuff. They come up with rubber tractor tires and they put out a bulletin about how the Russian scientists have just invented them. It drives me crazy, but we're the same way. Daddy invented tobacco in this country. They've been growing it in the south for two hundred years, but as far as this little corner of the earth was concerned, Jack Burdette invented it, just like you invented a fertilizer plant. You've been inventing things all your life. You invented the bottom of the spring and convertible Oldsmobiles and cotton brokering and Burdette's One Hundred Fertilizer. Hell, I'd probably be off lawyering in Atlanta if it wasn't for you, drawing up wills for rich fools in the city. You talk about moving us out into the world, but what you've done is keep us together on this ground." He spat and rubbed it out with his foot, as if it were a cigarette. "Sometimes I wish Daddy could see that," he said, "that it's these factories that're keeping us together."

J.C. rose and looked down the street. He could see the streetlights descending the hill that led to the offices. It seemed to him that there was a darkness down there, deeper than the rest of the night. He ran his fingers over his eyes, wiped greasy sweat away. "It makes me feel good to listen to you," he said, and he touched his brother on the shoulder. "I wish you could tell me what to do about Elizabeth."

"Maybe there's nothing to do but just keep on. Unless you're really ready to get rid of her. She's a strange woman, but there've always been strange women around here. Lois is strange. She likes to sing in bed."

"That's not too strange."

"Arias at three in the morning? Let me tell you it's a hell of a way to be conked out of sleep. It's got me so jittery I have to walk around after dark watering the grass."

J.C. laughed. "Y'all are crazy."

"Don't I know it, but the craziest is that I will eventually get used to it. You live in something a long time and it begins to seem natural."

"I wish that were true."

"Just let her live like she wants to, Jay. That's all you've got left to do." He began to coil the hose. J.C. started off toward the mass of bushes that separated their two yards. "Let me know how it goes," Bryce said.

"Okay."

J.C. found the path that they had used as children to cross through the narrow wood between the two houses. It was the first time since he became a grown man that he had taken it. Under the live oaks he stopped for a moment and listened to a flock of birds chittering in the branches above him. They sounded as if they were upset, angry. He couldn't tell what they were, blackbirds or cedar waxwings. Could something as powerful as what he had first felt for Elizabeth fade? If it could he didn't know how he could bear to go on living. He could live without her presence maybe, but he couldn't live without the feeling she brought. He slapped the side of the tree to feel the pain of a blow. There was numbness then a stinging hot as fire then a dull ache that rose up the palm. He rubbed his hand on his pants leg and hit the tree again. Again there were pricks of fire and then the ache. He hit the tree with his other hand, open-palmed. The skin stung and fire shot up his wrist. He hit first with one hand and then the other, slapping the corrugated immovable trunk so the small woods rang with sound. After a while the stinging stopped and the pain moved into his shoulders. He kept it up until he could not lift his arms to hit again.

The next morning he drove to Tallahassee and took a plane to Miami. There he caught a flight to Charlotte Amalie, then changed to the twin-engine ten-seater that made the afternoon run to St. Guillaume. He hired a taxi to her hotel and climbed the stairs two at a time to her room. She was not surprised to see him but she was surprised when he knelt at her feet and begged her to come back with him. Of course she would come, she told him, and there was a softness in her eyes that he had never seen before. He wondered if he had reached her at last. They made love in a welter of clothes she pulled out to pack. Some things have to come first, he told her, and she didn't complain that he was messing her things.

This is fine with me, she told him as he reared above her looking she thought like a wonderful wild horse. He thought once again that she was the most beautiful woman he had ever seen. Touch me, he said, touch me all over, I have to get all of my skin used to you again. She kissed him with lips that were first cool then hot. He remembered then the first time he had touched her skin, as he had grabbed her arm to keep her from stepping oblivious into traffic from a street corner in Honolulu. There had been no fever then, no spark, only the feeling as he grasped her arm just above the wrist that he was touching a cooler and fresher version of himself. She moaned under him and cried out, reached up and pulled his head down and bit him lightly on the lips. The room was full of a cool dry breeze that fluttered over them like the wings of a trapped bird. From where he arched over her compliant body he could see the shredded tops of coconut palms and beyond them the blue, indifferent Caribbean.

Later they ordered supper from the restaurant across the street. It was brought to the room by a muscular boy whose thin mouth expressed a relentless disdain. Nothing the boy could imagine mattered in the least to J.C. They ate, made love again, and in the morning took the plane back to the States.

17 If they were now to discover attitudes and affections, responses each to each that had never before crossed air between them, if there was a time, that would linger in memory, when breakfasts were shared and supper was followed by walks along the Course, when Sunday afternoons included drives to the beach south of Panacea and weekday evenings included sweet restful interludes rocking on the porch overlooking the owlish woods, these times, these attitudes, were not to last. Elizabeth built a house on the low triangular bluff above the point where the Course met the river. She said it was a summer house, called a camp in that part of Georgia, where the family could gather for picnics and nights in the woods, but when it was finished, she moved into it alone. She built it with her own money, had beguiled J.C. with that offer; with its board front porch, white interior walls and wide bedroom windows it was very like the cottage she had lived in in the hills above Pearl. Jack contracted a building crew and when they were finished Delight brought his truck around to haul her possessions over.

J.C., who had been only too willing to lay down his resistance to his wife, found himself jerking it roughly back. He was in the kitchen eating a bowl of vanilla wafers and milk when she came through with Delight to get her clothes.

"In other words," he said out of the tangled conversation he had been carrying on with her in his head, "it was just a gesture."

"What was a gesture?" she asked and continued through the house. Delight lingered in the doorway; J.C. glared him back out the door and followed Elizabeth. "Your willingness to come home," he said as he watched her climb the stairs.

"I didn't make a gesture," she said. "You made a gesture." She raised the hem of her dress, which showed off her bare legs, but it was only to check a torn place.

He climbed after her. "I wasn't making a gesture," he said. "I was giving in."

"To what?"

"To you, to all this."

278

"I appreciate it," she said, "but now I have to gather all these clothes."

"Why did you come back then?"

"Because I had run my string out in St. Guillaume."

"Were you in trouble?"

"No. I don't get in trouble."

"Only," he said, "because you never notice what you've done."

"But you do."

"I can't help it, it involves me. And it hurts."

"Poor baby," she said. "Here, help me pack this suitcase."

She began to stuff everything she owned, it seemed to him, into one of the huge red suitcases her father had given her when she finally graduated from Ashley Hall. He had to kneel on it to get it to close. As he did so he wondered if her father had had a premonition of what her life would be like.

"I thought you wanted a house for all of us," he said. "I thought you wanted a camp like the Poitevent's have down at the Gulf."

"I wanted a camp for me," she said. "You never wanted any kind of camp."

"So what? So what does that matter? I've got worries, I've got these major goddamn financial worries. I owe millions of dollars. Do you have any idea what that's like? It's like hanging out over the edge of a cliff by your toes. I jerk up out of sleep thinking the fuckers have come to get me. I've got to have some relief—don't you understand you're supposed to be my goddamn relief?" Couldn't she understand that? Was he just yelling into a son-of-a-bitching barrel? "I went along with all this shit," he said—"House down on the river, sweet fire-mongering Elizabeth come home at last because I thought maybe, finally, we could get along for fifteen minutes. I want to get something going with you, Elizabeth. I said to myself this time I will try to do what she wants, I will try to get along. Look, it's a beautiful cabin, I could go down there, I wouldn't mind."

"You would start complaining within ten seconds," she said. "You would stomp around on the porch and try to make everybody feel guilty for having a good time."

He thought, Goddamn it to hell I am never going to get out of this life alive. He said, "One day I am going to take you by the hand into those woods and shoot you in the head."

"You've told me that before."

279

"I don't *remember* it."

"Course not."

And so he pressed his heart against the impossible future. "I didn't tell you," he said, "that while you were gone—the night before I went down to get you, in fact—I spent the evening playing jacks with a little girl in the Quarter."

"A little colored girl?"

"No, a little white girl down in Undertown."

"How did you like it?"

"I loved it, she was a sweet little blond girl. Except for the color of her hair she looked like you did when you were a child."

"You don't know what I looked like as a child."

"Yes, I do, I know better than you."

She went into the bathroom and got the articles that she had so recently laid back out along the shelves and basin. He followed her there, too, speaking as he went. "I know what you were like as a girl. You remember when you told me about that time you tried on your mother's wedding ring, the way you went around wearing it after she died?"

"I wanted to be my daddy's wife," Elizabeth said. "I wore her dresses, too, and I cooked meals for my father, all the things he liked. He didn't even notice."

"Well, I understand that," he said. "I understand exactly why you did it. When my mother died I tried to get close to my father, too. I used to hear him crying at night and I would go sit on the floor outside his room. I wrote him a packet of letters all about Mama just like we weren't living in the same house. I understand what all that is like. It's not hard to picture you sitting up in your room in that house in Charleston; I used to sit up in the cupola and stare out at the territory, too."

"What does all this mean?" she asked.

"It means just what I told you when I went and got you: I think we can live together now, I think I have changed. I know what's important now. I thought that was what you realized when you agreed to come back with me."

"I didn't agree, I just came back."

"Ah, Elizabeth, don't be this way. Don't you see that I love you?"

"Yes, of course I see it. What is that supposed to mean?"

He sat down in the rocker that had belonged to his mother. "We've had this conversation before," he said. "I have heard those same exact words many times before."

"What—do you think people change?" she asked. "Do you think they all of a sudden become different people?"

"I had my hopes. I think I'm becoming a different person. I have something in me that wants to get better than I am. We all have it, all Burdettes; we're always trying to improve."

"You sound like something in *Ladies' Home Journal.*"

"I don't care, it's true."

"I don't care, it's true," she mimicked.

He had determined to keep the peace, but something in him, the same old thing, began to burn. "You've built a cabin on my land," he said. "I have rights there."

"Then throw me off."

He stared at her, remembering the look in her eyes in St. Guillaume. She told him that a hurricane had passed over just before he arrived. "*L'ouragan dépendance,*" she had called it, because the winds were only strong enough to blow down the outhouses. The love they made had been wild, famished, heartbreaking.

"I'm a very good man," he said. "I don't think you've ever known that."

"I've always known it," she said. "I wouldn't have married someone with a mean heart."

"You shouldn't have married anyone at all."

"To your way of thinking, I'm sure, but to me it was just another piece of the world to pick up."

"You could have married anyone."

She tossed her head and laughed. "You know that as well as I do. Those little navies would have shot each other to get a chance at me. Haven's being your best friend didn't stop you from showing up at my front door. Help me carry these bags."

He helped her, as if in a trance carried the massive suitcase down the curved staircase. Delight sat in the truck eating pork rinds out of a plastic sack. "How's it going, J.C.?" he asked, and for a moment a sliver of panic jabbed at J.C.—what was Delight in on, what privilege had he been given?

"How about a drink?" J.C. asked. "How about a big drink, Delight?" And he threw the suitcase into the back of the truck, the floor of which was streaked with rust.

"That would be nice," Delight said. "I can use a drink anytime."

"Yeah, I know.

"Do you have a phone down there?" he asked Elizabeth.

"I'm having one put in. I'll call you when it's connected."

He watched them back out of the driveway, Elizabeth with her hands in her hair, Delight already talking, saying something that J.C. knew he would never hear about.

Which was why—those words, he could rip air from here to Texas and never hear, words and everything else—five minutes later, pacing the dining-room carpet, which was the color of Spanish moss, he jerked open the bottom silver drawer, took out the .45 he had concealed there ten years before, walked down to the stable and from two feet away shot her mare in the dead center of the long white diamond between her eyes. The horse dropped like a sack of cement shoved from a truck. Hosea's son, coming around the corner, spilled the wheelbarrow load of feed he was trundling in. Before J.C. could speak—though he had nothing to say now—the boy spun and ran out of the stable crying Jesus. It's not that big a deal, J.C. thought, it's just a dead horse. Then his insides detached themselves from the walls of his body and he fell to his knees crying. He took the mare's head in his lap and pressed his face against the dry, warm cheek. How big a horse's head was, like half a body. He could see the skull under the flesh, bone that would shine on into eternity. He thought he would be willing to take anything living into his arms.

He was not exactly crazy then, not from then on, but the family concealed what he had done, if not from each other then from the town. When Jack told Elizabeth, on the front porch of her new cabin, and she slumped against him, he thought he saw all the years of her life collect in her face. All the years to come. If he was wrong about those years—the number of them at least—he was right in figuring that everything had changed. She did one thing about the shooting before the silence that was to last for six years fell between them. She drove in her red convertible Mercedes across the fields carrying in her right hand a coil of her own shit which, after she had climbed the tomblike stairs, she pressed against the closed and locked door of their bedroom. She came down, washed her hands in the kitchen sink and drove back to the river, where she lay out in one of her boats feeling nothing but the hugeness of distance until the night had swept the stars into the sky.

She lived alone in the cabin above the two watercourses and was visited by her lovers. Delight of the brandied breath and rough-hewn ways, a living extension of his animals, came in his truck. He smelled like a wild thing though he was self-effacing and often, even after years, shy. Rooley walked across the fields and called to her from the pines in back of the house. She ran into his arms like a schoolgirl. He smelled of turpentine and the sourness of uncleaned rooms. With his long hands he clutched at her desperately, crying her name into the midnight like a man lost and hopeless, shying from light. She gnawed the paint from his fingers and spit it into the straw beneath them.

She never let them stay the night; when they were gone she got up out of the bed or the water or the sweet straw and walked through the pines to look out over the fields. The night shining, stars or moon, the false dawn behind clouds, made something inside her clutch, bear down and give way, as if she participated in a new birth, spreading out over the lands. Canaan so big you would tire out before you crossed it end to end. This land like a state all to itself, seceded country.

He came in the night and stood outside her windows. On loverless evenings she left the blinds up so he could see. He stood, just out of the light in ferns grown up over ground she had burned back, watching her move about the scrubbed rooms. Through the wide bedroom windows that looked toward an angle of river in one direction and through pines in the other, he watched her undress and get into bed. Sometimes the moon shone across her body, leaching the color from it until she was as white as shell, phosphorescent nearly as bones. He thought she had become another being, a woman from a dream.

He was careful only to not approach too closely. In bushes he made what noise was necessary, not bothering to defend himself against snaps of undergrowth, the snares of cockleburs and vines. Nights in fall and winter he crouched on the bluff watching her as she rocked on the porch reading a book. She felt him, as a fish feels the human body slipping into the stream, but she never called out to him, never spoke.

He gained something like satisfaction from watching her, felt not a healing but a weathering take place, a smoothing down to the essential stone. She walked in the woods and he followed her, trailed her like a fey mongrel. Occasionally she called out, to the woods, to the beasts there, but he never answered. Once, as he squatted in a leaf-strewn depression under the bank, she urinated on him, but it was black dark; he couldn't tell if she had seen him. In her nightgown she would paddle in her canoe out into the river. The mixed waters of the two streams in daylight were the gray of a deer's winter coat but at night the water was dark as coal, flinging back the moonlight. He waited for some cue to reach him, some moment when the inevitability of speech overtook them both, when presence became overpowering, but no such moment came; she drifted in woods or boat, in places he could not reach, indifferent.

She took trips in johnboat or canoe down the river to fish and swim. She only occasionally went to town and then only for supplies. Her friends—the women who knew her—slipped away from her life, called once or twice, but put off by her unresponsiveness, her bright words tossed too high in the air above them to be reached, they left her to her peace, whatever it was. Mattie accompanied her on fishing trips and Jack still rode with her along the river trace on afternoons away from his flower stall.

And Jacey came, often during his last year in the public schools, then only once in a while after he entered boarding school in New York.

J.C. saw them, he saw Jacey climb the cedar steps carrying a meager handful of narcissus or day lilies like a half-bred lover. He watched Jacey push through the door and he heard Elizabeth cry out in her happiness to see him. He watched her settle him on a sofa, bring him food and drink, saw the arguments start. It wasn't long before they were on their feet, mother and son, ranting at each other. They accused each other of desperate, devilish acts. Jacey called his mother a whore and she accused him of caring about nothing but himself, of using everyone in his life. His son, become perhaps a kind of proxy for his father, threw things against the wall and stormed from the house. It was in these moments, even as a bitter blankness, a deadness rolled over him, that J.C. came closest to breaking into this world that excluded him. Though he did not understand his son's fierceness—they did not speak of the arguments at the main house—and though he was frightened by their intensity, mouthing just behind their speaking the phrases that splashed out of the lit windows, he wanted to run between them with shushing hands, stop this. But he didn't. He was grateful they were so deep in woods lest neighbors hear and call the police. Time and again Elizabeth ordered Jacey out of her house and time and again Jacey returned. Always his mother was glad to see him, always she offered him food and drink. But soon, as the crickets sawed and the tree frogs twanged their resonating strings, their voices would rise from the living room or the porch or the bedroom, the sound would come of a chair suddenly thrust back, a glass breaking, door slam-

284

ming, shouts, and Jacey would rush from the house into the darkness. Elizabeth came out later and if he was close enough he might see tears shining on her face. Once, she leaned her crooked arm against the side of the house and sobbed; he watched until the sobs died to silence and the silence died to the sounds of the woods night, rustle of leaves, winded branches, the break and plunge of a fish.

This is what Burdettes came to, he figured. The cabin was within the circle of ground the first Rooley had claimed as his own. Somewhere off this bank were the limestone foundations he had hewed out. In the stone of those foundations you could see the shells and bones of the small animals that had swum over the ground when all Canaan was a salt sea. But no ancient connections had saved Rooley Burdette; he had died mad, raving at Andrew Jackson like a brokenhearted Indian. And the others, Wheeler, James, Burleigh, on down to his grandfather Jackson, had raged against the dark blood that dragged them into the earth. His grandfather had fought Eustace over control of the lands. Still, now, the squat brick pedestals that marked the boundaries of their ownership rose out of the fields like the broken monuments of some ancient lineage. Once in the Solomons during the war he had come into a coastal village in which the natives lived around a high wrecked building. All that was left was a double row of broken columns and a few weathered blocks of coral stone. No one remembered what great chief had lived in the house that soared off those stones, but the people remained there just the same paying the homage of their presence to a glory that had fallen. So we stay, J.C. thought, honoring the gigantic dead. He should have let the house burn down. He should have moved off this land long ago.

One summer night as he lay on his belly under a wax myrtle behind her house the desire to speak to his father came to him. He got up without another thought in his head, mounted his horse and rode across the fields to the house. Dismounting under the tower, he walked up the path between the row of zinnias that were just coming into bloom. The flowers made him think of stars coming out behind the moon. He figured he would walk boldly in—time to change these ways—but when he reached the steps he hesitated, afraid of the life he might be barging in on, and retreated around the house to the front porch. He approached music wafting from the bedroom, sneaked up steps and knelt at the window where in the lighted room he saw his father and Mattie on the bed, the two of them naked, holding each other in their arms. As he watched,

Mattie pushed his father onto his back and took his penis into her mouth. He had never seen his father with an erection before; it was a penis exactly like his own. His face burned and he pushed off the sill to flee, but he turned back. Jack lay on his back with his arms thrown behind his head. Mattie's loose gray hair pooled in his groin. His father's eyes were closed and his lips curled back from his teeth; his chin jutted and he growled like an animal. Then Jack reached down and took Mattie's head between his hands and drew her up his body. He kissed her hard, lips sliding across her brazen face, his hips twitching against her. J.C. turned away the window and in a rictus of self-possession eased down the steps and around the back of the house. Breeze clattered faintly in the shell chimes over the back steps. The music played on, drifting down the open gallery, some soprano rendering despair. Carefully J.C. climbed the back steps, rummaged among a clutch of tools leaned against the house, selected a hoe, came down and went into the garden. Swinging the hoe like a bat, he broke the flowers down, row after row. What he didn't break down he trampled. He worked quickly, his heart throbbing like a sting, until the ground was littered with a raddled rainbow of blossoms. Then he threw the hoe against the porch, mounted his horse and rode back across the fields to the main house.

He woke the next morning to the sound of knocking on his bedroom door. The cold possessing hand of the night came back to him and he bounded out of bed and ran onto the porch. It was hot already; the cicadas sang as if in pain. He pulled his pajamas around him, came back in and stood behind his mother's rocker listening to the soft, intermittent tapping. Father, Father, go away. "What?" he said. "What?" but not loud enough to be heard. The rapping continued until he crossed the room and opened the door; his father stood there dressed in a pair of the overalls he wore when he was farming full-time.

"How are you this morning?" Jack asked and smiled.

J.C. stepped back to let him in. He returned to the bed, got in and drew up the covers. "I'm tired," he said. "It seems like I am tired all the time."

"We go through that," his father said. "It passes."

He sat down in the rocker and looked around the room. "It hasn't changed much," he said. "I like that except I can understand why Elizabeth is so fed up with this place."

286

"I don't need you talking to me about Elizabeth," J.C. said. He ran his fingers through his hair and lay back against the pillow. "What have you got on your mind?" he said to the ceiling.

"It was time for me to pay a visit."

"I thought you'd be out selling flowers."

"I've been resurrecting them this morning. We had a little vandalism last night."

"That so? Why don't you call the sheriff?"

"I thought I would come over and speak to you about it first." He ran his hands down both pants legs and patted the calves.

He sat back and rocked for a moment. "I thought that a man would get over his concern for his children, but I find out that he never does, not at least as long as he's got the energy to go on living."

"Bryce and Franken will be delighted to hear that."

"Umm. I'll say first off that I love you; that's never wavered. I say it first because there are other things I want to tell you that are not so sweet. Are you comfortable?"

"Just a minute," J.C. said, getting out of bed. "I want a glass of water." He went into the bathroom, ran water in a glass and drank it looking out the window at the green rows of cotton beyond the back fence. He noticed that two of the cedars by the spring were dying; he hadn't seen that before.

"You better take an Alka-Seltzer, too," Jack called. J.C. came back into the bedroom and threw open both porch doors. He stood behind his father leaning against the doorway. Jack swiveled the rocker around.

"We all know what you are doing," he said. "We know about your nighttime visits to Elizabeth's cabin. We all understand. We even understand about the horse."

"You ought to know about nightwork. You ought to be an expert on that."

"I guess I am. I know about being obsessed with a woman."

J.C. tossed the last drops in his glass over the porch rail. "Shit," he said.

"Your mother was insane."

J.C. started across the room. "Stop!" his father cried. "Stop walking around." J.C. came back to the door, stood there looking out at the spring.

"She drowned herself in the spring," Jack said.

"No. It was an accident. Everybody said it was an accident."

"They said it was an accident so I wouldn't go crazy. They thought that would save my mind, but it was suicide."

J.C. felt his skin crawl. He looked at the spring that he could see glimmering through the cedars. The surface was disturbed as if by a wind passing over, but there was no breeze.

"What did you do to her?" he asked.

"Nothing. I wrestled for a long time with what I thought I had done to her, but it never came to anything. She just didn't want to live in this world." He leaned forward and ran his hand over his face. "The Lord knows I tried to change her mind. I tried to make the world around her so beautiful that she would never want to leave it, but she didn't notice. I used to study all the little things she liked, that she had liked when we first met. She liked blackberry pies with a sugar crust and I made them for her, with my own hands. She wanted to see Hot Springs, Arkansas, for some reason and I took her there. As soon as she arrived she wanted to go home. She liked yellow dresses and I bought her yellow dresses. She liked to lie by the spring at night when we were first married and have me tell her stories. I remember I used to hold my hand in the water until it was cold, then run it all over her—she liked that." He pushed back in the rocker and looked at J.C. "But none of those things could hold her. Hell, she told me she was going to kill herself. I went and talked to Eustace about it and he wanted to lock her up, send her to the state hospital at Milledgeville until she got over it. But I couldn't bring myself to do that. I thought I could love her back. I used to lie awake at night watching her, in those last months. I was afraid of what she was going to do to herself. The night she drowned herself I had been up two days straight just watching her. It was like looking at a beast in a cage, she just moved around oblivious to humanity. I couldn't make it though. I fell asleep and she went out and drowned herself in the spring."

"Is that why you wouldn't come out of your room?"

"I was asleep. Hosea found her and called Eustace and he came over. He had to wake me up. I didn't even get out of bed to go look at her. I just rolled over and went back to sleep. I didn't see her again until they brought her home from the funeral parlor. She didn't look like anybody I had ever known. It was your letters that saved my life, that kept me from losing her. You brought her back the way she could have been. You never understood what was going on, none of you did. You saw her the way any child would see his mother, as beautiful and dependable and endlessly loving. And I needed after it was over somebody to see her that way. I needed to see her that way. Those letters saved my mind. They kept me going until I met Mattie and she could take over."

J.C. stared out the door. A flight of crows passed over, their shadows racing on the grass. "I don't know what I'm going to do, Daddy," he said.

"It's not likely that you would, in the situation you're in."

"But I've got to do something. I can't bear it having her live down there in that swamp. Bryce told me I should have an affair. I think he thinks I ought to get rid of her, divorce her and run her back to Charleston or wherever, but it's not that simple."

"You're hooked."

"I'm hooked. I don't care what she does, I just want to keep on trying to stop her from doing it."

Jack stood up, came to the doorway and placed his hand on his son's shoulder. They were the same height exactly, the wintry paleness of their skin was the same, they had the same gray eyes that seemed always to be imploring the world for one more chance. "There's nothing to do," he said.

J.C. looked him in the face. "There's got to be something," he said. "I can't just stand there and watch her. I have to do something."

"You'll do whatever you want to, whatever comes to mind. I just wish in the meantime, you'd leave my flowers alone. They're real important to me."

"I'm sorry about that. I didn't know what I was doing." He couldn't tell his father that he had seen him screwing Mattie. He was reluctant to think about it himself. "I'll pay you for them," he said. "I shouldn't have done that."

"Don't worry about the paying. Just the next time you come over stop to talk with me awhile. That's better than tearing up zinnias."

"I will," he said and for a moment it was as if all the grief that had stood between them for years was washed away, as if they had plunged deep in the spring and come up clean, pale-skinned and cool. For a moment, J.C.'s hand fluttered in the air between them. Jack waited for it to fall, but it stopped. "I have a lot of things on my mind," he said, "a lot of other things besides Elizabeth. If I could get somewhere with her I'd have more time to take care of this business that really needs taking care of."

"That's your problem," his father said, though not unkindly. "You chose that road a long time ago and you might as well keep walking it now. You still haven't learned that there's nothing down there you really want."

Jack walked to the bedroom door. "Life is too short for us to learn everything from experience," he said. "Some things we just have to take on faith. But you'll probably have to learn that, too, by the hard way you don't seem to be able to live without."

"Maybe so," J.C. said from the porch. He wasn't looking at his father, but out at the spring, where his mother had wound up. "Maybe so," he said again. When he turned around his father was gone. He didn't even hear his footsteps going down the stairs.

He had gone all the way to Hawaii, six thousand miles from this backyard, and he had found a woman there. At the edge of the war where men woke at night crying amid the sweet odors of tropical flowers. He had seen what an island looked like once they had finished taking it back from the Japanese. On Tinian the earth was churned up for miles as if by great plows. The bombs had splintered the coral bedrock; hunks of it shone in the black soil like bones. The woods stank; there were bodies in the jungles that would rot there forever. And Elizabeth had taken him in her arms and made him feel as if he would never die. Touching her he had felt as if the whole stream of his life gathered—power and beauty— in one moment. In a war there are times when time itself is a ribbon that breaks, when the threatened moment splits and we are flung down into the bright sunshine of a grassy meadow. All through the war he had kept a list of scenes and places, objects, that were capable of catalyzing his imagination out of the steel and salt and blood that multiplied around him. "Mountain meadow," he had written, "Cattaloochee Falls, garnets, the marshes at Sea Island, a pine wood at sunset, banana pudding." At night he read the list, stopping at a phrase, a place of memory where his mind could get off and wander. But, just as a starving man can't, finally, feed himself with visions of steaks and turtle soup, so he found that he could not save himself with a walk in a sun-washed meadow in the north Georgia mountains. In the end he couldn't even get there, anywhere beautiful. Until Elizabeth danced out brandishing sticks and a smile sweet as dew on the fields. When, in her white bedroom in the cottage in the hills, she had taken him into her arms, it had all come back—in words— the places of memory, that time on his way home from college when he had stopped by a stream in the Smokies and lain down in moss a foot

290

thick, that morning on the beach at Tybee when he was six when the lifting sun turned the whole ocean gold—he had it all, the smell of hoe-cakes frying in bacon grease at Eustace's, a fort made of palm fronds in the backyard of their house in Sea Island, the sixty-yard run he had made with an intercepted pass, the sweet, tart taste of the first yellow plums in June. Everything—everything!—had spiraled down into those arms; he spun his moments from there, his hope. Anybody could have told him, and perhaps Haven had, not to put all his eggs in that frail basket, but Jesus that is what he had done, no use to apologize for it now.

So I get up, he thought, and walk across this fine room where the carpet is the color of wheat and blood. So I step out into a morning in which the sun leans its hard yellow body against the world. So I stare through trees at the blue water where my mother drowned. So I will live in a new silence now, with other women, other arms. So I will learn how long it takes to recover out of grief and sadness a peaceful heart. God please save my soul.

PART
 FOUR

18 "The only things that matter," his grandfather said, "are Truth, Goodness and Beauty. If you can line up what you're thinking or doing or wanting with one of those three, you're all right."

They lay on the tower floor listening to Artie Shaw play "I Cover the Waterfront." Jacey was home from his second year at St. Crispin's. He said, "Well, Martha is beautiful and the truth of the matter is that I have a good time with her, so I reckon we'll do it."

"That's not what I mean, Polecat." Jack raised himself on an elbow to take a sip of sugar-cane wine. The wine was clear as water.

"Look at it this way then," Jacey said. "Martha's nineteen, I'll be sixteen in the fall, which is the legal age in this state for quitting school."

"You don't go to school in this state. In New York they probably keep you till you're twenty-one."

"I don't know, but I come from Georgia. All my business gets referred back here." Jacey turned over on his stomach. He raised himself so he could look at the partying women painted on the mat underneath him. They were large and busty, carousing under their own indifferent eyes. "It's not that I don't like school, though I don't, it's just that what I want to do has nothing to do with school, at least not St. Crispin's. I already know I'm going to be a painter. I've lived too close to Rooley not to know that already."

"Painters need schooling. Rooley spent six years in New York going to school."

"That's what I'm talking about. I'll go to school. I can take courses at the Art Students League any time I want to."

"You just want to run off with Martha Poitevent."

"Well, so what? You took up with Mattie."

"Not when I was sixteen years old."

295

"You didn't know her then."

"Slap your pockets, boy."

"What?"

"Slap your pockets."

Jacey reached back and patted his jeans pockets.

"What's in them?" his grandfather said.

"A pocket knife, a buckeye, a little bit of change."

"And that's all. What're you going to live on?"

"Martha makes money. She's on tour right now. They pay her to dance."

"They pay her enough for one room in some worn-out building in the New York slums. Everything else goes for food and expenses. You told me she has to buy those dancing shoes by the dozens."

Jacey picked up his Dixie cup and spit a stream of tobacco juice into it. He had started chewing the year before during the summer he spent painting cotton trailers for his father. He laid his head on his arms and stared at his grandfather's boots, which were the old lace-up clodhoppers he had worn when he was farming. "Aren't you ever going to get any new boots?" he said.

"I will when these wear out. I don't see why a good pair of boots shouldn't last you a lifetime." Jack drained the wine, got up and poured himself another glass from the sixteen-ounce Coca-Cola bottle on the table. "So are you listening to me?" he asked.

Jacey screwed his head around so he could see him. "I'm listening to you, but it doesn't make any difference. I'm a Burdette; I'm going to do what I damn well please."

"You don't have to swear about it. That's another Yankee habit you've taken on."

"Shoe school," Jacey said.

"What?"

"Shoe school. The guy who founded St. C made his money in shoes. That's why he named it St. Crispin's."

"Why?"

"St. Crispin is the patron saint of shoemakers."

"Have you ever noticed that you have the disturbing habit of drifting off the centerline of your conversations?"

"Yeah, but it doesn't disturb me. Why—does it bother you?"

"It's frustrating. But then you've come by it honest; your mother is exactly the same way."

296

"I know all about that," Jacey said.

"Have you gone to see her?"

"No. This is my first stop."

"Well, you'd better get on over and do your duty. She was gone all spring but she got back a couple of weeks ago. She needs to take a look at you. And you need to take a look at her."

She wasn't at the cabin. Her yard reminded him of a fishing camp on the Panhandle: boats up on sawhorses, a tangled net hanging from the limb of a Chinese elm, vegetable and flower gardens planted in rectangles made of two-by-fours set on the ground, a disorderly pile of pine stumps, pieces of river driftwood, piles of it on the porch and in the front yard. He walked around the house peering into windows. She had moved furniture from the main house: the old yellow corduroy sofa from the upstairs office, lamps, his grandmother's Morris chair, a couple of wicker rockers from the porch. Against the back living-room wall was the pearwood bookcase that had held his children's books: *Winnie the Pooh, Sleeping Beauty, Little Black Sambo,* the pale blue biographies of the country's heroes. She had stolen the biographies for him from the public library. And never been caught. He had learned all about glory from those books. He knew about that careening drunk Ethan Allen and his Green Mountain Boys, about Andrew Jackson, Rooley's nemesis, who got slashed with a British saber trying to protect his mother during the Revolution; he knew about Clara Barton, asleep on her feet in a ward full of wounded soldiers, about Tom Edison getting the hearing snapped out of his head when a baggage handler pulled him by his ears onto a moving train; he knew about Kit Carson and Lewis and Clark and he had once had a dream about General Custer's long golden hair. What was the name of Custer's horse? Robert E. Lee's horse was named Traveller, an intact survivor of four years of war. Three years after the war, during a vacation at White Sulphur Springs, General Pickett had accused Lee of destroying his life by making him charge an untakable hill at Gettysburg. Lee had listened to his tirade and turned away without answering, but when he was dying, a year later, he raved in his death dream about the same battle, cried out to Longstreet to bring up the men. Where were those books now? The bookcase was empty except for a Polaroid camera and a few magazines stacked on the lowest shelf. The room had a forlorn look the way unlighted rooms peered into through windows often do.

He sat down on the glider his mother had set on one end of the porch. The cedar boards had weathered to pearl. Ferns grew in the front yard thick as a planted crop. He was delaying and he knew it, but he lingered anyway, watching the wind frisk in the tops of the live oaks across the Okeekee.

He was still there when the exterminators arrived, bouncing in their truck down the double-track lane that ran along the river. They had come to fumigate, they told him, and he watched while they climbed over the roof setting their huge bubble of plastic over the house. It made the cabin look like one of the cloudy tents caterpillars sewed into the branches of pecan trees. The men set up their pump and blower below the front steps; Jacey stood in the ferns watching the canopy shudder and swell with the acrid penetrating fumigant.

"It'll be two days before anybody can go back in there," one of the men, a wiry youth who was going prematurely bald, said. The man looked familiar but Jacey didn't ask him who he was. Since he'd left for St. Crispin's he felt uncomfortable in Yellow Springs, as if he had discovered in himself another history that no one here was familiar with. It reminded him of the first days after their arrival from Hawaii when everything was strange and every step he took was penetrated by fright. The men didn't know where his mother was. "We told her it'd be Friday before she could move back in," the wiry youth said. He had a silent cough like an old man. Jacey mounted his horse and rode out through the pines to the equipment road that ran along the edge of the cotton field and on toward the main house.

He thought of stopping at Rooley's, looked in passing down the long terraced slope at his flagship house, but disturbing rumors had drifted north about his cousins: Alsace drowning a litter of bird dog puppies, accusing the minister of adultery, and Rooley vanished into the country for days, returning under the flag of a new beatific smile, either woman-happy or religious, both disruptive, preempting family cordiality—he and Jacey exchanged letters; Jacey had told him of his interest in painting, interest that at first was only pretense, even cynical, but that now had begun, to his surprise, to invigorate and sustain him; but he didn't want to catch his mother in Rooley's arms, didn't want to catch Alsace spouting searing truths.

He drifted north past the tobacco barns and rode through the Negro cabins, spoke briefly to Freeky Wilkes, a boy two years older than he who had taught him to fish, but Freeky, who had just returned home,

298

too, from basic training at Parris Island, was not himself anymore, erect and sheared, didn't want to be reminded how happy they had been when they discovered, at ages eight and ten, that antidisestablishmentarianism was the largest word in the world. "I don't know where your mama is, boy," Freeky said and looked at him with marshaled disdain, as if Jacey had just wet himself in public. He had learned to play marbles on the yellow clay in front of Freeky's house; they had taught each other to french kiss, one afternoon in a johnboat under some willows. He was almost sixteen, had been all his school life in the same class with everyone else whose birthday fell within the circle of spring or summer—making their year of age before the summer school bell rang—but he had always felt the difference, the eight-year-olds rushing from the last class, he following, still seven, walking in the next fall still seven. At St. Crispin's he had begun reading poems and he would have liked to tell Freeky about it, about how poets were able to talk about the most private events of their lives, their adulteries, their nervous breakdowns, their fear of their children, their love, without shame. In his age Freeky was laggard, too—they had admitted their fear to each other, and their secret delight at being pushed ahead of their time—but now he was a clean-cut fighting man, signed into the Marines by his mother, whom he had browbeaten into going along with him. "Your head looks like a cocklebur," Jacey said, wheeled his horse and rode away up the sand road toward the main house. When you miss a step with someone you have been close to all the secrets you haven't shared leap into the foreground. He hadn't told Freeky that he planned to live in New York with Martha and now he figured he wouldn't tell him at all.

He rode up through the avenue of live oaks that had been allowed, almost as afterthought, to flourish between the cabins and the stables—the ground between the two encampments had always been wooded; over the years as enterprise had dictated the thinning out of the woods between the settlements the oaks had been left so that now they formed a shaded drive like the ones leading from the main entrances of plantation houses in picture books. Jacey liked that, the moss hanging like pelts from the horizontal limbs of the live oaks, clumps of it fallen in the sand, a clear perspective depending toward the faded brick ramparts of the old stables; this nearly grandiose stage set leading nowhere particular from nowhere particular. One Christmas his father had cards printed up with photographs of the lane—called the Avenue in the family—and sent them out to friends and acquaintances. The dim reach of trees looked in the pictures like a new and different world, no home any Burdette had ever seen, a road leading into a past that was entirely a dream. Eustace and Bryce had teased J.C. so harshly that he never did such a thing again.

Jacey left his horse at the stable corral and walked up the lawn to the house. Sprinklers built their circles of dew on the grass. He had come in last night; his father had picked him up at the small concrete-block air terminal that had been built last year on land J.C. sold to the county. Jacey knew that the idea of an airport on Burdette land made his father feel special. He liked the idea of being hooked into that far-reaching public line. What irked his father was that the county board of commissioners had refused to name the airport after Langston Burdette; they named it Burdette County Airport, which, his father pointed out to them, was already the name of the county and not much of a compromise, if that, he fumed, was what the fools were trying to make.

He went through the kitchen, stopping for a quick look in the refrigerator—"Womb boy," his mother had said when as a child he stood transfixed before the open Frigidaire door, "you want to climb back into the light you came out of"—and continued through the house. There was mail for his mother on the hall table; he wondered who carted it down to her. Her books had never been put back on the library shelves; the spaces where they had been were still empty. The living room, with its array of accomplished Burdettes on the walls, its silk furniture, its eucalyptus fronds in a crystal vase by the back window, all as still and untouchable as museum exhibits, made him feel lonely; he closed the door carefully on whatever solitary presence hunkered there and bounded on his toes up the stairs.

The bedrooms were empty, everything in place. She wasn't in the attic, where in the cedar closet he stopped to try on his father's old Navy pea jacket, which still was too large. He climbed into the cupola and looked out at the sun-battered fields. The line of cotton bent in places and he could imagine the tractor driver making his small mistake, flexing the wheel slightly in his daydream against the line of the row so that each pass reiterated the momentary indiscretion, carried it in a breeze of cotton to the edges of the fields. The cupola smelled of sunburned dust, lifelessness. Martha was in Iowa, on tour with the second company of the Jouvence Theater. She wrote him that the country was like a sea, great rolling swells of land planted in corn; farmhouses, silos off in the distance.

"I try to imagine myself growing up in one of the farmhouses here," she wrote. "Each one is alone, hidden in a grove of trees, evergreen usually, out of sight of other houses. I can't imagine it at all. I can't picture what it would be like to be twelve years old standing on one of those back porches drinking a glass of orange juice and looking out over this endless, tamed country. What would I think about, what kind of references would I have? Dropped down here, Canaan would be like the grass islands in Appalachee Bay out from the camp; just a little dot in a sea of something else." Right now, he thought, I can't imagine myself growing up in *this* place. Where was I all that time? He got up, dusted the seat of his pants and went down the stairs.

As he crossed the back lawn to the spring, the one place he hadn't looked at from the cupola windows, he was thinking how he hadn't really gone anyplace in his life yet. Anyplace physical, he meant, another country. Hawaii had become a state, generating a legislature and bumper stickers just like every place else; it was no longer foreign territory. New York, St. Crispin's-on-the-Hudson, was the strangest place so far. And he thought, By myself I can't even manage a life there among the spruces and the birches, all that granite, without crying myself to sleep at night. A month after he arrived he had been writing letters full of miserable nostalgia; if it hadn't been for Martha he would have turned around and run home. But then if it hadn't been for Martha he wouldn't have been there in the first place.

A yellow Labrador puppy ran out from under the cedars. "Poitevent," he heard his mother call, but the puppy didn't stop, it ran up to him and pressed against his legs. He thought, Jesus Christ, she has named a dog after Martha. He picked the puppy up and carried it through the branches.

She lay on her back on the far side of the spring in a pile of peach-colored towels. Her white bathing suit was wet; through it he could see the shadows of her private body. He thought, Here I come, magnetized. The puppy squirmed in his arms and he put it down. The dog ran to his mother and licked her face. "Poitevent," she said in a dreamy, absent voice.

"Mama," Jacey said.

"Oh, Jacey," she said, "you've come for me."

She looked at him by turning her head only. It made her neck look scrawny. He walked around the spring and sat down beside her. She smelled of wine; there was a nearly empty bottle of burgundy propped on the towels at her feet.

"I got in last night," he said. "How are you?"

"Bold and sassy," she said, "bold and sassy." The puppy stood on her chest. She drew its head down and kissed it on the mouth.

"I went by your place, but the exterminators said nobody could live there for the next couple of days. Where're you staying?"

"I'm staying right here. Where else?"

"At the spring?"

"On these stones."

"It's a pleasant spot—plenty of fresh air, running water."

"The room service isn't too good, but the rates are cheap."

"I like your little dog."

"He's a pistol, except that he likes to pee everywhere." She held the puppy up by his front legs. "You like to pee on everything, don't you," she said to it. "Yes, I do, Mama," she answered for it.

"I used to do that," Jacey said, thinking of Hawaii.

Elizabeth laughed. "Whenever the Chinaman saw you coming down at the market he'd run and lock the doors. Peeing wasn't all you liked to do in public."

"I've gotten better."

His mother hugged the puppy so tightly that it squealed. She let it break free; it ran halfway around the spring, sat down and began to scratch fleas.

"I've been out here trying to see if I could still dive to the bottom of this spring," she said. "That's a very important thing to be still able to do. I can almost manage it. I think when I get it I'm going to invite all the ladies of Yellow Springs out here for a demonstration. It's the kind of thing they would appreciate, once they got over their fright. They all need to be able to touch the bottom of this water. How long are you staying?"

"I don't know. Martha's out in Iowa for a month. When she comes back I may go up to New York. I've got to convince Daddy that it would be a good idea. Why did you name the dog Poitevent?"

"He reminded me of Martha so blond."

The old divisive ambivalence came back; he recognized its blush as she spoke. "I don't think you should have named her that," he said, knowing as he spoke that no objection could make any difference to her.

302

"No way to resist fate," she answered. "It's all determined. I looked at that little pecker dog and Poitevent was its name. It could have been stamped on its forehead at the factory."

"Duke," Jacey said. "I would have named him Duke."

"That's because you don't have any imagination, Cortez. You're going to have trouble as a painter if you don't have any more imagination than that."

"Painting imagination's pictorial; I don't have to worry about talk." He felt the exhaustion of approaching defeat. "I've got to go," he said.

"No you don't; you're just mad because I'm sentimental." She pushed up on an elbow and looked him in the face. He turned away from her demanding gaze. "I miss you so much I named that little dog after the thing you hold close to your heart. Nobody can tell me I can't do that."

"Nobody can tell you anything, Mama," he said, looking through branches at the deserted fields. "You can't see six inches past your own head."

"Whoo, look who's talking." She ran her hands quickly down her body. As if, goddamn it, I am not even here. "You don't have the slightest idea what I'm up to. None of you ever have."

"That's just it. You don't think anybody but you has any idea of what's going on. You always think you're so unique, so goddamn different. Nobody's as special as you are. It's crazy. It's fucked-up."

"Don't talk like that around me. This isn't prep school."

"Shit—you see? Every time I get near the truth you get defensive, you try to change the subject, you start criticizing."

"Who's criticizing? I'm lying here by this spring trying to get my precious breath back and you come out here and start telling me I don't know how to live. I was living a long time before you ever saw the light."

She sat up and took a long pull on the wine bottle. "You want some?"

"Sure."

He took a swallow. The wine was frothy and warm, tasted of rust.

She looked at him, he thought, as if he were a sucker she was about to fleece. "You're so afraid you won't amount to anything—and you probably won't—that you have to come out here, less than twenty-four hours after you've come home, and torment me."

"I enjoy it, as long as you can defend yourself."

"That's not why you do it; you don't do it for the sport—maybe we could have fun that way—you do it for the hurt. You don't think you're worth very much so you want to make everybody else feel worthless, too."

It was the old accusation, the one that had driven him from her cabin in tears time and again two summers before. She was often not home these days when he arrived from school, off somewhere in the Caribbean or on an island in Maine. She wrote him once that she was down in Mexico shooting ducks, living in a village on the Gulf Coast. He had called home and been told by his father that as far as he knew she was right down the road at her cabin. Her letter carried a Yellow Springs postmark.

He took another swallow of warm wine and stood up. "Your life hasn't come to anything," he said. "You're nowhere."

"The reason you think that is because I am always in the same place, exactly where I want to be. You and your father think that you have to hustle down the road, fight Indians or something to get anywhere. I've been where I wanted to be all along."

"You don't make any sense." He was on his way out from under this circle of cedars, away from this woman, but he lingered, feeling emotion rise in him, the clap of blood that invigorated him. He knew he would pay for this argument, knew that the hangover would hammer him with guilt and regret, but he kept on, because the exhilaration of speaking to her this way pulled him. "You're the one who's always taking off somewhere. Nobody ever knows where you are. Where've you come back from this time?"

"I was visiting friends down in St. Guillaume."

"You don't have any friends there, you don't have any friends in any of those places."

"How would you know that? I have many friends."

"I know it because you don't have any friends here. As far as you're concerned everybody is just another sucker."

She smiled at him with bright red lips. "You're upset because you want to convince yourself you're not like me and you can't. Whether you like it or not you are. You're my twin."

"Bullshit!"

"Poor little boy, just coming awake."

"How can I be like you? You never give anything to anybody and I give all the time."

304

"My little Christian."

He flung the bottle into the spring. It sank, bobbed up, turned up-right and sank again, trailing a thin pink stain. "You'll have to go get that," Elizabeth said. "We can't have trash at the bottom of the spring."

"Who's this 'we'?"

"Go and get the bottle, Jacey."

He walked to the edge and looked at the bottle descending. It seemed to flutter in the refraction of light; the stain was a thin ribbon, suspended above it. He shucked shirt and pants, hoping as he did that this was not terminal proof of her ability to control him. He dove.

The water bit then soothed; it felt good after the heat of the day. The bottle was fifteen, twenty feet down; he blew his ears and swam after it, scissor-kicking, sweeping his arms in long digging strokes. He felt the faint press of the current rising upward, noticed that the wispy cedar roots along the sides seemed longer; they trembled in the current like strands of reddish hair. He caught the bottle just below his father's second mark, the row of pebbles wedged into an oblique crack in the limestone wall, and continued downward. He might as well see how far he could go. But it was too much. The old feat—now legendary—still eluded him. His lungs burned and he knew that if he made it he wouldn't have breath to rise: he turned and kicked upward, rising faster than the trail of bubbles that had always seemed to have a life of their own. I want a huge capacity for love, he thought, I want to give my life to it, and then his head broke the surface and he saw his mother lying on her back on the flags; she was not watching him, she was playing with the yellow puppy, licking its muzzle and pulling its paws across her face, cooing to it, saying words of love to it.

He hoisted himself up on the torn stone edge, letting the weight of his torso press upon extended arms: muscles bulged, his first permanent muscles, arrived last year by dream-flight, his body suddenly hardening, coarsening, new veins appearing as if they had wormed their way up out of the heart's core. He wanted to say, Mother, look at this, look how the hairs on my forearms have turned dark. They mirror new intent—what was childish has passed away. He wanted to say, Mother, I am leaving, I am going myself alone this time into a far country where no one knows my language or my name. I'm going to storm beaches. Look, look. As a child he had run across the light-washed Hawaiian room into her arms. She had held him in the bed at night, fit him into the common caves of her body where he belonged, which seemed made for his form, permanently. He saw his father writing letter after letter, yearning to get back through that door that had once been thrown open to him. To live fully—that was it, to live again in the time when all of life was an excellent energy, even repose.

He threw the bottle at her. It hit the dog, knocking it neatly off her chest like a little tenpin. She sat up and screamed at him as he climbed out and came at her. Screams weren't enough. He picked her up, carried her to the edge and threw her into the pool. She landed on her back, went under, came up and swam toward the far edge. This is funny, he thought, this is ridiculous, and then it wasn't. He ran around the pool and was waiting for her when she got there. As she tried to climb out he pushed her back with his foot. She paddled away on her back looking at him. "What do you want?" she asked in a low voice hissing with water.

"You drowned," he said.

"All right."

She flipped under and began to swim, down, toward the bottom.

He watched her go, diminishing in size but not in clarity, plunging down, on and on until the surface of the pool was no longer disturbed by her entry, until there was only the meager popping of her risen bubbles. Far down, where the blue mist reached up from the bottom, she curved in toward a narrow outcrop and vanished. He leaned out, looking and waiting; she didn't reappear, didn't rise. He ran around to the other side, peered down: he could make her out, something, crouched under the ledge. She didn't move, just something living stuck there, piece of body, his mother. She can't stay, he thought, she's going to die. He got down on his hands and knees but sticking his head under didn't help him see better. He rose, wiped his eyes—she was going to drown herself. "Judas priest," he said. "She's out of her mind." The puppy, lost dog, barked. Jacey dived, thinking, Nothing works, nothing, and swam downward, on his strong line of grief. Past all the marks of his father's excellence, he swam, lungs broken and seared, until he reached her. There was still ten feet of water between them and the bottom but he didn't try to win that prize; he grabbed her arms and turned upward. She pulled back; he spun in the water and shouted, six inches from her eyes: "I'm dying," and grabbed her cold face. She shook herself away from him and rose. They swam hard, side by side for the top; his ears stung with pain, a knife stabbing into his head; his lungs felt trampled, flattened. They broke the surface together and together fell back into a float. His head hurt; his mother looked up into the cedars. After a while she swam over to the edge and climbed out. He watched as she gathered up the towels, took the puppy into her arms and headed through the trees toward the fields. She hadn't said a thing to him. Nothing that would change him.

She woke early because this was the morning she planned to paddle the canoe down to Haven's. The house still smelled faintly of fumigant, a smell like rotten pecans. On the walls were sheets of butcher paper tacked in long strips from the ceiling. On the paper she had written in a felt pen an outline of the history of her life. The red sentences of the history were divided into paragraphs by green lines. Books were stacked along the wall under the paper, obscuring a few of the paragraphs at the bottom. In the top left corner, under a spiderweb which she was careful not to touch, she had written: "I was born on a sunny day in early February, Groundhog's Day in 1920. Whether you believe it or not, the bay was full of sailboats. I can remember the sails which were all white, like the wings of gulls. The people along the Battery thought they were clouds." Between some of the paragraphs she had drawn colored portraits of birds and animals. Above the writing, along the ceiling, she had painted a dark blue strip and dotted it with small white splashes: stars, she explained, a starry night in Charleston, the way the sky looked on the evening after she was born. "I used to gig flounders in the rain" was the next sentence, and she thought as she pushed herself up in the bed and squinted at the strips that it was a better opening than the date of her birth. "I used to fish for flounders in the rain," she said out loud, got up, took her marker from the bedside table and went to the wall. She was halfway down one of the middle strips in the middle of a passage about the Brazilian loafers her father wore when he went out to swim in the pool. They were canvas, the loafers, had thin red rubber soles and were soft as a bird's breast. She had completed a passage that read: "I stole them and hid them in a trunk in my closet. I thought that when I got old enough and my father was dead I would wear them." She stopped; In remembrance of him, she thought, but she didn't write that. She heard a sound outside and crouched down. The sound continued, a scrabbling noise, as if someone were climbing a tree. She went to the closet and got a shotgun, one of a pair of Purdys Haven had ordered for her. She walked through the house to the front porch. Three boys, ten or eleven, were trying to lift the johnboat she and Delight had laid across sawhorses

307

in the front yard. She walked to the top step and pointed the gun at them. The boys froze and the largest one, a child in a red shirt and a blond crew cut, stood up from under the boat. She fired over their heads. The shot cut leaves out of one of the water maples. The boys bolted up the lane along the river. She put another shot into the fair sky above them, broke the breech and sniffed at the wisp of smoke that curled out. "Good morning, world," she said, kicked the shells into the laggard azaleas below the porch and went back into the house. For the life that was in them, she thought, yes, not in remembrance. I didn't want to remember, I wanted to keep. She hummed to herself as she returned to the bedroom, took up her marker and began to write.

Message to the Unnamed Other:
From The Journal of Elizabeth Bonnet Burdette

On the way home from a plantation party one night I drove my father's car off a bridge into the Ashley River. There were four of us in the car: my boyfriend, Estil Johnson; Katherine Vareen; Joe D'Urban and myself. I still couldn't tell you what made me do it. We passed a big field where the moon was shining on the new corn and entered a patch of woods that descended toward the river. We were singing a song, a spiritual about crossing water. The road curved and we came around the bend through the trees onto the bridge. I wasn't drunk and I didn't have a thought in my head, but halfway across I swung the wheel to the right and we tore through the guardrail and soared out. The car began to turn over back to front, we hit I think on the roof, and sank. The water poured in the windows like we were the floodgates just broken. Estil was knocked out and I had to drag him out the window and swim him to the bank. I dove back in and met Joe who was diving for Katherine. We went down together—the water was a pure blackness—and found her trying to bash her way out the back window which was still intact. She fought us but we managed to haul her to the surface where Joe swam with her to the shallows. The three of them lay in the shallows like old alligators moored to the bank, like bedraggled puppies. I climbed up to a stand of sycamores and looked back down at the river where a faint stream of bubbles rose from the car in the moonlight. I wanted to split the world open and throw everything I hated into the hole. Estil, kneeling in the rank water, looked up at me and said, "What happened?"

"I saw some angels in the trees," I said and sat down. That was all the explanation I ever gave. After a while my friends climbed the bank and I lay with them in the grass until they got their wits back, then we walked a mile to a truck stop where I called my father to come get us.

After my mother's funeral I sat on the back steps with my coat up over my head even though it was spring and hot. Neither warmth nor green life could save me. Everything, not just my mother, was dead anyway. After a while I got up and walked down to the boat pier where a boy in a basketball shirt was fishing. He had lined his string of bass and perch in a row beside his chair. I thought what a sweetness must be in that boy for him to arrange his fish like that, side by side, so he could look at them and marvel. I could have stopped to speak to him, could have touched his pale hair, but instead I picked the fish up and one by one threw them into the water. The boy looked at me with such grievous shock in his eyes, but he didn't say a thing. I walked home thinking, Nobody in the world knows what I know, nobody will ever know.

The first time I saw my husband I thought, Here comes the circus. I thought marrying him might be like joining the rodeo, joining the bucking stock part, I mean.

He had the same moo cow eyes all the other men around me had, but there was something else, there was a depth to them, as if way back inside himself he was anchored to something powerful and permanent. I thought, Here's a bird that will catch fire and won't fly when he burns. He can have me, I thought, he can have me if he is willing to go through what I am going to put him through and that's everything there is on earth. I'm going to take him down to the low places, I'm going to take him to the mountains, up into the sky, away to the desert barrens where people are beyond tears; I'm going to make him understand what it's like to live and die in the same moment, I'm going to make him wish he was never born, make him wish he could live forever.

He appeared on my front steps in a car full of flowers: plumerias and hibiscus and bougainvillea and passion flowers, as proud and hopeful as if he had personally invented love about five minutes before he got behind the wheel. He thought he was the ocean and I was some dune beach he would wear away and rearrange; he didn't know he was splashing against pure hard rock.

As my father didn't know, but was the first to find out. My father had long skinny legs so his pants flapped when he walked. I teased him about it and he slapped me, then he cried in his guilt for hitting his daughter. I learned from that, I can tell you. He could have beat me and I wouldn't have stopped teasing him, I don't know why. But I learned how to manipulate him. In a way it was like learning the whole encyclopedia to have one fact at your fingertips. What I learned about my parents, I mean. I was born fully formed, popped out of the hot water ready for action. Poor parents, what could they do?

I bled the first time during one of my mother's teas when I was eleven. I came down the stairs, my hands dripping red, walked into the parlor and said, Mother, look at this awful mess. She rose crying—all the other ladies sympathetic, ah-ing, reaching for tears—crossed the room and hugged me. I said, Mama stop it; this is ridiculous, all my white things will be ruined. She wanted to take me upstairs, she tried to begin a long talk about what was happening in my body, about how I was a woman—it was very moving to her I could see, but I shushed her, went into the kitchen and washed myself with a rag at the sink. She didn't know I wasn't even a virgin; two years before I had let Jemson Puckett fuck me with his little pencil-thin dick on the white tile floor of my bathroom just to see what it would feel like. It hurt so much I wanted to scream, and I bled then also. I thought a baby would spring out of me overnight—I didn't care if it did, but I wanted to be surprised. I didn't tell that to my mother as she stood behind me at the sink, her fingers flicking at my shoulder like she didn't know whether to hug me or run away, and I remember that out in the yard where the spring was shoveling a new green life into Charleston, I saw two little boys pushing a huge beachball back and forth. It must have been four feet across, the ball was, and striped yellow and red. I had never seen the boys before anywhere in Charleston; they were, I am sure now, angels, blond-headed with skin so white it shone, come to let me know I was free to live. I climbed up on the sink, my behind dripping red, threw open the window and yelled at them to go on about their business now; I raised my sweet sticky hand to show them everything was all right.

Both my parents were tall and they both had eagle eyes, but only my father could foretell the future. The gift made him excitable and diffident and conservative. One night as we walked along the Battery, he said to me, With each gift we are given its opposite, equal for equal; the brighter the candle, the darker the darkness. He could see the future, but

310

he was haunted by the past. In the past he saw the death of dreams, the fallen moments when the arc of beauty frayed and began to falter. It made him want to preserve rather than extend. He saw happiness surely, but he also saw shadows move across the faces of the people he loved, and I am sure that he knew my mother was going to die. He saw her life snap like a twig and the white petals of it flutter down through the branches. He saw me soaring on my white wings.

When I was eight I wrote to the President and told him to pack up his things and go home. He wrote me back on stationery embossed with a red-tinted picture of the White House. He said, "It numbs me that someone your age would say this to me, though I admit the thought has crossed my mind more than once. I was born in a two-room house in a little town at the edge of the Iowa prairie. My father was a blacksmith who died when I was just a boy. My mother didn't long survive him, and after that I moved from relative to relative, leaving Iowa finally for the West. I made a fortune in the West as a mining engineer, but it was never my home. If I were to leave now the only place I would like to return to is Iowa. When I was very small I would peer through the paling of the fence at the back of our little cottage at the prairie which began at the foot of the hill. The wind had a way of punching at the field that made it seem as if a big hand were testing and judging the grass. I thought that hand would do the same to me, that if I didn't prove to be worthy, it would press me down into the earth. Believing that, I became what I have become. I too am afraid that before power like that, it is not enough."

The funniest thing my husband ever said to me was when, after the first month together in my cottage above Pearl Harbor, I asked him how he liked being with me and he grinned and said, "Babe, it's like loving dynamite." We both roared.

I love to touch all the creatures that live in the sea. When I was a child you could take a boat out to the barrier islands and gather scallops in the shallow water near the marshes. Now there are no scallops, as soon there will be no oysters. Folly Beach used to be littered with sponges. They are stiff and coarse as shredded canvas when dry and soft as a baby's skin when you wet them. On the island beaches I found the blue glass balls covered in hemp netting that the Japanese used as fishing buoys; they had floated halfway around the world. I imagined setting out holding one or two, floating off into the sea to some paradise country that existed on no known map.

I remember all this, the way the shore was, the glistening lapis lazuli glass of the floats, but I do not rake down through an ugly present to reach it. In magazines they talk about the disappearing wilderness, they say the wild animals are dying out, we will be alone with pavement before long. I know this isn't true. The fact is we must work constantly not to be overrun by wildness. I have seen a raccoon step into the headlights on a street in Charleston, a city founded in 1650 A.D. Into the backyards of all these houses in all these little towns creep at night the savage creatures. They lie in the grass watching us move about our well-lit rooms. They will be there when the last tycoon has been pounded into the dust. Delight laughs when anyone asks him where the wild game is. The animals are only biding their time, he says, they're waiting.

And more than that, I mean more than that: I sneer at the silly cringing folk who are afraid to love the life in front of them. The only possibility of happiness is to take the bitter with the sweet. To love them both the same. Jack loves his fine music but I have seen him plunge his hands into the innards of a slaughtered hog and marvel at the colors. I never saw purple until I saw the torn breast of a dove.

Delight and I went out to the coon dog trial near Fayton. They put a coon in a sack and dragged it behind a tractor around the pond as a pack of hounds raced after. The sack was slung over the low branch of a water oak and the hounds, skidding in the loose mud, rounded the dam and launched themselves into air. One was faster, better leaper, fiercer teeth, and hurtled into the air snapping, becoming, for that coon, the accurate angel that would tear it to pieces—but the sack was too high. The coon was taken down and chained into an apple box, set on a pole at water level in the center of the pond and the dogs were sent out swimming, two by two, to bring the little bastard in. Then you could see the heart of the hound: the long swim in the cold, the bitter welcome, nothing that wanted to come lightly. But one, a saddle-shouldered bluetick hauled up from Florida in a wire cage in the back of a pickup, starved and whipped and cringing around the hips before its master, scarred along the jawline and across the shoulders, a full hand taller than any other dog, swam toward the coon, its shovel head gliding along the surface, black eyes fixed and gleaming. The coon washed its little monkey paws, reared on high legs and fell back tugging on the chain. It clicked to itself, making the small noises of an old woman shooing away the dark. As the bluetick reached the crate the coon leaned forward and raked blood into the flesh below the dog's right eye. As the dog came on anyway the coon bit, three quick times, stitching perfect holes into the red ragged lip, attempted to leap over the rising, forward wrenching shoulders, was caught, its white breast clamped between the gulping slathering jaws; the winged wall of ribs cracked and, for an instant, its heart beat live and open inside the dog's mouth before the whole front of its body was torn loose. The dog writhed in the well of blood, scrambling halfway into the box, disemboweling, tearing out the throat, bursting the eyes, cracking bone on bone, devouring, scrabbling deep into the body, through the body, into the ghost behind the body, on and on, until . . . until it heard finally the man's voice calling over the water and, awakening, fell away and swam slowly back to shore, kneading the thin taste of blood in its mouth.

I sit on the blue velvet hassock before the streaked mirror turning a knife in my hands. I press the flat of the cool blade against my cheek, draw it closely downward to my jawline. There I level the blade until the edge bites barely into my skin. I press until in the mirror I see the beaded line of blood rise. This is not mutilation, nor is it provocation; it is an assay, a weighing of possibility, of possibility and hope, a peering into the dark dream I will someday inhabit. My death comes to me like a cloud in the night, I feel myself easing down into the softness of it, the sibilant caress of it, the warmth and the mystery of it. It must be better since we keep it for so long. I will one day sink into the sky of my death, I will ride the long even swells, I will be alone but not lonely, bodiless, thoughtless, dreamless. I feel as if the edges of my body are fraying and dissolving, as if, like those blank days at the edge of the ocean when the sky and the sea are the same color, I am becoming one with the air around me; I am the scent of tea olive wafting through the open windows, I am the buzz and rattle of a bluebottle fly beating against the sill, I am the lick and start and caress of the wind itself, the river tarry and roiled, groping its way along the margins of the land, petting and caressing and calling the trod-upon earth. I am the bitter taste of a camphor leaf, I am the yellow sweetness of the tulip tree blossom; I am the gouging fin of the catfish, I am the soft gray body of the slate-shelled mussel; I am the decoder of mysteries, the detective of the high and low notes, the mystery rider, the one who is known to all. I am the Christ and I am Judas, the murderer and the broken body. I am every feeling that has ever been felt, every thought, every gleam of light shining through the crooked branches of the live oak and I am the eye that perceives the light. I am the darkness and the endless anguished cry of the broken heart, the mother weeping over her drowned child, the father fumbling through his tears to touch the cold face of his dead son. I am the daughter who died, the daughter who lived, I am the inconsolable one, I am the song of mourning and of hope; I am the mystery of birth, I am the baby's cry, I am the gasp and croak in the throat of the dying patriarch. I am among the bodies piled under the willow trees awaiting burning, I thrust my pitchfork into the heart of a crying child.

There is only a thin line of blood separating me . . .

CONVERSATION

Mattie: Don't you think you can sit still long enough to shell a bushel of butterbeans?

Elizabeth: I don't know; I'm not sure that I can.

M: You'd better learn to still your heart.

E: If I did that I'd die.

M: If you did that you'd learn something about yourself, which I can't see happening the way you live.

E: How do I live?

M: Like you're trying to catch a fast horse.

E: I think you're talking about my husband.

M: I'm talking about you.

E: You don't understand me.

M (Laughter): You're not that hard to follow.

E: So what is it I am?

M: Spoiled.

E: That's all?

M: In your case that's enough. It hasn't crossed your mind yet that there are other human beings walking around on this planet.

E: I see the people. I spend my life looking at the people.

M: You look at people as if they are animals in a zoo. Once and a while one's cuddly enough for you to want to take it home.

E: I can't be bothered.

M: And that is what you hold to, darling, that nothing can bother you.

E: If anything could, I'd change.

M: The only chance we have for satisfaction in this life is by being of service.

E: I am of service.

M: To who?

E (Laughter): To my own hot heart.

M: That's not enough.

E: It'll have to do.

I am an example, I am the woman in long skirts tied around her waist leaning down to pluck a Jupiter shell from the shallow water of Apalachee Bay. I raise my head and see Delight on the beach striking fire into a pile of myrtle sticks. He works intently, finding satisfaction in the small change of dailiness. Delight knows the tracks, he knows the spoor of every creature running in the woods. At night, in his sleep, he calls out in the voices of doves and wood thrushes, he hisses like an otter. I am fascinated by the deftness of his large hands, the way he can quickly braid twine into rope, weave a snare. I bring him my fair body as a gift, as I have brought it to all my lovers, in exchange. We lie together in the cold moonlight; our voices are so small under the immensity of this Gulf sky. I am often so tiny, a grain. The only thing I never am is nothing.

On the afternoons my mother went out to meet her lover she dried her washed and wrung out handkerchief by pressing it against the mirror in her bathroom. The handkerchief looked like a large white lace postage stamp affixed to the corner of a silver envelope. In the mirror my mother's stately beauty was reflected, as if the still perfection of herself was what she was sending trapped and permanent to her waiting lover.

I remember the way we sweated, that night dancing on the pier at Isle of Pines, the way our slick faces seemed to have become parts of the same lovely machine, touching and sliding and glistening. I kissed the salt of him, the bitter stink of his lust.

When Haven's mother died he called me weeping. "I held her head up," he said. "She was drowning in her phlegm and I held her head up, just like she was trying to slip away underwater." My husband and I attended the funeral. She was buried in the family cemetery at Willows near the stand of red cedars her father had planted to remind him of the Cedars of Lebanon. Haven has never been the same since his mother died. He wastes away, a wraith on his farm, riding out every day to put flowers on her grave. I went to visit him and he said, I see black ships, I hear the call of the captains, I have never been able to save anything worth saving in my whole life. I asked him who had ever done that, saved anything, anyone. He looked at me as if I had cursed him and walked away under the flowering water maples.

Sometimes in the night when I hear singing coming from the grave-yard of the Burdettes, from the banks of Yellow Spring Course, from this tarry river, I think it is Haven, the elegant boy he once was, diffident and gracious, at sufferance to his lovely courtliness, his endless courtesy, and I want to rise up and run to the window to call out to him, to speak some soothing prayer into the darkness, to lure him into my arms, to feel again his delicate strong fingers caressing my breasts, trailing into my secret hair, finding me, converting me to fire.

Dear God, I'm going to eat you alive.

In the garden of my mother's house: the clown faces of hydrangeas; the sweet yellow ovoids of the mock banana, like the eyes of ghosts; the lacy, fragile blossoms of azaleas; the tender white easily bruised flesh of gardenias; day lilies, the pods of which my friends and I ate at tea parties on the dirt-floored carriage house; morning glory, mother of the five-pointed star; moonvine, blooming only at night; iris like prostitutes in tissue petticoats; Japanese magnolias, the sweet-smelling early blooming flowers as pale as if worn out and wan from their long winter trek; mi-mosa; althea; amaryllis.

The maid said, "You had better do what I tell you because I am speaking for yo' Mama," and I said, "Nobody speaks for my Mama, even my Mama," and I punched her in the belly, the first time I ever used physical force against anyone. I was eight years old and I could smell the bay which smelled like all the sumps in the world, and already men were a mystery to me, the long muscles in the legs of my teenage cousin that haunted my dreams, my father squatting next to the pool so that I could see his testicles bulged against the khaki pants, the brawni-

316

ness of his forearms which reminded me of the legs of crabs, the way the hair bristled at the back of his neck—J.C., dressed in white, climbed the steps with flowers in his arms; he said, "You will probably destroy me," and I said, "You will handle that chore yourself, I'm afraid," and then he looked at me as if he were disappointed.

I am not turned away from the town ladies, as men would think, because I find their talk too simpering sweet; I find their talk anything but sweet; it is instead raucous, violent, aggressive and accusatory; it frightens me.

My father, the admiral's son, would not know me, though he lives, puttering about the Reservation that is Charleston, whirling checks through his tills. Sometimes when I was a child and the phone would ring, I would pick up the receiver and gurgle and shriek into it, making noises from the night and from the woods, broken, lost, creature noises, just to give whoever sat silent at the other end of the line the quick knowledge that the world was still untamed. (As I would tell you now that the world lies wild and rolling at my feet, as I would ask you why this is—I look out my bedroom window past the angle of porch at the wind shaking the tops of the live oaks across the river the way a mother would shake an intractable child; I see the martins whirling around the gourd house, flown in just this morning from Saskatchewan; I hear the splash of a beaver's tail, the hollow, questioning cry of a barn owl; I lie down on my soft bed and the room fills with dreams, the white moments, music that has traveled over the great empty spaces of the world to reach me; I heard Schumann and Bach, the majestic questerings of Brahms; I see the shadows rise up the wall, they are friends or corpses, I can't tell which, they do not stagger but move slowly, there is, in the sky, a whole fleet of clouds that look like gentlemen shaking the rain from their coats; across the river, I know this, the white trunks of the sycamores are dirty at the bottoms like the muddy legs of horses; the leap of a bass makes a heavy flapping sound like the wing of an eagle beating the smooth black water; across the stillness of the evening I can hear every sound; I lie lazy in the arms of the world, a child still, wondering, amazed . . .)

Years ago I saw a solar eclipse. All the shadows went out of focus. The bitten sun shining through the tree leaves threw clusters of white

317

brush strokes on the ground, each mirrored and held by its equivalent dark stroke. I held my hand out and the shadow was out of focus; along the length of my shadow fingers the sun made a creation: the lower knuckle dark, the middle knuckle lighter, the tips all light, white and shining.

In a diary dated August 12, 1887, my grandmother wrote: "I have seen him walking on the road when there was no one there, and I cannot understand how I smell the scent of tea olive, I feel the red dust on my wrist, I taste the sweetness of a peach, and he is nothing."

Grown old, she traveled from town to town carrying, like an antique brooch, the faint and singular hope that he might be living there, unnoticed and uncared for among the rise and fall of other people's lives.

My son thinks he will be a painter. I see already the picture he will paint of me: I stand with my arms open, screaming, there is blood on my dress; behind me a figure, sexless and defeated, lies across a bed. I will be the demon who prevents rescue, that will be the role I play in his desperate art.

When I left for Washington in 1937, I know my father cried. He came down the long stairs wearing a white shirt and white trousers. It was Monday morning and I could hear the fish sellers crying their wares in the park. His eyes were red though his face was wiped clean. He said, "Lizzie, Lizzie," in a soft voice and then stood very still looking at me. I could hear the fronds of the cabbage palms ticking against the living room windows and out on the gallery the maid swept away the dew. I knew he would come the rest of the way down the stairs, that he would step through the narrow rectangle of golden sunlight soaking the old carpet and take me in his arms. I knew he would do this and I knew I would not resist him as I had spent all the years doing. He raised his hand, it was as if it drifted up; it stroked the air; I thought, He is caressing me before he gets to me, he is touching already the memory of me. When I drove the car into the river he said nothing, he never spoke of it. I told him that I had seen angels in the trees and he looked at me a long time and his hand rose in the same manner, shaping a form in the air between us and then falling, as it did then, that morning before I left. I took a single step toward him and the thing that held him broke; he stumbled down the stairs and took me in his arms and kissed me, full on the lips. It was one more moment when time stopped, when I held the still heart of the world in my hands.

In the early morning I rose, went out and swam in the pool. The water was the color of young limes. The big curved iron pipe with the little spin wheel on top that fed the pool always looked to me like a penis. I would touch it and a shiver would run through my body. It was very early, I think before six. The eastern sky which I could just see beyond the buildings of the Exchange was rose. As I swam, slowly on my back, I saw a man come into the lane. He wore a shirt of striped colors, a garment like something torn from the back of a clown, and he walked with a slight limp, his head held high as if he were watching birds. I swam to the edge of the pool and watched him come on. He stopped at the lane gate and looked across the yard at me. He had the face of a child under wild gold hair tossed around his head, though his body was old, shrunken under the long shirt. I started to speak, but something said don't break the silence. He said, "The world is a paradise," and smiled. It was the sweetest smile I ever saw. I dove, and when I came up he was gone. I called out, but no voice called back. Then I heard the singing for the first time, inside of me, but large, filling the world. And then the silence came again. I thought, Ghost or Lord, I will follow you. That is what I have done.

The world is a paradise.

19 On November 3, the day after his birthday, a day when the spruces outside his window were soaked with cold rain, Jacey packed everything he could get into the two gray suitcases his father had given him for his first trip north, said goodbye to his roommate and his best friend, and after attending vespers at the school church, boarded the 5:55 train from the Hyde Park Station to New York. Martha met him in the Oyster Bar in Grand Central, where they shared three bowls of fish chowder before taking the bus down to the apartment she had rented on East 7th Street overlooking Tompkins Park.

The apartment was two narrow rooms, one behind the other, and smelled of roaches and old sweat among other undifferentiated though persistent odors. They made love on the bed Martha had bought along with all the other furniture from a Puerto Rican used-goods dealer who also lived in the building. Afterward Jacey lay in the bed looking out the barred windows at the elm trees in the park. The lower halves of the trees were lit by the streetlights and their dark tops shook in a wet east wind. They reminded him of the oaks outside his bedroom window at Canaan. At this moment no one in the world but Martha knew where he was. She was in the kitchen making cabbage soup from a recipe she had parsed out in the Ukrainian restaurant downstairs. He thought, I am sixteen years old and living with a grown woman in a walkup apartment in the largest city in the world. The thought was terrible, then it was fine. He got out of bed and did a few quick jumping jacks. The room was small but he figured he could manage a cartwheel; he couldn't quite: his heel grazed the wall and he landed in a giggling heap in the corner. He got up, raised the single-paned window and looked down in the street. Three men in dark clothes ran up the sidewalk shouting to each other in Spanish. Their heels clattered like hooves over the metal plates covering a torn-up patch in the pavement.

Martha called him from the kitchen and he went out and sat down to soup with her in the little alcove she had made with a Chinese screen to set the kitchen off from the boxcar space of the living room. He said, Why are we eating twice? She said, Because I have to bring you into the world I live in. Here I am, he said. The soup tasted like nothing he had ever eaten before. As he ate Martha sewed ribbons onto a new pair of toe shoes. She held the shoes up after every stitch for his approval. He took a spoonful of soup and she held the shoes up. He took another spoonful and she held the shoes up again. She wore a look of infinite coyness. They both began to laugh at the same time. They laughed until he got up and came around the Formica table and took her in his arms. They made love on the kitchen floor with the silk ribbons of the dancing shoes hanging down from the table over their heads.

In his mind he threw paint against fences, walls. A warehouse on West 21st Street was painted white down one whole block and he walked beside it, flicking imaginary paint off his fingers at it, full of fierce terrorist nonchalance. He signed up for courses at the Art Students League and got a job busing tables at a fish house on First Avenue. He came home at night smelling of turpentine and the ocean. Martha was the principal dancer in the Jouvence Theater's second company. Quick on her feet, athletically sexual, her technique was flawed. She danced anyway like something deranged.

No Burdette has ever done this before, he'd say to himself as he walked past vegetable markets on the Lower East Side. He'd stop and dip his face into fruit, into the excellence of southern vegetables: collards, mustard greens, black-eyed peas, rutabagas, okra. Any hint of the South hammered his chest; he'd nearly stagger. Even before his life was arranged he bolted to the Museum of Modern Art to see *Full Fathom Five,* Pollock's 1947 breakaway. I was two years old when he painted this, he thought, standing in front of it. The brushstrokes, luminous slashes of cadmium yellow and alizarin crimson, the gun-metal field itself, were held back by the bulging net of muscle-poured lines—"It's as if my own life is in there," he told Martha, "just like that, I felt just like that up in those spruce fields outside the school, like I was some piece of color burning behind all those branches." Some piece of color, little piece of fire now, walking New York streets so strange. On his pilgrimage to Pollock's old studio on Eighth Street he thought how he had tormented with a broom the old dam bear at Bernard and Delight's zoo. The bear going crazy, knocking over her house. Something poked him at St. Crispin's, poked him now. He found the old cemetery on First Street where the Dutch founders were buried. There were oaks growing up out of the seventeenth-century graves; they looked as if the strong burgher fingers were trying to pull them back into the earth.

The streets of the East Side were narrow and the fronts of the buildings were laced up tight with fire escapes and steel balconies. Trash cans clattered at night, and from the park which smelled of dog shit came screams. One night as he crossed the street to the apartment a man got up out of the gutter behind a Chevrolet and grabbed his coat. He had a white frost of beard and his hands were crimped with arthritis. "I want your light," the old man said, but when Jacey fumbled in his pocket for a restaurant match he stopped him. "Not that—your *light,*" the man said, and Jacey, confused and frightened, pulled his sleeve free and ran into the building.

"I'm scared," he told Martha that night in bed. "I don't know if I can live here."

"You're just homesick, boy," she said and laid her body across his, bearing him down with the weight of, it seemed to him, their unreadable future.

He claimed art as his province but he noticed in himself, as he had not in the airy studios of St. Crispin's, a resistance to it, an inhibition and reluctance that he seemed unable to break down. He took life classes and painting classes and chafed at the exercises his teachers made him do. He wrote letters to Rooley in which he complained that New York was cold and that the abstract expressionists were out of favor. "They're making *arrangements* now and I don't understand and I think they're mostly unpainterly and ugly," he wrote. Rooley, who had become a Pentecostal Christian, urged him to go to church and give his body and soul to Christ. "The spirit will do the work," Rooley wrote. "Just surrender, let the child come out."

The child was the last thing Jacey wanted to let out. "You shitting me, boy?" he said to his distant cousin as he walked past the Hell's Angels outpost on Third Street. "If I shit something like you," he answered, "I'd pinch his head off." Along the curb the Angel bikes were racked like swords. In fair weather the huge tattooed men lounged on sofas on the sidewalk administered to by women. He thought his mother would like that, wouldn't mind being a part of it, if they let her bring her bike. Then he didn't know. Between a bookstore and a shoe repair shop he stopped because the street ahead of him had gone white. A blankness descended and he couldn't see.

He woke up on the sidewalk with a black woman kneeling over him speaking to him in a Georgia accent. She wore a coat that looked as if it were made from the skin of mongrel dogs. "You're gonna be all right, honey," she said. "Just lie still." He raised his hands to her and touched her face, which was as cold as the winter day. Though she held him in her arms until an ambulance came, he could not bring himself to speak to her.

It was nothing physical—the doctor told him that. He was as well nourished as any boy the doctor, a short man in a crew cut, had ever seen. "Which makes it mental," the doctor said. "And I can't do much about that." He offered him a prescription for tranquilizers, which Jacey refused. "I'll ride it bareback," he said, put his clothes on and took a cab home. When Martha came in from class he was in the bed. She looked at him once, then undressed and got in bed with him. The minute she touched him he burst into tears. She held him in her arms for a long time while he cried.

It took his father two weeks to find him. He flew up to bring him back. Jacey watched from the bedroom window for the cab. When he

322

saw his father get out (wearing a tweed overcoat he had never seen before) he raced down the stairs and met him in front of the building.

"Can we go up?" his father asked and Jacey told him no. They went around the corner to a delicatessen, where Jacey ordered blintzes and an egg cream, items unheard of in south Georgia. His father made chat out of Canaan, the fall crops, relatives. Then he gently said, "Don't you think it's time you went back to school?" To J.C. his son looked haggard and drawn. He wanted to reach across the table and touch his clouded forehead, take him all the way into his arms in fact, but he restrained himself, afraid to.

"I'm *in* school," Jacey answered, tracing with his forefinger lines through a water ring.

"Have you run away from us?"

"Not away."

"You're only sixteen."

"I've got a social security number. I've got a work permit. I take classes at the League."

"They'll let you in so young?"

"They'll let anybody in—anybody who's serious."

J.C. spread his hands open on the table and looked at them as if they had just that moment taken form. "Are you sure this is what you want to do?" he asked.

"I'm not sure," Jacey said, feeling a chill shoot along his bones, "but I'm not going back to St. Crispin's."

J.C. wanted to tell his son that last week he had seen a raccoon on the back porch. From the bedroom gallery he had watched it climb the steps and sniff at the back door. "It was just like a little dog," he wanted to say. "You should have seen it," but his son's manner, the impenetrable armor he wore, drove him back.

The school had called him at work. As the principal's explanation wormed out of the wires he had been hit with a rage so fierce that he threw the electric shaver he held through the window. He put the phone down thinking he would kill his son and the whole Poitevent family. As he dialed their number he remembered that Artis Poitevent owed him money for a horse he had promised to buy and never had and he intended to get every penny of it back. But Artis answered the phone in tears, having just read Martha's letter that told her family she had moved into

323

an apartment with Jacey. "J.C., this will kill her grandmother," he said. "This will kill her."

"I don't know about Estelle, but it might kill me," J.C. said.

"Go up there and bring them back," Artis said, shirking, as J.C. knew he would, any responsibility for action.

"Why don't you come with me," J.C. suggested.

"I can't," Artis answered. "I couldn't bear it."

It took ten days for J.C. to discover their address. He got it finally, after several phone calls, from Jacey's roommate, a boy from Oklahoma who had spent a week with them during Christmas break a year ago. He immediately sent a telegram which said, "We love you and are very concerned. Family emergency. Please call."

There was no answer. He sent another telegram telling Jacey when he would arrive in New York.

"Martha's parents are distraught," he said now.

"Martha's nineteen years old," Jacey answered. "She's a professional dancer. Besides, you told me New York was the big leagues."

"Nobody makes it to the big leagues when they're sixteen."

"Here I am."

"Scraping tartar sauce off've plates and living in sin."

"Daddy," Jacey laughed. "You don't worry about living in sin. What about you?"

"I don't live in sin. I'm married. I've been married for seventeen years."

"Ha."

J.C. looked around the room that was filled with strangers. "I could make you come home," he said.

"How could you do that?"

"You're under age for life on your own. You're still legally the ward of your parents. I could make you come with me. The whole legal power of this state would help me."

"Some power."

"It's my right."

Jacey's hand shook and he felt his upper lip rise off his teeth. "And I would make them all know how it is with you and Mama," he said. "I'd let them know how you live." He looked away through the front windows that were streaked with rain. "And anyway, you couldn't watch me close enough to keep me from leaving."

J.C. felt as if a gout of flesh were ripping loose inside him. Gout, sheaf, plain, territory of flesh. It fell a long way, as if his body were a well. What his son said was true. "Why do you hate us so much?" he said.

"I don't hate you at all."

J.C. shook his head. "I can't believe it," he said. "Not twice in one lifetime."

"Oh shoot, Daddy." Jacey stood up and walked out of the restaurant, leaving his father to pay and follow.

J.C. caught him at the corner. They stood in a trickling rain looking up the street. "I've always liked the way everything you need is packed in together," J.C. said, glancing at bank and grocery store. He nodded at passersby as if they were on the Square in Yellow Springs. Jacey thought of how sad the fall made him, especially up here, in the North, where the trees burned themselves alive. In south Georgia what failed in season was only a portion of what grew; the live oaks and the sweet bays remained, and the pines that never changed. In Georgia, the winter, cold and wet as it was, was something you could nearly hold your breath through, spring about to screech around the corner any minute.

He had pushed out ahead but now he followed his father into a Minute Cleaners, where he had his suit pressed. They sat side by side on a bench in the back room while the launderer worked on the clothes. Jacey was embarrassed to see his father sitting in shorts and T-shirt in this nearly public place. It didn't seem to bother J.C. at all; he read a magazine, slipping his fingers under his black garter to massage his heavily muscled calf. At forty-six his father's body was still trim, muscular and trim, though the crisp rusty hair that bushed out of the top of his undershirt had turned gray. Jacey didn't want to look at him. When a woman stuck her head through the curtain and his father spoke to her, invited her in in fact, Jacey cringed and swiveled in his seat so he wouldn't have to face him. I have abandoned my life, he thought. This had better work, because there's more than miles now between me and what I was. When the cleaner, who looked more like a wrestler than a small businessman, came in with the clothes on a hanger Jacey could not look at his father's face. He watched a point on the wall while he dressed.

They had dinner that night in the main dining room of the St. Regis, the hotel his father always stayed in when he was in New York. The dinner was late because Martha was rehearsing. Jacey met her uptown, waited in the lobby of the practice studio. Dancers drifted by him as he sat on a short leather sofa next to a desk that was piled three feet high with dance magazines. Most of the dancers carried their gear in small canvas satchels thrown over their shoulders. Years of *pliés* made their feet splay slightly outward as they walked—webbers they would have been called at St. Crispin's, duck walkers. Martha came out with three other girls. She wore a fisherman's sweater with a leather vest over it and a stocking cap with a long blue tassel hanging down the back. For a moment as she approached he saw how dancing had transformed her; her back was straight and her movements seemed to depend from the waist as if she had collected energy there and radiated it to arms and legs. It seemed impossible that she had ever lived in Yellow Springs and he wondered if this was happening to him, if this move to New York was not a breakaway at all, only one step down a road that he had begun to travel a long time ago. He felt panic rise in him and for a moment he wanted to fly home with his father, not back to St. Crispin's, but home, to Canaan, to the high room of his grandfather's tower where he could look out over country he was known to. The feeling vanished when she spoke to him in the familiar accent of south Georgia and by the time they had run down the wide staircase and out into the mizzling rain, he was happy again, so excited that they raced the twenty blocks from the studio to the hotel, chasing each other through the crowds.

His father paced in the lobby before the golden portals of the elevator doors kneading his hands. Jacey rushed up the marble entrance stairs after Martha. She stopped when she saw J.C., whirled with a question in her eyes as if she had misunderstood where they were going, but Jacey kept coming; he grabbed her around the waist and spun her, took her hand and ran up to his father, who had halted under a large gilt mirror watching them.

"Hello, Dad," he cried. "How is everything?"

His father looked at him bleakly, then smiled. "I never thought of you getting lost before, but I was just thinking of it now," he said.

"I've got Martha to lead me around."

"Hello, Mr. Burdette," Martha said. She dipped her head almost as if she would bow to him. And then it was as if a great cloak drew around them or as if they stepped into a force field that drew them into another country. It was only the familiar country of Yellow Springs, but as they moved across the lobby Jacey felt as if he were being drawn back into

326

another time and place. His father's voice contained the modulated tones of the country he had fled; Martha's too, and for a moment Jacey lost his bearings; it was as if they were walking into the restaurant of the Hotel Burdette, as if across the room there he could see his aunts and uncles waving from a cluttered table, as if he could still hear the Sunday seraphics of the church choir and smell the heavy balm of the camphor tree in the Square.

His father moved ahead of them after the waiter, twitching his shoulders. Jacey figured he knew his father's whole repertoire of twitches and quirks by heart; he knew the long, leg-straightening stride, the way he pressed his waist with the insides of his wrists, the way he jerked his head to the side as if he were about to spit. He laughed at the thought of his father spitting on the royal-blue St. Regis carpet. Martha looked a question at him, and he took her fine bony wrist between his fingers and held it up as they walked as if he were offering her hand to the room, to kings about to take it. The sullenness and resentment of the afternoon had abated, and when his father engaged the waiter in conversation about his origins Jacey listened with enthusiasm. His father had a habit of questioning passing service people, waiters, cabbies, elevator operators, as if they were setting out on a long voyage together and he thought it best to get to know each other well at the beginning. He wanted to know where they were from and what their home life was like and what their fathers had done, and what their children were up to. As he questioned the waiter Jacey felt a tenderness in him, a delight almost, and the tug he had felt earlier that day, the feeling that he wanted to go home with his father, came back. But it was not frightening to him. Martha sat on his right eating a piece of celery, biting the stalk just enough to break a morsel off, and he remembered he had seen her eat like that a thousand times before.

In the morning he would stand at his easel in the drafty League classroom, surrounded by people who up until two weeks ago he had never seen before. They spoke in accents that were as foreign to him as the accents of Brazil, but the paint on his fingers would be familiar. Cobalt and crimson make a fine black. An ultramarine line would make cadmium orange explode. Naples yellow mixed with alizarin red made a color like something invented by Degas. He had spent a year at St. Crispin's drawing light bulbs, tennis shoes, bricks. He had done it, chafing and angry, until he could put life into each one. He moved on to oils, to

327

figures, to the reach of an extended arm, the curve of fingers grasping the slope of a neck. Now, in New York, he had stepped backward—safer there—mixing colors for hours learning how to make what he needed. As he mixed colors, scraped them off the Formica board he used for a palette and mixed again, the urge to fling them on the canvas would come so strongly that he would have to leave the room and walk around outside. His teacher had told him that before he let him use the full palette he would have to paint for weeks—weeks!—with only one color. He would have to paint with it until he knew everything about it. "It's the same with dance," Martha told him. "You start off every class doing simple *pliés*."

As he raised his water glass he saw the crescent of yellow at the bottom of his middle fingernail; he wondered if his father had ever had to wait, had ever had to practice the same moves over and over. When his father was his age he was already a thousandaire, a moneymaker, pinhooker on the tobacco market. He was speaking now of the cotton picking which was just winding up. "Two steps ahead of the rains," he heard him say. "We had to cannibalize one of the other pickers for parts, we were so rushed at the end. Couldn't even wait for parts to come. We tore a picker down and used her guts to keep the others running."

Was his father in a dream? The smile that had settled on his lips seemed to be one that he could have found in a monastery somewhere, someplace where men discovered serenity. Beatific, that was the word. He presented it to them as a kindly man would give food to starving travelers.

"What was the emergency?" Jacey asked and took a sip of water for the dryness that filled his throat.

"Your mother." The smile continued. "I'm afraid she'll have to be hospitalized."

Jacey felt a shocking chill as if a winter door had just blown open. He maintained his composure by rearranging the silverware by his plate. "Why?" he asked, not looking up.

"She doesn't eat. She's wasting away."

"Maybe she's not hungry."

"It's worse than that. Eustace found her unconscious at the cabin. He took her to the emergency room. Apparently she had gone so long without food that she just fell out."

"Oh, poor woman," Martha said, tears springing into her eyes.

His father's smile faded but his look was still mild, detached. "What are you going to do?" Jacey asked.

"The doctor thinks we ought to send her to the hospital down in Tallahassee."

"You mean the sanitarium."

"I mean the sanitarium."

Jacey passed a hand over his face and looked at his father straight on. "How will you ever get her there?" he asked.

"I can't do it by myself. She won't listen to me. You'll have to help me."

Martha pushed back slightly in her chair, reached under the table and took Jacey's hand.

Jacey felt the weary stubbornness that for the last few years had come over him in his father's presence. "I can't leave my classes," he said.

"You left St. Crispin's all right."

"I don't want to talk to you about that. It was necessary."

"Pleasure-seeking—excuse me, Martha, it's no reflection on you, but your parents are sick over this. Your grandmother may not survive it."

"She never survives it," Martha said. "Every time one of us gets out of line it kills her. In the last twenty years she's died a thousand deaths."

J.C. drew his mouth into a line. "Don't you think this is a little different?"

"And scary," Martha said. She drew her legs up in the chair and smiled sweetly over the tops of her knees.

"I don't think you are ready for this," J.C. said to Jacey.

"For carrying Mama to the hospital? I'm sure not."

"No," his father said impatiently. "For this—New York. You need to stay and finish school first. Why don't you go back up to St. Crispin's? When you finish I'll be glad to finance your studies here. My father would be paying for me to go to school right now if that was what I wanted to do. Education is very important in our family—it's an open checkbook. You just go back up there. You can even take weekends down to see Martha—she's got enough to do without having to maintain some living arrangement with you. Her career is just getting off the ground. And you need to finish your studies. Then if the painting doesn't

329

work out you can go to college. I know they'd be delighted to hear from you at Harvard. They have a wonderful art department. It would be the easiest thing in the world for me to set up a meeting with some of their art people. Have you ever been to the museum there? Some of the finest paintings in the world are at the Fogg."

As his father spoke Jacey pressed back in his chair. The words were projectiles that stung and bounced off him. He realized he could survive the attack. "I can't," he said out of a face that felt frozen.

"What you can't?"

"I can't go back." How could he explain that for him there was no way back down the rope, even a rope so short as two weeks in New York City. "I didn't do this on impulse," he said. "I've planned it—we've planned it—for a long time." But as he spoke uncertainty crept in. Could he say no to his mother? How could he? "I'll call Mama," he said, "but I can't go back to school. This is what I want to do. This is it."

Something in his father seemed to collapse. His shoulders drooped and he took a long drink of water. But he pulled himself together and looked at his son. "I can't pay for your staying here, none of your schooling," he said. "You're on your own."

"That's fine," Jacey said. "I wouldn't have it any other way."

His father made a sharp guttural sound and got up from the table.

"Where are you going, Daddy?"

"I can't stay," he said. "I'm sick." He strode out of the room, his arms twitching at his sides, his hand making little circular motions as if he were calling small beings out of the air around him.

Jacey did not believe his father was through, and he wasn't. As he saw him into an airport cab the next day his father said, "This will probably kill me, you know," in a voice that might have been commenting on the weather.

Without Martha next to him Jacey felt vulnerable and he said, "No, it won't," in a voice that implored his father not to mean what he said.

"I love you, son," J.C. said through the open window and then he sat back in the seat before Jacey could reply. Jacey gripped the sill, unsure of himself. His father leaned forward again and said, "Come home whenever you're ready. If you come home all this will be forgotten."

Then the cab sped away. Jacey stepped out into the street and watched it accelerate through traffic. The cabbie drove as if his father were threatening him with a whip. When it passed out of sight Jacey walked over to Second Avenue and caught a bus home.

Within days the letters began, from his father and—to his surprise—from his aunts and uncles, too. Everyone suggested that he come home. Bryce wrote about the cotton crop and about the fishing trip they had taken to the Florida flats when he was twelve. It was the only time they had ever done anything like that, but Bryce described it as if such adventures were a way of life for them. With his aunts it was love, love, love and a hint of tears on every page. Lois wrote bright, spry notes describing her garden and the new pool she'd made Bryce put in. "The last fall flowers are blooming," she wrote, "and they make me feel like a lost little girl. I think I would never want to be away from a place as beautiful as this." That was as close as she came to addressing his defection. Louise wrote terse paragraphs lauding Burleigh's football exploits at Georgia Tech, adding P.S.s that suggested he haul his ungrateful carcass back up the Hudson. He even got a letter from his old Little League coach—a friend of Martha's father—who reminded him of the great days of twelve-year-old baseball and told him that Martha's parents were in despair over the situation. He showed the letter to her and she laughed and told him that Mr. Jacobs had always tried to look after her. "He's always been my father's emotional henchman," she said.

When they got a phone the early-morning calls began. His father was always friendly, always wanted to know how things were going, always carried a report on his mother. His mother, who was not a part of this plot, wrote him that she was getting married again and moving to Texas. "I have finally conquered this country," she said, "and now it's time to move on."

He called his grandfather to see if what she said was true.

"She's still out there in the cabin," Jack told him, "drinking a lot and working on her book."

His grandfather laughed when he told him of his father's tactics. "You got a rocky row," he said, "but you shouldn't figure it to be any different. As determined as your father is, you'll just have to get used to living your life around him."

His father's tenacity amazed them. Mornings they waked to the ring of the telephone. They stubbornly refused to unplug the device when they went to bed. Somebody might want to call us, Jacey explained vaguely, but what he meant was that he did not want to give in to the idea that his father still controlled him, from a thousand miles away in Georgia. To Martha he said, My father wrote letters to my mother by the hundreds. He recited as best he could remember the passages he had read from his father's letters to her. Martha suggested that they leave the line open. That way, she said, he can just shout into the phone every time he wants our attention. Cookies and bags of boiled peanuts arrived from his father's secretary. She also included poems she composed. One of them read, "O my sweet, you can't be beat/Why don't you turn this way your little feet." Jacey tacked the poem on the bathroom wall.

He began to dream of his father. Always in the dream he received a message that his father was dying, but he was never able to get there in time. He couldn't move fast enough. The dreams would often wake him up and he would get up, climb the four flights of stairs to the roof and look out at the city. The Brooklyn Bridge was a web of lights to the east. He could see a long way uptown; lights burned all night; he tried to find patterns in them at first, then began to just enjoy the light against the black hulks of the buildings. They're my new stars, he thought, looking up at the obliterated sky, they have taken over from the stars of south Georgia. From the lights of buildings he fashioned constellations of his own, bright pockets of explanation that he hoped would sustain him. But the patterns changed, the same lights were not on each night. In the street below women ran by cursing. The drunks retreated to doorways, collected themselves and drifted south toward the shelters.

Once in a while Martha would join him on the roof. They would sit with their legs dangling over the tin parapet looking at the sky. Or they would recline against the low wall and look uptown at the lighted buildings. Martha, who had lived there two years already, picked out landmarks.

His mind ran with images of his father, memories of their drives across the lands on Sunday afternoons, of duck hunting on Oyster Bay in Florida, of going shopping together in Atlanta. From the streets below came smoke and cries, obscuring fog. Through the trees he could see the yellow and red neon lights of a Puerto Rican boys' club across the park. The boys—who looked like men to Jacey—stood around the entrance smoking and talking in small groups. They often shouted at the passing traffic on the avenue and to Jacey their voices were full of malice and an impenetrable knowledge. He would crawl across the space that separated him from Martha and climb into her arms. He was not the man he wanted to be, the man he thought he could become by going to New York and studying painting. He was afraid all the time, making connections that revived his memories of a childhood in south Georgia.

He had done the same thing his first year at St. Crispin's, wandering in the woods above the playing fields, turning in his pockets the small pieces of limestone he had pried from the wall of the spring. He had written letters begging to come home. His father had written back of his own homesickness that first year at Harvard. Reading them Jacey found enough strength—if only just barely—to stay. It was not that his father had felt the same things he felt; it was that he admitted he had, that for a moment he took down the wall of years and experience that separated them.

But now, but now . . . he huddled on a winter night on the pebbled roof of a tenement in New York City. Was this a tenement? He didn't know enough about such things to be sure. Before he came here he had never even known anyone who lived in an apartment. In the small towns of the South anyone could find a house. One day he would live like his mother, alone in a cottage in the woods. And Martha would be where? Under soft skin her body was as hard as wood. In her groin were muscles as hard as tennis balls from the dancing. He had never seen muscles like that before. She walked as if her body were held upright by a hook in the sky, as if she were attached to some planet far away and her feet only barely touched earth, this foreign planet.

One night he unwound the wire that held the door shut and walked out into the freezing air of December. The roof was seeded with pebbles embedded in asphalt. The night was rich with lights, disordered and vivid. Only the Brooklyn Bridge, swinging eastward, seemed to carry any promise of order. He leaned out over the tin skirts and counted lights with his fingers. The wind blew straight out of Canada. He thought he would fall, forward or back, sprawled dead or exhausted: either, defeat. Even your bones, he thought, even your skin can stop being familiar. He wanted to dig with his hands into his own body until he found some piece he could call Jacey. He took off the loden coat and scarf his father had paid for, he took off the moccasins his uncle had given him and the wool socks and threw them all over the edge. He took off shirt, pants and underwear and threw them away. He didn't watch them fall, stepped back naked and held himself in his arms. This is not much of a gesture, he thought, as long as I can go back inside. He laughed, felt better. The only way to live is to love the fear. He walked to the edge of the roof and looked down into the street. The dark naked tops of the elms shivered in the wind. Through the branches, across the park, he could see the Puerto Rican toughs standing outside their neon storefront. This late they still wait for what the world is going to bring them. God save them, he thought, and God save whoever crosses their path.

But they did not end, the images of his father striding across a field, the memory of his testicles bulged against his trousers as he squatted in the front yard talking to the plant manager. In the dreams he howled and fought toward home. They spent Christmas in New York and took turns crying through the gray blowing day. They pulled themselves together to take the calls from their families. This might not be the way to do it, Jacey told Martha, but they went ahead and cooked the old-time Georgia meal. Jacey wanted to remember every bit of it so he wrote it down in his sketchbook: sweet potato soufflé, oyster casserole (that Martha had to make three times before she got it right), two kinds of greens (mustard and kale), black-eyed peas (soaked back into life), a chicken (no turkey) stuffed with celery dressing, white rice with gravy, biscuits (round and flat, pale yellow), syllabub, mint tea. He drew Martha at the stove, he drew her eating a drumstick, he drew the table full of food. We are an extraordinary couple, she said, and for the moment he believed it. Do you think this is a tenement? he asked her, and she glanced around the room as if she had never seen the place before. Hadn't you thought of it before? he asked. No, she answered, I never noticed; what do you think? I have no idea, he said—we're the first people I've ever known who lived in an apartment. Whatever it is, she said, it'll have to do.

He said, I guess so, and went into the bedroom and lay down on the bed. They had pushed it against the front windows and he lay looking out at the wind gashing the rain. No snow, he said to himself, we have come all this way and no snow. Then he thought of his mother and the old chill raced through him. When he wished her Merry Christmas on the phone she had said, I don't pay any attention to that. He hadn't argued, let Martha take over. You come and go, he said, meaning himself. Two nights before he had crawled into Martha's arms and hung there like a baby. He thought manhood was a prize he could win and he was afraid he would lose it if he grabbed at her love. She got out of bed and danced a figure from her new ballet, but he called her back. Tell me how much you love me, he said, tell me again and again. Martha, understanding, indulged him. She took his face in her hands and kissed him on the lips until the fear became a small animal disappearing over a ridge. I can do this now, she said, tracing with her long fingers new lines into his sixteen-year-old face, but I can't do it forever. I'm not strong enough to hold you up and me, too. I would if I could—you're a sweet romantic mama's boy and that touches me, it does—but I can't. You're going to have to find your own strength to walk.

And so he did. If what rose up in him was never as distinct as the ravening purposefulness of his grandfathers Langston and Rooley, if he had no venal enemy Andrew Jackson, no pure-hearted tract of ground to break his back and will against, he had at least the city of New York, founded by the blond-haired Dutch, he had art, paint vibrating on a canvas, the violent abracadabra of Pollock, de Kooning, Rothko and Clyfford Still—and he had himself, mind in which the kinked lines of his past shuddered and blew out sparks, life in which memory (mother-lust, father-fear) was always liable to come stomping and wheezing out of the most tangled woods demanding tribute, solace, a place at the table. As we sometimes come to believe, as if it were true, that the world itself is a world of intention, of directed mind containing both joy and the probability of malice, only to discover, in the kneaded ashes of our own hot hearts, that the world, vale of trees and running strangers, holds nothing more than the propped facades of our own minds, the wisps of dream we have colored and shaped, nothing out of nothing, nothing with nothing, from nothing, for nothing, of nothing—only, only for the moment just only, the variegated and relentless self which it is perhaps our whole duty to dismantle, give away piece by piece to the nothing that is and the nothing that isn't—so; so he discovered it was only himself he walked around on the way to work, to the restaurant where he bused tables until they let him become a waiter, uptown to the League where he drew until his eyes went out of focus and his hand could not control a line, to Janis and Castelli and Fourcade and Allen Stone where the burning paintings hung, to Martha's rehearsals, to her performances where her transformation into winged, erotic beings made him cry out, to their two shotgun rooms where he swept and mopped and cooked and threw new covers on the bed; he read Whitman and Proust and Joyce; he joined a rugby team and dislocated his shoulder; he saw every one of Buster Keaton's movies, wept when Marilyn Monroe died, mooned over southern vegetables in Balducci's, wrote letter after letter to his grandfather and Mattie, to his uncles and his cousins, reassuring them that his life had purpose, called home Sundays, thought, Maybe there is evil in the world, maybe not, wondered whether he would live or die. He didn't think: This is the underground railroad and I am running for my life, he only thought: I am running.

He loved working a job where he took his pay home at night. He loved the whole idea of honest exhaustion and money at the end of it. Where he grew up, when he was a child, they paid a man a dollar for every hundred pounds of cotton he picked. The strongest man might make three dollars a day. In tobacco season it was four dollars, working dark to dark. Now he brought home tens and twenties, folded bills he had smoothed out at a table with the other waiters while the busboys closed the place down. Change your quarters for bills, change your ones for tens and twenties. One night he made seventy-three dollars. On his way home he stopped in Brendau's, a restaurant on First Avenue, and had a chocolate malt and a plate of potatoes. A woman with blood in her hair drank soup from a bowl. A dark-skinned man sang a muttery song at the ceiling. A couple in identical Maine guide jackets fed each other pudding. For a moment there was no loneliness in the world, none that could get him. He thought that presently he would rise from the red booth and walk out into the city-harnessed night. Even in New York you might see leaves blowing up the sidewalk. This spring he would discover that the elms outside their window were everything you could ask an elm to be. This summer the rain would, for a moment, find diamonds in the light. Tonight he would walk down the street and the shadows, the late cabs passing, even the Puerto Rican toughs leaning against the wall by the club would hold no danger for him. He was a man of some illustrious means, a pocket full of silver, a blond woman who danced, paint like a rainbow, house with a bed in it. He had a place, and he could live in that place.

Martha was not fierce, she was not selfish, she did not harbor secret resentments. She sat sometimes by the window looking down at the street and when she finally turned back to the room, her eyes were calm. At night she prayed on her knees beside the bed like a child. It wouldn't hurt you to do it, Buster, she told him, but she didn't press the issue. As far as Jacey was concerned, God had never knocked on his door. He knew the good Baptist hymns and they sang them together sometimes as they walked down the street but that was for the sport. Martha didn't talk about religion, even when others did. She did not suddenly announce—as Rooley might—that the stars were the handiwork of God and she didn't mark the Lord's retribution in the trials of men. But each night in the pale light blown in from the park she knelt on the square of rug by the bed and said prayers, her lips moving with the silent words. He sat against the headboard with his knees pulled up whispering, "Our

Father . . ." trying to make the words out. In the old Sunday school days he had memorized Bible verses with the other children. In a Christmas program when he was seven he had recited the first Psalm in which everyone was advised to shirk the councils of the wicked. At seven, evil was easy to avoid. Nowadays who could tell? He hadn't been to church in Yellow Springs since the night his mother had tried to burn down the house. In himself he felt the pull of something dark, like the gravity of a planet just out of telescope range. He had been joyfully obsessed with his parents all his life and now they were like wolves he must keep running from. He leaned down until he could look in Martha's face. Her eyes were closed; there was no tightness, nothing held back. He wanted to take her head in his hands, let the thoughts flow into his body.

"What are you talking about?" he asked her one night when she had finished and crawled up beside him.

"I'm trying to give in to something larger than myself," she said.

"I'm afraid everything larger than myself wants to eat me."

"In your case that might be true."

"Can you do it?" he asked.

"What?"

"Give yourself away."

"It's very difficult," she said. "I'm not especially inclined toward a belief in intangibles. And I don't usually want too much help when I think I have things in hand."

He thought what a wonderful, flawed dancer she was. Her bones were bigger than a dancer's should be, but there was a delicacy and energy in her that made audiences gasp. When she moved the life seemed to spurt out of her. Her flawed technique would come to haunt her, would as she grew older seem to lodge like unerasable weight in her bones, a cross-purpose diminishing excellence as the energy failed, but that time was still distant. Once, splurging after a performance, they took a cab back to Tompkins Park. As she nestled with her head on his shoulder he noticed her lips moving: it was another prayer. Thanksgiving. At St. Crispin's she would have been laughed at. His mother would have laughed at her.

But he did not mind her praying. "You're serious," he hesitantly said, as if she might deny it.

"I'd be crazy not to be," she answered and pulled the quilt over them both.

He pushed up so he could see out the window. The maples were blossoming and he could make out in the light from the street their little red chicken-claw flowers. "What about all this life out here?" he asked. "How can belief mean anything to all that?"

"I don't do it to affect any of that stuff," she said. The city light made her blond hair look silver.

"But don't you think if there's a God he'd better tend to some of this?"

"I don't know. What do you think?"

"I think he's got his work cut out for him. Those JD's down there would just as soon kill me as look at me. I don't think they're salvageable. And last week somebody kidnapped one of the Hell's Angels, tied him up with wire, poured gasoline on him and set him on fire."

"My God."

"Your God is right. And that little guy who runs the store on 6th Street—the one with the Caribbean bananas and the hot peppers —his son got shot in a holdup last week. He's paralyzed from the waist down."

"That's terrible."

"I know, but where's God, where does he enter in?"

"I don't know. I don't understand it either."

"But aren't you supposed to have an answer for things like that? Doesn't the church have a position on deadly capers?"

"It does, but I'm just as baffled as you are. I had a cousin—you don't know him, he lived in Vidalia—who committed suicide. He was only fourteen years old. In his bedroom one morning before school he took down his .22 rifle and shot a hole in his heart."

"Jesus."

"He was schizophrenic. His parents had brought him home from the asylum for the weekend. If he got better he could start the eighth grade, but he shot himself instead. The church would say he's in a lot of trouble for doing that. Suicide is choosing against God. It's an act of the ego, extreme selfishness: I can't have my way so I won't play." She reached across him and took a sip of water from the glass she kept on the table. Then she dipped her fingers in the water and dripped them over her face. She lay back. "I don't see it that way," she said. "I don't believe Arnie Gates is now roasting in eternal hell."

"I'm glad of that. But how can you reconcile a belief in God with a church that's going to damn your cousin to hell?" Before she could answer he said, "I don't know—I think I want to be on the side of the losers. I want to go with the dark folks."

She laughed. "You just say you do. You'll never go with them. You never would have started hanging around me if you wanted to dance with the devils."

"But I don't believe in God. I don't even think about it. If you didn't get down on your knees I don't think it would ever cross my mind."

She stroked his hair. "It's not churchy," she said, letting her fingers trail across his face, "though I would like to follow what it says to do in the Bible. It's just that there seem to be things—behavior—that I have to keep away from. Not exactly because they don't fit into some kind of thought-out or imposed moral system, but because I get screwed up if I do them. I have to try to let people do what they're going to do, whatever it is. I couldn't make love to two men at once"—"I'm glad of that," he said—"and I pretty much have to do what they tell me to do in the company, even when I think it's stupid. Otherwise I get tangled up inside, I don't know what fits anymore. The problem is that I don't seem to have a nature that wants to control itself. On my own I'd run wild, do anything. So I pray. For strength. I try to admit how weak I am. Sometimes even that's hard because I get to thinking I can do what I want and take the consequences, whatever they are. That's when suffering arrives."

He slid his legs under hers and raised them so that they made a tent post under the covers. "I've started wondering about what we're doing," he said. He had not wondered about it until just this moment, not consciously. "In the last few years of his life," he said, "Pollock started giving his paintings titles again. He'd stopped when he got into the drips, everything was just numbered. When a painter starts numbering his paintings you know he's really moved into abstraction, representation is gone. But in the last three or four years of his life he started using titles again, even for the drip paintings. He did *Blue Poles* in 1953. The last painting he worked on was called *Fragrances*—isn't that wonderful?"

He sat up and leaned down and began to massage her ankles. Even there, in the smooth depression behind the bone was a hardness, trained flesh. "What I mean is, Pollock was the wildest of the wild. He was drunk all the time. He opened the door and let all the demons out. In some of those canvases it looks like the paint was laid on in a typhoon. I don't see how he kept from blowing apart."

"Maybe he did. Blow apart."

"No, I don't think so. I think in the end he was trying to get back. Not back maybe, not a retreat, but somewhere else. I went up to Castelli's yesterday and saw one of the late paintings; it was called *Scent*. I think the gallery owns it; it's not for sale. It's different from the drips. He used a brush or a knife and there's a scheme going on, not just some unleashed fury. It's like something had started to come clear, like he had found a road." He laughed self-consciously. "I keep getting the idea that once we accomplish whatever it is we're supposed to do in this world God—or whoever's there—takes us up; we finish and blip, we're gone."

"So you're afraid to straighten up."

"Yeah. I'm afraid that if I settle down and fly right—as they say in Yellow Springs—God'll jerk me off the planet. I don't want to go."

"Like your mother."

"No!" He whirled on her, pushed her body away.

"Jacey!"

"I don't want to hear that shit. I have enough trouble living with it as it is. Fuck God and my mother, too."

"Oh, sweet."

"I'm going to be somebody else, Jackson Pollock, too wild to tame."

"Wild Elizabeth."

He stood up in the bed, bounced up and down. "My mother doesn't do shit," he cried. "Pollock made great art."

"Come back down, you're going to break the springs. It doesn't matter."

He dropped, leaned over her and began to rub her legs. The skin was smooth and foreign. "It does matter," he said, his voice hard and whispery. "Sometimes it's the only thing that matters to me. I walk down the street and all of a sudden I see Mama leaping out of a bookstore. She's always just about to jump around the corner. I run up to Castelli's to see the paintings to remind myself there's still something that can be made out of madness."

"You aren't mad."

"I'm a Burdette. I'm a Bonnet, too."

"Your granddaddy's not mad."

"My grandmother wound up face down in the spring."

"She wasn't you. Your mother's not you. Neither is your father."

"I'm them. I'm nobody else."

She reached between them and took his penis in her hand. "I don't think of this as being interchangeable."

He pressed hard against her, trapping her hand. "Deaf, dumb and blind," he said, "and relentlessly opposed, I'd find their tracks and follow them."

"Follow this," she said, reached back and spread her cunt. He leaned down and made sounds into her ear. He stroked the back of her legs. She turned her face and he kissed her on the side of the mouth.

"For the life that's in it," she said.

"Damn, Martha." He drew away.

"What is it?"

"My mother says that."

"Oh, Jacey. Don't go away."

"I can't help it." It was like the dim, drizzly light under some of Pollock's paintings; there it was, miserable and ubiquitous, no matter how you danced.

"Don't leave me now," she said.

But he was gone, a rabbit in front of dogs. "I have to do something about her," he said.

"You don't have to do anything."

"But how can I save myself if I can't save her?"

"She doesn't need saving. She's doing what she's supposed to do."

"That's just God talk. Last fall I opened my trunk at school and found all her underwear packed in with mine. All these silky panties wadded up under my shirts." It was as if he had opened the lid on a corpse. He had reeled back in terror and run out of the house. He ran through town into the country, where he walked until he came to a road leading through a stand of white birches. He followed the road until he was far back in the woods. His heart pumped so hard he thought he might be having a heart attack. To save himself he sat down on a crumbling stone wall ringing a pasture that was grown up in raspberries and alders. Beyond the field the woods continued, birch and spruce, unbroken into Canada as far as he knew. "I am you," she had said and he had tried to drown her. He threw himself on the ground, imploring no God, rolled in September yellow Hudson River grass, his penis risen, hot as a fire.

With ravening fingers he ripped his buckle loose, pushed underwear and trousers down his legs, kicked them off over his sneakers and began to masturbate. The whole earth seemed soft as a breast. A woman danced in front of him naked, her body shielded only by the force of her will. Violently, in the pure murderousness of his lust, he pried her into the light. As the black heat exploded in his groin, he cried out, jackknifed, trying to catch the semen in his mouth. He lay back and kneaded the sexual grease into his face. It dried on his skin, tasted from his fingers of bitter salt. He closed his eyes. The dark shape of his mother faded, the sound of her cried-out name flew off into the empty air.

"It's all gristle," he said now, "there's no meat."

"I don't understand you." They lay on their sides facing each other, her legs drawn up.

"It's a mindless mystery," he said.

"What? Jacey, make sense."

"I think she has driven me crazy. I see little sparks of light, words jump out at me. You know that guy in Yellow Springs they call High Lift? He drank some bad white liquor and now he takes these high slow steps like he's avoiding cow pies. He told me that his head is full of voices that don't come from any people he knows . . ."

"Would it be better if they were familiar to him?"

"No, shit, but that's what's happening to me."

"You're hearing voices?"

"Sometimes at the restaurant I'll leave a table and I'll hear the customer calling me back, but when I turn around he hasn't said anything."

"That's just nerves."

"That's just a sign of my life falling apart."

She pressed herself against him, pushed him onto his back with her body. "I like crazy boys."

"No," he said, squirmed away, wrenched a pillow between them. He looked up at the ceiling, remembering the geckos that had chirped there when he was a child. "It's come back on me," he said. "It's just come back on me."

"Shove it off." She turned onto her back and stretched her arms above her head, pressing her hands against the headboard so her muscles stood out. Athlete, he thought, Olympian.

"I've dreamed of looking at the world," he said, "but I was afraid to leave the backyard. I was afraid if I went out in the street they wouldn't let me be a Burdette anymore; I would have to come down out of the trees and walk around with the rest of the sweaty mortals." He stroked her cheek but she turned her head away. "Do you know why I don't know how to drive?" he asked. She didn't answer. "Everybody I know when they get to be fifteen wants to hop in a car and drive away. Not me; I didn't want to get behind the wheel. You know why?" She shaded her eyes with her hand and didn't answer. "Because if I knew how to drive I'd have to get into a car and go somewhere, just like the rest of the grown-ups."

She shifted in the bed, pulled the pillow around her face, framing her loose long hair. "For somebody who wanted to stay put you've come a long way," she said.

"I know. Isn't that amazing. At St. Zapato's I used to read Walt Whitman. The guy wanted to embrace everything. It thrilled me, the possibility did, but when it got to be my turn to go to the courthouse to get my learner's permit I strolled off whistling in the other direction. If it hadn't been for you I'd be out there riding a John Deere with the rest of the cotton pickers. My grandfather says a man doesn't come into wisdom until he has stayed in a place long enough to outlive boredom. I was never bored at Canaan, but I didn't want to leave."

"You just said you wanted to look at the world."

"But I wasn't through looking at the ground I was raised on. There's a place in the swamp where the river widens out, it bellies out into a kind of lake. When I was a kid Delight used to tell me there was a man living on the other side who had a hand growing out of his knee. It used to scare me to death, but at the same time I wanted to see what he looked like. Now I'm old enough to know there was never anybody there, but I still want to go back and look for him."

"Jacey, everybody grows up."

"My mother hasn't. She's never given one minute's notice to what being grown up requires. She's down there right now in that house in Lazarus Swamp. She's probably talking this very minute to the man with the hand growing out of his knee."

"Jacey!"

"It's *true*. You know what she used to do? She used to write messages on little slips of paper and throw them out the car window. We'd be on a trip and she'd be tossing these little folded slips out the windows. She liked the idea of somebody picking the message up and reading it—that's

343

why she did it. She thought she could change lives that way. 'Indefatigable'—that was one of her favorite words, indefatigable. Can you imagine some Negro sharecropper unfolding one of those little pieces of paper and reading that word: Indefatigable. 'My, my,' he'd say, 'I'm gone live diff'rent from now on.' "

He was full of energy now and it drove him out of the bed running to the kitchen for a glass of cranberry juice. "Do you want anything?" he called to her. She told him no but he brought her an apricot anyway. He crawled over her, paused to kiss her once on the forehead with juice-cooled lips. She was still closed to him, he saw, but his mind was running with thoughts of his mother, Canaan. "I can't wait for the now days to become the then days," he said. "I want the past to hurry up and get here."

"That's because you're still such a child."

"Ah, you're pulling rank. You tottering twenty-year-olds *know* life."

"We know you'd better grow up."

"Why? My mother hasn't."

"And you're the one who can't stand being like her."

In Central Park he stared at the boots of the mounted policemen. He lay under a tree just off the path to the zoo looking up into new leaves until he was afraid the tree would fall on him. He had tried to kill her; just like his granddaddy, just like his daddy, he was capable of that. And it's me, he thought, me who would die. He would flee to another country, but no one there could help him. There was only this place, Martha, complex art. For a moment, brief as a rainbow, he thought, It's all right, I can live with it. If I'm her, fine. Then that thought was swallowed up by something greater: It hates me; that thing in her—that thing in me—hates me. He felt the hairs on his arms rise; he reached across the space that separated them and touched her sex, struck his fingers into the soft, downward-lying hair.

"Let's do this now," he said.

"All right."

"Let's do it my way."

"Only if we do mine first."

His voice choked in his throat. "Okay."

This life here was a kind of joke, he thought, some vaudeville story I am telling myself. A pearly, nearly tangible light filled the room. From

344

behind the open windows he could hear trees beating their leaves together; even the wind was strange to him, even the wind.

She turned on her side toward him, frowning. Nothing on her body sagged, it was as if she were carved out of one solid piece. "I'll do what you want," she said, "but we don't have to talk about it. I don't want to hear it in words."

"Fine." He touched her then, hard as stone himself, he mounted her, slid his penis between the lips of her sex into the wet striated glove of her body. She arched against him, directing him with tugs of her hands, shifting hips. He buried his face in her shoulder and pumped, thinking of nothing, thinking of green woods seen from cliffs, of Confederate soldiers standing at the edge of a misted clearing. She came suddenly, crying out as if in surprise and anguish, teeth bared, spittle collected in the corners of her mouth. He felt as if powerful cold hands were squeezing his head.

He waited only until she had come back enough to place her light, grateful kisses against his neck before he slid down her body into a crouch between her legs. "Now this," he said and pressed her thighs open. "Do it to yourself." She spread the lips of her sex with her fingers and slid the middle finger of her other hand into the groove they made, pressing down on the mounded flesh above the clitoris.

"Is this it?" she asked. "Is this enough?"

"Yes. Wider."

He crouched over her supported on one arm, his face close enough to smell her, not touching her, masturbating. He would like it if he never had to touch a woman. Her hand vibrated with a determinate palsy, her head arched back on her neck, she cried, "Now? Now?" and he answered, "Yes, go, yes," forced, as if wrenched up with all the rigid muscles of his body, the gout of semen loose, burning like lit paper in his guts—he came on her belly, followed the spurt of juice with his own collapsing body, glued himself with the splashed seed against her. He found her throat and arranged a few dry kisses there. She held him, stroked his hair.

"I love you," he said, because he did, and because he knew that if anything human could save him, she was it.

20 Elizabeth thought, Well, I can lie day and night and what would it matter? Light was what she wanted in this room as she had wanted light in every room she had ever lived in. She had painted the walls white and kept the curtains pulled back. She was quiet these days, quiet enough to become one of the animals. They came to the porch, raccoons, skunks, otters from the river. She left fruit peelings and berries for them. From her window she would watch as they went about their business on the porch. I have become a part of the woods, she thought, I have merged with all this.

She lay in the glider looking at the tops of the trees, which were draped with the golden light of an early-spring sunset. Around her on the grayed boards lay her notebooks. She had been cross-referencing them, marking passages notebook by notebook that seemed to tell a story. It was the story of forty years; which gets more significant all the time, she thought, as she raised herself to take a sip of wine. Her husband no longer sneaked around the corners of her house. She was alone now usually, a forgotten woman. Increasingly these days the journeys she took were in her head. Without leaving her room she could take trips back to Hawaii, to Texas, to the islands south of here. "Yesterday morning in Mozambique I had a native boy paint my feet black," she wrote. "In Wales I climbed Mount Snowden and picked a bouquet of the small blue flowers that grow there. It was dusty and dry last spring in Tehuantepec; the pipes broke and we had to drink water from the streams."

Her husband had told her once that De Soto had crossed this river on his way north. Often she imagined she saw him, leading his ragged band of clattering Spanish through the trees. She could hear the clanking metal, the crunch of a sword breaking branches. At night she called from her bed to whoever was out there, whoever moved with light or heavy tread among the ferns. She was known to walk out into the fields at night and lie down among the cotton rows. The voices in her had long been silent; she heard now only the groanings of the earth, the wind that seemed to be always telling a sad story to itself, the fluttering chorus of the three-pointed cotton leaves. In spring she picked the white and pink cotton flowers and carried them back to place in bowls of water around the cabin. Sometimes she would not bother to carry them back; she covered herself with blooms as she lay in the sandy ground watching the stars.

Looking at the night sky became her passion. She found that she was content to lie for hours looking at the constellations. At first the stars seemed nothing more than random notations of light, without purpose or depth, but as time went on she began to piece together a world in the heavens. She knew some of the arrangements already, the Pleiades, Cassiopea, the long V of Taurus, Orion's great stride, but she was happier to make up her own figures, gods and kings. She discovered the Holly Tree and the Exhausted Lovers, and the Great Motorcycle, Preacher Major and Preacher Minor. On a Wednesday night in May when the air carried the scent of tea olive, she discovered the Veil of Islam and the Drowned Girl. In September, one night when she had stuffed her ears with cotton from the burst bolls around her, she discovered the Fort of Hope and its companion, the Viny Well. In the dead of winter, on the first rainless night in a month, lying bundled in two Hudson's Bay blankets, she discovered the fraternal twins, Jake and Ralph, and the Simple Sons. The air was so clear that night that the shooting stars, which fell in all seasons, streaked long yellow lines across the sky.

"I am not a hermit," she wrote in her notebook, and she was not, certainly not that. She often had visitors, Jack and Mattie, Haven occasionally, Rooley once in a while—though since he had become a Pentecostal, every phrase he uttered was sprinkled with the sugar of the Lord—Delight often. She bought a television set and she and Delight watched animal programs together. They liked the programs about wild African animals and Delight, as drunk as she was, did not mind when she pretended to have walked the very ground the programs were filmed on. Once again, her husband's own obsession had given her freedom: his tortuous reasoning that brought him to a point at which he forced himself to swear off his nightly visits to her cabin gave her the freedom to allow Delight and Haven to share her bed. Rooley was now monogamous; Alsace wanted a child—at thirty-seven—and he got her pregnant; the past was past as far as he was concerned and he would not even speak of the days when they lay on the attic floor watching the sunlight creep across the multicolored boards, whispering to each other like children.

But Delight had no such scruples. In his rusted pickup he crossed the fields to her cabin. They lay on the living-room rug drinking wine and watching lions chase down antelopes. Delight's bald head seemed more rough-hewn than ever, the bones harsher under the rufous skin. The drunkard panic was on him now, except when he was drinking; it pulled his eyes into slits and made him afraid of noises, woke him up at night clawed by fear, but with the wine in him he was fine. One night as they lay in the johnboat he said, "I wonder about the wind."

She had never wondered but now she did. She loved his remarking on breeze. "You're simpler than I am," she told him and hugged him. She began to wonder about the wind and about the river current, about photosynthesis and the distance starlight traveled before reaching the earth. Where, she wondered, do the rice weevils come from and the potato bugs? There had never been rice in this spot and if anyone had planted potatoes—as she did now every year—it had been generations since they had done so. But there were weevils in the sack of rice in the cupboard and the coppery backs of potato bugs gleamed among the wide leaves of her plants. And what was it on earth that kicked up a wind? Haven said the wind was caused by the sun which heated the air and made it move about, but she was not convinced. Better, she thought, the legends she had heard in Hawaii, that personified all natural forces, at least gave them a god's hand to get them moving.

"Do you think animals think?" Delight asked one night, and they began to scrutinize more closely the beasts that ran across the television screen. The lions, lolling in the shade of acacia bushes, seemed to be ruminating over something. Elephants, the narrators said, were emotional, and even vultures with their sinuous necks and their black penetrating eyes seemed to have opinions, especially about jackals and other scavengers. She had, years ago, looked into the eyes of a raccoon and seen intelligence there. If the intelligence was not human, that did not disturb her, she thought these days that her own intelligence might be something other than human.

When she visited Alsace she stroked her swollen belly and wondered aloud what might be growing under that roundness. "What do you expect it will be?" she asked and Alsace looked at her with alarm.

It had become easier for her mind to skitter away from the established order of things. "I will create my own Linnaean system," she told Delight and giggled at the grandiosity of her desire. Just as she had ordered the stars, so, she thought, she would order the vegetable and animal kingdoms. If she never got very far with this project, if, as she sat by the window watching the yeoman robins and mockingbirds and the vicious, bitter jays, she found herself more often than not content to let them remain on whatever branch of phylic listing they already occupied, she was not unduly disturbed. She had to communicate with others, she figured, and calling a chicken by the same name everybody else called it was not too much of an imposition. But with Delight, the new orders would sometimes overtake them. They did, after all, occasionally at least come up with new names.

Delight always smelled of the zoo, a smell that was so foreign to any odor she was familiar with that the scent of him was liable to send her into a wandering reverie. Deep in the fur of bears and raccoons was a mystery she could not understand. He raised his fingers to her nose and let her smell the wildness. "How do I smell to you?" she wanted to know, and he would blink and try to describe her odor. She let him lick her skin for the taste of her and she licked his, tasting the grease of bears and the dusty, rooty smell of squirrels. Once he arrived stinking of skunk and she welcomed him into the house to have the odor living indoors with her. Later she had to wash the rugs with tomato juice to get the smell out, but that evening they had sat with the lights off in the living room breathing the pungency of the skunk.

"Your body is *full* of animals," he told her, sententious with drink. That was fine poetry, she thought, and probably true.

In the late afternoon she liked to climb down the bank and sit with her feet in the river. The water near the bank was fretted with roots, obstacled with bony cypress knees. The river was so stained with tannic acid that even close to shore, only inches deep above the white sand bed, it was still dark, only in the shallows next to the bank transparent, ticked and run with bream fry.

Crouched in the bank's declivity, smelling sassafras, her riding boots discarded on the bank behind her, her feet in the stained water, she watched for the rise of fishes, for deer easing out of the dense swamp across the river to drink. She discovered that she could sit silently for hours at a time. This was a wonderful discovery to her, a woman who had lived as if random sparks blew across her always. "Never confuse movement with action," she had told Delight, and though she knew that she herself had often done so, her silent vigil at the river's edge seemed now a kind of action to her, internal, observant. A woodchuck waddled out of the myrtles and cruised the far shore. A nutria, black as coal, poked its head out of the water, swiveled to look at her, dived back. She watched, in the early morning and evening, squirrels high in the fork of a hickory scratching fleas.

What kind of time, she thought, would apply to a woods world like this? Beyond the woods behind her cabin the cotton grew, trained to her husband's merchandising rhythms. For months—years?—the rows of cotton represented, for her, the only human ordering she saw. She did not count her stargazing, her new phyla, the mechanism of her house, the television tuned to *Life in the Wild.* She did not count the long nights with Delight, drunk and firing a pistol at the stars. I am beyond reason, she thought, I have passed into the mystic realm though I probably will not be drawn up to windy heaven like Enoch or Moses. She thought, I am forty-two and I have escaped both responsibility and the electric chair. I have found the break in the trees that leads into another country.

She was thinking this last night as she and Delight crossed the field to the pond. They liked to sit under the sycamores and look at the moon on the water and drink their wine. On fine nights Jack's music drifted across from the tower. As they walked along, she wrapped in her Hudson's Bay blanket, Delight swaggering in his ankle-length black wool overcoat—his anarchist's coat, he called it—she was thinking that she would like to begin a series of letters to the friends of her youth. Letters of the moment, she called them to herself; she had in mind writing detailed descriptions of the scenery around her cabin—extensions maybe of the lists and nature diaries she had kept for years. "I would like to tell Lacey Pinkney," she said as if they had been speaking about the project, "exactly what a pile of worn cedar boards looks like. I want to describe a corn snake to her. She's probably never looked closely at a snake."

"No snakes now," Delight said. "Too cold."

"I don't mean to pretend there are snakes out in the wintertime," she said, "though it would be interesting to describe what they do in cold weather."

"Curl up in a big ball," Delight said. "A bunch of them twine themselves together like string. B and I dug up a nest of garter snakes once when we were putting in a ditch. The ball was a foot in diameter, made entirely of garter snake bodies."

"I would have loved to have seen it."

"It scared me to death. I ran halfway back to the house. I thought maybe they were like coachwhips, would start rolling after me."

"Coachwhips don't really do that, do they?"

"I don't know. The only one I ever saw just shimmied off like any other snake." Delight pressed two fingers against the side of his nose and blew his nostril clear. "I've heard though," he said, "that if they won't bite their tails and roll after you, they'll stand up and come on—whoo, I hate damn snakes, hate 'em. Bernard and I used to argue about them. He thought they'd be a fine attraction at the zoo, and he was right, they are. I can catch a snake as well as I can catch anything else, but I don't like it. I did it, because he wanted it, until I ran over the phantom rattler."

"The phantom rattler?" He had told her the story before, but she liked to hear it.

"Yeah. I was coming down a sand road when I saw a big diamond-back—it must have been seven feet long—stretched across the ruts. I didn't want to stop for him and I didn't want to think about him being in the woods, so I hit the brakes and skidded right over him. I stopped and looked back to see what I'd done, but he was gone. I couldn't believe it. He should have been a mess of skin and meat. I backed up and got out to look for him, but there was no sign, not even track. Then I thought he must have coiled up around the axle. I got down on my hands and knees to look. He wasn't there. He wasn't in the floorboards either, hadn't crawled in. He was a vanished snake. I felt like my heart was going to break out of my chest. I got back in the truck and drove home as fast as that pickup would go. I've never touched another snake since, at least not to catch it wild. If Bernard wants snakes he can catch them himself."

She laughed and took his hand, which was rough and creased in the palm.

They came to the ridge and sat down under the trees. Branches creaked over their heads. Around them the long grass—yellow in daylight—bent over as if a huge weight had just been lifted off it. Delight put his arm around her and they looked down the long shallow slope at the pond, which was black and faintly stippled by breeze. Winter was the time of whooping, dust-blowing winds—between the rains—but the breeze that blew over them was gentle, if cold. She pressed herself against Delight, enjoying his bulk. He passed his hand over his face and shook it as if wiping something off; he took a long swallow of wine.

"We're going to lose all this," he said, solemnly.

She raised her head and looked at the stars that she had named and ordered—for her own protection, she thought. "What do you mean?"

"J.C. is overextended and the price of fertilizer has fallen. I don't think he'll be able to hold on."

"Fallen?"

"The oil companies have come into the business. They've bought up so much material that the price has dropped; companies like ours are getting squeezed out. It's an old story."

"So we'll lose the plants?"

"So we'll lose everything. The farm mortgages are what gave J.C. the money to get the plants."

She couldn't believe what she was hearing. "This land?"

"If J.C. doesn't get out right this minute. He can probably still sell to one of the oil companies, but he has to do it quick. In six months nobody'll want it."

They had been drinking wine since early afternoon. She had paced herself, she thought, as she always did, pursuing the queenly euphoria that drink brought while at the same time resisting, fighting the small skirmishes that marked her retreat. She clung now to what clarity she had—could he be speaking the truth?—as another part of her—defiant, spiteful—relished what she was hearing. She looked up into the sycamore above her head; only the branches were peeled; they shone whitely above her. She was about to speak, but as she stared at the bony limbs of the tree she remembered, for the thousandth time, the night on the Ashley when she had driven the car into the river. There was white in the trees that night, different trees than these, oaks instead, but among the branches for an instant she had seen a white shape floating, larger than a bird, not human but living. She was too drunk, she told herself, too drunk to figure this hard news out, but what were those branches, slowly treading wind above her head? They were too white, weren't they too white, weren't they glowing? She squeezed her eyes shut but behind the lids she still saw the interlocking, rachitic shapes of the branches, the memory of white as she soared over the river to fall. That white shape that floated like a ghost at the edge of her eye had been there always, some way or another, window, being—she had no idea—angel, hope or heaven itself, untouchable, like the jacket of a small boy who ran down the street crying. She would never know, she would never catch it, life wasn't long enough, she could not get free enough.

"I have to go," she said and stood up.

Delight fumbled with the bottle and got clumsily to his feet.

"I have things to do," she said and started off between the trees.

He came along behind her, stumbling as they reached the cotton rows, stopping to untangle his feet from the leftover stalks. "Have I said

352

something I shouldn't?" he called as she strode ahead. "All that stuff is true; it's just awful."

"It's not awful," she called back. "It's just . . . unusual." She laughed and continued across the field, putting distance between herself and human sounds.

She lay on the glider through the afternoon and into the evening. When it got dark she rose, made a supper of biscuits and honey, fixed a cup of tea, came back out and lay down again. She picked up a notebook and read through her list of Georgia flowers. She had managed to live her whole life in places where every season made a flower. Here, in this zone perched like a cap on the tropics, it was very close: camellias in winter barely made up the slack between the last zinnias and geraniums and black-eyed Susans and the first crocuses and forsythia. She thought, I could have made these notebooks a parade ground for genius, copied the bright sayings of Einstein and Goethe and Anaxagoras, but instead I have written down the words painted on the sides of boxcars. Her book was nearly complete; on butcher-paper scrolls and in notebooks she had written down what she knew of herself and the life around her. She had read that on the day they finally reached the Oregon coast, Lewis and Clark had been so exhausted that they had gone straight to bed instead of going out to look at the ocean. Her tiredness was like that, but she would still get up and walk out into the waves. One more time at least, she thought.

It was after midnight when she saddled her horse and rode across the fields to the main house. Canaan, Canaan, she sang, you bonny bloody ground. She let herself in the back door with the key she still had and climbed the stairs to her husband's bedroom. The door was open; from within the room she could hear the soft sibilance of his snoring. She thought, That was new, snoring. She dropped to her knees and crawled across the carpet to the side of the bed. He lay on his back, two pillows crushed around his head. Beyond him another form lay: a woman sleeping on her side facing the wall. The woman's head was a mass of curls; the curls looked like worked metal in the window light. She stood up and leaned over them. With her fingers she stopped lightly, for a second, her husband's mouth. He stirred and turned on his side without waking. From her pocket she took the small silver gun her father had given her years ago. It was a miniature carved replica of the gun that had killed

353

Billy the Kid. She placed it in the depression her husband's head had vacated. Then she walked out of the room and out of the house, mounted her mare and rode back across the fields to her cabin.

There are a few mornings that are like no others, mornings in which the dogwood blooming outside the bedroom window is more full of light than any tree could be, mornings in which the uncut grass in the front yard is a green that has never been seen before on earth, mornings in which the voice calling from the pine woods is a voice of such sweetness that when you hear it you feel your heart might break.

It is such a morning, she thought, come up fair at last, washed clean by rain, and more than rain.

She loaded the johnboat with books and notebooks, with clothes and provisions, with the scrolled sheets of butcher paper from the bedroom wall, shipped paddles and lantern and poled away from the ferny bank in front of her cabin. I am so surprised, she thought, that I have been able to live my life this way, walk out the door and go adventuring. The sky, with the sun sunk deep into the blue, made her grateful. She poled into the deep, momentarily paled water where the Course met the river, then let the boat drift. By the time she reached the end of the wide reach called Billy's Lake, where the river cinched itself to crawl through Lazarus toward the deep water south of Canaan, she felt as if she had been alone for days.

J.C. shouted himself awake out of a dream in which he had stood naked in front of his mother sporting a chest full of glossy black hair. He was not in fact a hairless man; the brindle mat of curls that had appeared in his late teens had always been part of his pride; he was even pleased when the hair began, shortly after his fortieth birthday, to turn gray, though the gray seemed, so far at least, selective, settling in a patch over his left pectoral muscle—but in the dream he had been a boy, thirteen or fourteen, old enough to feel shocked embarrassment at being viewed naked by his mother, and the black hair, unlike the hirsuteness of any Burdette he had ever seen, was as thick as animal fur. His mother, seated in a brocade chair on the front porch, had laughed at him with all the force of her well-bred condescension, her gray eyes alive with appreciation of his ludicrous position.

He looked at the sleeping woman beside him, Jane, his secretary.

Her long, persimmon hair covered her face; she slept with her hands drawn up under her chin like a child. His shout had evidently not been loud enough to wake her. As a child he had waked himself up shouting only to find that what in a dream had been loud screams were, back in waked life, only squeaks and whispery cries. He rolled over onto his back, felt something hard under his head, reached for it and found the tiny silver gun Elizabeth had laid there. He knew its significance—nothing nice—immediately, but his mind struggled self-protectively to find an undisruptive place for it. What is this? he almost said aloud, turning the gun between his fingers. It was, he knew, a Colt .45, three inches long, carved from a block of Colorado silver: one of Elizabeth's treasures, one of the trinkets she kept in her velvet box that had once rested on the dresser across the room. She told him that it was a replica of the gun Pat Garrett used to shoot Billy the Kid. The actual gun, he had informed her, was hanging on the wall of a haberdashery shop in Atlanta. She had believed him, the corners of her mouth had turned down, she had grabbed her tiny silver gun away from him. Now in my hand, on my pillow. Ah, Elizabeth. Certainly she could not be upset that he slept now with this hennaed girl. His last secretary. Not now anyway; this wasn't the time for more domestic strife.

He got up and padded barefoot to the bathroom. There he showered and shaved, filling the room with steam. As he shaved he thought of Elizabeth. Maybe he was glad she had done this, had found him out. Now they would talk. Anything to get his mind off the other. The other danger. This empire that was breaking up and whirling down the drain. Oh God, oh God, why have you let this happen to me? I have been as good a man as I could, I have gone forth into your world and mastered it, I have taken my dominance over the lesser creatures—why do you hide from me now? This morning he and Bryce would meet with the bankers. They would beg for an extension of the mortgage deadline. If the bank carried them another quarter things might change. But things would not change, J.C. knew. The oil companies were in it now. Even if the big corporations decided that agricultural chemicals were not going to pay handsomely enough, their decision would take years. They had already bought up potash mines in Florida and Louisiana; they had their own sulfur wells in Texas; a divestiture now would take years, years. By the time it came about he would have been under long ago. They had driven the prices down; they were large enough to control production to

355

an extent that would still make it profitable for them, or if not profitable their assets would be covered by their holdings in other areas. He had only this land, this stretch of soil that was stapled together with mortgages, about to be torn along dotted lines. Why, oh why?

There were long vertical lines in each cheek, marks of age and worry that had never appeared in his father's face. As he stretched the skin with his fingers to shave he thought that possibly his mother would have looked like this had she lived. The lines, the chin which seemed always about to crumple, the lines at the edges of the eyes like marks creased in by a fingernail, these must be the features of her own age. He was looking into a ghost face then, the face of a woman who had been dead thirty years. So he carried her forth across the earth. In the dream she had laughed at him with an impenetrable disdain. As she laughed the skin on her face had swelled and split until he was looking at teeth and skull, the sopping flesh over her bones.

He turned abruptly away, went to the window and cleared mist to look out. Spring was coming, the dogwoods by the back fence were struggling into bloom. This winter there had been ice in the spring, thin sheets of it, a few inches stretching from the curbing. Why has this happened? Maybe it would be possible to stall the bankers another quarter. If they let him keep the land they would have a chance of getting their money back. He felt a tingling rise up his spine. Elizabeth, you bitch! Why assault me now? And then he thought maybe she could help him. She had an answer for everything. If she had been interested enough to sneak into his bedroom she must still be interested enough to speak to him. She would tell him something. Maybe he could suddenly come to believe that her way of life made sense.

When he returned naked into his bedroom to dress, the freckled woman who sat against the headboard combing the ends of her hair with her fingers was a stranger to him, or, if not a stranger, her force of being was so weak, it seemed to him, that he could hardly see her, couldn't bring her into focus. Her endearments dissipated in the air between them, didn't reach him.

He drove in his ten-year-old farm car, an unwashed blue Chevrolet, along the sand track that skirted the swamp woods. The road had never been improved; he, out of resentment, wouldn't have had it done, she didn't care. He followed the grassy tracks under the planted pines and

356

drove a mile through them before he saw the house, nestled among its ferns and pines on rising ground next to the river. This was Rooley's spot, he remembered, almost anyway; somewhere on the other side of the cabin among the oak scrub were the tabby foundations of his house. He pulled up in front of the cabin and got out. The front door was open. He called her name—a protection of sorts—but the silence told him she was not there. He walked through the rooms touching the furniture, saying her name under his breath. She had stripped the bed. The blue-striped mattress seemed to contain a loneliness that made him turn away at first. He rubbed the coolness out of his arms and after checking the kitchen, the spare room that was filled with locked trunks and a few old rockers she had taken from the storage shed at the main house, he returned to the bedroom. Except for the denuded bed the room did not seem emptied. Maybe she has gone to the laundry, he thought, though her car, a navy-blue Jaguar this year, was parked outside. He checked her closet, which was bulging with clothes. He was about to close the closet door when his eye caught on the brass buttons of his Navy tunic. What was this doing here? He took it from its hanger and tried it on; it still fit; his daily exercises had kept his form as slender as in the old days. He buttoned the blouse up to the throat and looked at himself in the oval mirror over the dresser. On the table beside her bed was the photograph taken of him on the bridge of his ship. It had been an arranged shot—no one ever wore a dress tunic on watch—but he had never told her that. He cupped his hands in front of his chest, holding absent binoculars just as the man in the photograph did. His cap was missing; maybe she had that, too. He found it wrapped in tissue paper on the shelf. The headband, still, seventeen years later, carried the faint scent and stain of his body.

He placed the hat on his head, pulled the bill low in the way he had liked to wear it when he stepped off the ship into port. Looking at himself in the mirror, for a moment he could feel the old days, the war, the smell of grease and diesel fuel, hear the great heartthrob of the engines, the pounding of the three inch 50s. His ears still rang from the guns. His nose looked polished; his face had gotten older, there were lines in his neck now, a coarseness of skin. He had depended all these years on the fact that he had once fascinated her. This incredible creature who sleeps next to me. She had broken his heart so long ago. Broken it as absently as her foot might snap a twig during her morning walks. She had not even noticed, had never owned up to a thing. He sailed the hat at the wall. It hit the lamp, knocking it in a crash of breaking bulbs to the floor. He went over and picked it up. It was a lamp that had belonged to Jacey as a child—a boy in blue overalls holding a paintbrush. He set the lamp back in place, got a broom and dustpan from the kitchen and swept up the pieces. When he finished and emptied the dustpan in the kitchen, he came back and lay down on the bed. There were paint marks on the wall. Everybody in this family is a goddamn artist, he thought. It must have been a big painting, because the marks, green and red, were around the edges of the wall. He had stopped spying on her two years ago, so he wouldn't know. He held the caseless pillow over his face and imagined smothering to death. If he got drunk enough someone could do it in his sleep, he guessed, but he was not a drinker, always a light sleeper. Except after a night of lovemaking; such as last night, he thought, when I didn't hear her come into the room. Was she trying to tell him she could have shot him? That the jig was up, flee for your life? No, not that. She wasn't the kind of woman to get derailed over her husband's escapades, such as they were. Elizabeth would be last on any list of jealous women. And then the thought came to him that she was gone, and he knew as surely as he lay there that she was gone for good. He sat up in the bed. My God, my God, why now? He ran out of the house to the riverbank. The johnboat was gone. He had never gotten over seasickness. Not for a minute in three Pacific years. Hawaii, Ulithi, Eniwetok, Peleliu, the Solomons—he had dragged his nausea with him everywhere. Oh, Elizabeth, it could have been so fine.

He climbed down the bank and waded out into the water. Across the river something swirled on the surface, snake, or turtle going under. The river, curving around a bend under maples, disappeared into trembling patches of sunlight. He unbuttoned the tunic and threw it downstream. It fell open onto the surface, arms out, floating in the current. For an instant he thought that it might not go under. He didn't want to see it sink. He scrambled back up the bank, got in his car and drove away through the pines.

Under the fence and out, she thought, looking up from the bottom of the johnboat at the sagging strip of chicken wire suspended over the river. In the middle of the fence a rusted sign hung. It said FLORIDA STATE LINE in teary black letters. It was late afternoon, fifteen miles maybe behind her. The sun lay down in the trees, throwing up a barrage of orange and yellow light. The river was dark, except for where here and there the sun cut through a break in the pines. She had gone far enough for terrain to change, though here, in this passing spot, it had for a moment changed back. Toward the line, the land swooped down into rocky swamp, small headlands of limestone, or pushed up among grasses, banks shelving suddenly down into willow sloughs. But for the last mile or so, the ground had become sturdy again and the pines, yellow and longleaf pines, had come back.

She knew all this, had years ago logged the features of this country into her notebooks. She had no need to check the books now, nothing at this moment she needed to add to her lists. I'm done, she thought, and the thought for a moment pleased her. Ahead, beyond the redoubt of Haven's plantation, was the wild woods, the Florida jungle full of bears and panthers that stretched twenty miles to the Gulf. Only in the last stretches would the jungle give out, fading among cabbage palms and wax myrtle scrub into the quivering fields of grasses that were the land's final negotiation with the salt sea. Beyond them, beyond, too, the last heaved afterthought of earth upon which the town of St. Luke's clung like a dirt dauber's nest, the Gulf leaned in to collect the river. It would collect her, too, she thought, downstream traveler, like a Burdette in reverse.

On the bank nearest her a robin swung in the branches of a bush she didn't know the name of. In Georgia, the robin was a winter bird, its sudden absence in late March was the first animal sign of coming spring. This bird was late—it was the end of March—it had hung around still. As she watched it, riding the wind that slowly swung the branch, she thought that she now had no need to put anything into its place. Robin which is a harbinger of winter, flying in with frost on your wings. As a child Jacey had chased robins in the backyard trying to spear them with the sword his great-uncle had dragged back from the Civil War. He had never been able to kill one, but morning after morning he had tried, stalking them between the camellia bushes, throwing the sword like a spear. The sword, she realized, had probably been a fake. The great-uncle had spent the years after Second Manassas in a prison camp in Maryland. Nobody would have given him back his sword. He'd probably bought it from a shop or from a widow, something.

She laughed out loud. The sound rang across the water, startling the bird. It fluttered out of the bush and settled on the low-hanging limb of a pine. "You're no fake, Mr. Robin," she said, waving her arm at the bird. The boat turned slowly in the current; she was traveling feet first into Florida. Water to water, she thought, and wished she had a drink. She dragged her hand in the water to feel its coolness. Summer would come again, around the next bend or the one after. The smell of honeysuckle and tea olive would fill the air. She decided she would not stop at Haven's as she had planned.

The banker was a short portly man in a charcoal suit. His dun hair grew back in a single receding curve from his high, unmarked forehead. He was waiting for J.C. and Bryce in the boardroom of the Yellow Springs Bank, a corresponding institution to the Farmers and Mechanics Trust in Atlanta. As J.C. led them into the room the man stood up and came partway around the mahogany table. He kneaded his hands lightly before shaking hands first with J.C., then with Bryce. They sat down, the banker at the head of the table, J.C. and Bryce a few chairs down, leaving space between them. From a satchel the size of a small suitcase, Bryce took several folders. The banker, a Mr. Waverly, had a single folder in front of him; it was lined up along the edge of the blotter just beyond the axis of a blue enamel water pitcher. When Bryce had the folders out, and had opened them to the pages full of figures, J.C. said, "I think we still have a few ideas about how to solve this situation."

The banker pursed his lips and scrutinized the space between J.C. and Bryce. "I'm afraid," he said, "that from here on out, the ideas will have to come from us."

On the wall opposite was a portrait of the bank's founder, Will Severn, a narrow-faced man in a high collar. J.C. remembered that his grandfather had once threatened Severn with a horse whipping for not tipping his hat to his wife. The banker patted the extended fingers of his left hand. "Your time has run out," he said and uncurled a smile that seemed to J.C. so full of incongruent reassurance that he wanted to cry.

That night her life became magical. She drifted past Haven's in the stillness just before dark. The world seemed as she peered over the gunwale to have hushed itself in anticipation of great doings. The hedgelines of ligustrum and azalea that ranged out from the gazebo seemed to Elizabeth to have the particularity and import of lines on maps. The Chinese elm at the end of the porch below Haven's bedroom window shook sud-

360

denly with a breeze that did not touch any other trees. The house was lit up, almost early it seemed to her because there was still light in the sky, swirls of orange, ambiguous as blown smoke in the west, but no one was about. She thought she could hear the quail chirping in their pens but she was not sure. A dog barked and fell silent; no one noticed her passing.

Beyond the last bend of tenanted land, where a rail fence stretched its awkward anglings across a field grown up in dog fennel and blackjack oak, both as yet unleaved, the light seemed to gather and swell in the sky. She thought, This must be a phenomenon accompanying fatigue. She was tired, not from the day's activities, which had included nothing more than the regular unfastening herself from whatever tangle of branches or sandbar her boat drifted into, but from the night, and nights that had gone before, from her whole life. It's worn me down, she said to herself as she leaned back on a sofa cushion in the stern and peeled an orange for supper. Then the sky blazed up, the way light will suddenly strike us when we become conscious of our blinking. She did not know whether she was seeing things, but the greenery, the massive drooping oaks, the slender, barely leafed poplars seemed to soften, caressed by a light that held something, color and the promise of shapeliness, back. Two white gulls flew up the river following the course. They seemed birds of good tidings, greeters from the wide world of oceans and solitary skies, and in her heart she welcomed them as sisters. The riverbanks were sandy and as the night fell they seemed to glow as if brushed with foxfire. A single star blossomed in the south. She fell into a sleep in which dreams swam up like pale, heavy fishes. She stood on the North Shore road in Oahu shouting *Campesano* at a convoy of passing trucks. She crossed a vast room carrying a folded newspaper to a country inn where three men sat around a table in fur coats looking out a frosted window at the snow. Someone needed to get up and go out—someone wanted to get up and go out—but no one did. Her coat turned to feathers, to wings. She saw the wall of a ship side rear above her and felt the surge of the bow wave. The sawmill clatter of planes warming up at Hickam Field. Her father said, "You are too young for that, much too young." J.C., naked and painted like an Indian, ate a grapefruit at the kitchen table. Pale blue lightning flashes streaked his cheeks. Her son spoke to her in the lovely, muddled voice of a deaf child. Dogs barked.

She woke—she seemed to come awake—to the sound of her parents' voices. Across the moonlit water she saw them sitting at a glass table conversing quietly under budding poplars. Her father leaned across the table to feed her mother a peach. She ate it from his hand like a pet. "That's wonderful," he said. "That's just right. You are doing fine, my dear." Her mother smiled—Elizabeth could see this—in the liquid way of a woman eaten by lust. Her face was smeared with juice. Elizabeth stood up and called to them, whacking the water with her paddle to catch their attention. They turned and looked at her without surprise. "Mother, Father," she cried, "I love you." Her parents smiled and waved as they would at children diving for coins. From his vest pocket her father took a flower and tossed it to her. It fell in the water between them, floated there shining with a light that was unearthly. "We're in Italy," her father said loudly. "We've been touring the ruins. You would be amazed at how the stones still cling to one another. Your mother has caught cold, but I'm sure it's nothing serious." Above their heads, above the new crumpled leaves of the tulip poplars whose flowers she knew tasted sweet as honey, stars fell, the tiniest of lights, stretching their yellow threads across the sky. Seeing them she thought she was going to have it all tonight: stars, the moon, the fragrance of new leaves, her parents in conversation, the decipherable news of dreams, but when she looked back they were gone; the sandy bank, darkly speckled with last year's drifted leaves, was empty.

She would have poled over to look for some sign of them, but a languor overtook her and she lay back against the cushions and looked up into the sky. Geese flew in a broken V high up in the heavens, heading north. Their frayed cries seemed the cries of old men. I take my apostate course here, she thought, everybody heads north except me. We will spend the summer with the locals, the bats and bluejays who have no villas on the wind. How fine it was to be abroad again. Out in the wide world, putting miles behind her. She stretched and brought her arm to her mouth and licked her skin. It tasted faintly of copper, faintly of salt, faintly of a bitter perfume. The air was full of sound: voices, cries, the trailing notes of familiar songs. Far up ahead a beaver whacked the water with his tail. The sound rushed by her ricocheting off the wall of trees behind her. And then, as she knew it would, some weight of being seemed to rise out of her and soar off above the pines. Good, good, she thought, I am coming awake. I am coming awake, she thought, as sleep overtook her, a real sleep this time, dreamless and inviolable.

• • •

When he got home the next afternoon there was a telegram for Elizabeth on the hall table. He read it leaning against the door. It said: "Father dying. You are welcome here." The afternoon light shining through the glass muntins in the side windows made narrow rainbows on the rug. When he was eight he had pried one of the muntins loose and taken it out into the yard to try to catch the colored light. His father had given him a whipping. "You'll have to bury the old guy without her," he said aloud, crumpled the telegram and thrust it in his pants pocket. He climbed the stairs with a feeling of physical tenderness all over his body, of almost weightlessness in his legs, went into his room and lay down on the bed.

He lay at a still center while the world roared overhead. Once on the flying bridge of his ship he had seen a Jap Zero zoom so close he could smell the cordite of its guns. The speed of the plane had interrupted the sense of movement he felt on the rolling ship. Now he felt the same sensation, as if this time, the planet itself were roaring by. For a second he was overtaken by vertigo and he sat up ready to run to the bathroom to vomit out his nausea. Then the feeling passed, the world slowed down and he lay back on the bed. Outside he could hear Burleigh calling to his dogs. The dogs left artfully concealed piles of shit all over his yard. He felt a stab of resentment and for a second wanted to bound up and scream threats down at his nephew. The maid had changed the bedclothes but he could still smell his secretary's perfume. It was a perfume he had never known the name of but which he had first smelled when he was a teenager. It had a cloying candy sweetness and made him think of hayrides and the wrenching awkwardness of adolescence. He hated it.

And not only that, he thought, anger suddenly bright like a light switched on, not only that: everything. He sat up and took off his shoes. They were good English shoes, the color you'd get if you could mix a deer's hide with blood, and he loved them. They had stiff rubber soles and they fit like gloves. He had bought his first pair of English shoes on a trip to New York just after the war. They were for him a sign of success, of his important place in the world. He thought how strange it was that someone like himself—a Burdette, lion of Georgia—should need these small proofs of his importance. He had known for years that there was a hypocrisy threaded into his life, a hypocrisy that was expressed by his habit of driving unwashed and out-of-date cars while at the same time purchasing English shoes from New York. It was best exemplified in his

363

attachment to Elizabeth. He knew this, had thought of it often. She was his beautiful jewel, this woman whom no other man had been able to hold. But he didn't hold her either, hadn't really come close. Where in God's wild world was she? He took the telegram out of his pocket, smoothed it out and read it again. It was signed "David." Her older brother, the heir of her father's banking domain. He had met David once, during the years of Elizabeth's Hawaii life. They had had lunch together in the coffee shop of the Biltmore Hotel in Atlanta. They had not been able to break through the stiff formality that surrounded them. J.C. had felt the whole time that he was about to career off into great racking sobs. David, a thin man whose thinness was accentuated by his height and by the way he hunched his shoulders, had been vaguely sympathetic, but they had not spoken directly of the problem with Elizabeth; they had talked business. After a light lunch they parted with affirmations of their intentions to see each other more frequently in the future, but they had never met again. Their only contact had been over the telephone and at Christmas when their families exchanged gifts of haberdashery.

He thought that he had better call David, but when he picked up the phone he dialed his son's number in New York. He let the phone ring half a dozen times, hung up and dialed again. Martha answered on the second ring.

"I knew it was you," she said gaily. "You're the only one who calls twice."

He felt the same old dis-ease in talking to her, as if any minute she might say something that embarrassed him. "Have you heard from Mrs. Burdette?" he asked, feeling the rasp of formality in his throat.

"We hear from her all the time," Martha said. "Why?"

"She seems to have gone out of town and I just got a telegram from her family that her father is dying. Is Jacey there?"

"He's at work. Would you like me to call him?"

"I'll do that." He realized how much antipathy he felt toward this girl who always seemed to know exactly what she was doing. "What's the number?"

There was a brief silence and then she slowly gave him the connection, pausing after each number as if he were a child writing it down.

"Thank you," he said. "How are things up there? Still dancing?"

"A day at a time. You still building empires?"

"Bigger than ever." He squeezed the receiver, wanting suddenly to

364

clap it against the table. "If I miss Jacey would you ask him to call me?"

"Of course." There was another brief silence, then she said, "We love you, Father Jay."

He felt a knot of tension, that he had been unaware of, partially unwind. "Oh, thank you," he said quickly. "I love you, too. If I miss Jacey," he said again, "please tell him to call." He didn't want to break the connection.

"I have to go now," Martha said. "I was in the tub."

"Oh," he said coming back from a distance. "Yes. It's important. Tell Jacey."

Then he rang off and sat on the edge of the bed staring at the strip of chestnut-colored wood between the rug and the wall. He thought, I'm not going to have any money. Oh my God. He was not sentimental about this ground, unlike his father, who when J.C. was a child would as they crossed a field stoop and grab a handful of pebbly earth and stare at it as if it might contain rubies. He had not sung praises of land, land, land. Big deal, land. It was money, sovereign armor against the world's poison. And power, yes. And most of all just moving on. No stopping here, boss, this is an express train. The Dixie Special, bound for glory. He had ninety days to raise an interest payment of two point seven million dollars. They had to sell the land. And then Bryce said, We'll get jobs selling flowers on the Square like Daddy.

He couldn't think, couldn't think. I'm going to spend the rest of my life staring into strange places, unable to figure out how I got there. He thought, All right: One, I am sitting on a chenille spread. Two, I am wearing herringbone trousers. Three, my belt is a little too tight. It's a belt I bought at Brooks Brothers in Atlanta. Oh God, he thought, I am going to call Jane again. I can't live without arms around me.

He got up and rushed like a man running for a train onto the balcony. He caught himself on the rail and stared out at the spring where his mother had drowned. In the fading daylight, in the darkness under the cedars, the water looked green. He could imagine her floating face down in that cool water. He could imagine it and he did for a moment, before forcing his mind away. Perhaps the death of his mother was what he had wanted Elizabeth to exorcise. Once when he was fifteen, a year before she died, his mother had come to Parents' Day at the high school. It was the only time she did such a thing. J.C. showed her his classrooms, introduced her to his teachers and took her to lunch in the cafeteria, where they had fried ham, turnip greens and cornbread. His mother said she supposed the school served food like this because of all the country children. Afterward they walked down the hall to the auditorium in which the Drama Club was to present the first act of *As You Like It*. As they walked his mother took his hand and held it tightly. This was not, as far as he was concerned, a motherly thing to do, and at first it unnerved him. Then he liked it. They walked down the hall, his knuckles brushing against her cotton-covered flank, and he felt proud and happy, as if she were his fine beautiful girl who had come from miles away to see him.

Elizabeth woke to the faint knock, knock of the johnboat against the hull of a half-submerged houseboat. The houseboat lay stern down in the water near the bank. The bow was draped by the new gold leaves of a young willow. She pushed the johnboat against the bank, tied it with the painter and stepped onto the canted deck of the houseboat. The boat was rusted out, its pilothouse awry; it had been there several seasons, though she had never seen it before. She felt a rush of anticipation and dread, as if, like Ishmael, she might find a tattooed savage snoring inside. She made her way through scattered debris into the mainhouse, which she saw had been a place set up for partying. A bar leaned on its side against one wall, burst cushions lay on the floor, and the walls that had been painted with a scene of mountain serenity were ripped and scarred. A single gold curtain tassel hung from one of the portholes. A drawer full of blackened cutlery lay against one wall, and there were streaks of what looked like grease congealed on everything. In Washington after college looking for a place to live she had seen apartments like this and they had given her a chill that lingered for days. The fact that human beings lived in such squalor unnerved and frightened her. Her childhood had been rosy and privileged, even the floors of the galleries were waxed, and the sight of embedded and intractable filth gave her a feeling of impending doom, as if her bright world smelling of tea olive and fresh blackberry pie was a lie, about to be swept away.

She called out in a loud voice to the ghosts of whoever might have abandoned this scene. This place had been blasted not by poverty, but by something else, a storm, neglect, a broken mooring, but the picture in her mind was one of crouching, humiliated shapes moving about this room, lying down in the stinking refuse. She wanted to run, into the clean golden air of the morning where she could hear the cries of the early birds, but she forced herself to stay. She sat down on a warped wooden bench that ran along one wall. It is time I faced things, she thought. She ran her hands down her legs and squeezed her thighs, soothing herself with muscle tone. What if I had to make do with this? She had never had to make do with anything; she had always had the power to bring change to her world. She felt a moment of intense loneliness, as if her connection to everything she held dear had snapped. She understood that love was a choice you made, nothing more. Beyond the kick of blood, the rushing in the veins, it was only a choice: I will or I won't. She had said no because she would not be restrained. But this refusal of restraints was more than a choice, she knew that. She did not say with her mind I will not follow this broad-shouldered man who would like me to come with him to eat strawberries and vodka, she only shied away, as a butterfly would if you tried to touch it. So how could I change now, she thought, stretching her long legs into a welter of ruin. How can I change?

She got up and looked out a broken porthole. A school of mullet swam upstream, their silver backs just breaking the water. They swerved together toward the far bank, turned and raced away downstream, as if in panic. She had dreamed she was walking in a red dress through the pineapple fields near Wahiawa. In the distance, coming toward her like beaters in a pheasant hunt, was a line of men. They were in shirt sleeves and they carried long bamboo poles. They swept the air with the poles and gave cries that were like the shrieks of carnivorous birds. This was one of many dreams, in a night that had been fantastical. Why should I want to change, she thought, when I have a mind that works like mine does? She knew that the ropes that bound her to the world were fraying. She was at home with drunks and criminals, all those who could not accept the world as it was. This movement, no—action?—catalyzed by her husband's loss, was really only one more step along an old line. What could she do next? Let her boat drift out into the open sea? She would die, alone in the Gulf. God wouldn't transform her into a gull or a dove and draw her up into heaven. She couldn't swim away like a fish. She could return to St. Guillaume, but Marcel was married now and McCracken had retired from the charter trade.

She walked outside and stood on deck looking down at the brown current which tugged gently at the canted hull. Everything gets worn away, even you, Elizabeth. She could return to Hawaii and perhaps from

367

there travel to islands farther west. There were undiscovered outposts yet, perhaps. Perhaps Rufino, her old gardener, if he was still alive, would take her in. With fingers that seemed to have stiffened in the night, she touched her face, her breasts, pressed her palms flat hard against her thighs. "I am Elizabeth Bonnet Burdette," she said. "What I need I find in me." She whirled a step, nearly fell, caught herself, leaned out to see around the next woody bend. "And you can't have it," she cried. "None of you." The sun lay its tattered golden coat on the water.

J.C. woke into a room streaked with sunshine. Jane lay beside him, flung defenseless in sleep. For a moment, looking at her, he surged with happiness, but then his mind came back. As a child he had waked in a room in which the sun bounded off the walls. Here, in his parents' bedroom, the light entered more hesitantly, bringing shadows with it. He had not been able to reach Jacey. His son was too busy to come to the restaurant phone and later when he tried the apartment again Martha told him he had not come in. The fact that his son didn't want to talk to him made his stomach hurt—what had he done? The boy was the victim of vast mood swings. Sometimes when he called, Jacey chattered on like a small boy, telling of his adventures. He had a brightness, a sweet heart that drew J.C. in. They would both get so excited that J.C. would begin making plans to take the plane to New York. But then, in the middle of conversation, Jacey would fall silent and when he spoke again it was out of a merciless self-righteousness and an adamantine, undissolving anger. J.C. would feel himself close against him; their conversations would die away into senseless, bitter skirmishes that left him gasping.

But this time he hadn't been able to get through. Jane woke and kissed him. She always woke quickly, like a child, and she always woke full of ardor. Her green eyes were as clear as if she had only blinked instead of slept. She said, "I love to wake up beside you. It's like sleeping next to a warm engine. One of those good engines that runs something big and necessary. You make me feel like a girl again."

He stroked her thigh absently, thinking of his son. "You are a girl again. Still."

"To me I'm an aging woman. A spinster secretary."

He looked at her. Everyone comes to their sad conclusions, their little fumbled pieces of emotional handwork. "I should be feeling old," he said. "Everything's falling apart and I'm forty-seven years old." He *did*

368

feel old, if that was what the listlessness, the disinterest that had descended on him could be called.

When they were in Hawaii Elizabeth would often, just before coming to bed, go to the back door and call out into the darkness for nonexistent pets. "Here, Kitty," she would cry. "Here, Kitty Kitty Kitty." When he asked her why she did it she said she wanted to make sure there weren't any lost beings out there. "I just want to make sure every stray within hearing knows it can find a home with me," she said. Which is what he was, he thought, a stray. Circling in the dark, hoping for someone to come out and call him in.

He did not say this to the slender young woman beside him. She would not have understood, he thought, that a man who was the sole, if about to be displaced, proprietor of 25,000 acres of Georgia heartland could find himself as lost as a stray cat. But then maybe with things the way they were she could understand. Maybe scared and lost was the only way she saw him. He didn't know; he didn't know what she thought. And the knowledge scared him. He felt so alone he took her in his arms, squeezed her until she cried out in pain. "Don't break me," she said. He released her but it was only to move with a coarse dexterity to the parts of her body that were the emblems of lust: her small breasts, the sleek, coppery hair at her groin, the thin, wetted lips of her sex. He pulled her thighs roughly apart and mounted her, thrusting so deeply in that she cried out in pain. No cry deterred him, but as the first semen jerked from him the phone rang and though she held him, tried to wrench him back, he forced himself through the orgasm and grabbed the receiver, abandoning with a rush of despair the moment of release.

It had rung the fourth time; it was his son, who told him, No, he had not heard from Elizabeth lately and did not expect to. Why? J.C. asked him, Doesn't she contact you? His voice was coarse and breathless. It took all his strength to mask what was happening in the bed. "I think she's too far gone," his son said. "I think she has jumped ship."

"Thank you," J.C. said and hung up. He looked without seeing into the face of the young woman, which was full of pain and embarrassment. I will kill her, he thought, I will find her wherever she has gone, and kill her. The woman beneath him was sobbing.

21

She called her brother from the Charleston airport and he drove out in the gray weather to pick her up. Sometimes when we see our kin again after years apart the senses that respond are not the ordinary senses of sight, touch, etc. Other maybe more deeply embedded senses take over and we respond from other venues. So it was when she saw David in a rained-on gray suit striding lanky and feverish toward her; a room that she had kept closed inside herself opened up. It was not as if she saw the boy who used to scratch nervously at his long forearms or who tripped into the swimming pool when he tried to catch a friend running by. It was simply that an internal space opened up and swallowed him. He took her in his arms, but that meant nothing; she had been in his arms all along. She could feel through their clothes his hesitancy, the old fear of what she might do when he got close to her. She hugged him hard, reached up and brushed his lank sandy hair out of his eyes.

"We're so glad to see you," he said. "It's so much harder than we thought it would be."

She didn't know what he was talking about and instinctively didn't want to know because she *did* know as if it were a message she had memorized ages ago—she made him, for a second, into a complete stranger, someone who couldn't say anything that mattered to her. "What are you talking about?" she asked.

"Daddy's passing. Didn't you get the telegram?"

Help, murder, police. It was as if every cell in her body clenched. "You don't mean he's *dead*," she accused. You mean something else entirely. Idiot.

"Yes. He's not dead. He's dying."

"Of what?" Terminal silliness. Impacted pride.

"Old man's cancer. Hodgkin's disease." He washed his empty hands, looking at her with beggar eyes.

"I didn't get any telegram," she said. "I've just come off a river in Florida."

"I sent it to Yellow Springs. I wanted to let you know. He's slipping away from us."

A wave went over her this time and she felt her scalp tighten and

370

her hands go numb. "I've always wanted to visit the truly miserable," she said through lightly clenched teeth.

"You've come to the right place," he said, looking around for her bag.

In the car she said, "I came here to straighten out my bank affairs. I'm on my way to Hawaii again."

"I'm sorry." He looked at her with the same solid wondering sympathy, his lips a little open, that he had offered her all her life.

"There's nothing to be sorry about. It's never been the kind of situation anybody should be sorry about."

They drove in along the Battery. She rolled her window down, as she always did, rain or shine, when she came into a town. From the other side of the seawall, which seemed almost monstrous to her, she could hear the ocean slapping breastwork, heavy absentminded pats. In the park a salt wind lifted the leaves of the live oaks. The trees looked like women shaking their hair. The houses along the park were freshly painted, though the woodwork on the upper galleries was haggard and worn. On the corner of East Bay and South Battery someone had thrown out a rolled-up rug. Big snake half curled in the gutter, it had been gold, she thought, taken up from the stained parquet, rolled by servants, carried out and thrown down among the new spring leaves, still useful maybe—this was another world.

"I feel like a little old lady," she said as they turned between the stucco gateposts of the Lane of St. Louis.

"I feel scared as a boy," David said. "I've been scared ever since Daddy lay down. He wouldn't go back to the hospital. What he really wanted, he said, was to go to a hotel. In Columbia. He said he wanted to die among strangers."

They pulled into the ell made in the tabby wall for cars. David shut the car off but he made no move to get out. The big yellow house reared up past the tops of winded live oaks. David stared out the windshield at the yard where the mist on the grass looked like frost. "It's frightening to me," he said. "He's so angry. And he's always been such a mild man. Now he thrashes around. I think if he wasn't so weak he'd jump out of bed and strangle us all. Every time I come near him he makes a grab for me." He passed a hand over his face. "At least he was like that until last week. I'm forgetting: he's changed now. I think I saw something give up."

371

"He just caught on to you."

"I'm afraid for myself," David said as if he didn't hear. "I see myself in him. I keep seeing myself lying there all wasted and angry, everything come down to brittle bones."

"Why, David, you're a poet."

"I'm a middle-aged banker who's all of a sudden afraid of dying. I'm afraid really to go in his room. We've got him downstairs in the old guest room—I'm afraid to look at him. The skin on his face is drawn back; it's like he's melting. His head is bruised, I don't know from what. He used to dive into the pool and swim three miles without looking up. I used to sit in a chair and watch him; it made me feel so good to sit inside that swim."

"What?"

"It was like during the swim—it'd take him an hour—I was safe to think and feel anything I wanted to. Sometimes I wished I could jump on his back and have him carry me along." He stopped and pressed his hands flat on the windshield. He had the masculine version of her long, knuckly fingers. "I thought he could carry me anywhere, across the bay on his back, across the whole Atlantic even. Now he looks like a little drowned rat—agh, I don't mean to say that. Everything seems wasted."

She thought he must be talking about something he wasn't saying, but she said, "It's only wasted if you think something's dying out," and patted him on the cheek. His skin was prickly with colorless beard. The big gray and blue articulate houses had shouldered to the very edge of the lane, impervious as stone cliffs. Between them the gray air shone; she could smell the sump of the ocean. In the old days her mother had planted flowers along the lane, which in other cities would have been called an alley, though it was an alley fronted by mansions. It was paved with ballast stones that had been carried in the holds of sailing ships. "I have come out of the wild woods to be here," she said. "Out of the darkest kind of wilderness."

"Wherever," he said, "it's fine with me. I couldn't stand this without you."

She took his moist hand, bent across the seat and kissed it, nipped it in the fleshy part below the thumb. "Ow," he said and stroked her face.

"I want to see Papa," she said.

They crossed the yard arm in arm, climbed the front steps which were painted the dark evergreen of live oak leaves and entered the hall of the old house. The hall smelled of camphor and ageless dust and the faint, eroded scent she associated with her mother. David let her go and led the way to a narrow door at the far end, where he knocked carefully and entered. Her father lay in his carved bed against the far wall. A woman in a white nurse's uniform sat reading before a coal fire burning in the grate. The curtains were half pulled and the light that came through the sheers was gray and nearly luminous. She crossed the room and stood over her father thinking, This is how we step back into time. He lay on his side, curled up, facing the wall. She bent down and kissed him. His frailty made tears come into her eyes. He began a slow-motion thrashing, trying to turn, his thin arm pumping against his side. "Lizzie," he said, "Lizzie," and cried as she knelt on the bed and took him into her arms. He is so light, she thought, I could throw him if it came to that. She pressed him close, smothering his face against her throat, and through clothes she could feel their hearts beating, both hot and quick, beats banging against each other, as if, automatically, the way hands rise waving farewell, their bodies sought a connective rhythm, tried to get in step. She realized she could hold him as tightly as she wanted and he couldn't do anything about it. He nuzzled her throat and she smoothed his thin waxy hair. "You've come back to me," he said into her ear.

"Lover, lover," she said and kissed him on the lips which were white and cracked and tasted bitter, like quinine.

David stood apart, his arms folded over his shallow chest, a foolish look on his face. She wanted to pick her father up and hand him to him. She wanted to say, Look at this strange thing life has done. She wanted to carry her father out into the street, up the steps to their neighbors' houses, she wanted people to gape and wonder at this exotic creature fashioned and tooled for death.

She eased him back on the pillows. His lips thrust out in a perch mouth, working words.

"What?" she asked, bending close.

"Come home," he said. "Come home."

"You've got *that* on the brain, Papa. I'm here." She patted him.

Except for the bed which was the bed her parents had slept in there was nothing she recognized in the room. All the furniture was old, covered in velvet and brocade, a stiff plush sofa against one wall. Perhaps there was an era in her family she had missed. The nurse, a gray-haired woman with a poorly mended harelip, looked on meekly smiling. Elizabeth got up, went to the tall windows and drew back the curtains. Rain glistened on the screen roof of the swimming pool. A green, lichenous moss grew in patches on the roof. The water was dark green, cold-looking in the misting rain. She had grown up here in the closed society of this silly town. Her father had said, If you cannot accept how we live here you must go away, and she had gone away, a long then a short distance into the wide world. Perhaps she had always been circling back. Following the only dream that had ever moved her she had stepped away from the circle into the dark woods, found treasures there and dragged them back into the light. Whatever else was there in the world to do? I would like to tell you, she thought, addressing everyone, what I saw there in the alien world. I have seen a hawk tearing the eyes out of a cat. I have taken the head of a newborn child into my hands and shaped the skull into beauty. I have seen men beg for love. I have seen women suckle on their own breasts. There were many things I wouldn't do. I know exactly what is going to happen to everyone.

She turned back to the room.

"Where is Mary?" she asked, meaning David's wife.

"She's gone shopping." David shot a risky, retreating glance at their father, the way a skittish horse will eye the bridle. Elizabeth walked over and touched the old man's forehead. Her fingers caressed the pulse, which beat its staggering rhythm. It's what they call God, she thought, this thing that moves.

"J.C. called," David said.

"What did you tell him?"

"That you were on your way over here. Was that all right? He didn't know where you were."

"That was fine. I don't mind if he knows I'm here." Let him come, she wasn't going anywhere. "When did he say he would get here?"

"Tonight."

She took her father's hand. The skin was so soft she wanted to rub herself against it. He opened his eyes.

"From here on out," she said, "I'll be taking care of you. You can rest easy from now on."

"Joker," her father said and a wet smile soaked like solvent into his crusted mouth.

She swam on her back looking up through the torn screen into the leaves of the oldest live oak in the yard. Its branches were as big around as barrels. She thought of a party she had attended on Molokai with Kaui where they had served a ritual liquor made of kava roots that cut the legs from under anyone who drank it. She wondered now if she had put control at last behind her, if all the time her refusal to join the life of her husband was not just a way to maintain control. What a horrible position to be in, she thought, where I am trapped in a life I have to first get control of before I can let it go. It was like those rodeo cowboys who chased down calves that they tied up in ten seconds flat then let go. Tie it, then release it—go on. But that was the way it was. She swam, slowly moving her arms underwater, her legs joining in rhythm, two opening and closing Vs in the cold green water. It was the first stroke—except for a miserable dog paddle—she had ever learned. She did it these days when, swimming laps, she grew tired. These days, she thought, were not these days at all but actually the dear dead days when she had swum in the spring behind the main house at Canaan. Had she marked that place, that scarred property, as much as she needed to? The old fire tracks had been erased, the 150-year-old clapboards crowbarred out and replaced, the kitchen walls replastered and painted. She had wanted to live in a room the color of the tiny blue asters that bloomed in the road ditches in the fall. Her husband said no, no, no. She could only get along with men who were at odds with the world, some world. J.C., however, had only been at odds with her. She had gotten off the river at St. Luke's, the site of the first Spanish fort on the Panhandle, now a decayed mackerel and oyster town, hitched a ride to Tallahassee and caught a plane to Charleston. How easy it was to step back into the world, no matter how far you leapt out of it. Just turn the corner and there it was again, smelling of diesel fuel, washed with the lemonade light of streetlamps.

A car pulled into the parking ell and her sister-in-law Mary got out. She reached back in for two large sacks of groceries, negotiated the gate and started across the lawn. Elizabeth watched her—for a moment unnoticed—as she crossed the wet grass in her mannish, shoulders-forward way. Before the rehearsal dinner for David's wedding, as she and Mary dressed in her bedroom in the big pink house she had grown up in in Savannah, Mary, so frightened she gasped for air, had stripped and shown her body. "I'm as hairy as a grizzly," she said, "and I'm terrified David won't like me." Elizabeth was surprised her brother didn't already know, hadn't apparently reached under her fine clothes—it made him seem vulnerable to her, a little sad, poor brother—and Mary was certainly right: Elizabeth had never seen such a hirsute woman's body. The ginger hair roved across her belly to the wing bones of her hips. An inch-wide trail of it crawled to her navel. Her nipples were encircled with crowns of hair, and a faint clump of curls grew in the depression between her breasts. "I wanted to shave it off," Mary said, "but I was afraid it would grow back even thicker."

"You could dye it," Elizabeth suggested, restraining herself from touching the errant curls.

Elizabeth had thought no more about it but the next afternoon as they drank champagne at the reception in the living room of the old house, her brother red-faced and unable to stop laughing, Elizabeth saw that the hair on Mary's forearms, which she had not noticed before, was blond, so blond it was nearly colorless, and she wondered if Mary had taken her advice.

She thought of this now as Mary saw her, acknowledged her with a nod and continued across the lawn, up the back steps and into the house. In a moment she came out tightening her belted sweater around her waist and walked over to the pool.

"You're the only person in the world who would go swimming in weather like this," she said, standing a few foresquare feet back from the edge of the pool. It was from Mary that the reproaches would come, the reproaches for never paying any attention to her kin.

"It's warmer here than out there," Elizabeth said and splashed a little curl of water over the edge of the pool. Mary moved back frowning, seemed about to walk off, then changed her mind. "We don't really need your help with all of this, but David is happy that you're here," she said, pursing her lips, licking the top one with a pearl tongue.

Elizabeth dove, swam strongly the length of the pool underwater, turned against the algae-slimy wall and swam back, breaking the surface again at the same spot she'd left. "You're stoutening up nicely, Mary," she said. "It becomes you."

"Something does," she said.

Elizabeth didn't want to punch at her sister-in-law, felt, as she had since her first morning on the river, a calmness that seemed enduring, but still, she liked to play.

"Won't you come in," she said, cupping a handful of water. "You must need to relax."

Mary retightened her sweater and swept her hand over her flounced, tarnished hair. "We have too much to do to think about relaxation at the moment," she said.

376

"I suppose," Elizabeth said, falling onto her back floating. "Do you ever change the water in this pool?" With her ears underwater the words sounded far off, disconnected from her.

Mary spoke again but Elizabeth couldn't hear her. She pushed back upright.

"What did you say?"

"Do you know how long your father has been ill?"

"Most of his life it seemed to me."

"A year and a half. For a year and a half he's had this cancer."

And you haven't been here, you haven't paid a bit of attention. "I've been having a pretty good time," Elizabeth said. She was beginning to feel a little cold. "I wish I could tell you," she said, an earnestness coming into mind and voice, "I wish I could tell you what my life is like. You wouldn't believe it, but you'd be interested."

"I don't have the time to listen. *I* don't even have the time to stand here talking with you."

"You'd better move on then," Elizabeth said, but it was to Mary's already retreating back.

Elizabeth started to slip under—green salving water—when she thought of something and pushed herself back up. "Do you and David still live here?" she called.

"It's our house," Mary shot over her shoulder, turning slightly as if to watch her words. "We live here, in our house."

"Sneaky people."

Mary whirled around and slogged back through the mushy grass to the edge of the pool. "You disappeared," she said, her hand coming up as if she were about to shake her finger at Elizabeth. "You vanished and nobody ever heard of you again. Your father gave the house and everything else to us."

"I can imagine it," Elizabeth said. "I can imagine how you went about it." She made a slurping sound with her mouth, a kissing sexual sound.

"Minx," Mary said. "You were never any good, Elizabeth."

"That is certainly the truth. Are you sure you wouldn't like to come swimming?" She had paddled to the edge of the pool and now she stretched her arms onto the concrete apron, her palms turned up. "I think a swim would do you good," she said.

"You're a terrible person," Mary said, starting to turn away.

"Don't hold back, sweetheart."

She pulled herself up onto the edge and sat with her back to her sister-in-law. She looked over her shoulder at Mary, who had begun to fidget. She felt warm, her skin burnished by the cold water. A breeze touched the pool roof, hummed lightly in the mesh. Her husband was expected at nine.

"Would you hand me that towel?" she said, indicating the blue puddle of cloth on the patio table. Mary huffed over and brought it to her. Elizabeth reached for the towel but instead of grabbing it she dropped on her back between Mary's legs. She grasped the woman's ankles and looked up the flared wool skirt.

"What are you doing?" Mary cried, trying to pull away. Elizabeth held her long enough to look up her skirt before she kicked free, stumbling against the table.

"I wanted to see what you looked like up there," Elizabeth said. "I've thought about it for years. You look pretty clean."

She rolled over and stood up. "Now I want to take you swimming." She advanced on her sister-in-law stretching her arms out like a wrestler. The woman backed away, turned and ran for the house with Elizabeth behind her. Elizabeth caught her, slapped her on the back of the head and ran by her without stopping to the top of the steps. Mary started to come up, then turned and ran across the yard toward her car. Elizabeth bounded down the steps and caught her halfway there by the tail of her sweater. She had her almost to the pool when Mary slapped her hard across the forehead with the back of her hand. "Help!" she yelled. "David, help me, please!" Elizabeth moved in under her sister-in-law's swinging arms, grasped her around the waist and half-walked, half-dragged her to the pool. They tottered on the edge, as if for a moment the rounded, slightly upturned lip of concrete had become a tightrope. Then Elizabeth bent her knees, put her shoulder into Mary's stomach and pushed her in. As she went over, arms flailing, Mary's index fingernail caught and gashed Elizabeth's neck, then she hit with a huge splash that drenched her.

Elizabeth paused for a moment to watch Mary go under (arms thrashing down in the green), then she dived cleanly in after her.

She swam away from the thrashing woman, and it was as if for a moment she were back in the river dreams, not in their particularity of parents eating fruit at a glass table, of her child running after her with a red handkerchief, but in the air of them, the mood, the daze of another

378

world. She porpoised and swam over to her sister-in-law. The woman moved energetically, but Elizabeth could see (underwater, eyes wide open) that it was to no purpose; she didn't know how to swim. Elizabeth surfaced into Mary's cries, which were frantic, death-fearful. She approached her but she couldn't get in under her thrashing arms.

"Mary, Mary," she cried, "I'm here," but the woman did not respond to her. Her eyes were wide open but she didn't seem to see.

Mary went under dragging at the water as if she were pulling it down on top of her. Elizabeth followed her down, dived for her feet, grasped them and thrust her up. She was easier to handle underwater. Elizabeth came up behind her as Mary's arms crashed down on the surface of the water, flapping as if she were trying to fly out of the pool. "Swim, Mary," she cried, paddling around her. "You've got to swim, so swim." Maybe she could by force of will get her to swim. Maybe to save her own life Mary would galvanize strokes out of ignorance. But she did not seem to be able to manage it. The woman dragged herself under one more time, and this time as Elizabeth followed her down she saw that her mouth was open; she had lost the ability to tell the difference between water and air. Elizabeth slipped under the still-flailing arms, came up behind, grasped her around the chest and kicked upward. When they broke the surface Elizabeth pulled Mary's head back with her arm under her throat. The woman stopped struggling, as if the right button had been pushed. Elizabeth towed her to the steps at the shallow end, scrambled out and hauled her onto the concrete. Mary moved under her arms, wriggling, twitching—a sea creature, already reverted, Elizabeth thought.

She sat back on her heels and looked at the woman, who lay sprawled on her stomach, one of her arms curled under her abdomen, the other flung outward above her head. Like fucking, Elizabeth thought, like love, and she remembered years ago when she had hauled Jacey ninety feet through the ginny water of Yellow Spring, the way his heart shuddered under her pressing hand, the sweet smell of his mouth under hers. She thought it strange to remember this now and she bent down and kissed Mary on the back of the head. The woman's hair smelled of a candy shampoo and the pulse in her neck throbbed under the skin. "Mary, Mary," she said, "you're not that hard to beat. Once I get you out in the open." She looked at the house, which was blurred by the misting rain. Her brother stood on the steps silently watching. What did he think he was seeing? They looked at each other across the yard—too far apart for eyes to pull the other in, but close enough to understand each other.

Mary pushed up on hands and knees. Her head hung down between her shoulders swinging slowly from side to side. A line of phlegm fell from her mouth onto the concrete. She turned her head and looked at Elizabeth, who sat back on her haunches beside her watching. There was sadness in her eyes and wonder and dismay. Elizabeth saw her humanness, if that was what it was. She touched the woman on the cheek, trailed one nail lightly to her chin. She knew when she was on the river that if she came back to civilization she would want to embrace everyone. To keep from doing it, she thought, to keep from taking everybody into your arms, you throw them in the nearest pool. Anything to keep from fessing up. She got up and helped Mary to her feet. The woman was too beat to protest. She leaned her head against Elizabeth's shoulder, let her steer her toward the house. David came down the steps looking embarrassed.

"We have so many problems here," he said, "so many problems," in a variation of his old-time litanies.

They might get a real look at me, Elizabeth thought, passing the exhausted woman to her brother. She hugged herself in her black bathing suit. I have wandered three days in the wilderness—was that long enough? How could this have become a planet in which you could spend a day watching a hawk drift over wild pine woods and not be able to tell of it? She had come down a cliff trail once in Maui and seen a field of rocks turn to jewels in suddenly flashing sunlight. From a beach in Molokai she had watched a school of whales trail out over the level ocean for half a mile. Look, friends, there is nothing more beautiful than the flower of the Cherokee rose, white-petaled, gold in the center smelling of pepper and the wind.

As David took his wife in his arms a moany cry began from the house. A high, weak, frail, penetrating cry, it came from her father's bedroom. David smiled over Mary's shoulder. "I didn't tell you," he said. "The pain gets so bad that Papa can't keep from crying out. Sometimes he cries all night long. They give him drugs but he cries anyway."

"We should take him back to the hospital, David," Mary said, coming to herself. "It's just not right to keep him here in the house." Her voice had a petulant, peevish edge and Elizabeth noticed in her upturned, coming-to face that one eye was higher than the other. She had never seen that before.

"It's going to be all right, darling," David said and touched his wife with his hand, tentatively, as if she might be fiery.

Elizabeth left them on the steps, got her robe from the kitchen hall and went into her father's bedroom.

The old man lay on his back under a wrinkled sheet with his fists against his temples crying. The nurse, who had just administered a shot, leaned over the bedside table putting her equipment away. Elizabeth crawled on her knees onto the bed and bent over her father. "Tommy," she whispered, "Tommy Bonnet," addressing him by his Christian name for the first time in her life. I have loved everyone, she thought, but they have never understood it, and she kissed her father's bruised and sweating forehead. The purple marks at his temples and on his forehead, fading up into the sparse hair, looked like stains, a little like the wen on the forehead of Jimmy Givens, a boy she had gone to kindergarten with. O, Jimmy Givens, she whispered, I should have kissed you, too. Her father smelled sour, like just-spoiled milk. He opened his eyes as her lips touched him and he began to give off tiny, wheedling, disjointed cries.

"What are you doing, Papa?" she asked, taking his fists in her hands, remembering as her fingers closed over the bones how small they were, small for a man, always unnervingly delicate.

"I'm singing," the old man said.

Elizabeth laughed. "I don't know that song."

"Oh sure you do. I used to sing it to you all the time." He relaxed his hands, let the ends of his fingers curl around the backs of hers. She moved away until she was sitting with her legs over the edge of the bed.

"I wish I could remember something important to say," the old man said. "I keep trying to remember what somebody famous said about dying, but nothing comes to me. Do you know any famous statements?"

"How about 'Bury me on the lone prairie'?"

"I don't think so; I've never seen a prairie—oh." He closed his eyes and began again to moan.

Like love, she thought, like sex, for the second time in ten minutes. Everything makes me think of it. Even that nurse hunched there over her needlepoint, so lonely.

She said, " 'Sweetest love, I do not go for weariness of thee . . .' "

He opened his eyes again, bit his lip. "Not that," he said. "It's not like that." Then the drug or exhaustion took effect and he closed his eyes and drifted into unconsciousness.

She sat beside him until the late rainy afternoon turned to night, until her brother came in carrying a book to spell the nurse for supper, until her father's wheezing, cinched breathing became a rhythm and a sound she was used to.

He drove with his arm out the window, pointing the .45 straight ahead along the hood. It's going to be so simple, he said out loud, thinking of the Jap Zeroes and their cowling guns, aimed at whatever the pilot faced. He had seen the lines of .50 caliber bullets walk up the deck, over gun housings and superstructures, striding giant steps. Once a string of bullets had slapped holes in the bulkhead beside him. They had hit before he could move, spraying gray forecastle paint instead of Burdette blood. For an instant, to sense at least, the lesson of his mortality came clear to him, but as he dived to the deck already he was thinking, Not me, ha, not me.

North of Savannah he had left U.S. 17 and driven the state roads toward the shore. Well after dark he stopped in Beaufort, South Carolina, and had a sandwich at a filling station. It was cold even for late March. Wind had blown down dogwood petals from a tree at the corner, whole flowers littered the concrete under a streetlight. Sunday, it was later than he planned, the churches had closed for the day. Only an old man up the street in farmer's overalls leaned in to look at something in a drugstore window. The gun was under the seat. As his car was tended to he had stayed near the driver's window in case it slid out and was noticed by the attendant pumping gas. The world clears right up, he thought, I know exactly what I'm doing. This is in fact what I should have been doing all the time. He had not stopped to visit his Savannah plant, which was actually across the river in South Carolina, the South Carolina plant. He didn't have to think about it now. What he could do was imagine that solitary farmer studying hair permanent ads sprawled on the pavement with blood across his face. Or this grease monkey in tattered gray coveralls and a boot-camp haircut wiping the dipstick with a dirty rag, imagine this man at the instant when the bullet cut off the lights in his body and he was dead before he fell, everything giving way at once, like a sledged steer. I can in fact turn life into death, he thought, and went into the station and bought a Coke. He drank it down so quickly his nose and throat stung. He went out, paid with a credit card, got in his car and drove away.

He had raced across south Georgia, his old run through pine barrens, but now, less than a hundred miles from Charleston, he began to take his time. He had loved this coast always, coast of wild barrier islands, white sand roads, huge sheltering oaks. The memory of the sunlight on the marshes, shining gold as a wheat field, had been one of the triggering memories he carried with him on his slip of paper through the war. He had learned to swim on Tybee Island, off the coast from Savannah, on a beach trip he took with his parents when he was five. When Jacey was young they had spent vacations at the Cloister at Sea Island. Elizabeth had been there, but each morning she got up early and ran off down the beach, spent the day alone in the weedy dunes at the north point.

He reached between his legs and got the gun. He had taken if off a Marine in Tinian during the staging for the invasion of Japan in 1945. He and Haven had done that. As far as he knew, except once when he killed her horse, it had never been fired. He sighted along the hood and when the yellow diamond of a CURVE sign rose into his lights, he fired. The gun kicked hard and in the running wind he almost dropped it. He pulled off the road just beyond the sign and walked back to look at where he had hit it. A thumbnail crescent of metal was missing along one upper edge. He thought that wasn't bad for a moving shooter. Back up the road was a wayside park, a few picnic tables under oaks, and he walked back to it and sat down on one of the concrete benches. He laid the gun on the table and ran his finger around it, setting its outline. The table smelled faintly of ketchup, old pickle juice. Beyond a row of young planted pines a cornfield stretched away into mist. Jane had said, Why won't you let me come back, and he had said, Because I don't know if I'm coming back myself. She asked him what he was talking about but he couldn't say, wouldn't say. It will be a difficult journey, he told her, and she turned her mouth down and looked away. She had brought him coffee and toast slathered with homemade blackberry jelly. She wanted to lick his fingers but he wouldn't let her. Why can I get what I want where I don't want it?

But that was in the past, he thought, raising the gun and sighting it into the cornfield. He said softly, "Khew, khew," then pulled the trigger. The sound of the gun was nothing like the sound he made with his mouth. He fired again, leveling onto the fence posts he could see between the thin pine trunks. The gun kicked hard into his palm and wrist. He could feel it in his shoulder. Firing the gun made him feel better, and he moved his aim to one of the sapling pines and cut it in half. When they were kids Haven had once suggested that they become robbers in Mexico. He wanted to buy a jeep and lay out along the federal highways and rob the tourists. Tourists, he had argued, would be so buffaloed by the Byzantine procedures of Mexican bureaucracy that they would never be caught. They could ride away across the mountains in their jeep to strike again on another road. It was a good idea, absurdly appealing, but they had never attempted it, just as they had never sailed to Bimini in the sixteen-foot Snipe Haven wanted to buy from a man in St. Luke's. They had never done any of that stuff, none of it but go to war. But war, he thought, raising the black gun in both hands, was enough. His ears still rang with the sound of the three-inch 50s. He had arrived on Saipan a month after the invasion and the whole island still reeked with the stench of bodies. On any walk in the jungle you could bring back bones. Once he had looked with a flashlight into a Japanese water-catchment tank and seen a pile of bodies. From the shattered and stinking carcasses of murdered natives the red eyes of rats peered up at him. He had reeled back crying out for his own life. He remembered how glossy the leaves of an old avocado tree drooping over the catchment looked, as if the tree had drawn up the blood into its veins—he remembered this as he remembered, suddenly sweating, how he had run blindly across the littered invasion beach into the lagoon. He had fallen to his knees in the shallow water where two hundred yards out, over the shoulders of the ragged reef, the guns of shattered tanks stuck out of the surf. He had dropped to his knees and plunged his face into the water, which was as clear as a spring, eyes open peering into the sting of the eroding salt.

He fired the rest of the clip, hitting nothing, and laid the gun on the table, thinking, Have you ever stopped the car to get out and look at the flowers growing along the field rows? There is a long grass in the ditches that every spring makes small blue flowers. The flowers have no scent and they are shaped like the wings of butterflies. In the wind they flutter. Have you ever kneeled among them, have you ever held them to your face?

He stood up and said aloud, "You have to have something more going for you than an empire. The banker will come and take your land away. The banker will take your factories away." In the movie *African*

Queen, the Germans burned a native village to the ground. Where there had been houses and gardens there were smoldering ruins; families fled into the bush. He said, "It can all go very suddenly," and thought, Mr. Profundity is at it again. Did the ache in his left shoulder mean he was walking on the edge of a heart attack? He released the clip and shot the chamber. May the smell of cordite give me peace. He pressed the barrel against his face, ran its warm metal over his skin, then placed the muzzle in his mouth. He held the gun very still, then sucked on the barrel; the sudden bitter taste made him spit, hack. "O, Mr. Romance," he said and swung the gun in an arc, following the hope of movement. From his pocket he took another clip and clicked it in. He didn't fire again. He walked back up the road to his car, got in and drove off into the foggy darkness.

He came in along the broad mortared wall of the Battery and he was thinking of what the shells sounded like as they fell on Fort Sumter. The street was newly paved; he followed a passage of fresh asphalt marked by kerosene flambeaus. The sweet smell of the flambeaus and the sharp, ironic smell of the tar was just enough to make him feel at home. Off to his left, the park under streetlights, each of which was surrounded by a huge nimbus of mist, looked frozen and still. He swung over and parked next to a concrete bench with the name of a fruit company lettered along the back. He got out, climbed the Battery steps and walked along the sea-wall. The tide trailed a soughing line of phosphorescence along the bottom of the wall. Vague lights, far off, red and green, came and went in the harbor. A boat horn sounded a long way away.

This was not the first time he had come to Charleston about a woman. During his sophomore year at Harvard, he had spent part of spring vacation here visiting Kathleen Harper, a brilliant laconic Radcliffe freshman who never seemed to quite understand why he was so mad about her. Her father had just died, a doctor who killed himself with pills, and the house resonated with the tension of unresolved grief. Kathleen's mother was a starved, brilliant-eyed woman who resented his being there. He woke in the mornings to the sound of her shouting. She stood on the back steps below his window shouting at a dog, at the absent milkman, at the ridiculous azaleas. She could hardly bring herself to speak to him at all. And Kathleen, who, a month earlier when she learned of her father's death, had come to his room and pressed herself into his arms, now, at home, retreated from him into a crepuscular silence and suspicion. She caught him, at seven in the morning, rifling her bureau drawer. He slept in her room—she slept in a guest room—and he did not see her standing in the doorway as he rummaged through the chains and pendants, the crushed handkerchiefs, looking for toothpaste. She had laughed in bitterness when he tried to explain and turned away from him. Her mother played wild broken-tuned pieces on the piano, rising up glassy-eyed, exhausted. Kathleen avoided him, and though he tried again to explain that he had done nothing sinister, he was unable, in the face of her grief, to confront her deeply. He repacked his bags and took an evening train south. That spring at school she avoided him, finally dissolving from his life. He heard the next fall that she had married an old high school friend and moved back to Charleston. She lived in a narrow house on Tradd Street that was so close to the street that two men could not pass in front of it abreast. He didn't know if she was still alive, blond and singing "Embraceable You" to herself. She was right, he had not been looking for toothpaste.

And now as he walked on the wet slate, a cliff of dark buildings ahead of him, the huge soaked live oaks—which always seemed to him somehow like giant beings kneeling—in the park to his left, he saw a man, a hundred yards away, rise from the shadows below the steps onto the pathway. He craved no human contact now, wanted his mind free to run up other trails, he wanted to become a tiger, free of importunity, gunsel, clicking time like the rungs of a ladder he climbed toward the death's head he came to embrace. They would raze Canaan from the face of the earth. It was no more important than an African hut burning at the edge of the veldt. His wife might live in the woods, but he could not. He had watched through her cabin window as she rolled on the floor in her ecstasies. In the beaten ground beneath the windows were the tracks of animals, raccoons, skunks, cats. He looked out at the bay the waves of which made small sounds, perhaps of longing, perhaps of succor.

It was because he was looking at the sea, because his thoughts were edging along the barriers of memory that he did not realize until he was twenty feet away that the man walking toward him was his son. It was the boy Jacey, his son. J.C. choked the impulse to run to him. The boy was taller, dressed in dark clothes, thinner than he had ever seen him. He carried a cane which he ticked against the sea rail. He wore a white panama pulled down over his eyes.

386

It was something huge come to get him, J.C. thought, his fate or his death, the meaning of his life. That was why you had kids—one reason—to find out what your life means. The figure stopped, stood still, then slowly raised the cane and shook the silver knob at him.

"You came on the plane," J.C. said. "You just arrived."

"I came on the plane," Jacey answered. "I just arrived." He turned as J.C. came up to him and leaned over the rail, bent and spit into the water. "You can smell the ocean from every room in the house," he said.

"I didn't know that, but I suppose you can."

J.C. leaned out beside his son letting his arm rest just touching Jacey's dark sleeve.

"You didn't come home Christmas," J.C. said.

"I know. I couldn't get away." He reached down with the cane but the water was too far away. "How's Rooley?" he asked.

"He's stopped painting entirely. He said he wouldn't make any more graven images. Their little boy's a pistol."

Jacey ejected a tough bark of laughter. "Riever Jesus."

"I haven't heard that word in a long time."

"Which one?"

"Riever. Is your mother here?"

"She's taken over from the nurse." He turned and looked at his father. "Did you know she's been on the river for three days?"

"I haven't heard from her since she left. How is Martha?"

"Martha's always fine. I can't keep up with how fine she is."

It was difficult to concentrate on what his son was saying. His body still seemed to be hurtling forward, as if the journey from Canaan were still roaring on. He thought, But this is what a son is for: to bring you off the hard road and wrap your old bones in a cloak. "I feel old," he said, surprising himself.

"So do I," Jacey said. "And I'm just eighteen."

"I felt old at eighteen, too. I was a freshman at Harvard and I used to look out my window at the elm trees. There wasn't a single evergreen tree in the Yard, and it used to drive me crazy; I thought that winter that I was going to be lonely for the rest of my life."

"There's a guy who lives downstairs from us who's got a chain saw that he fires up in his room. It makes an unbelievable racket. I think he does it for the company."

"He probably does. Strange New York."

"It's like living in a fire drill. Or it was when I first moved there. We live just a few blocks from the Hell's Angels. You can walk by their place—they've got sofas out on the sidewalks—and watch them roar off on their bikes. Last week one of them killed another one with his bare hands."

"My Lord." Son sporting raffish hat and cane, it is possible to rake off the mask and expose the murderous beast. In his mind he spoke, said, *Beneath the seat of my car is a .45 automatic. A short while ago I blew apart a pine tree that was as big around as your ankle. I am going to kill your mother.* Out loud, as he looked out at the lights that might have been the lights of Sumter, he said, "Every time I come here I wind up thinking about the sadness of the Confederates. The Yankees shelled this city for two years. These fine houses. What must those men and women have thought as the bombs fell on them? They'd been so bold, it had all seemed so easy and right: whip a flag in the air, fire a few shots at that ugly Yankee fort, cut loose into a new life entirely. By the time Sherman marched in here the women were wearing dresses they'd woven out of the stuffing of sofas."

"You sound a little like Granddaddy."

"He's never been to Charleston."

"He talks about Canaan that way. Mattie calls him Old Consecrated Jack."

"It's funny," J.C. said. "I never really thought of Canaan that way—and your granddaddy didn't either when he was young—I didn't *hallow* it, it wasn't some sacred place"—he raised his arm to touch his son and let it fall between them—"any more than your paints are sacred, but I depended on it." He wiped his face with downward descending palm. "You never know how much you depend on something until it's not there anymore. While it's there you can feel independent as hell. Then it goes and you're sitting on the edge of the bed at three in the morning shuddering."

Jacey raised himself on straightened arms, lifted his feet and for a moment balanced horizontally on the rail. He leaned an inch too far forward and tipped toward the smacking sea. J.C. caught him around the waist and drew him back, held him a moment against him.

"That's all right," Jacey said. "I wouldn't fall."

"Sometimes I can't quite tell."

Jacey scuffed his feet against the walkway. "Uncle David said that the roof of Granddaddy Bonnet's house and the Battery walk are covered with the same slate."

"That's one of those remarkable facts that touches me deeply when I'm in the right mood."

Jacey flung a hand at the park. "All this touches me. I feel like it wants to pull me down into it." A car passed carefully negotiating the torn roadway. The beam of its headlights rose and fell in the mist.

"They all used to leave this place in the summer," J.C. said. "The rich ones did, to plantations on the high ground. Our most ancestral land is fifty miles up the Ashley from here. The Mennonites own it now; it's a big communal farm."

"Did you ever go back there?"

"My grandfather took me once when I was a little boy. The only thing I can remember is how angry he got because the Mennonites hadn't kept up the graveyard. I think he almost got in a fight. That feeling—of being pulled down—is I reckon why the Burdettes moved on from this place. It was probably suffocating them. At least I think that's what would happen to me if I had to stay here. I can understand why your mother got out." He pushed his hand along the rail, which was slick with water. "She never understood how alike we were."

"It's hard to see."

"You think?"

"She never followed any of the rules and you follow all of them."

"That sounds a little like an insult."

"No. I admire both ways. But it's hard to see where the common ground is between them."

"I suppose so." He felt as if he could reach out and take the whole Atlantic into his arms. Wide suffering, poetical, pathetic sea. By day Sumter lay like a brown log on the horizon. Beyond a foreground filled with the sails of pleasure boats. He remembered lying in Kathleen's bed listening to the horn of the tourist ferry, a white tiered boat, as it put out from the yacht basin. And now in Hawaii, the great sea road where the battleships anchored was a national monument. You could ride out in a launch and look down through the oily water at the gun turrets of the *Arizona*. Over a thousand men were buried down there, too deep and too lost to bring up. Maybe if you put your ear to the water you could hear them tapping with wrenches.

He gripped the rail, which seemed to him the exact same circumference as the butt of a .45. Once when he was fifteen, alone in a dove field, he had been peppered with birdshot out of nowhere. Someone beyond the trees was shooting high. Bent over pulling a passion vine off his boots, he hadn't even heard the shot. He had looked around at an empty field, trees far off; his fingers were sticky with drying bird blood. What kind of instrument was he capable of being? He was a man who had hammered his competitors out of business. James Alvin, a man he had gone to high school with, had taken him to court to try to stop him from buying up all the cotton in south Georgia. He wasn't able to, and James Alvin went bankrupt. There were men in Yellow Springs who crossed to the other side of the street to avoid speaking to him. His own father, the man who was responsible for his mother's death, had spent years raving at him.

"Sometimes I want to jump in the ocean," his son said. Could everyone read his mind? His father said, I know what you are thinking; his wife said, You're as easy to read as an apple.

"Why?" he asked, turning his body toward Jacey. "Why do you want to do that?"

"I've begun to see things that frighten me." He looked at his father with eyes that said, Can I trust you? Will you hurt me if I tell the truth? J.C. looked away, dodging secrets.

"Anything in the world is capable of scaring us," he said. He wanted to feel the heft of the .45 in his hand again.

"I'm not prepared enough."

Why was his son speaking to him in this way? For years they had passed each other as strangers, scouts on unrelated missions.

"In New York," his son said, "the only territory you have is the one you spin out of yourself. Everybody knows it and everybody's trying to devise something that'll hold them up. Maybe Martha's not, but I don't have what she has. She's a believer. I have to paint like a maniac for days to feel safe for ten seconds."

Was this his son? What could he say to him? They once had Canaan, but he had lost it. Did he know the bankers had come? "When I was an undergraduate at Harvard," he said, "everybody was upset about the lack of a true American myth. The Depression had wrenched us onto swampy ground. A lot of folks became communists for ten or twenty minutes. The place bloomed with artists and social critics. In the Southern Club we used to laugh at them. The Depression wasn't new to us—

390

we'd been in it since 1865." He hacked a ball of spit and swallowed it. "We all had places to go back to, even if the place was only the imaginary country of the South itself. That was very important."

His son looked out to sea. The mist had turned cottony; it was becoming fog. "I don't think I have Canaan anymore," Jacey said. "I think I've lost it."

"You have," J.C. said and felt the hairs on his arms rise.

"What?"

"Lost Canaan. I've lost Canaan."

"I heard about that. Granddaddy told me."

"It's just happened."

"It's been coming awhile, though."

"I never saw it. I was standing on the tracks whistling, looking the other way."

His son raised his eyes and looked him in the face. The boniness of feature that marked all the Burdette men was fully on him now. He looked, to J.C., as if he had never been a child. "You have never been able to see what was going on around you," Jacey said. "You've never been able to see past the backs of your own eyeballs."

J.C. dropped then clumsily to his knees and took his son's hands in his, but even as he did so a shadow seemed to rise out of the white mist, a shadow that as he saw it he knew was thrown there by his own mind. Momentum is momentum, he thought, and I will not stop. I can't stop now any more than I ever could.

He kissed his son's fingers, tasting the bitterness of tobacco, like gall. He could feel him try to draw away, but he held him. "You have to love us," he said. "It is what you have to do no matter what. You have to love us."

Gently, perhaps more gently than he intended, his son disengaged his fingers from his grasp. Jacey raised his hand, oddly, as in benediction, then swept it out toward the blankened bay. "I'm afraid," he said, "that the truth is I don't have to love anybody at all."

J.C., on his wet and creaking knees, looked up into that face built of his own blood. We can draw a strength from the world by changing it, he thought. When nothing else would help, love lifted me. If not love then, death. He felt as moony as a schoolboy.

22 They found her sleeping in the bed with her father. Not sleeping, lying cupped against him with her eyes closed in the odorous room that was lit by a single green-shaded lamp by the empty nurse's chair. She did not open her eyes when they came in, led by David in his undershirt. The old man, drained down to childhood, was curled in his raddled sleep, small littered breaths escaping; his lips shone with petroleum jelly. She lay with her head slightly raised against the back of his neck, and though she kept her eyes closed, it was as if she could see them standing silently, without leaning, a look of dismay and fright on her husband's face, her son's face stern, resisting his revulsion, her bewildered brother kneading his hands. What is it to you? she asked silently, what discovery here takes you up into its arms? She had dreamed of the white gulls flying over the river. She would get up tomorrow or the next day and go away. She would cross the Pacific to stand on the edge of the last ground that could be called American. Why couldn't there be a far enough place, endless territory? There was nothing left but sky and ocean and she was not a bird or a fish. They had cornered her in her father's bed, her still-lean body pressed against the loins that engendered her. She almost laughed out loud and perhaps a smile flickered on her lips and went out. I have gotten away with giving nothing, she thought, nothing but the presence of being itself. Here I walk past the gate and pluck a tea olive blossom: look at me. I call to the animals at night: hear me. Taste this oil on my skin.

"He's really sinking fast," David said in a quick breathless whisper as if he were watching something speed toward him.

"He's so small," Jacey said, and then he said, "Granddaddy . . . ?" the word rising into a question at the end. He would call out forever, she knew, he would run from place to place seeking arms that would hold him.

"Don't wake him," J.C. said.

"Mama," Jacey said, "Mama, are you awake?"

She opened her eyes and looked at them. She had not seen her son in a year, maybe longer. How nice it would be if they all got into bed with her. "Hello," she said and smiled, flicking her tongue between her teeth. Her son reached over her father's crumpled body and took her in his arms. She thought for a moment that he was going to lift her off the bed. They hugged each other strongly as the old man shifted and moaned underneath them, kicking his feet at the blankets. I will you my sense of smell, she thought, I will you my way of looking. I will you the love of touching everything in the world. Her son smelled of turpentine and tobacco and unwashed trousers. He drew back, his face gone simple. She slid out of the bed, edged between bed and window, came around and took first her brother than her husband into her arms.

"You are the luckiest man in the world," she said to J.C., kissing him in the creased center of his chin. To lose your empire.

"To have seen such performances," he said, drawing back and smiling.

"I'm grateful for such an audience." She caressed his cheek, probed with one finger the line of bone beneath his eye.

"Don't you want something to eat, Elizabeth?" David asked.

"Of course I do," she said. "I want some peaches."

"We don't have peaches, but there's honeydew from California." Her brother rubbed his skinny arms.

"I'll stay with Granddaddy," Jacey said.

"Fine," she said to them both.

She turned and bent over her father, with light fingers touched his hair into place. His hand twitched against his throat, he made sounds. She hummed one complete breath over him, rose and led them from the room.

Jacey sat in the nurse's chair tracing on a small triangle of limestone the raised shape of a fossilized leaf. He hadn't known that his grandfather collected fossils. The room was full of them. They were on the dresser, along the windowsill, half a dozen stacked like wood chips on the table under the lamp. Leaves and bugs pressed in slate, the flattened carapaces of marine crustaceans. His grandfather, knees pulled up, looked like something left after the blast of a water hose. He had never seen this man before tonight. When David had brought him—almost by the hand—into this fetid room, he had recoiled at the shrunken shape struggling in the sheets. His grandfather hadn't known him, hadn't wanted to know him. It was too late to thread himself into that creaking life.

"He's out somewhere," David had said. "He's off visiting another country."

"Where are my songs?" his grandfather had cried. "I think they're in the electricity."

"Yes, sir," David said. "Can I get you something, Papa?"

"Catholics hate America," the old man wheezed as his eyes roved the room behind them.

"I have a difficult time understanding all of this," David said, picking at his navy wool coat sleeve.

He's a homosexual, Jacey had thought, one of those queer hometown men who marry scentless, plain women for cover. David smiled with half his mouth, the lower side containing like a tiny purse a wet ball of skin next to the crease. He had long thin lines like razor cuts straying from the edges of his eyes; they creased his thin and satiny skin. I looked up at him, Jacey thought (he had been sitting on the bed), and I saw this stranger who looked like my mother, stranger whom I was part of, and I thought I'm never going to get down from this high place I have hung myself in. David scratched the underside of his arm, which was as white as a frog's belly. He had looked at Jacey as if the boy might tell him what to do.

Jacey rubbed the fossil and looked into the air above his grandfather's head. There seemed to be a haze. Earlier he had walked down the lane to Church Street, along Tradd to Meeting, on to Lamboll and Legare. In a house beyond an iron-fenced yard on Legare he saw, through lighted front windows, two women playing with a balloon. Through the open window he could see them batting it back and forth. They ran around the room after the balloon, which floated across the light. The women kept disappearing as if they had fallen to the floor, then one or the other would rise and swat the balloon. He stood grasping the iron spears of the fence palings for twenty minutes watching them. He thought the sweetness of Martha's body would drive him crazy. The hard stone under the sweet flesh, flesh that smelled like apricots.

Last night he had made love to a Puerto Rican woman who claimed to be a Cherokee Indian. He had drunk too much in a lesbian bar on 7th Street, had touched, in a moment of drunken irresistible tenderness, the tensed back of a woman sipping vodka; the woman had spun on him with murderous eyes, shouted at him, "Prick!"; he had reeled back terrified and appalled into the arms of the Puerto Rican, who gathered him in, patted his face, and led him across the park to her apartment. There, in a litter of electrical wire and broken appliances, they had made love. The

394

woman was short and had the body of a wrestler. She was nearly hairless, lank black strands at her groin he dipped his mouth to, smelling bitter, like almonds. As he licked a wet line into the intersection of her thighs, he saw in the tender, honey-colored flesh of her body Martha's skin and he was forced back from his own excitement into thoughts of her spare body stretched across their bed. He wanted too much: romance and distance, his father's reflexive dogmatism, his mother's dance with the beasts. No. He wanted to be like those two women playing with the balloon. He wanted to live forever in that moment when they waited crouched against sofas as the balloon drifted across the lighted air.

Martha had said, I will go on tour and when I come back I will have decided what I want to do. Maybe I won't come back to you, maybe I will. I don't know.

He said, Burdette, Burdette/Nothing's over yet.

She said, You have the most beautiful pecker in the world.

He said, How in the world would you know?

She said, I was sixteen but I wasn't naive.

He said, I was thirteen, I was only thirteen.

The Puerto Rican, who called herself Connie, had pulled away from his body saying, "What's the matter, *corazón?* Can't you make it with me? Are you impotent?" She put the accent on the o: imp*o*tent.

He didn't know. Fear took hold of him, but it was fear as soft as a down pillow. She sat astride him, reared above him, her bright, wrestler's muscles rippling across her shoulders, her hands squeezing fleshy fists; for a moment Jacey thought she was going to strike him, but he didn't resist, he lay trapped between her spread legs, his arms at his sides. His head swam with drink. The air seemed sprayed with caramel, a caramel light, a broken streetlight at the corner twitching on and off. The woman pressed both hands open against his chest, pressed as if to stop his heart, her lips drew back from long yellow teeth, then she swayed, her hands fell loose and she began to cry. She pressed her head into his shoulder and sobbed. Oh my Jesus Lord, Jacey thought as he held the woman's unruly head against him. After a while he crawled out from under her, dressed and left her there, without a goodbye, sprawled akimbo on the floor, the tan light dense and motionless in the cluttered room.

His grandfather stirred, began to make light clicking noises in his sleep. Jacey got up, went to the bed and stood over him. His head was like a bird's, the papery scalp showing through thin white hair. Beneath the skin he could see the bones of the skull which would shine forever in the grave. His mother approached strangers in the street and asked them if they had anything to tell her. She called to animals from the back door of her house.

The old man stirred again and woke. He blinked clotted, wandering eyes. "I don't have on any underwear," he said.

Jacey laughed and touched his grandfather's forehead. "I don't either."

"Well, it certainly is strange to kick around under these sheets without any underwear on."

"Mattie said I was just like a field nigger."

"That's how I see it." The old man coughed silently. "Who's Mattie?" he asked.

"She's my other grandfather's common-law wife."

"You like her?"

"I love her. She's never cheated on herself a day in her life. Did you sleep well?"

"I didn't sleep at all. I was talking to Jesus." The old man slowly rubbed his forehead with the knuckles of his right hand. "We just had a very delightful conversation."

This, Jacey reckoned, was the madness of drugs. But he said seriously, "What did you say to each other?"

"He told me that my life was worth living. He told me I hadn't made as many mistakes as I thought. I told him he was looking well for such an old man."

"Is that really possible?"

"To look well?"

"No. To talk to Jesus." Before his grandfather could answer, he said, "I once knew an old colored woman who talked to Jesus. She talked to him while she worked in the yard. She said that he sat up in the chinaberry tree and discussed her neighbors with her. I have a cousin who's a Pentecostal and I think he speaks in tongues."

"I'm dying," his grandfather said. His hands, which lay on his chest, fluttered up for a moment and dropped. "I'm dying," he said again, "and because of that the Lord comes to me. I don't care about the world anymore."

"That's a good way to be."

The old man's face seemed to crumble and then his body was

396

wrenched by a huge spasm of coughing, his knees knocked as if he were beating time and his hands grasped his own birdy shoulders. Jacey leaned over him, terrified, and took his face in his hands. The skin was hot and cold, in patches, like summer pond water; the bruise across his temples burned. And he thought, My body is already a ruined house haunted by ghosts. "Grandfather," he said, "are you all right? Are you living?" Martha in the bathtub turning on the hot water with her toes; Martha licking grape jelly off her long fingers.

"Oh my God it hurts," the old man cried and he beat on his chicken chest as if he could drive out the pain with the bones of his hands.

Jacey pulled one wrist away—the old man opened his eyes and looked at him in surprise—he felt the pulse, holding the hand away from his grandfather's body with a desire to know if he was dying, with a desire, too, to prevent him from touching himself, with a desire, too, to hurt him, to prevent him from doing what he wanted to do, to control him. Now, he thought, in this life, my heart is broken. She will touch another man. —It doesn't matter to me if you take other lovers, she had said. —I don't, he said, and it matters. —Not to me, she said. —It would if I could tell you what it means. She took me to the river and there she touched my body in all its parts. She made me feel everything. I thought I would die. I wanted to die. Martha said, —You can't make a mother out of me. —You'd be surprised what I can make a mother out of, he said.

His grandfather groaned and began to make spitting noises. Jacey tipped a glass of water to his lips, leaning into a still center in the thrashing, balancing the glass so it did not spill, letting careful drops fall into the old man's crying mouth.

David cracked the door and came in. He looked at his father, reached but didn't touch him. "He's like that again and again," he said. "It passes."

"I don't think I can deal with this," Jacey said, backing away. Light seemed to wash past him and it filled the space between himself and his grandfather, a nacreous, mineral light. His mother told him she saw white wings in the oaks. *Did* she means birds? She collected nothing living. He had kissed the bitter face of a Puerto Rican charlatan. He had told Martha he might die without her.

He left the room, careened down the dim hall, through a lighted doorway into the breakfast room and through to the kitchen, where his mother and father sat across from each other at a small checkered table.

"The son and heir," his father said, looking at him with shocked eyes.

"Granddaddy's not doing well," Jacey said.

His mother got up straightaway and left the room. As she passed she stopped to kiss him once lightly on the neck. "You don't look so good in dark clothes," she said, feisty as ever. He spun a second in resentment but it blinked away. Her kiss felt necessary.

When she was gone he sat down in her chair and looked at his father; the skin on either side of his nose was white and his eyes had the distance of the prophets in them. They sat without speaking until his father got up and poured them both cups of coffee, asking as he tipped the enamel pot if he wanted cream. Jacey nodded yes and remained seated as his father served him. It was a small thing, not objecting to being served, and he could tell that it pleased his father. But it was not enough to break the silence between them now and they sat for a long time at the table under the harsh white kitchen light, speechless and stunned by love.

On the hard, spinsterish bed David led him to, J.C. lay on his back looking at the red blinking light of a distant radio tower. The .45 was in the bedside drawer under an open handkerchief. He held his arms up and spread the fingers of both hands. He could smell the ocean, even through the closed windows. I can't believe this is happening to me, he thought—Yes I can. "Into many a green valley/Drift the appalling snows"—how romantic Auden's line had seemed the first time he read it from a book opened across the knees of his ship's executive officer, Billy Kopeski. That had been in the long lake reach between the locks in Panama. He had wished a fever would strike and kill him. After Elizabeth refused him the world was no place he wanted to go back to. Not for that moment anyway. The excitement would rise again, but it would never have the pure leaping curve of delight that it had had before the war. From the deck of his ship the whole world of America hung above him like ripe fruit. He was canny enough, energetic enough, dedicated enough to take and eat what he wanted. There had never been any doubt about that. If it came to hustling his father off to the reservation he would do that; if the friends of his youth turned against him, so be it. He was the likely Burdette, no panjandrum: conqueror. Once in Atlanta passing the freshly constructed, high-rising red brick edifice of the Henry Grady Hotel his father had stopped their brisk walk to sweep his hand at the new exuberant city fronts on Peachtree Street. "Only a city that's been burned would work so hard to forget its past," he said. They had spent the afternoon watching the city go up in flames in the Cyclorama at Grant Park. Coming back into town his father had pointed out to him the landmarks of the battle, which were obscured now by the bricks and streets of well-to-do neighborhoods. Somebody goes on making up a myth, Dad, no matter what happens. Old Burdettes endlessly connecting, endlessly justifying. His father would say, You don't understand.

They talked now. He rode his horse across the fields and sat on the back steps with the old man talking about the past. His father said he wanted to be remembered as a great plowman, but only, he added, if greatness became an issue. There was always music around the old man now, some aria or concerto drifting down out of the tower fading out among the spindly bodies of zinnias and Constitution roses. His father said, Everything is marvelous, even that squirrel in the sycamore there, little tree rat scratching fleas. He's got that big cloak of a tail that when it gets cold he can wrap around himself; but in the summer he can just wave it along like a flag, no trouble about getting too hot. J.C. said, Maybe when I get old I'll sit in the sun and think about things. Don't misunderstand me, his father said, you can't survive by looking back at the past and wondering; you have to have something up ahead. And it's a good idea to have a play-pretty going for you in the day you're in. I know that, J.C. said, but he was thinking about his shattered empire and the conversation drifted away into trivialities.

I have a gun, he thought suddenly and sat straight up. I have my little exploding repair kit which is my hope for the future. What do you think of this, Daddy? He got up and went to the window. The roofs of olden houses gleamed in faint misted moonlight. It's always like this, he thought, the hero always gets up and ponders before the moonlit window. How I hope things will go well. How I wish they had gone differently. His father had an answer for that, too—However things go, he said, they always go well. That's cutting the world an awful lot of slack, J.C. had said. Sure, his father said, but what else is there to do? We've got to make our little camp and keep it clean. The light in his father's eyes seemed to shine back from a country very far away. No one can accuse me anymore of killing your mother, he said, not even me. If I ever see her again it'll be in a time of sweetness, we will be very easy with each other.

They will be able to accuse me, J.C. thought and stroked clear lines into the fogged panes.

In the kitchen Elizabeth had made him a cup of coffee, but it was too late for amenities. Like a bad actor he wanted to cry, Enough already! and rear back disgusted. Ho, ho, Elizabeth, you don't know the half of it, sashaying around your daddy's kitchen. This is not even your house anymore; your mustachioed sister-in-law has taken it away from you. What's neglected dies, Elizabeth—even you ought to know that. Dies or turns on you.

She had come straight up to him and put her arms around his neck. The yellow kitchen shone with light, reflected from the night panes. She stroked his face and had him sit at the table. Can I fix you something? she asked. Would you like an omelet? No. Then he relented and took a cup of coffee. He had thought, She has never let me relax around her for five minutes, unless she was fucking me. In Hawaii, she knelt at the window looking fabulously out as if miracles were about to spring into life on the lawn. He had to be careful, because she might do something that would turn his head. As she nearly did when as he sputtered a few evasive sentences at her a tiny ball of spit flew out of his mouth onto her sleeve, and she, without breaking the train of his speech, picked it off with her fingertip and put it into her mouth. Watch that, he had said silently, you're going to bite off more than you can chew. She had said, I had a wonderful time on the river but I won't be going back there again.

Where now, he said despite himself.

Hawaii, I think. I'm going back to the islands.

Reflexively he had thought, What about us, what about your obligation to me, but he held his tongue, secure now in the heavy peace his gun brought. You have direction, he'd thought, you have meaning: let it go.

He looked out the window at an ell of shabby brick wall that was lit by window lights from the house next door. A dark glossy vine crawled across the top of the wall, like something coming over. Then his thoughts went away, as they had so often (forever! forever!), to their early days when she was an antelope running on the beach, when she sang every song playing on the radio, when every eye turned toward her, and all who could got up and followed.

She said, "Among a thousand creatures in the dark I could find you." Coming up on him as he sat in the window seat in this guest bedroom. Her fingers touched him low along the back, rose to his shoulders and kneaded the stiff muscle.

"I'm no creature," he said and twisted her hand off him.

"Oo," she said. "Oo, what a barbarian."

"I'm too tired for that business," he said.

She knelt beside him and leaned her torso down onto the window seat, looking out. "I used to sit at this window," she said. "I thought I could memorize everything I saw. There's a tree down there with a white blaze on it where they cut a limb off and filled the cut with plaster. At night I thought it was a ghost. I talked to it because I thought talking could make it friendly toward me."

"Where's your old bedroom—is this it?"

"No and yes. When I was twelve I moved up to the third floor, to a little yellow room under the eaves. It was there," she laughed, "that I planned my desperate capers."

"You must have spent a long time at it—planning capers, I mean." Her hair was still perfectly black at forty-two and it shone in the window light like something polished.

"I dreamed and dreamed. I dreamed until I couldn't tell the difference anymore between dreams and the world." She pushed up on her elbows, took his hand and stroked it, stretching out the fingers. "You never believed that," she said, "that dreams could become as sharp as the obvious world—but you lived it all your life."

"I don't know. Your dreams were different from mine."

"Does that matter?"

"It's the *only* thing that's mattered. Couldn't you ever see what a huge difference it made?"

"I suppose not. I was looking at other things." She touched his face with the tips of her fingers; he could feel the nails lightly on his skin. "You are so beautiful," she said. "There has never been another man anything like you."

And, he thought, wily crafty clever to the end. I have a gun, he said silently, that lies ticking under a lace cloth. The whole world is about to change. Out loud, he said, "Have you ever wanted to just take the world up in your hands and fiddle it into something fine?"

"That's a romantic notion," she said. "You can't do that with the world."

"What else have you been doing?"

"Not that. Not anything like that. My father—that man moaning himself to death downstairs—told me a long time ago that if I couldn't abide by the world as it was, I would have to go away. He meant his

401

world and he didn't think I would go. But I did. I packed one of my mother's suitcases and I went away. I couldn't change him; I couldn't change any of this." She leaned forward and pressed her face against a windowpane. "All along this lane," she said, "the ladies planted gardens. They already had the proper lovely flowers in their yards, but they came out into the street and planted gardens. You should have seen the flowers; there were all kinds, little wildflowers they had dug up in the mountains, exoticas from South America and the Caribbean, mosses from Scotland, all jumbled up and wild as heaven. I didn't think about it at all, then I wondered why they did it. Being me I'd come out at night and lie down in the flowers like a cat. I'd crawl around in them. The women didn't know what it was. I knew why I did that, get dirt and perfume in my hair—a voice would call me and I'd have to go out and rub the regular life off my skin. And then I started thinking about the ladies, those proper women coming out in the morning or at dusk in loose stockings and old aprons, down on their knees coaxing fresh life into those wild plants."

She licked a V onto the pane. "I figured it out," she said. "The best those women could do was make a little wilderness outside the gate. And I loved them because they could at least do that. I understood why they came out before breakfast and got down on their knees among the flame pinks. They needed exactly what I needed: to throw themselves down into the wildness of the world. I don't know why it happened to me but somehow I saw that if I wanted to do that every day of my life I could— nobody was going to stop me. It's so curious how we protect ourselves from enemies who aren't looking our way: nobody on earth is really watching. Even you weren't. You loved what I did and you only tried to stop me because you got afraid. I saw you looking at me that night when I danced with the sticks. I saw you looking at me all the nights. What fascinated you was that after all these years of Burdettes transfixed into their reverent paralysis by their great and mighty ground, there was someone in the world who came from even purer stock—perfect high-bone southern royalty—who didn't care at all, who'd do anything. But it wasn't me you saw—it was you. . . . ."

"Bullshit," he slowly said. And thought, No explanation can get the half of it. "That's madness."

"So?"

"So? Don't you see that in this world it's impossible to live that way?"

"But I have."

"At tremendous . . . *devastating* . . . cost."

"To whom?"

"To me, to Jacey—to your father down there, that guy you abandoned. I wish I could have talked to him, he'd understand what I mean; he was the first one, the first man you seduced and left. You haven't done anything in your life but leave a trail of rotting carcasses behind you—nothing—agh, fuck!"

She continued, as if she hadn't heard him. "I used to love those women, Mrs. Forrester and Mrs. Rainey and Gloria Pinckney, and all the others; it used to break my heart to watch them giving so much love to those wild flowers. There was something about them—the women—that was so fragile, so sweet—and so untouchable. It wasn't just my wild nature that drove me away from this lane. The day I left, the day I took the taxi to the train station, I cried. I cried all the way to the station, I cried while I boarded and I cried, I guess I cried, nearly all the way to Washington."

"That justifies what?"

"Not a thing. I wouldn't have come back if they were dying and the only thing that could save them was one more look at my pretty face."

"No. You would never do anything."

And it was again as if she couldn't hear him, could not receive the harshness that had come into his voice, not see the way his jaw set in the faint light from the garden. That was ivy not wisteria climbing over the wall. He thought of galax, the mountain evergreen highlanders put on caskets.

"I don't think I need to hear your justifications now," he said.

"I'm sure you don't, sweet man." She rose from her knees and kissed him on the cheek. She let her head rest against his for a second, until he could smell her, sweet and bitter at the same time. Then she straightened up and said, "I want to go down to see Papa again. I'll come back in a little while."

He sat in the window seat until the sense of her presence faded. A wind had come up; it bucked against the windowpanes. He reached up and swiveled the sash lock shut. He was not a man of waking visions, but it seemed to him when he looked back at the bed looming white under its chenille spread, the frail parson's table beside it, that the room had gotten larger; everything was farther away, growing fainter and less recognizable.

And I have let my mother slip away, now you. She sipped camomile tea and looked at her father, who hugged himself in the big bed. Her mother had been laid in the ground under a blanket of yellow roses. She died in the kitchen, in April, as she washed a pot of the season's last mustard greens. Elizabeth had been coming down the hall when she heard her mother say sharply, "Here now, stop that," as if she were correcting a child, and then she heard her fall. She ran into the kitchen and found her lying below the sink clutching her heart. Elizabeth had not paused to touch her, raced to the phone and called an ambulance. Then she knelt beside her mother, who had stopped breathing, who was suddenly dead, and removed the green shreds of mustard that clung to her hands and wrists.

"I ate them," she whispered to herself. I ate the little bits of greens I picked off her. The skin under her mother's skin was blue, like a puddle of water in a clay yard. She had not tried to resuscitate her mother, but she had held her eyelids open and looked at her eyes in which her reflection faded and died. Her mother's eyes were blue, the same blue as her own, the color of clouds sometimes when the sky is clearing after a rain. Just blue, she thought, make it just blue. She had seen her mother's death seep into her eyes, fill them and put them out. And she was gone from them, too. She was fourteen.

She tapped her fingers on the edge of the bed, then snaked her hand onto her father's wrist. She linked her fingers around the frail bone and grasped him, lightly. "Why can't I make life go from me to you?" she said. The pulse in her father's blue bruised temple shuddered and beat. "I forgave you as we went along. I didn't leave you because you hurt me." She lifted her hand and looked at the faint blue pressure marks her fingers left. "Everywhere I touch you now makes a wound," she said, "even kisses do." Where were her notebooks? Her scroll of papers on which she had written down the story of her life? She didn't need that regalia anymore; thinking of it was only a reflex. "You would love Hawaii, Papa," she said, but as she said it she felt the islands slip away from her, slip away from the net she had woven them into years ago.

"There's no far country," she said. "I'm not going there."

"I am," Jacey said from under the bed. His hand appeared, then his head, and he pulled himself out. He got up and came around to her side of the bed.

"You scamp," she said.

"I didn't want to be disturbed," he said, jiggering the lint out of his hair, "but I wanted to be close by." He grinned hugely, pulled up a chair and sat down beside her. "How you doing, Mama?"

Instead of answering she said, "Do you think you're in vaudeville?"

"I do what I can."

He took her hand and kissed her fingers. "Don't, you silly boy," she said and drew back from him, sensing danger.

"I was listening to Granddaddy breathe," he said. "It's not like any breathing I've ever heard before. He starts and stops, gets loud and fades—it's like he's imitating a whole bunch of people at once."

"You interrupted me making my peace."

"That's always the way it is. The day Dee and Bernard's bear died I was at the store buying feed. I missed the whole thing. Dee told me the bear grabbed his head just like a man would and fell over. He had a stroke and I missed it."

"A bear. You can see a bear die anytime you want to."

"Well, you're the woods queen. You ought to know."

She slapped him across the eyes. He folded right up, collapsing into the chair and himself like a tension hoist when you punched the spring. He put his head on his knees and cried, building into the tears something big that fueled them, folding his hands over his head like a prisoner. "I can't take it, Mama," he said. "I can't get loose." This minor chord now?

"You're so stupid, Jacey," she said. She glanced at her father, who moved in the bed, twitching toward his death. His Vaselined lips gleamed like a starlet's.

"There's no problem getting out," she said. "The problem's getting back in." Did she say that? Yes she did.

"I want them both," he said.

You child, she thought, you graven image. Everybody calls out Help me, lead me out of the woods. Why don't you jokers just sit there awhile? "You don't know anything yet," she said. "You haven't even had a baby."

He raised his face full of tears. "What does that have to do with it?"

"It's just one thing, one of a million things you don't know about."

He wiped the tears with the heels of his hands. "You can't pull that on me," he said. "I've been on my own for three years, in New York for

405

God's sake. I've been living with a grown woman the whole time. We've made a life."

"Something, something—not a life. Everything that's important to you is still circling around you." She laughed. "Like a wolf."

He shuddered. Like the devil walking over his grave.

"Why did you come back," he said, "that time you went down to the Caribbean?"

Sweet boy, born to unravel this mystery. "Because I needed your father. Because I needed his obsession with me. I wanted to be loved that hard."

"But you never loved him back."

"Which was very tough luck for him." I am going to walk out of this life, she thought, without having been understood for a single second. She was suddenly angry. "You dope," she said, "neither one of you people has any idea how much I loved you." Agh. She wasn't speaking a language anybody could understand.

Then she smiled and traced with her forefinger the line where his hat had been. "You wanted something different, didn't you?"

"I wanted a story I could follow. This one hasn't made any sense at all."

"Are you sure it has to?"

"I don't want philosophy, Mama."

"What do you want?"

"A place to stand. I want to grip down and hold."

She pushed her hair back hard until she could feel the skin pull around her eyes. "This will seem crazy coming from me," she said, "but anyplace you are is a place to start."

"But I can't see the ground. It's like when I used to swim in the pond—I couldn't tell where the bottom started."

"Then you keep swimming."

"But I'm tired."

"Then you drown. Or you grab something that will save you."

She reached down and gripped his thigh close to the groin. It was closer than a mother could get away with, but she held him there, her strong fingers clutching the flesh through the cotton pants. His body stiffened.

"I dream of you at night," he said, his voice hoarse.

"Everybody dreams of me at night, somebody like me."

406

He had seen Mattie hold a chicken up by its feet and whack its head against the chopping block to stun it for the ax. "You are stupendously crazy, Mama," he said.

She looked at him with lighted eyes. "I could unfasten your pants, fetch your little cock out and take it in my mouth. You wouldn't be able to stop me. Something in you would give way; you would enter a zone in which any kind of preventive action would be impossible. We would move, for a moment, out of time." She flexed her hand, nudged the sack of his testicles with her knuckles.

He flinched. "Oh, God," he said, "have mercy."

"No mercy now," she said. "Not in this moment. I will stand up and take off this fine burgundy dress and you will see that my body is beautiful. You will never forget it. Wherever you go you will take me with you. I will wrench your life to pieces." She began to unbutton the front of her dress.

"No," he cried. "No!" and pushed up out of his chair thrusting her hand away.

She grinned at him. "Why not?"

"I don't want it." He shoved the chair at her, oddly, almost as if he were placing it under a table he was excusing himself from, and stepped back. "I don't want this at all," he said.

Like a scared horse, she thought: his eyes. "There," she said, "you have it."

"What?"

"There's no place for you here, with me or any of this. You have to make your own."

"I can't."

She laughed her silver laugh. "Root hog or die."

"I can't."

"Sink or swim."

"I can't."

"Fish or cut bait."

"Mama!" His tone was sharp, the voice continuing to implore, but into his eyes had come something like a smile. "You're relentless," he said. "You're like one of those snapping turtles that won't let go until sundown."

"I exactly am—from time to time."

He leaned down and kissed the side of her mouth. She wanted to leave a mark on him, slight like lipstick, but then she figured she had done enough marking already. She pushed him gently away from her and stood up, as the boss will when the interview is over. "You've got enough in you to last," she said.

"Yes," he said, the faint edge of chill slipping along the easy laugh he gave her, "what with being a Burdette and all."

"Bonnet, too—whatever that means."

"Yes." He glanced at the old man, who had begun to blink himself awake. "I'm going for another walk," he said.

"Yes, you are." She wanted her father now. "Adios."

"Umm." He went out, closing the door lightly behind him.

She turned to her father and placed her hand flat on his cheek. The skin was cool and dry. He stirred and she slipped her fingers up covering his opening eyes. Under her skin she could feel the lids fluttering and thought, This is where the last life lives, it's left a residue here. She raised her hand and watched him swim up out of his cloudy sleep, his head stretching back until his Adam's apple was sharp against the thin flesh of his neck. He raised one kinked hand (fingernails still trimmed: kind nurse) and scratched below his ear, tending, she was glad to see, to his continuing simple needs. It's nice to know we can pay that kind of attention right up to the end, she almost said out loud. He blinked her into focus and said, "It's a longer life than any of us suppose," and laughed, a coarse, otherworldly laugh that if she had been a superstitious woman would have made her shudder.

"I've been talking to you," she said, letting her hand drift to his chest. They had walked along the Battery when she was a girl, she in her white starched pinafore, he in his navy suit. He would flap his bony arms for her, like a chicken, to make her laugh.

"I can't hear the people anymore," he said.

"I've never been able to."

"I hear the angels calling to me. You wouldn't think so, but it surprises me that they know my name. Isn't that silly?"

"I love it."

"You would." His eyes, red and full of the final dense smoke of his disease, seemed to bring her, for a moment, into a stronger focus. "Nobody could ever teach you anything," he said. "You were a daily surprise."

"I probably still am that."

408

He rolled his head. "Oh my, it's so close."

"Yes." She smoothed his brow. "What do you see, Papa?"

"Fruit stands. And men in aprons smiling at me. Your mother is around there somewhere. And Daddy. He came out of the bank and said, 'Wait till you see what they've got here.' "

"Oh, Papa." How big the house of memory is: how we move so gaily through the rooms, our hands caressing all those we have loved. My life has been a gift every minute of the day, every minute. I will tell you about the mysteries, Papa. I will hold you in my arms and blow my breath into your mouth.

She rose and lay her body across him, pressing him down. He did not resist her, perhaps no longer could. She pressed her mouth against his, tasting the digressive, ruined breath. He trembled, gasped, tensed. A long shudder rose up his body and died. She felt the sparks of his life flicker. She held him down as the last faint charges went off in his body. She held him down until he was still.

Then she got up, straightened her dress and, bending down to put out the light, looked into his face. She was not surprised to see that already he was a million miles away.

She thought she rose on a current of love. Up these stairs with their worn moons of wood. She thought she would go up to the widow's walk to feel the night on her skin, but she stopped at the door of the bedroom to see J.C. He still sat at the window, wrapped now in her mother's old quilt. The look on his face was the same as in the photograph she had always kept. Eagle delight. Between clasped upright palms he held something covered by the quilt, like a book just closed. She had come quietly but he looked up.

"I was just thinking," he said, "how you have always fascinated me." His eyes searched her. "You look like some little schoolkid leaning against that door."

He turned back to the window. "I would love to have grown up here," he said. "I would have been wild about this place, all these old bricks. You can hear the church bells ring."

"All over town. St. Michael's. St. Philip's."

"I would have loved to go to a church with a saint's name. With the Baptists it's places: Bethel, Berea, Shiloh. We're too scared of ourselves to give our heart to somebody who lived."

"I talked to the saints when I was a child."

"Yeah. I would have liked that."

She laughed. It was as if her soul had begun to leave her, hovered at the edges of her body, a mist. "I feel better than I ever have in my life," she said. "I've gotten to the place I was looking for."

"Too late."

"No."

She was—forgive her, Jesus—in love with everything. She could live in a hole and play into eternity with the shards and sticks she found there. It was the way she used to be, looking all afternoon at the gulls. "I could take you down the list," she said. "I could become a magician and pull the world out of my pockets. You name it: doodle bugs, puffballs, mica, cedar wood. I could give it to you. I've got it all."

"You're still jeering at me." He raised his eyes and she felt a rush of electricity in her, the first wild moment of the fall, but he lowered his glance and the moment passed.

She said, "Do you want to go up on the roof?"

"What for?"

"I want to feel the air. I think it's clearing."

He hesitated, then said yes.

As she climbed the attic stairs ahead of him she felt her heart beating, not fearfully—she was ready now—but exuberantly, in response. She had spent two—was it three?—days on the river, she had caught bream and cooked it guts and all over a driftwood fire, she had heard the songs of every bird the Okeekee River was home to, she had seen her mother and father sipping tea at a table in Venice, she had squatted on the gunwale of a ruined houseboat peeing into the water. Waves, waves—gusts of happiness swept over her. Something cried, "This is exactly what I had in mind!" She turned; her husband trailed, the quilt draped over his shoulders; she leaned quickly down and kissed him on the forehead.

In the attic instead of switching on the light she took him by the hand and led him in the dark through stacked boxes, hoop trunks, past the row of pinewood cabinets she had crawled in as a child, up the narrow permanent stairs. She released him to unlatch the trapdoor, which she pushed open onto a flat space that was swept by a cold, moist breeze. He came up after her, the quilt tucked around him, climbed heavily behind her into the railed square. A waist-high balustrade, painted white, kept anyone from falling down the steeply slanted roof. The house was higher than any around it; to the east and south they could see the bay and the long oily reach of the Ashley River; the city of spires ranged behind them. The wind whipped the oaks in the yard below them; the new leaves of the sweet gum by the pool were ripped off and strewn around the lawn as if fall had lurched back out of hiding. She thought, If you live in memory you don't have to explain anything: everything follows naturally from everything else. Her father had gone on, leaving behind him a voice that connected past, present and future. The hot days at Folly Beach when they waded in the surf picking up sand dollars, the time in Maine when he had slapped her for sassing the maid, the light, apologetic kisses he gave her mother when anyone was watching. Death drew a ring around the past.

She said, "It snowed once when I was a child. Mama left the car windows down and when I came out in the morning there was a crescent of snow on the steering wheel and a little drift in the seat." She sat down with her back to the rail. He sat opposite, pulling the quilt around him, drew a square-nosed pistol out from underneath it and let it dangle in both hands between his upcanted knees.

"You goose," she said brightly. She reached to touch the gun, but he drew back.

"No."

She watched him as he turned the pistol in his hands. "I remember that snow," he said. "I was in high school. We went out between periods and built snowmen, each one about three feet high. There was just enough snow to do that." He chuckled. "We had to scrape the grass clean for thirty feet around to build a single snowman."

They fell silent, both looking up into the sky, which was whitened by mist and streaked by the reflected lights of the city.

"I keep leaving my body," she said. "I can't stay with it."

He raised the gun and pointed it at her. "Why," he said, "can't you for five minutes come back to reality. You're going to die without ever having touched down on this planet."

She felt the gun on her, like God's eye. At last, she thought, I'm playing the Palace. Was it only her granite ego—speechifying still: nobody can kill *me*—that prestidigitated fear away? It had better not be. "I wish I could do something for you," she said. "Would you like me to suck your cock?"

411

"No!"

"I could tell you the story about the time I climbed Mauna Loa."

"I don't want to hear it."

"I used to go out in the hurricanes. The bay boiled up like soapsuds. One time a sheet of tin sailed right over my head and sliced a ginkgo tree in half."

"That's not news, and you're lying. You can't tell the difference between the truth and lies."

"Somebody needs to be that way."

"And you're the one."

She leaned down and licked her kneecap to taste the sea salt. "Shooting somebody's really not that imaginative," she said.

"So what?" He laced up a smile. "Are you trying to keep me from doing it?"

"Of course not," she said, her voice husky. She wanted to repair him, finally, once more, always. "Why don't you let me have the gun. I'll do it for you."

"See what I mean? You never once let me have my way with you."

"All right. What do you want me to do?"

"Let me think a second."

She waited while he brooded, the gun on her but his eyes looking a long way past her. Her mother had never gotten old. Which she didn't know anything about either, getting old. But as she lay on the bed these days, queued for heaven, she could feel her face sagging away from the bones. It had always been possible to get up and take a trip, find a randy man. But then you come to a stop. Who cares why it happens, whether inertia or a rock? Lacey Pinkney would keep building her breasts until they tipped her into the sea. Sonnie McKinnon would chase Tommy Pope forever. Rooley had become God's water boy. Delight was afraid of the dark. And there was her son, who had dreamed that he could be saved by his mother's body. You must hold life lightly, lightly.

It wasn't movement, she thought, it was action. It wasn't action, it was rest.

She stood up. The gun, like a blind dog, nosed up as he said, "I haven't decided."

"Yes you have."

She crossed the short floor to him, bent, as the gun came up—he would not shoot—and kissed him on the mouth. She could feel the hard muzzle of the .45 press against her breast, but every fear was gone; she was gone.

She rose and stepped over the railing, pulling up her dress to give him, gladly, one more flash of her fine legs. She took off her shoes and threw them ahead of her down the roof.

"I'm going to kill you," he said, standing behind her. They were close enough to touch but he didn't reach for her, pulled no trigger.

The roof was steep—slick slate—but by sitting down she was able to descend to the edge. She stood up, balancing on the iron rain gutters, which were still choked with last year's leaves. She turned and looked back at him where he stood, pressed against the railing, the quilt drawn close around him. He shifted the gun into his left hand and waved, a look of absentminded foolishness on his face. She smiled at him, the old mocking, understanding smile, her chin tilted up. Then she turned. Below her the murky screen of the pool roof was streaked black by the rain. It was too far to reach. But that's never stopped me before, she thought, as she flung herself outward, arms spread, almost flying.

Jacey would tell Martha the story a thousand times. He would tell how as he crouched on the garden wall he heard his father's cry, which was the cry of a sorrow that could never be repealed. He would tell how he saw his mother leap into the air. He would tell how if the pool had not been between them he could have gotten there in time to break her fall to the concrete. He would tell how he lifted her anyway, smoothed back the mask of blood. He would tell how she spoke words to him that he was unable to understand. He would tell how she died in his arms, still speaking. And then he would stop and they would look out, at the Gulf, or at the Caribbean, or at the indifferent city streets, and the silence would wrap its arms around them like a lover.

EPILOGUE

Canaan was broken up and sold, to Arab businessmen, to rich northerners who planted the fields in pines. The Main Street houses were sold; J.C.'s went last, purchased, with stables and twenty acres of ground, as a winter mansion by a doctor in Connecticut. The furniture and paintings were sold. On the last day J.C. walked through the empty hollowed rooms which smelled still of the undecayed scent, he thought, of his mother, just long enough to feel the tears rise, then he hurried away.

Eustace, remembrancer, link to the last wild times, died, at ninety-six, blind and mindless; Ransome died; Ethel died.

Delight and Bernard lived on at the zoo, renters, nearly charity cases. Anyone who saw them knew they had no place to go. Bernard joined the church and became a deacon; he was elected over three other candidates for the at-large seat on the county commission. Delight drank, and drink had its way with him.

Rooley and Alsace moved west, taking their child in arms, leaving paints, their forlorn house and the memory of Elizabeth behind. Only once in a while, in the high country north of Phoenix, as he wandered among the cliff houses of the old Indians, did Rooley let his mind drift back to the lost time when he held the black-haired, incorrigible woman in his arms, when he raved to paint, when he felt the pure thrust of Burdette blood that he wanted to wrestle like Jacob's angel until it told him its name. Then he swept his arms at whatever sky was above him, at the wagon tracks scored into the desert floor a hundred years ago, fell to his knees and cried for what had been. He let his fine God lift him up, sang to himself the old words from the Negro churches: "Precious Lord, take my hand . . . . " and he rose, into a new country, a country without rain, without trees, without sweet blue springs, and he made there, with his wife and child, what life he could.

J.C. took a managerial position with the conglomerate that had bought his fertilizer plants, but he left after two years. He could not, unlike his brother Franken, work for another man. He and Bryce moved to Atlanta, where he got a job from the governor as head of the Historic Development Commission. It was through J.C.'s efforts that the main house of old Canaan was entered on the National Register of Historic Places. He was gossiped about, he knew, but he was a Burdette, Old South, and was taken in. If at parties and receptions he noticed the whispers from across the room, he did not acknowledge them, and though he knew, in the nights, that what was broken in him would not mend, he walled himself off from it, would not speak of it, to himself or anyone else, raised it finally to a shining platform in memory, like a deer stand in a lost green jungle, that he gazed at from a great distance, unable to see who stood there, unable to see their weapons, unable to remember what hunt, what prey. Everything that was, and had been, was unreachable.

Jacey, devotionist, who would have burst his own breath to force life back into his mother's body, wandered. To New York; to Charleston, where he lived for eighteen months in his mother's old room; to the Caribbean, trailed by Martha, wife now, ex-dancer, half nurse, half keeper, where he met Marcel, who taught him to fish in the clear sea, to dive, and who told him stories that made him burn and weep; on to Mexico, where he was jailed for drunken disorderly conduct in Veracruz and Ciudad de la Carmen; to the West Coast; to Hawaii, where everything had changed; on finally to the low calcimite islands of the Micronesian archipelago, where he and Martha took jobs teaching painting and dance in the American school on Guam.

He took a certain bitter pleasure in climbing the high cliffs at the south end of the island and looking out over the Pacific, his mother's ocean. He had all her notebooks; in one of them she had written: "In the winter I could stand at the edge of one of those tropical cliffs and watch the wind blow the rain like a sail." He didn't know which cliff, or even which tropics. She had once driven her car off an Ashley River bridge, following, she claimed, the vision of white angels floating in the tops of a stand of oaks.

The great ultramarine swells he regarded, that broke their coarse heads against the gray rock, were anchored in the Marianas Trench, the deepest water in the world. A rip in earth 35,000 feet deep, depth the final bulwark between the last American outpost and the rest of the world. On weekends he swam alone with snorkel and spear along the decaying western reef. The reef extended out beyond the narrow sandy lagoon for nearly a mile. He would swim to the far edge of it, through the clear, light-bristling water, to the point where the coral shelved sharply downward into the depths of the great rift. There was the uneroded light, there was the faint curl and press of waves against the ocher reef, and then there was the darkness depending endlessly downward. He would hang there, at the marled boundary, as his breath came back, looking into that salt unfathomable night. No sun will ever shine there, he thought, and that is fine with me. And then he would kick, hard, legs a white flash in the sunlight, and swim downward, as far as breath would take him, farther, to the very edge of his life, into the dark.

The old man Jack, who never took a penny from the empire, bought his old overseer's house, his garden, the land his tower stood on and the strip of grassy field along the south side of the pond. Still not as social as he had hoped he would become, grown older—too old to worry about, he told Mattie; I believe I have slipped under the wire and gotten loose—he lay on the floor of his tower listening to music. It was Schubert now, and Brahms, those masters for old men. As the great chords rose in the final movement of Brahms Fourth Symphony he would get up and look out over the land. It might be spring, late May, after the last sweet flowers had already come into bloom. In the old days he could have told among the mingling scents, among the fine odors of sweet bay, tea olive and magnolia. Now he was old and could not; they were all the same to him. If it was summer he could hear the buzzing of insects and the provocative cries of the heartless jays; in fall he loved the blue skies which were clearer then than any time in the world, and in winter the rains came, the austere, chill, relentless rains, elemental tears that swept the land clean. Through his fathers he could reach back to the oldest times, patriarch by patriarch, back to the first day when Rooley Burdette had lashed his horse running through the wild woods. But the patriarchs were gone and would not return.

He would sigh and turn back to his tower room. He had his music that would not die, he had his flowers that bloomed each spring as if the world were an outrageous paradise; he had that gray-haired woman down there, sweeping dust off the porch. She would love him, he knew, as long as she lived, and he would love her, and that would be enough. Ride on, Rooley, he thought as he settled himself on the floor, ride on, boy. Ride on.

416